FULL
ELLIS

OBJECT DATA
[002-C4PD]

STOP

34.857500,
-111.841139

ANALYSIS

KROSS

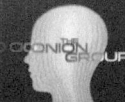

First Edition, December 2024
Written by Ellis Kross
Edited by Sidonie Lailler

ISBN: 979-8-9919643-0-2
Kross, Ellis, 1983—
Full Stop
I. Title. Fiction. GameLit/Psychological/Thriller

ISBN: 979-8-9919643-0-2 pbk.

Story by Ellis Kross
Book design by Izzy
Cover artwork by gremlin (istockphoto.com)

"Fan Service"
Artwork
by
GrandFailure

This is a work of fiction.
Names, characters, places, and incidents are the products of the author's imagination.
Any resemblance to actual persons, living or dead, is entirely coincidental.

Printed in the United States of America

PUBLISHER'S NOTE
This is a work of fiction. Names, characters, places, and incidents either are the
product of the author's imagination or are used fictitiously. Any resemblance to
actual persons, living or dead, business establishments, events, or locales is entirely
coincidental.

TABLE OF CONTENTS

③

①

②

④

full stop

ellis kross

4. THE RESIDENT

THIS GUMMY GAL, DOLORES, WAS AT IT YET AGAIN.

Hawking and spitting loogies at nurses and staff members, wildly swinging punches, raking their eyes, tugging at their hair, kicking at anyone who stepped within her vicinity of holy "nope."

Three orderlies, including Rook, were called to help assist the nurses on the 3rd floor where one particular resident was giving everybody a hard time.

Rook, who was admired by many, if not, all of the residents at Mother's Grace for his carefree, easy-to-get-along-with spirit that never came off as superficial or condescending, like some of the other orderlies who'd smile at the residents while mouthing expletives through their teeth. Not only did the residents find comfort in Rook's company for his cool mannerisms, but also it was, first, the soft and tender tone he used when he spoke to them. Not once did he ever speak in a raised or overly punctual voice, like most orderlies or nurses, who talked to residents as if they were deaf, dumb, and barely understood En-ga-lish, making sure to articulate each and every syllable slowly and coherently, volumes full blast and broadcasted for the entire floor to hear. What the residents really liked about Rook was that, if they didn't pick up whatever he said, if he said it too softly or quickly for them, Rook never treated their inability to hear as an annoyance or a good waste of breath or like some at Mother's Grace, a grievance, as if repeating oneself was no different than a slap in the face, an insult to one's character. A last ditch effort at a power-grab. Secondly, the residents tended to gravitate toward Rook for one reason and one reason alone: He carried a tragic look about him, a deep sense of *longing* that often pulled his face inward, including his eyes which coated with thought. Rook's unbuttoned tragedy attracted those who were most vulnerable whether it be, in various degrees, residents longing to reconnect with a past loved one, a son or daughter or spouse or pet, a loyal dog or an affectionate cat, who either passed away or abandoned them, or longing to be as noble as those larger-than-life, albeit flawed and redemptive, characters in their favorite TV shows that they watched in the recreational room. When they found themselves in Rook's presence, they understood the longing, and if they didn't know any better, they could easily mistake a similar look as the one they witnessed whenever they looked in a mirror.

When the orderlies arrived at the 3rd floor, Dolores was juking around in her wheelchair and using her mouth as if it was a machine gun to fire loogies at any nurse who attempted to grab her.

Rook approached the chaotic scene and stood behind one of the nurses.

Dolores misfired.

The nurse ducked her shoulder.

With little time to react—milliseconds—Rook stood his ground and not once did he flinch or make any attempt to move out of the way of the loogie's path. The loogie hit him on the side of the cheek. A thick and phlegmy loogie that crookedly ran down Rook's face, his chin, as well as his neck, dribbling past the V-neck collar of his scrubs.

The nurse stepped farther away, revealing the latest victim.

Dolores's eyes swelled greatly from the sight of the loogie on Rook's face, and she nearly wept.

"Rooky Boy," cried Dolores. "I'm so sorry—"

Rook held up his hand, signaling to Dolores that he was fine, no harm, no foul.

It's done, his hand said, loogie under the bridge.

The two other orderlies managed to wheel Dolores, who was rather deflated and dismissive after spitting on the one orderly at Mother's Grace who didn't treat her as if she was a halfwitted nuisance, back to her room without any uproar.

Rook excused himself and washed his face in the nearest restroom. The loogie even rolled down his scrubs until finally settling along his right breast. While carefully stretching the collar, he removed his shirt and grabbed a paper towel from the dispenser and ran the towel underneath a running faucet until it was damp. Then, he wiped the loogie from his chest. He pulled the paper towel from his chest. His eyes immediately crossed the jagged scar, which was the shape of a six, maybe five-point, star along the right side of his upper abdomen. The sight of the nasty scar embodied a strange yet undeniable power over Rook, more or less, a stark *reminder* of his past, Joshua's past, and those who hunted him down as if he was a rabid animal that needed to be put down. If anything, the scar made Dolores and her latest "episode" seem like an occupational hazard of a job, which had given him so much satisfaction over these past couple of years. Nothing personal, he told himself.

Adjusting his shirt, Rook stepped from the restroom; and as soon as he turned his shoulder, he suddenly sensed a presence moving toward him.

Blindsided, Rook bumped into a slightly older woman, whose skin lotion smelled of coconuts. Oddly, smell was the first—or second—sense of the five-ish senses that he picked up. The next sense: sound. She let out a lively "*Oh!*" during initial contact. Rook couldn't tell whether it was a laugh, cry, or a verbal billow of pain. She grabbed hold of her chest and breathed a sigh of relief.

Once the surprise wore off, a beaming smile curled across her face; and for a moment, as the two made eye contact, she appeared to glow, as if her soft, porcelain skin sparkled like a diamond held underneath the rays of a sun. Both of her eyes went from sad—one might describe as *depressed*—to radiant, as though also smiling at Rook, who was completely lost in her beaming sad-ish gaze.

"Sorry," the startled woman said, clearing her throat. "I didn't see you—"

"Na. . . no. . . " Rook stuttered. "It's my fault."

3

The two shared an awkward pause, which forced Rook to desperately search for something to say to her, anything that wouldn't make him look like a weirdo in front of a woman, who obviously, based on her facial responses, found him attractive, dare he'd say, interesting!

As she waited for an audible response from Rook, who was combing through his churning thoughts, pushing past his first and most immediate observations, she, too, found herself at a loss for words.

The 40-ish-somehing woman, who was standing right before his eyes, checked every single box in his questionnaire of datable and, fingers crossed, "it" women. Her hair was pulled back, as if she was about to go for a run or jog. Based on her lean and toned physicality, he leaned toward run. She probably ran between three or four miles, maybe more, every other day, possibly in a shaded area, like in a gym or on a trail with a lot of trees or canopy; however, she wasn't at all muscular and masculine, like the growing number of women he crossed whenever he wasn't at Mother's Grace, or spending hours sculpting in order to achieve one of those Amazonian booties you'd find on a PhotoBag model. The features of her face were peculiar and oddly shaped, both eyes slightly sunken into the sockets of her skull, the bridge of her nose straighter and more upright than the average type, and her entire profile didn't at all correspond to glossy mag standards of modernity. She had the shadowy face of a 1920's silent film actress. Tragic yet hauntingly beautiful. The face of a woman who, during that time period, would steal the vocal gaze of any decent fella whenever she strutted on by, casting spells of random catcalls.

"So," she said before the awkwardness ventured into that "weirdo" vibe, "is it normally this wild around here?"

"Oh," Rook uttered, his voice still on the same level as a thought. He spoke more loudly, "You mean Dolores?"

"Is that her name?" she asked, glanced over her shoulder, and saw the spitter-kicker being wheeled back into her room. "She looks *really* upset."

Rook waved off the recent episode.

"She's actually pretty sweet," he said. "You just caught her on a bad day."

"A bad day, eh? I can definitely relate. I know a thing or two about bad days."

"I'm Rook," he said, as the awkwardness started to creep back in.

"Autumn."

"Nice to meet you," Rook said and warded off the awkwardness by talking. "So," he said, smoothing out the tremble in his voice, "what brings you here?"

"My mother. . . " she said and then quickly corrected herself, ". . . what I meant to say is that my mother and I recently admitted my father to Mother's Grace."

"You make it sound like a prison sentence."

With tension building, Autumn laughed an uncomfortable laugh.

"Unfortunately, we can no longer take care of him," she said, her lips tightening. "He does this thing where he'll wander off in the middle of the night. Once, police found him clear across town. So, he gave us no other option than to. . . " she paused, as her eyes swelled with tears, ". . . put him in, you know, a home where he can be watched twenty-four hours a day."

"It's not as bad as they make it out to be—" Rook clarified *they*, "—people, that is."

Autumn smiled at Rook, this time a closed and nervous smile.

Rook asked, "So, what's your father's name?"

"*James*," she said. "James Piper. You know him?"

"Sure," Rook said, his voice slightly higher in pitch. "I know Mr. Pepper."

"Piper?"

"What'd I say?"

"You said Pepper. It's Piper."

"I did, didn't I?"

Autumn gave Rook a half-nod.

"He's really quiet."

"He can be," she said, "but once you get to know him he won't shut up."

He mimicked Autumn's closed smile, as if he combed through his thoughts once again, but this time couldn't find a single strand.

FOR several weeks, after Rook boldly asked for James Piper's daughter's phone number when he saw her a second time, which was two days after he accidentally bumped into her in a hallway outside a restroom, the two had been sending cordial texts back and forth until last night, when a provocative image popped up in his text messages. From the time Rook acquired her number—moments leading up to the big ask when he watched her walking through the parking lot from a window inside the recreational room were filled with more anticipation than a gripping horror-thriller, and yet, despite all the hype, wrung nerves, and knotted gut, it was relatively easy after he dropped a few lines of small talk mostly related to the weather (*How about the storm last night?*), which led right into an off-the-cuff comment, like "*We should exchange numbers*" after mentioning a brand new coffee shop that recently opened across Mother's Grace—they had only seen each other twice in public outings, the first time for a couple of drinks after he asked her if she wanted to grab a coffee, of all times, around happy hour—deliberate or not, you be the judge—but she was in a frisky mood for a stiff drink, and then, the second time, when the two went out for dinner and a movie. They had dinner at, of all places, an oyster bar—again, deliberate or not, you be the judge, since oysters were a known aphrodisiac, and it was still a "R" month—and then, afterwards, watched a flick of Rook's choosing: A shoot-'em-up action blockbuster filled lots of gunfire, explosions, muscular men flexing their guns, smoking hot women getting naked around that steamy fifty-minute mark, lots of stunt work, and then more hot, sweaty sex. Again, was it deliberate on his part to suggest a caffeinated beverage during a ripe time of day when Autumn, who spent her days crunching numbers like a professional wrestler, was dying to unwind and stretch her toes and loosen her metaphorical collar? The oyster bar, deliberate? The movie? He used the good ole trump card: He played dumb.

During that slow, sleepy time after lunch, which took place around ten o'clock in the morning, Rook pulled up the image of Autumn. The photograph was a selfie, which she snapped following a jog on a treadmill inside her neighborhood gym. The angle of the selfie prompted a second viewing, then a third viewing, a fourth, a fifth—the fifth viewing done with the pinching of his fingertips along the phone's screen, which blew up her tell-all cleavage—and by the time Rook and other orderlies were ready to escort the residents to a special event inside the auditorium, which some of the residents were buzzing about all morning, he lost track of how many times he had viewed the image.

Rook hid his arousal with a slight adjustment of his waistband and forced himself to pocket the phone and it wasn't until after the guest speaker, best-selling author Stanley Pruitt, known for his popular **BLACKOUT** series, arrived on stage to read several chapters and excerpts from his latest pageturning futuristic novel, *9/8/48*, which was over a thousand pages long and looked as thick as a tree trunk, and later, afterwards engage in what was only destined to be a riveting Q & A, that he was tempted to view the seductive image yet again.

With his phone switched to silent mode for evident reasons—if there was one thing that the majority of the residents hated with a unifying passion that resulted in overwhelmingly landslide victories, it was smartphones, and if Mother's Grace was run and governed like an *actual*, functional democracy, then smartphones would cease to exist and if they did exist, they'd be banned into oblivion and if by some unexplainable or supernatural phenomenon they eked their way into reality, they'd wind up on a shady black market somewhere or, in this case, snuck into Mother's Grace via grandma's birthday cake like contraband, and the only forms of communication expressed within the confines of Mother's Grace would be either through those two fleshy parts of the mouth called "*lips*," or, for the hearing impaired, by way of sign—he reached his hand into his pocket and barely poked the phone from the lining, his touch awakening the phone.

In the briefest of glances, he noticed a circled number ① over the icon of an envelope.

Word-for-word, Rook carefully read a text from Autumn:
"If you're not too busy later, we should get together after work."

He read it again, this time pushing aside any opinions and dissecting the text message from a neutral perspective. The two words stood out the most: *Get together.* On the surface, it was a common expression used to indicate two parties meeting up to hang out or whatever. The more he zeroed in on those words and why she specifically used those words, especially after sending him a photograph of herself posing in a way that screamed *"Undress me now and have me forever!"* he began to feel queasy, not in a sickly way where, at any moment, he was going to puke out his guts, but in an exciting, incredibly anxious way where he felt an urge to text her back with a resounding "YES! I'M FREE!" in all caps, drop everything that he was doing, and *get 2-get-her.*

As the reading event came to an end, Rook stood next to the snack and beverage table in the very back of the auditorium and continued to stare at the text, wondering whether or not it was an innuendo for sex—more than likely, based on last night's text, it was and even if it wasn't and Autumn wanted to grab a bite to eat or, hell, go see a movie *(perhaps another one of those awesomely-toxic and very male-driven action flicks with big guns, gratuitous violence, hard boners, and thunder thighs that begged "Give me more please!" from audiences who were trying to blow off steam, instead of wasting hard-earned money on hidden agendas and insulting lectures by out-of-touch actors who lived in cozy bubbles where issues were solved by teams of lawyers and handlers?)*, Rook knew that he was venturing into a warm and frenetic realm where, if he played his cards right, as in strategically not dumbly, then he could revel in her flesh and have her forever.

"It's not going to write itself," a voice said in front of Rook.

With his frozen thumb hovered over the keypad, Rook looked up and saw the author, Stanley Pruitt, grabbing the top plastic cup from the stack of cups. Stanley's loyal and saintly patient fans scuttled back to their self-assigned cliques with their recently autographed hardbacks clutched like rare artifacts—and *yes,* after much demand, *physical copies were back, baby!*

Startled, Rook inserted his phone back into his pocket while Stanley poured himself a cup of watered-down coffee and checked out a spread of donuts that was so colorful that one could easily mistake it for a gay-pride event.

Nodding toward the stage, Rook asked Stanley, "They pay you for this kind of thing?"

Stanley half-grinned.

"Not enough."

He lifted his finger to his mouth, as though hinting at Rook not to repeat the comment.

"Quite a fan base," Rook said, acknowledging the electricity among the residents. The grinning faces. The clinging of their novels, like prize possessions. The reserved excitement.

"Believe it or not, despite the pay—or what little pay—I actually enjoy doing these kinds of events every now and then. You'd be surprised by how many. . . " Stanley paused, moving his eyes upward in thought, and said as if he was a diplomat, ". . . passionate readers I run into whenever I'm out in public. Here," he looked around, basked in the seasoned vibe, "I feel more—"

"Safer?"

"Sure, but I was going to say *humble*."

"How so?"

"The way I see it. . . " Stanley said, more thoughtfully, ". . . most of the people in here have lived stories so remarkable that I could only dream about writing. If anything, they inspire me to become a better, more grounded writer, which is much easier said than done. This may come as a surprise, but believe it or not, regardless of my success with the *Blackout* series, I'm still trying to write my great American novel."

"Well," Rook said plainly and grabbed himself a blueberry donut, "good luck with that."

"Nice talking to you," Stanley said and waited for Rook to fill in the blank.

"Rook," he said finally.

"Stanley."

"Nice to meet you."

"Same," Stanley said and held out his hand.

With his other hand, he shook Stanley's hand, a firm and resolute shake. He pulled his hand away from Stanley's. His fingers barely grazed the side of Stanley's fingertips, causing a shock first, then a strange force from friction, both similar to a pinprick-like sensation from static electricity one might experience while running a hand along the screen of an analog

TV, or that other sensation one felt while touching the exterior of a balloon after rubbing it against clothing material or forcibly raking socked feet along a carpet.

The hair on Rook's arms stood stiff like the quills on a porcupine. Tiny bumps of gooseflesh spackled across his arms and spread across his entire body, causing his skin to tingle. He was struck by a wave of nausea.

Since Rook's mind was occupied for a majority of the morning by all things Autumn—not the season but the individual—he hadn't eaten much for breakfast or lunch. He pushed aside the strange sensation and parted ways with the author, whom Rook figured was charged by shaking all of those papery hands, and ate the rest of the blueberry donut and left the auditorium. He returned to his phone and with the conversation with Stanley lingering in his mind, didn't show an urgency to respond to Autumn, even though, moments earlier, he had drafted several responses.

An hour passed, and that wave of nausea returned, this time as brutal and relentless as a tsunami.

Rook excused himself after assisting a nurse with an automatic lift that didn't work half the time and rushed to the restroom where he ran his hands under warm water, which momentarily pushed aside any urge to vomit, thus keeping a five-year vomit-free streak alive.

Afterwards, he walked to the nurses' station where he bummed an anti-nausea pill from one of the nurses, Sandra Brown, who was working her last shift at Mother's Grace before she went on an indefinite sick leave. Rook was rather reluctant about asking Sandra, considering she recently received a devastating diagnosis from her doctor about the C-word, ovarian, that ugly, awful C spreading like corruption, undetected, had already started to move its way to her belly and the doctors were worried that, if they didn't catch it in time, then Sandra's chances of surviving grew slimmer by the day.

Without any hesitation, Sandra gave Rook one of her pills and then moments later, after he thought about how he looked, bumming a pill from a sweet lady who needed it way more than he did, the other C, his conscience, started to eat and twist his insides; Rook returned the pill to Sandra, who firmly held out her hand and told him in her lovely, sassy Sandra Brown tone, "Sick is sick, Sugar, and from the looks of you. . . " she said and acknowledged a lack of color in his milky white face, ". . . you need it right now more than I do. Besides," she winked at Rook, "I got plenty of refills."

Even diagnosed with one of the worst stages of cancer, he thought, and she still manages to hold a smile.

Rook thanked Sandra and later downed the pill with a chug of lukewarm coffee leftover in his thermos.

Another hour passed and then another.

The nausea wasn't quite gone, but rather lingering.

Autumn sent Rook another text: "Thought about you when I read this article xpndnc.pruitt/982048."

Curious, he clicked on the link. He was redirected to the news media site called XPNDNC, which delved heavily into conspiracies and not actual fact-based current affairs. Based on what Rook had told her yesterday about the author visiting Mother's Grace after he learned that she was an avid reader herself, the article was about Stanley Pruitt and a peculiar scar in the shape of a starfish on the top of his head. Rook was somewhat confused about the article and he never saw any scar on Stanley's head due to the fact he was wearing a baseball hat. He only skimmed through the first couple of paragraphs of the article—a so-called "journalist" using way too much flowery language and opinions—before he decided to close the window. He noticed one of the orderlies, Frank, who looked preoccupied by something other than work.

On a whim, Rook pulled Frank aside and bluntly asked him if he could take the rest of his shift.

"Something tells me you got other places to be."

"Yeah," he said, miserably, "the wife's been on my back all goddamn day about calling the AC guy to fix the unit. He cut me a deal a few months ago, but I swear the fucker sold me a lemon."

"What'd you say?" asked Rook.

Frank's head jarred backward.

"Serious?"

"Dead-serious."

He flicked his head at Rook.

"Sure you're up to it, man?" asked Frank. "You look like my weekend warrior cousin the morning after one of his epic Saturday nights."

"I'm good."

"Shit, man," Frank said, relieved, "that's a helluva solid. You run it by Claire yet?"

"It's already done, if it's okay with you."

"You're tryin' to get your ass out of a jam, aren't you? I know what it is. It's that girl you've been talking to, right? Is she too much for you?"

"Nah," said Rook while maintaining his composure. "I need new brakes in my car. I can use the extra money."

"Whatever, man," Frank said, more mellow, the recent news as smooth as a toke.

"Bring it in," said Rook.

The two slapped hands, their shoulders bumped in a bro-hug.

"*Roo-key* Boy to the rescue. You're a live saver."

"No problem." Frank walked away, his movements more exaggerated, peppy. Rook said from behind, "You owe me one, Frank."

While walking, Frank rotated around, backpedaled, and casually waved at the remark as if he was volleying it back at Rook, "The hell I do."

In a similar fashion, Rook playfully smirked at the gesture and didn't think anything of it. He returned to his phone and texted Autumn. As with Frank's remark, he didn't think too much about his response. In the text, he wrote that he had to "work late" and was "asked to fill in for a guy who called out sick." He deleted the word *sick* and instead, kept it simple: *Asked to fill in for a guy who called out.* He ended the text by writing, "Maybe later, if it's not too late"

Before sending the text, Rook made sure to add in a "?" at the end of the text.

Minutes later, Autumn texted back: "Sounds good."

Rook breathed a little easier, a slight weight lifted from his chest.

That night, with only a couple of hours left in the shift, he made his rounds through the quiet hallways of Mother's Grace when, all of a sudden, he heard the sound of a stairwell door closing. Since it was well-past visiting hours and most employees used the elevators, he decided to check out the noise. He entered the stairwell and leaned over the railing and caught a door on the floor below him, the 7th floor, closing.

Startled by yet another noise, which he soon concluded was the distant rumbles of thunder, he investigated.

When Rook arrived on the 7th floor, he saw, not an employee of Mother's Grace, but rather one of the residents wandering down the hallway. He caught up with the resident, who was none other than Autumn's father.

When Rook stood in front of James and obstructed his path, James looked at Rook with a vacant expression, as if he was staring *beyond* Rook and peering into an entirely different universe. His beady dark eyes fluttered from side to side like an insect. Rook couldn't tell whether he was sleepwalking or chasing after a ghost.

"Mr. Piper," Rook said, concerned by James's eyes, "you need to return to your room."

Mr. Piper—James—looked away and proceeded to walk away from Rook.

Strangely, Rook, who, as part of his job, was to make sure all of the residents were resting safely in their rooms, never walked after James.

Normally, reactively, he'd ushered a resident back to his or her room if it was well past visiting hours, especially while caring for a resident with an onset of Alzheimer's, and it wasn't at all unusual for a resident to wander off in the dead of night, wearing a very similar expression on his or her face. Tonight wasn't normal. The entire day wasn't at all normal. From the moment he arrived at Mother's Grace to the moment he was *zapped* by what Rook could only describe was electricity after shaking the best-seller's hand, he didn't quite feel like himself. Even before his arrival at Mother's Grace, Rook backtracked, with Autumn's text, Rook felt as if he was changing. For the better or worst, he wasn't so sure. But he did feel different, both inside and out.

As James continued to shuffle his way through the dimly lit hallway, Rook was moments away from walking after him when he heard a commotion coming from the other end of the hallway. Two nurses were arguing with one another. Rook was drawn to the rumbles of thunder, which sounded closer, louder. In the corner of his eye, he saw more flickers of lightning. Then, shortly after, he heard more rumbles, some of which rattled the very foundation of the building.

A nurse hollered out, "*Switch off the valve!*"

He redirected his attention to the nurses, ignored James, and checked out the commotion.

Shitty water was running from one of the rooms and pooling all over the hallway.

The other nurse raced back into the room and helped out the other nurse, who was struggling to turn off the water from the busted toilet, which had a crack running diagonally across the tank, gushing out water.

Another nurse was consoling the eighty-three-year-old resident, Bryan, who felt guilty about the crack in the toilet. The word circulating around the floor was that Bryan hadn't been able to go "*number 2*" for three whole days—the nurse, Willow, blamed it on all the sweets Bryan had been eating and insisted that he add more fiber to his diet, which would provide him with relief. According to Bryan, the toilet was clogged and started to overflow. In an attempt to the flush the stinky turd, the tank behind the flusher-thingy suddenly cracked and that crack spread like a fissure across the entire toilet, including the bowl, causing the water to spill out like a broken dam.

Instead of helping out, Rook was drawn to yet another flash of lightning.

A *clap* of thunder immediately followed the bright flash of light!

The entire building suddenly lost power, which prompted a generator to kick on.

After the unnerving moment of pitch-blackness, a couple of emergency lights switched on, not entirely lighting up the hallway, but providing just enough light to find one's bearings.

Transfixed by the violent storm approaching, Rook robotically walked to the window at the end of the hallway and watched the night darkness before him.

A streak of lightning suddenly cut through a cloudy black sky and stretched and fingered its way toward the earth.

The clapping sound that soon followed jolted Rook. A similar, if not the same feeling he felt after he shook Pruitt's hand, rushed through his body. His skin tingled. His eyes in a daze rolled over white, as he stood in front of a window.

More streaks of lightning flashed through the darkness. More thunder shook the foundation of Mother's Grace.

With each flash and clap, Rook's body jolted, resulting in his skeletal structure, including his cheekbones, to swell and protrude and distort his face.

Remnants of *her*—his unholy ghost—stirred underneath his flesh, like a massive parasite worming its way through his body. Flashes of lightning brought her closer and closer to the surface. He placed his hand underneath the shirt of the burgundy scrubs and ran his fingers over the scar on his upper abdomen, reminding him that she was gone, had been gone, and what he was experiencing was not her, but an interference of electrical signals, the mind tricking itself into believing that a piece of her still remained inside him when, he told himself many times before, she jumped into someone else along his travels.

As Rook focused on his breathing, he managed to push aside the overwhelming panic that nearly crippled him and redirect his focus toward the nurses, who were rushing to clean up the water leak. He pulled himself from the window and walked past several unlit bedrooms until one of the residents called out his name, "*Rook.*"

Surprised by the name, he stopped in his tracks and then backpedaled a couple of steps until he found himself standing at the doorway of Ruth's room.

Ruth, who was one of the residents on hospice, laid in bed, wide-awake, her eyes aimed directly at Rook.

In the dark room, a lamp cast an orangish glow on Ruth's pale, sunken-in face. The hospice nurse had stepped out for a second, and according to Ruth, she told that "*uppity bitch* (the hospice nurse) *to grab my pack of nips from Dylan downstairs* (an orderly who stole Ruth's pack last week before she took a turn for the worse). *If those damn cornrows haven't already cut off*

*the blood supply to her head, perhaps she can do me a favor and lace my
nips with fuck-it-all and finish me off herself.*"

As flashes of lightning and claps of thunder grew farther
apart from one another, signaling a passing of the storm, he
entered the room and walked to Ruth's bedside where he
took a seat in a creaky wooden chair.

Ruth said weakly through her gravelly, cancerous voice,
"Some storm, huh?" When Rook didn't respond as fluidly as
she expected, she moved her head slightly along a flat, greasy,
damp pillow, her marbled eyes that nestled within the deep
sockets of her skull pointing at Rook. She said more wor-
riedly, "You look like you're at death's door."

Wearing a look on his sweaty, pale face, he said through
his phlegmy, strained voice, "Yeah. You're the second. . . "
he cleared his throat, ". . . you're the second person to tell me
today."

"What in *Dante's Inferno* are you doing here then? I don't
give a flying shit about what you pass along to me, but the
others, that ain't cool, Rook—"

"I'm not contagious," Rook said over Ruth. "I think it
might've been something I ate."

Ruth's voice lowered, deep and dark. "You sure?"

"I wouldn't be here if I wasn't." He flicked his head at
Ruth. "The last thing I'd ever want to do is get you sick."

Ruth burst out laughing. The sudden outburst brought on
a violent coughing spell, which, in return, forced Rook to
grab a damp towel to wipe away the spittle from the corner of
her mouth.

"You're funny," she said with an unlikely tenderness in
her voice.

"So, what are the doctors saying?" asked Rook.

Ruth dismissed the question, didn't have time to answer
questions.

"The hell with 'em," she said with a bellyful of anger
slowly climbing upward. Deep inside, she had an entire wine
cellar filled with bottles of aged hate, covered in red, dusty
rage, ready to peak at any moment. With a curl of her lip, she
said to Rook, "They're saying I'll be dead by the end of the
week."

A warm, ethereal energy settled like an invisible blanket over their bodies, an unlikely bond gradually connecting the two, Ruth approaching the end of her journey and Rook enduring, not the beginning of his journey, but rather caught in the very middle, a halfway point, and together, the two jigsaw pieces fit not perfectly, but with inappreciable exertion, expediently; and, as he witnessed a door opening inside Ruth's eyes, welcoming not him, but her, his unholy ghost, a pathway manifested before him, a way out of the madness.

Sincerely, Ruth asked, "What's bothering you, Rook?"

"Do you have any regrets?" he asked, as tears brimmed over his eyelids.

Once more, Ruth burst out laughing, but this time it was weaker and tepid and could pass as a sputtering sigh.

"This is what you think about? *Regret?* Everybody has regrets, Rook. I wouldn't be human if I didn't have regrets and anyone who tells you different is full of shit." She made a noise with her mouth, moved her death-stitched eyes back to Rook. "That's the thing about shit. It has no regrets whatsoever. All it does is pass right through you—"

"But did you ever feel like you were supposed to be somewhere else? Or even do something else? Like you turned your back on a moment that could've changed the course of your life?"

"You're talking about Destiny, eh?" she said disdainfully. Then, more mockingly, "Yeah, and I was destined to be a violinist for one of the most revered orchestras in London. Destiny arrived all right, and he was six foot five, blue eyes, lush hair as dark as the other side of the moon, and a genius, too, like crazy-mad-scientist type of genius. But from what I learned, Destiny doesn't give a darn about you and your dreams or desires. Destiny will pull a goddamn Houdini and leave your ass cold in the winter with a child you neither wanted nor asked for because Regret and Destiny are roommates living in a one-bedroom flat with a leaky ceiling and an asscheese for a neighbor who constantly plays nu-dubstep to drown out the sad reality that *you are alone*. This is where I'm supposed to be, not because Destiny or Regret put me her, but because this is the consequence of my actions. The way I look at it," she said, weaker, and looked up at the ceiling,

"Regret, Destiny, whatever the hell you want to call 'em, they only exist in those who are too chickenshit to grab the world by its ball and look the world directly in its eyes and tell the world that its grift is finally up. I'm here now and *I see you for exactly what you are. . .* "

As Ruth's words cut right through him and left him with a gnawing ache deep in his stomach, he reached out his hand and touched the top of Ruth's frail, bony hand.

A force, similar to the spark from earlier, but much heavier, like a warm, staticky draft of air, was extracted from Rook and flowed into her. Both of her eyes softened, the brownish irises lightened into an earthy green shade.

Feeling the weight lift from his body, Rook heard a *clinking* coming from the hallway outside the room. He turned his shoulder, only to find the slouched silhouette of a woman standing at the doorway. The stranger stepped forward and revealed herself.

"*Sandra*," said Rook.

With a labored breath, the nurse, Sandra, entered the room.

"Rook," said Sandra. "There you are. We need your help with a leak."

He released his hand from Ruth, stood up, and parted ways with Ruth, who patiently smiled at him.

"Goodbye, *Joshua*," she said.

As Rook left the room, Sandra pulled him aside.

"Who's Joshua?" she asked.

Rook shrugged his shoulders and said, "Beats me."

He exited the room while Sandra stayed behind and watched over Ruth.

"*Rook! What are you doing?*" said one of the nurses. Rook found several of the nurses on their hands and knees trying to sop up the puddles of shitty water with cotton towels. "Get over here and help, will you?"

He grabbed a handful of towels from the janitor's closet and rushed over to help the nurses.

WHEN Rook arrived back at his apartment, he couldn't get out of his scrubs quick enough. He tossed them in a partially-full laundry basket—three days ago he washed a load but that lingering funk hovering over the basket told him that he might need to adjust his schedule—showered, then after-wards, threw on a loose, holey T-shirt and sweatpants and plumped himself on the sofa in the cramped living room and relaxed over the middle cushion after spending a majority of the day on his feet. He switched on the smartTV and flipped around a couple of channels until landing on a nature channel by way of voice command.

Only a few minutes of watching a documentary on *jellyfish*, he received a text on his phone. His insides stirred from the thought of Autumn sitting alone at a bar or, in similar fash-ion, on a sofa, longing for his touch.

Flexing his heavy eyelids, he forced himself from the sofa and slid the phone from the coffee table as if his index finger was a hockey stick and read the text from Autumn.

"Wanna come over?" read the text message.

While staring at the text, he thought about replying to Autumn even though earlier in the day he specifically in-formed Autumn that he had to work late and that he proba-bly didn't have time to, as she put it so ambiguously, "get to-gether."

Instead of replying, he pulled his attention to the package that he received a couple of days ago.

Rook honed in on the two letters, C and U, while he drifted deeper into thought.

From the moment he added the trendy product in his shopping cart to the moment he finally hit that "COMPLETE ORDER" button after days of keeping it in the cart as if he was waiting for the price to drop but in actuality he was somewhat appre-hensive about whether or not he wanted to return to such an unusual place that upended everything that he knew to be true, he'd be lying if he said that he wasn't looking forward to exploring all of those new enhancements, as well as fea-tures—"*Levels within levels, get outta here!*"

FULL STOP

For weeks, the anticipation built and built while scrolling through clever-catchy ads on his phone or watching cinematic spots on TV.

Finally, after weeks of anticipation, the product arrived in his mailbox. The packaging in near mint condition and appeared as if whoever created, wrapped, handled, and delivered the product took great honor in making sure the buyer (Joshua Lamb, or as the name on the address read, *Rook Carlowe*) was pleased. He didn't open it, though, not yet, at least. Instead, he told himself that he'd use it whenever he wasn't so damn tired.

MOTIVO LOCO

TWELVE-year-old Juan da Gama watched his papá kneel down on one knee and rest the weight of the upper part of his body onto his elbow and pick up a whole pacana from a stack of chewed-up twigs and leaves and with his flat stubby fingers, brush off leftover debris and use that curled, veiny ball of a fist to crack open the shell of the nut with two pump-like squeezes, making it look effortless.

Even though the pacana was from Western Schley variety—what his papá pronounced as sly or *astuto*, "like a serpiente," he'd say while motioning his rocky hand in a wavy zigzag pattern to demonstrate the slithering of a snake—which was best grown in much hotter climates such as the southwest, where "*sly* pecans" were less susceptible to a host of diseases, one in particular being the fungal disease, scab, more common in the southeast, and similar to a Cape Fear or Desirable pecan, known for a thin and easily crackable shell, opposed to a Stuart or Elliot, which often required a special nutcracker, he couldn't tell any difference in the variety of pacanas for his papá and the two beating hearts of his instrumental manos were mighty enough to shape and mold the world.

As the pieces of shell scattered along his coarse palm, Guillermo, or "Memo," as the other workers called him, used the fingernails of both his index finger, as well as his thumb, grown slightly longer than his other ones, which Guillermo trimmed on a weekly basis, to remove the pacana from the remaining shell. He split the two kernels apart, gave one to his hijo, Juan, and kept the other to himself.

The two ate the kernels, Guillermo savoring every bite of the pacana for the trees were carriers of old stories shared through the very fruits they produced.

"*Necesito sal,*" said Juan after tasting the pacana.

His papá cracked open his mouth and revealed a toothy smile, patted the young chico on the back, and ordered him to run off and finish watching his cartoons back in his house along the edge of the orchard.

Before Juan parted ways, Guillermo climbed back onto a rickety tractor, let out a grunt from the mild exertion, and gave his hijo permission to listen to his cartoons as loud as he desired. In a more animated way, he specifically instructed Juan, "*Ruidoso.*"

On the way back to the house, Juan heard the rumbles of engines from afar. He followed the sounds to an opening in the aisle of rowed trees where Juan witnessed clouds of dirt billowing up from the narrow road in the countryside.

While witnessing the owner of the estate, Señor Blanco, and his heavily armed and militant-like entourage, speed toward the main house, a range of both emotions and thoughts rose up inside Juan and provoked him to disobey his papá and further inspect what was always, according to his papá, off-limits and met with a resounding "No," whenever he inquired about visiting Señor Blanco.

Juan looked over his shoulder and watched his old papá riding away on a tractor, collecting pacanas to later sort the goods ones from the bad. Juan told himself and then, to make his point, convinced himself that his papá would never find out.

On a whim, Juan decided to defy his papá and follow the entourage to the main house where he witnessed Señor Blanco's bodyguards exit from four black SUVs, each of the guards carrying assault rifles and dressed in all black, Señor Blanco's own ejército de la sombra. Last to exit was the owner himself, as elusive as an exotic bird, Señor Blanco, attired in an all white suit.

As Juan crept closer toward the main house, he used pacana trees as a way of cover, darting behind one tree, then another, hiding his body behind the tree, poking out his head for a peek at those guards, who were keeping a close eye for any potential threats, especially snipers ready to pick off Señor Blanco or his younger and more ruthless and yet highly fashionable hermana, Liliana, who rarely visited her hermano.

Juan managed to get close enough to the main house to further inspect a remaining group of armed bodyguards. Two of them, he pointed out, were escorting a weak and bound man into the main house.

Once the rest of the guards entered the house, two of them stood watch at the entrance of the house, most of their attention focused on the road ahead and not the orchard.

Eager to get a closer look, Juan slipped past the guard's range of vision and crept around the side of the house where he snuck into the house via patio door, where the help, or *la ayuda*, used to bring supplies, including produce, to and from the house.

Cautiously, Juan stepped into the house where he heard the group of guards, as well as Señor Blanco himself, walking directly toward the courtyard. He dodged *la criada*, a rather petite lady who was carrying a stack of clean folded hand towels to one of the guest bedrooms, and scurried into the main office where he hid behind a doorway. From where he stood, he had a perfect angle at the courtyard.

Kneeled in front of Señor Blanco was the same frail-looking man from before, the one who was bound. He was yelling and screaming with cries of desperation being emphasized throughout his pleas.

All of a sudden, Señor Blanco ordered his men to bring *la rata* to his *estudiar*.

First, the word, *rata*, caught his ear.

Rat.

Then, the next word left Juan spinning in his own thoughts.

"*Estudiar?*"

Juan glanced over his shoulder and realized he was standing inside what looked like a study, with massive bookshelves lining the walls, one book grabbing his eyes, the novel *Pedro Páramo* by author Juan Rulfo. Several golden items stood out among a wide-range of both Mexican and American literature, like Steinbeck and McCarthy, as well as English literature, such as Dickens and Orwell and many others who were unfamiliar to Juan: a set of golden nutcrackers and sheller devices laid out on burgundy velour, as well as the statue of a golden bass, which was perched on a table behind an executive desk with the golden emblem of a lion's head, made of varnished oak, sleek and glossy, said to be a sentimental gift from President Shaw of the United States to Señor Blanco's padre, who passed it along to his hijo, Daniel.

As the voices closed in, the footsteps more pronounced, Juan faced forward; and as he took a glimpse into the hallway, he witnessed a snapshot of the whitely dressed Señor Blanco and his group of hired muscle storming their way toward the estudiar. He rushed back into the room and the first hiding spot that he could find was the executive desk.

Once Señor Blanco and his men entered the estudiar, Juan crawled underneath the desk.

The bodyguards dragged la rata, who went by the name "Hugo," or, as his fellow amigos at Policía Federal Ministerial, Inspector Agustin Rivera, toward the center of the room.

The obstruction of the desk made it rather difficult for Juan to clearly hear Señor Blanco and his bassy, muffled voice; however, as he leaned closer to the wavy opening at the very bottom of the desk, he managed to catch the gist of the conversation. According to Señor Blanco, the "new *presidente* has a real hard-on for me and my *empresa*, no?" From where Juan was cowering, he could only make out Señor Blanco's waist and down, most of his focus pinpointed on the flashy gold-feathered penny loafers, which matched the hiking boots he commonly wore, Señor Blanco being an outdoorsy man who enjoyed fishing and hunting, mainly Mexican pronghorn.

With his heart pounding against his chest, which made it harder to breathe, Juan watched the penny loafers turn and face the desk.

"*Cojones oro*, no?"

When Señor Blanco returned to the previous matter, his empresa, which, according to Señor Blanco, was a front to smuggle drugs across Mexico/United States border—"*business is booming*, no?" Juan overheard him say in broken Inglés to a bodyguard—Señor Blanco asked Inspector Rivera, who, before his cover was blown by a member of the revival cartel while he was executed the Nuevo Vera way, used to be a mule for Señor Blanco, whether or not his new *jefe* was ever going to show his face in public—"since his cojones are so *grande!*" he emphasized.

Señor Blanco was referring to the many assassination attempts against Presidente Guzmán, who, through an executive order, recently gutted and replaced the previous federal agency due to corruption. As Señor Blanco described to the inspector, the only similarity he shared with Presidente Guzmán: the two were surrounded by "*hienas,*" as if the insult was indirectly intended for not only inspector's ears, but also his bodyguards, who couldn't be trusted.

As his heart pounded harder against chest and made it more difficult to hear and even comprehend what Señor Blanco was saying for he could hear his pulse echoing against his very own eardrums, Juan thought that he heard Señor Blanco mention "*Chupacabras,*" a notoriously ruthless gang that worked with Nuevo Vera, and how he could deliver Agustin to the gang, who was well known for gutting their enemies like cerdos and hanging their rotted corpses, with intestines hanging out and all, upside from bridges.

As Señor Blanco walked toward the table of nutcrackers, he claimed that he needed to "*enviar un mensaje*" to Guzmán as a show of strength.

Inspector Rivera attempted to stand to his feet. Two of Señor Blanco's bodyguards grabbed him by both shoulders and slammed him back to his kneeled position on the floor.

By Señor Blanco's side was what looked like to Juan as the golden pacana shellers from earlier gripped in his hand. Similar to a pair of scissors, the sheller device had two blades that were specifically designed to snip the ends of a pacana, thus making it easy to crack open without destroying the kernel inside.

Señor Blanco leaned down toward the inspector's level and reminded him: "*¿Quién es el rey de* Nuevo Vera?*"

The screams began when Señor Blanco snipped away at the inspector's nose.

As the bodyguards reinforced their grip around the inspector's head, tiny pea-sized pieces of flesh and then, finally, cartilage, which required more effort from Señor Blanco, fell to the floor. Each piece of the nose was thicker, clumpier, and bloodier.

Juan covered his ears, but the inspector's screams penetrated his hands, causing the terror to flood through his veins.

"Maybe next time," Señor Blanco said, "your president will think twice before he sticks his nose in other people's business!"

Señor Blanco tossed the bloody sheller to the floor.

The bodyguard then handed him another object.

As soon as he removed his hands from his head and heard the faint *click* of a safety being switched off, he suspected what was about to happen next.

Before he had a chance to cover his ears once more, the gunshot *rang* out!

In a sudden flinch, Juan jerked his head away from the thunderous sound. He removed both hands from his ears and heard the *thud* of the inspector's body falling to the floor. He carefully opened his tightly closed eyelids and saw the same statue from earlier, the golden bass, now dotted with blood splatter.

Mindful of his movements, Juan rotated his head back around.

Once more, he flinched, not from the sound of gunfire, but rather, the gruesome image of the inspector's bloody face lying on the *Leucaena leucocephala*-patterned rug. The majority of his nose was missing, cut-off, one piece at a time, exposing part of the bone, as well as dark cavities of his skull. The bullet went in and out and left behind a gaping hole in the upper part of the inspector's forehead. Clumps of his brain matter were scattered in piles along the rug. Yet, despite clearly being dead, the inspector's eyelids remained open, like windows without any blinds, staring directly at Juan. A death stare frozen in time.

Carefully, Juan moved his eyes toward Señor Blanco, who was towering over the inspector's body. He couldn't see Señor Blanco's face for the bottom of the desk obstructed the view; however, Juan was able to get a close-up of the gold Luger hanging by Señor Blanco's waistside.

Juan had seen the pistol twice before, once when Señor Blanco was target practicing behind the main house and then another time when Señor Blanco visited his papá while he was dumping *fabricantes de dinero* into these large burlap bags, the handle of the gold Luger protruding from his waistband. He was so stylish—so *fresco* and incredibly confident, Juan thought whenever he saw Señor Blanco, and as he said to the inspector moments before he pulled the trigger, a hombre who was forced to show strength and send a message to the inspector's superiors—but the moment he witnessed Señor Blanco towering over the corpse of a man whom he knew as "la rata," Juan thought about his papá and how he specifically warned his hijo not to go anywhere near Señor Blanco.

WHAT defines happiness?

Is it the lie we tell ourselves everyday while the world around us burns to the ground?

The knockoff fireproof veil that protects and shields us from the flames of truth?

Or, is it a willingness to ignore the certified grade-A bullshit and make the best at what little we possess while crafty pyros peer down on us from their flame-retardant castles?

In order to make sense of these never-ending queries, first one must delve inward into his or her own life and well-being and only then, answers will begin to rise over the black smoke and in that glimpse of light, everything will be crystal clear. First, I'll start with myself. What I know for certain: A happy girlfriend helps make a happy life. But what makes her happy? I'd say that can be the easiest and yet, at the same time, the most difficult part. Difficult, not finding a thing or things that make her happy, but the willingness to sustain what makes her happy, especially in an age where you're walking straight through a fire hose.

On the drier side, an upset girlfriend creates a life so miserable that your own thoughts begin to turn on you, proving that you're an enemy, the outlier who doesn't belong, based on every little thing you say or do, a dire threat to her survival, as well as those close to her—her immediate family members, they scorn you—you're something that needs to be put in check or worse, don't let the door hit your ass on the way out. Even if you're strong enough to survive a verbal lashing on a daily basis, you might as well be living in a hell where each and every room is padded with eggshells, each move you make is carried out with precision and the utmost caution and delicacy, as if you're a highly-trained NAVY Seal utilizing stealthy tactics to infiltrate the base of a known terrorist, each word spoken no different than a live grenade, ready to explode at any moment, and each breath out of your mouth, not only feels, but also smells like a wet fart after Taco Tuesday. Don't mind yourself—What am I really saying?

I'm just passing gas through my mouth hole.

Or, should I say manhole? She minds everything I do or say. Like she has a gun pointed at my head, the hammer cocked, her finger on the trigger, and if I wake that three-headed beast during that *certain time of the month*, then I might as well let her pull the trigger, get it over with, all of that brain matter splattered over furniture and walls. Backy Boy once called it his last "*masterpiece.*" His "*middle finger to the world.*"

The only downside: I'm still alive, hole in head and all.

My thoughts are one-sided, patchy and fragmented.

Don't worry.

She'll gather all those pieces of me, use a special tool to scrap me off the wall, and then put me back together, like Frankenstein's monster.

And all that remains of me are remnants of what she created: A "thing," stapled and stitched together, rebranded and enlisted back on the market, only to be auctioned off by a smiling grifter with his hair slicked back with 10W-40 wearing a tuxedo that he lifted from a dumpster.

As the cardboard sign reads: "*Take me back!*"

And she'll buy you back for dirt-cheap.

That's the whole message she's trying to send, that I don't deserve better, that she's the best I can do, that even worms find me revolting.

So, the next time when I'm lounging around in what she'd call a tomb, waiting for her every command, don't mistake that ghost of an echo for a heartbeat.

What was once a heart is now a car battery, plugged into my main arteries, and resting inside a squared cutout in the center of my chest.

And that awful smell coming from my mouth isn't a case of bad breath.

It's the toxic fumes from a wobbly exhaust pipe.

2

WHILE Pepper chatted with the rail-thin car mechanic inside the automotive repair store, Under The Hood, Rook nibbled on the plastic cupful of frozen blueberries that he left in the freezer the night before and scrolled through suggested headlines on his cracked phone.

One of the articles he stopped on was about a forty-year old male who was struck by a vehicle yesterday afternoon after he walked into oncoming traffic. According to the report, the victim, Walker Huey, was wearing the latest version of *eLusion*'s contact lenses, VR-SKP, while he was hit by the driver of the minivan, Michelle Isham, a single mother of two who was dropping off her two children, an eleven and fifteen year old, at the RC. When paramedics arrived on the scene, they couldn't resuscitate Mr. Huey, who was pronounced dead before arriving at the hospital. Several eyewitnesses claimed Mr. Huey aimlessly wandered into the street, which was part of the ongoing phenomenon known as "ghost walking." The report ended with a pun by the journalist: *"Guess he didn't C where he was going."*

With his eyes glued to the screen, Rook kept scrolling through headlines, one being a new viral trend on the Internet where people snuck into funeral homes and filmed the dead in caskets, and then another being new "WARNING" labels that the FDA was going to start slapping on the front of products that contained sugar, such as cereals, breakfast bars, and cookies, in order to address and possibly get a handle— no pun intended—over the "obesity" crisis in America. Also included on the warning labels were graphic and slightly exaggerated photos of what the body looked like after consuming too much sugar: Love handles, double chin, hair loss, etc. Between the headlines were advertisements, each one creepily tailored to Rook's Internet searches. He clicked on the social media app, *Traxx*, which was also littered with pop-up ads and didn't operate as efficiently as it did before the tech company went "public."

Startled by a horrific thought, Rook pulled himself from his phone and frantically searched for any lines or marks along the side of his face, red ones that might indicate that he was—or had worn—a headset, but he doesn't find any.

More relieved, Rook returned to his blueberries. Since the shop was only a mile and a half from where Rook and Pepper lived—exactly three minutes from the point he pulled out of the driveway, plus tack on an additional five minutes to wait for his girlfriend as she made last touch-ups to her appearance, such as primping her hair or making sure that her face looked presentable for a nine-fifteen appointment or adjusting her loosely-fitted dress to cover up a small but noticeable baby bump—the frozen blueberries melted into a perfect bite.

Not too soft, Rok thought, but not too crunchy.

By the time Rook finished snacking on his frozen blueberries, Pepper handed off her keys to the mechanic and parted ways.

She exited the shop.

The electronic bell above the entranceway made a *chirp-chirp* sound, pulling Rook's attention away from a news article on his phone that pertained to a headline (updated) about the best-selling author Lionel Wilhey, who was the latest victim of a strategic seek-and-destroy campaign after receiving swift backlash for his latest novel, which was summarized as a struggling author who turned to AI for assistance in finishing the rest of his novel after suffering from a bad case of writer's block, only to later realize that the author himself was stuck inside the fictional story generated by AI. According to three posts on Chatterz, which were mentioned, as well as highlighted by the journalist, who, not only used AI to help write the news article, but also cherry-picked the only *three* posts that she could find while tirelessly scouring through the social media site in order to legitimize a "cancellation," readers alike had already begun to cancel Lionel Wilhey and were planning to purchase the book, only to film themselves burning the book in what readers collectively hashtagged as yet another "#BookBarbeque," which, in return, generated yet another backlash and controversy, dividing the Internet, leaving many stuck on the fence with the spelling of the hashtag and whether the correct spelling was "barbeque" with a letter q or "barbecue" with a letter c.

He carelessly placed the phone in the other cup holder, which further spread the spider web-like cracks on the screen.

As Pepper anxiously waited outside the entranceway, Rook drove the car toward the front of the shop where, after witnessing the two car mechanics watching Pepper from inside the shop, he decided to exit from the car and rush around the other side of the car and chivalrously open the door for his girlfriend.

About a mile down the road Pepper checked her purse but couldn't find her medication. She even had the water bottle ready to wash down the pill.

"Maybe you put it in the wrong pocket," said Rook.

More upset, Pepper argued that she always put the pills in the side pocket.

"Always," she emphasized.

"Do I need to turn around?" asked Rook.

Pepper checked the time of the dashboard.

The time read: "9:07."

Depending on the traffic, which was more sluggish than usual, they were at least five minutes away from the credit union.

"I don't have time," she said, digging through her purse. "You're gonna have to drop me off and then drive back to the house and pick up my meds yourself."

Rook was a sentence, no, a comment, no, two words, no, better yet, one word away from starting an argument with Pepper.

Considering her doctor's advice about stress, how it could easily trigger a seizure, and how any unnecessary stress should be avoided at all costs, Rook swallowed his words and afterwards, he could feel each one sitting in the center of his chest, burning and slowly climbing up his esophagus.

Rook remained mostly quiet throughout the rest of the drive, except for when he fired several of those balled-up words at other drivers who weren't driving in a way that met his standards and expectations, only to ricochet off the interior side of the windshield and further upset Pepper: "Look at this *fuckin' bitch* pulling out in front of traffic," or "What the *hell* is this *no-good, entitled piece of shit* thinking?" or "What kind of turn is that, *moron?*" or "Why don't you stick that phone up

33

your *ass*, you fuckin' clown!" or "Nice signal, you *inconsiderate* asshole!" or "Pay attention, *idiot!*"

Rook didn't exactly utter all of those remarks, maybe half of them while the remaining remarks flared up inside his head like a headache.

Worried about, not only her own safety inside the car, but also Rook's, Pepper grabbed the top of his white-knuckled hand, which was gripped over the gear. She interlaced her fingers with his until both of their hands connected like two jigsaw pieces that didn't quite fit properly; however, when pressure was applied, the two made it work, regardless of misshape and unevenness. Her touch alone pulled him away from the madness all around them, the chaotic morning rush, and helped lower his blood pressure and yet, even though the frustration was brushed away from the surface, it was still present, more or less, subdued, as if it had been pushed farther down into Rook, internalized, like a tiny membrane that started to knot and swell until it was cut off from blood or oxygen, only to soon form into a ball of blackness, dark and sketchy, driven by a gnawing hunger for development, and the only thing that stood in Rook's way from accessing what could only appear as a new organ ready to be discovered and exploited, was a door, cracked open, just barely, and it was only a matter of time before it opened completely.

After Rook dropped off Pepper at the credit union where she worked as a loan officer who was meeting with an important client, he drove back home where he grabbed Pepper's prescription bottle of anti-seizure medication, Levotrigine, which was sitting on the kitchen countertop.

Before leaving the kitchen, he pulled a coupon for a "10% discount off the next oil change" at Under The Hood from the magnet on the refrigerator door and slipped the coupon in his breast pocket.

Lastly, he eyed the 2024 calendar hanging from the side of the fridge, each particular month with professional-looking photographs of rare or exotic birds, the month of April showcasing the *Irena Cyanogastra*, or Blue-mantled Fairy Blue-bird, and grabbed a black Sharpie from the utility drawer to the right of the sink and X'ed out yesterday, April 7th, from the calendar.

He placed the Sharpie back in the drawer and made a pit stop in the bathroom to take a piss. When he finished his business, he turned on the faucet to wash his hands. At first, the water was slow to come out, which alarmed him. As he twisted the other knob, the blue one (cold), the water suddenly spat out and splashed his shirt. He managed to soak his hands with enough water to wash off the soap. He made a mental note to give Christian a call whenever he took a break from work. Christian, who was considered by his past neighbors as a jack-of-all-trades, repaired the garbage disposal last year and ever since, they hadn't had any issues with the sink.

Pressed for time, he decided to grab another shirt from the bedroom closet instead of drying the shirt with a towel, which would take more time. As soon as he removed a black collar shirt from the hanger, his eyes caught his father's golden bass statue stuffed inside the cardboard box on the floor.

Immediately, Rook was baffled by the statue and wondered what it was doing in the closet, if Pep had put it there—*Who else would move it in the closet?* He began to think if he moved it into the closet and forgot about it. He had been so busy over these past few days—Friday being a shitshow with him angry-painting the baby's room after he got into a heated argument with his girlfriend over the color of paint, then working on Saturday, and then spending most of the Sunday with Pepper at the lake—that he never realized the statue was missing from the living room. He left the statue in the closet and finished dressing. With the two items in his possession, Pepper's meds and a coupon for the oil change, Rook finally left the house.

On the way out, he made sure to lock the door behind him.

After taking a couple of steps from the front porch, he suddenly heard the rumbling of thunder in the sky. He drew his eyes to the clear blue sky. Searching for a storm cloud but not finding any in sight, he furrowed his brow in confusion.

He pushed aside the creeping thought and ran into one of his neighbors, Jay Mackey, who lived across the street.

Right before entering the car, Rook waved at Jay and said, "Sup, Mack Daddy! Is it supposed to rain today?"

Since Jay was practically deaf in his left ear, Rook had to repeat himself.

"Don't think so, Rook," the seventy-nine year old said and then asked Rook if he watched the game last night.

Lately, Rook hadn't found the time to watch any of the Dragons' games during the season, as he explained to Jay, with work, with Pep, who didn't care for basketball, but mainly, with the baby on the way and all the preparation, the painting, baby-proofing the house, and whatnot.

Rook stopped talking due to the throbbing of a sound system, and it wasn't until he turned to the approaching flashy white hatchback that Jay soon acknowledged the neighborhood nuisance. The sound of the music was muffled; and yet, it was still loud enough to drown out their voices. His next-door neighbor's cousin, Juan, who, as Rook suspected, was at least fifteen years younger, parked the hatchback in front of the neighbor's house. The blaring rap music caused the trunk to rattle like a maraca from the vibration of the bass.

As his neighbor's cousin turned off the ignition and stepped out of his vehicle, Rook parted ways with Jay and made his way toward his car. Before he entered the car, Juan gave him a look that could easily pass as a glare, as if, in a way, he was challenging Rook, provoking him to say something to him.

PEP first spoke about her disorder after one month into our relationship, which was the average length for most relationships in my early thirties that could be best summarized as precarious.

According to Pep, she had a family history of epilepsy. Her mother, who suffered from substance abuse, not only passed down the neurological disorder, but also the bad gene, or what you may know as the "addiction gene." *Sex, sugar, booze, drugs, weird fetishes*: the list ran at least a mile long. Anything that provided those selected few who had the naughty gene with hits of dopamine or flooded their brains with endorphins. In the beginning, Pep was upfront about her past history with drugs and alcohol, which she believed might have contributed to her diagnosis when she was twenty-nine. She decided to kick the habit—

not like Pep had any other options, except for a visit from Death Himself—after she was discovered in Blue Heights, barely clinging to life inside a dilapidated house scheduled for demolition. Whatever clothes left on her body were either ripped or ruined. She had bruises all over her body. Traces of blood on her thighs. Needle marks on each one of her forearms. One of the workers found her right before he was about to drive a wrecking ball through the house. Soon afterwards, she was rushed to Gabriel Memorial where her stomach was pumped of alcohol and other things. When she was questioned by a detective, she couldn't remember what happened to her the night before. From the condition of her body, someone might've taken advantage of her. Police never found the suspect or suspects.

During her recovery, Pep found exercise, in particular, running, to be a useful outlet to help maintain sobriety after a friend asked her if she wanted to participate in a marathon.

After Pep competed in the marathon, especially after the people close to her advised that she should *not* participate due to her disorder, the same with swimming, and how family and pseudo-friends warned her to stay out of the water since her disorder put her at higher risk of drowning, she sought out marathons around the state like a fiend jonesing for a fix.

Eventually after her health returned, she incorporated running into her life and one year later after she sobered up, the fitness routine was her new drug of choice. She said it provided her with enough relief to forget about drinking; and after a run, any thought of alcohol disappeared. She could even be around other people who were drinking without feeling as if she was going to leap out of her own skin.

I told myself, when we first started seeing each other after her friend, Betsy, who worked in set design, introduced her to me backstage at the *Three V's* concert, that Pep's scars weren't any deeper and darker than mine.

After I developed a connection with Pep after a couple of months of spending time with her, I told myself that I'd love her unconditionally, with or without her disorder.

I convinced myself, "Who doesn't have a disorder these days?"

In a society governed by order, who in the hell would want to be normal? To be a part of the very corrupt system that once held its boot on the back of those who were a different shade than me—and in a matter of speaking, still does, but in a more careful and covert way that fleshes itself out through the burden of time?

Pep put the *dis* in disorder, as if she disrespected its very definition of disorder by not letting it define her. "We don't always wrap ourselves in bubblewrap?" she'd say whenever she teased the Epileptic Community, and she'd say *community* with the same disrespect that she felt about her disorder. Or, she'd prod: "Not all of us wear life jackets." She reminded herself that only an unhealthy and dysfunctional society preferred to group us, based off a certain disorder or our appearance. Which begged the question: Is it normal for society to stick a label on everyone and everything? Or, is society the one with the disorder and those of us with disorders are the normal ones who have no desire in being lumped into a category? Pep compared herself to one of those analog TVs with rabbit ears and every now and then she'd receive a bad reception and the screen would appear all fuzzy and scrambly and if the screen didn't clear on its own, she'd have to give herself a thump on the side of her noggin to properly function.

As Pep transformed into a woman who was carrying life inside her, I was forced to ask myself if my relationship with Pep was all for show. A way of blending into society, giving the impression to those around me that I was whom they considered to be a normal individual.

Ever since I learned that I was going to be a father, I found myself stepping into a new role, not the role of a father—such label, regardless of its connotation, was mandatory—but rather one that I loathed ever since I was a boy on the verge of adulthood. The role of Mr. Approval. But I asked myself, "Why do I need approval from a society that sticks their filthy noses in other people's business?" Who are they to tell me when and how to raise a child?

3

AFTER passing along Pepper's medication, as well as the coupon for the oil change to the receptionist inside the credit union, Rook drove past a new development where the average cost of a house was in the million-dollar range. He wasn't scheduled to install track lighting fixtures inside the newly built home until later in the morning. He instead stopped by a rundown apartment complex located on the opposite side of town.

Once parked, Rook waited anxiously inside the car and tried to convince himself that, once James arrived and he was officially declared a father, everything would be much different and he would finally straighten up his act, that he wouldn't have to drive all the way out here in a shady part of town anymore, that he'd no longer have to tell lies to Pep about working earlier than he was expected, that he wouldn't have to worry or lose any hair over getting caught or covering up his tracks, constant checking his phone, his texts, making sure that Venus didn't send him a risqué selfie, as Rook specifically warned her not to but, of course, she did anyway, especially whenever she was feeling hot and bothered. The weight of the secret would finally be lifted, he thought, from my shoulders, from my face, from what little soul I have left.

Slow to exit the car, he switched the ringer of the phone to silent and headed up to the third floor of the complex where he took in a deep breath before he knocked on the door to apartment 3E.

Midway through the third knock, Venus answered the door wearing nothing but a transparent dress that she was sporting during what she called a "Try-on" video for her subscribers.

As he scanned her voluptuous body from head to thigh, he reminded himself that the break would be clean and that, when the moment arrived, there'd be no hard feelings.

Before Rook could compliment the dress, Venus reached her arm through the doorway and grabbed Rook by his collar and pulled him into the apartment and closed the door behind her.

Afterwards, since Rook was scheduled to work in about an hour, there was no pillow talk, no cuddling, no heart-to-heart.

The two had an unspoken agreement about the relationship and Venus, who was almost half Rook's age, making her twenty-two years old, even though Rook thought she added on a couple of years to make herself seem older, was fully aware of Rook's commitments elsewhere and how he had a son on the way. She didn't know where Rook lived either, so she said—and Rook made it clear that he had no intention in crossing the two worlds and avoided the topic whenever it organically manifested during small talk, which took place during that awkward silence before sex and very rarely afterwards.

While dressing, Rook struggled to zip his pants. The zipper was snagged on the denim and the harder he pulled on it, the deeper it stuck.

With white satin bed sheets loosely draped around her body like a veil, Venus rested on her side and propped up her head and watched in amusement while Rook yet again attempted to zip his pants. As Rook continued to struggle, he zeroed in on the zipper and for a second, he felt as if he was gripping a miniature train between his fingertips and attempting to force it back on the track. In a distance, he could hear the *horn* from a steam engine. And in that moment, he began to sweat and his hands started to shake.

"Easy, Zipper Man," Venus said and waved him closer to the bed. "Here," she said, holding out her hands, "lemme try—"

"I can manage," he said.

She rolled her eyes at Rook, who, after yet another failed attempt, walked over to the bed.

While Venus messed with the zipper, Rook's eyes fell onto the psychedelic poster of a wavy-looking, layered face on the wall. Beyond the many layers of the face was what appeared to be a celestial being hovering in deep, dark space.

With a couple of jiggles of the zipper, she managed to zip Rook's pants with no problem.

"There you go," she said, her voice pulling him from the trippy poster. She gave him a half-smile and said, "A side piece can be handy after all."

From the look alone on her face and how she was lying there on the bed as though begging for him to remove the pants yet again, Rook resisted the sudden urge and instead, leaned down and kissed Venus on the lips. By the way her phone kept chirping on the nightstand, he knew he wasn't the only one. There were others, he knew. Two, he guessed after their names slipped out of her mouth when they were grabbing drinks at The Molehill last month.

Rook checked the message on his phone.

He had two of them, and both were from Pepper.

"I gotta run," he said.

"Okay," Venus said, her voice deflated.

Rook sat down on the bed next to Venus.

The words dangled on the tip of his tongue.

Clean break, he told himself.

As he looked into her eyes, he saw the future and in that future, Venus was still in it and she was no longer a "side piece." She was his main piece. She was his everything.

In five years, she'd be one of the most beautiful women on the planet.

But *what if* she wasn't?

What if she let herself go?

What if she stopped taking care of herself?

He swallowed the words and left the apartment.

When he arrived back at his car, he waited until he was inside before he responded to Pepper's texts, which mentioned the meds and the coupon, Pepper thanking him for dropping them off, and then, to show her gratitude, using several emojis at the end the text, one, a red heart, another, red lips. Rook responded by entering an emoji of an eggplant and a peach and then right before sending it decided to erase them. He typed in a donut and a hot dog, deleted them.

"What am I?" he asked himself. "Fifteen years old?"

He instead maturely responded with a "You're welcome."

While he had Pepper's attention—he could imagine Pep sitting at the desk in that stuffy office, scrolling through on-line clothing stores for attire to wear during her pregnancy—he sent yet another text to her: "After I dropped you off, I finally saw the guy who's staying next door. What a jerk."

All of a sudden, Rook's phone rang.

The name of the caller read: "**Pep**"

Before answering, he turned on the ignition and drove away from the apartment complex.

"Yah-es," Rook said animatedly after making a right-hand turn onto the highway.

"The guy you're referring to in the text: Did you mean Nicholas's cousin?"

Without thinking, he turned on the speaker: "Drives a hatchback?"

"Yeah," she said. "That's him." Pep paused, listened. "Where are you?"

"Driving," Rook said without missing a beat. "Fixtures aren't going to arrive until an hour or two. No point staying on site. Thought I'd go on a food run for the boys—"

"You didn't say anything to him, did you?"

"No," Rook said, hesitant. "Why? Should I?"

"The other day..." Pepper said and sighed, "...right before you returned home from work, Angela stopped by the house to use my phone since her battery was dead."

Rook said, "Which one is Angela?"

"Nicholas's wife," Pepper snapped at Rook. "They've lived next door for how long and you still can't remember their names?"

Trying to hold in his frustration, Rook said, "Why'r you so concerned whether or not I said something to this guy, who, by the way, comes and goes at odd hours throughout the night? Just think about it for a second, Pep: What's it going to be like when the baby arrives? Is he going to be over there making all kinds of noise, preventing *our* baby from sleeping?"

Pepper said, "Think about how they must feel. Angela gave birth around eight months ago."

"She did?"

"Do you not remember?"

"I forgot," Rook said, drifting off.

"She's been telling me how hard it is trying to find baby formula—"

"Have you spoken to Nicholas's cousin?"

He heard another sigh on the other end of the phone.

"He showed up at our house," Pepper said, more quietly.

A flash of anger rushed through Rook.

"Showed up, how?"

"When Angela was using my phone, he just barged right in, like he owned the place."

"Did you tell him to leave?"

"No," she said. "Angela and I were in the kitchen—"

"And he just walked into the house?"

"Yep," she said.

"Why didn't you tell me earlier?"

"I forgot," she said. "I didn't think anything of it at the time. He was looking for Angela—I guess—and I think he might've saw her follow me into the house."

"I'm going to say something—"

"Please don't, Rook," she said. "I think Angela said he was temporarily staying with them."

Another pause crept up into the conversation, this time tenser.

"There was one thing that rubbed me the wrong way," Pepper said, thinking. "When he was standing in the living room, he was staring at the bass statue—"

"Makes sense now."

"You found it, didn't you?"

"I was wondering why it was in the closet. . . You didn't think he wanted to take it, do you? If so, he won't get a lot of money for it."

"It was just strange. That's all. Besides, I know how much it means to you, with your father passing it down to you. . . "

"You told this guy—"

"Juan," she said. "I think he said his name was Juan."

"You told *Juan* that it wasn't real gold, right?"

"No," she said. "He left right after Angela used my phone."

With Venus on his mind, Rook said spontaneously, "Why don't we take off this Friday and go somewhere this weekend?"

"What?" Pep's voice raised an octave. "You're serious? I have appointments—"

"Cancel them."

"I can't, Rook. . . "

"Well, all I'm saying is just think about it. . . " he said, ". . . this may be the last opportunity we have to go somewhere before the baby arrives."

As Pep thought about Rook's proposal for a potential weekend getaway—just last week, he mentioned the mountains and how a detox from the city life would be a good reset for the both of them—Rook ended the conversation by asking her how everything went with her appointment.

43

RIGHT before Pep found out she was pregnant I asked her if she wanted to move in with me, since the lease for her apartment was almost up, and she was still on the fence about whether or not she wanted to continue to pay an exorbitant price for rent in a less than desirable location plagued by overdevelopment and traffic, which was becoming a headache. She decided to take, as you may call it, a "leap of faith," and start a brand new chapter where she was no longer the main character of her story, but rather the main character of our story.

I'll never forget that second weekend after she moved in when she asked if I'd like to paint the bedroom with her. Originally, she wanted to paint our bedroom *saffron* and thought the color would help brighten up the overall mood, which was already gloomy to begin with, considering the room only had two windows and any natural light that managed to slip through was predominately obstructed by an overpowering oak tree along the backside of the house. In the beginning, I protested and shared my distaste for the color and stated my case that I wasn't too thrilled about sleeping inside a bottle of mustard, which, when she brought home the bucket from the hardware store and tested out the color, looked more like a bottle of honey mustard. The color alone made my skin feel sticky.

The next option: *Rose madder*, red being a color of passion, and even as I stood at the doorway and tried my best to imagine those fours walls covered in all that passion, I still wasn't comfortable with the color; however, a lack of protest only provided Pep with enough encouragement to commit to the color.

Halfway through painting the room, I accidentally spilled the bucket of paint onto the sheet of plastic. We managed to salvage enough paint to finish another wall the next day. It was what happened after the cleanup that I'll never forget: Dabs of red paint randomly smeared on the side of Pep's face, one of the straps from the loose overalls hanging precariously over her shoulder, a glint that somehow traveled galaxies through her eyes and lit up her glowing skin. The one thing I adored about Pep was that she was a woman of wit and class, and except for the privacy of our bedroom, never saw any point or reason in showing off her body whenever we were out in public, and whenever she did, it was often subtle or inconspicuous, a glimpse of her cleavage whenever she wore a blouse or on lazy

Sundays, which mostly consisted of chores around the house, a bellybutton whenever she knotted the bottom of a worn Bobcat T-shirt, or in this case, a shoulder, open and bare, providing me a glimpse of what she offered. We ended up painting the entire bedroom with our bodies rolling around in red paint.

Two weeks later she missed her period.

Soon, my role as lead character was going to turn into a supporting role, and I was perfectly content with taking a backseat in the story and passing the torch to someone else.

In the words of my father: "*You can't keep trying to fight the world when the world has already thrown in the white towel.*"

In other words, what Bill was trying to say before cancer ate through him was that the world tried to create a magical yet functional place where ideas could grow and flourish like fruit on a tree, but ultimately failed for temptation of greed snaked its way underneath our noses and rotted away the willingness to express oneself without judgment of our peers and any of those expressions were nothing more than calculations and algorithms intended to destroy, not create.

And if the world ever pulled its head from the sand, which it did from the time to time, he'd tell me, I'd lose every time for each day that passes leads me one step closer to defeat.

At times, whenever I find myself alone, I think about Bill and I wonder if he's present. In a gust of wind. The notion only of Bill sending messages via wind seems so absurd and only exists in the movies and has no bearing in a scientific reality and yet, at the same time, nobody, including scientists, have any answers to the ultimate questions of where we go after we die. Sure, the body dies, the flesh breaks down and eventually, decays, but what about the soul, is there a soul, and if there is a soul, then where does it go? Or, did Bill take another form, like a bird or a cat? Or, if a soul does exist, is his soul in a better place, and if it is and such a place exists, a place far better than this one, what kind of souls reside there? I know, for sure, a place like that wouldn't allow a soul, like mine, whose body once carried so much hatred in his heart. A person who was desperately searching for love to drive out all of the hate inside him, but soon realizing that it was the curse of Self who was the one preventing himself from loving. I blamed Bill for, at times, his worship of Self, Peggy for all of her insidious ways, or anyone who had wronged me in the past. I thought the death of my father would rid the hate from my body and soul. But after his death, the hate was still there; and much worse, it was way much more stronger than ever before and it felt as if his death had given it strength.

For years, the hate went dormant, occasionally rearing its raw, tumorous head whenever the opportunity presented itself, until I met Pepper, who, from the moment I made eye contact with her, vanquished the hatred with a katana forged by her very spirit.

When we first met backstage—she was eight years older than me but didn't look her age—all of the hatred that I had been carrying inside me was yanked from my chest as if her presence alone drove it out of me, leaving behind a massive hole that was ready to be filled with her love. And she did. She filled the crater deep inside my chest with nourishment, strength, and willingness to further understand me and my dreams, which would eventually turn into *our* dreams.

Before I found a chance to confront the hatred, ask it what it had been up to these days, what hole was it hiding in, I no longer saw any advantage in fighting with it, the hatred, which meant I no longer sought any purpose in fighting with a world that openly flung its hatred, carelessly and unapologetically, as if it was a pastime. Pep was my sun, and I was her pale moon, whose light shone the brightest whenever she was within my reach. She was my world, overalls and all, and I'd do anything to defend her and the life that she carried from the deliberately constructed sickness, which was desperately trying to claw its way inside the both of us.

4

AS five o'clock approached, Pepper tidied up her desk before logging out of the computer.

Ready to call it a day, Pepper made two phone calls before leaving the office, one to the car mechanic, who told her when she dropped off the car that it'd be ready for pickup by the end of the workday. When Pepper called to ask if the car was ready, the car mechanic, not the same one whom she had spoken to earlier but a different and more incompetent one, informed Pepper that the car was *not* ready and wasn't going to be ready until next morning. When she inquired about the delay, he told her that Elroy, the other guy, the professional one, had a family emergency and that he was short on help.

The second call was to Rook, who was running late, his excuse being that the deliveryman never showed up at the house and that he had to borrow Jorge's truck and drive all the way out to Spartacus to pick up the set of lights—Rook stretched out those words "*all the way*," as if they belonged to a faraway galaxy that took many light years to reach—and now, he was in the final stages of installing the last fixture of lights and that he wouldn't be able to pick up Pepper for at least another thirty minutes, an hour tops, he stated, as he held the phone away from his face and braced himself for gale force winds.

"By the way. . . " Pepper said, surprisingly not upset as she sat back in the chair and tried to make herself comfortable, despite having already planted that seed of aggravation, ". . . I went on Book-It and found a quaint little rental overlooking Hyde River."

"Hyde River, huh?"

With her mouth closed, she answered with a rolling hum, which sounded as if she was sampling from a sweet dessert.

"Kind of a haul, is it not?"

"I gumshoed it," she said. "It's roughly six hours away. We could leave earlier in the morning and be there by lunch."

"Any flights?"

"Yeah," she said. "Glad you mentioned it. I checked—"

"And?"

"Freaking outrageous," she said. "In all my days of flying, I've never seen the cost of flying this high before."

"What else is new? It makes you wonder. . . "

"Wonder what?"

"If it's all deliberate."

"Please don't start with your conspiracies, Rook—" One of the contractors was speaking in Rook's other ear. "Listen, Pep," he said, "I gotta finish up here. We'll talk about this later, okay?"

One of Pepper's coworkers walked past the office. Pepper, in return, draped the phone over her shoulder, cupping the microphone.

"Hey, Regina," she said, "are you clocking out?"

Rook's muffled voice said over Pepper's shoulder: *Pep, you there?*

Regina stopped, arched her neck backward like she was doing the Limbo, and stuck her head into Pepper's office.

While making a face, Pepper asked, "Can you give me a ride home?"

"Sure," Regina said, her voice higher in pitch.

"It's no problem?"

"Not at all," Regina said and then clarified, "Are you still staying at Ravenbrook?"

"Not anymore. . . " she said and suddenly corrected herself, ". . . well, technically, I still pay rent there. A freaking waste, I know. Now, I'm right off Spring Grove, with Rook."

"Oh yeah," she said, remembering. "That's right. I drive right past there on the way home."

Pep? Hello!

Regina waved her hand, indicating Pepper to follow.

"Great," Pepper said with elation in her voice and held the phone back up to her ear, "Hey, Rook, Regina's going to give me a ride home."

"She doesn't mind?"

"Not at all."

"Is she around?"

Pepper hit the speaker button.

"Tell Regina I'll make it up to her," he said with his voice reverberating through the speaker.

Regina leaned back into Pepper's office and said more assertively to Rook, "You can come over to the house and stain my new deck."

"That seems like a job for Harold."

Regina teased, "Harold wouldn't pull his sorry ass from the couch if the house was on fire."

The comment caused laughter from both Pepper and Rook.

From the corner of her mouth, Pepper said to Regina but, actually, was speaking more indirectly to Rook, "He still hasn't finished baby-proofing the rest of the house."

"We still have plenty of time before the little man makes his live debut."

"Well," she said, her voice drawn out, "not that much time. . . "

Sensing a tension between the two, Regina chimed in, "You best listen to your girl, Rook."

"*Yes, ma'am.*"

Finally, Rook thanked Regina once more and promised Regina that he'd stop by the house when he and Pepper returned from vacation, which prompted Pepper to defend her boyfriend's comment, saying that it was only a "we'll see," which often led to a flat-out "no."

Rook ended the call.

Pepper tidied up one last time before she and Regina left the credit union.

By the time Regina pulled up to the house, it was already dark outside. Pepper thanked Regina for the ride and after Pepper stepped out of the car, Regina asked her if she needed any help walking her to the house. Pepper waved off Regina's offer: "I ain't that pregnant," she said.

"What is it now? Twenty weeks, am I right?"

"Twenty going on twenty-one," Pepper said.

"Yep," Regina said. "Your ass is pregnant. Just wait till the cravings hit you. For me, I remember I wasn't as hungry when I had Clementine. But Zachary, a whole other story. Twenty weeks. . . " she remembered, ". . . he was about the size of a bell pepper—"

"They've already started," Pepper said, "the cravings—"

"Any food in particular?"

Pepper thought for a moment.

"Chicken," she said, recalling her last meal. "I know," she said, "pretty generic. In the past, I never really cared much for chicken. But now, for some reason—"

"You can't get enough of it, huh?"

Pepper answered with a smile.

Over a globe of silence, Regina asked, "You talk to Dean yet about a maternity leave?"

Pepper paused, her face more serious.

"Not yet," she said. "I'll work as long as my body will let me. . ."

"How about your other place, the one off Ravenbrook?"

"I'm still under contract," Pepper said, "but the lease is up next month."

Regina sighed and said, "It's a big step, Pepper."

"Well, I practically live here now."

Regina asked, "How's the transition going?"

Pepper sighed.

"That bad, huh?"

"No," Pepper said, looking down. "Don't get me wrong. Rook is great. It's just sometimes it's hard to know what he's thinking—"

"Harold's the same way," Regina said. "As long as we've been together, you know what the one thing I've learned about him?" Pepper waited for Regina to give her the answer. "I find it's best not to know what's going on inside that head of his because I'm scared of what I might find. Not knowing is the better than knowing. *'Ignorance is bliss,'* you might call it. So," Regina said with a sigh similar to Pepper, "we just get by; and sometimes, it's better that way."

"I don't know if I can live like that—not knowing. Maybe it's just the curiosity in me."

"Don't be," Regina said, her tone dour. "Otherwise, you might not like what you find."

Pepper nodded, smiled.

"I better get going," she said.

"A'ight," Regina drawled. "Just make sure you take care of yourself."

"Will do."

Before Pepper exited from the car, Regina stopped her for a moment: *"Claire. . ."* Regina said, causing Pepper to freeze from the sound of the name, ". . . we're all proud of what you're doing. Keep up the good work."

Once more, Pepper answered with a smile and closed the door behind her.

Regina waited outside until Pepper was safely inside the house before deciding to drive off. Once she flipped on the front porch lights and blew Regina a kiss goodbye, Regina drove away.

As soon as she closed the front door behind her, she immediately felt a strange sense of déjà vu while she stood in the foyer. She flipped on the first light switch, which lit up half of the living room. She placed the house keys in the clay bowel on the table in the foyer and walked into the kitchen and placed her purse on the countertop underneath the hanging cabinets.

As soon as she flipped on the overhead lights in the kitchen, she found herself yet again in a strange state. Several of the cabinets were randomly opened, both the upper and lower.

Confused by the mess in the kitchen, Pepper walked into the living room and flipped on the closest light, where she noticed the cushions on the couch were disorganized. One cushion jutted out slightly, as if someone had looked underneath it and didn't put it back in its proper place.

Immediately, she felt agitated and couldn't help but wonder if Rook had flipped the entire house upside down to search for her meds and then left in a hurry without tidying up.

With her knees, she pushed the cushions back into place; and right before she exited the living room, she saw one of the cabinet doors open below the bookshelf next to the fireplace.

She vaguely thought to herself: *Why in the heck would he be looking* for my meds *in there?*

A couple of Rook's "criminal justice" books were lying on the floor. Even though Rook was no longer pursuing to become a lawyer, he still kept the books. He had tons of them, books on law or the ins and outs of law, both civil and criminal. Pepper insisted that he should donate them, since he no longer had any use for them.

She placed the books back on the shelf, closed the cabinet below, and returned to the kitchen where she pulled out her phone from her purse and sent Rook a text message.

"Do you want to pick up dinner?"

As Pepper waited for a response, Rook, who was tightening up the last screw in the mount, which secured the lighting fixture, heard a *chirp* coming from his back pocket. He put aside the screwdriver on the top of the ladder and responded: *"How about the leftovers from last night?"*

Pepper checked the fridge and pulled out the large Tupperware packed with leftover chicken and white rice with broccoli that she prepared the night before. She peeled back the corner of the lid and gave the leftovers a whiff. She mildly shrugged in agreement.

"Sounds good," she texted back. Then: "How much longer are you going to be?"

As she set the Tupperware on the countertop, her eyes crossed the knife holder. She paused from the sight of the knives in the holder. Shrugged off the very thought.

Before returning back to work, Rook texted: "Give me 30."

Her phone *chirped*, pulling her eyes away from the holder.

Lastly, Pepper texted an emoji of a smiley face along with a chicken drumstick.

Since the leftovers would take every bit of thirty minutes, she pre-heated the oven to three hundred and fifty degrees and then dumped the remaining leftovers into a two-inch deep pan and added a cup of water and sealed the pan with a sheet of aluminum foil.

While the oven was heating, Pepper stopped by the bedroom and changed into a more comfortable outfit, T-shirt and sweats.

Thirteen miles on the other side of town, Rook finished installing the light fixture.

He flipped on the light switch: *"Let there be light!"*

And there was light.

Meanwhile, back to Pepper, who flipped on the bathroom light switch.

She turned on the faucet and dampened a facecloth and removed the makeup from her face.

While running warm water over her face, the baby started to kick.

Caught off guard by the sudden kick, Pepper rubbed her lower abdomen as a way of calming the baby. As indicated by her OB/GYN, it was entirely normal for the baby to move— or kick— during its development.

"How's it going, my little man?" she asked in a motherly way.

She suddenly pulled her head up from another *chirp* coming from the kitchen.

348°.

After drying herself off, she walked back to the kitchen where she read a text message from Rook: *"On the way home."*

349°.

"That sure was fast," said Pepper, as she replied to Rook's text with a thumbs-up emoji.

Behind her, the oven made a *beeping* sound, startling her.

She rotated around and once she acknowledged the glowing blue number 350° on the control panel, she placed the covered pan on the top rack inside the oven.

As Pepper made her way to the fridge, she suddenly felt another kick, not from the baby, but from her heart, which pounded against her chest after being startled by an intruder wearing a ski mask. The strange man in black clad was standing at the edge of the kitchen; and in his gloved hand, Pepper saw, as her eyes flicked toward the knife holder perched on the countertop—first, a quick glance to her left and then, once she caught a glimpse of the empty narrow slot, her eyes faced front—he was holding a butcher's knife.

She suddenly darted toward the set of knives.

Didn't care which one.

Anyone.

A fish knife.

The intruder was one step ahead of her.

He slid his hand over the top of the handles protruding from the knife holder as soon as she made an attempt for one of the knives and with his free hand, pushed the blocky wooden holder across the countertop. The holder clipped the side of the toaster and crashed against the corner of the tiled wall, making a *clinking-thud*.

With her nerves wrung by the deathly clamor, she backed away from the intruder, who was pointing the butcher's knife at Pepper. She looked into his sweaty, beady dark eyes, and then shot a glance at the blade, which was shaking from either his nerves or his tight grip—Pepper couldn't tell which for he remained in a defensive stance, his chest inflated, both shoulders puffed out as if he was ready to absorb a blow. She thought to herself that he had a chance to cut her, but he didn't. Which meant he wasn't here for her.

In that very moment, as she stood in a nearly paralyzed state, the only thoughts that crossed her mind: *How did he get inside the house?* She had locked up the house before she left for work earlier in the morning. A window perhaps? The backdoor?

How long had he been hiding? And where?

Inside the hallway closet.

The thought alone of this man standing behind the closet door made her skin crawl.

How much did he see?

Did he watch her undress?

The words, as thick as honey, dripped from Pepper's mouth: "Wha. . . what do you want?"

Pepper stared him dead in the eyes.

She remembered his eyes, those eyes, the ones from before.

"Where is it, *perra?*"

Pepper cried, "Where's what?"

"*La estatua.*"

More frantically, she shook her head, as though she was conveying, not the answer "no," but rather a confused "what."

Pepper's lack of verbal response forced the intruder to clarify: "The statue."

"I don't know what you mean," said Pepper.

"The *pez.*"

Pep digested the word *pez* and immediately she thought about *pescado.*

"Fish?"

"*Sí,*" he said and readjusted his grip around the knife. "The fuckin' bass, bitch."

He leaned slightly toward Pepper, causing her to cry out.

"Okay," she cried. "Okay. . . "

She reminded herself that if he wanted to cut her then he would've moments ago, when she reached for a knife. She then pieced together the clues, first, Nick's cousin, Juan, who displayed a keen interest in Rook's statue when he barged into the house after she let Angela use a phone, and then, secondly, the intruder's eyes and how each one held the same keen interest, almost one of arousal.

She'd never forget those eyes.

The intruder shouted out, "Where is it?"

"I'll show you," she said with her hands up. She motioned toward the hallway. "It's in my bedroom. . . "

The intruder took a couple of steps back, allowing Pepper to exit the kitchen.

Once more, her eyes flicked toward the overturned knife holder.

"Don't do anything stupid, *comprender?*"

When Pepper didn't respond, the intruder stepped forward and once more, showed her the blade and held it close enough to see the etching of the maker along the side of the blade, as if he was reminding her what he was going to do with it if she did anything stupid, such as her making an attempt toward the other knives or even worse, her attempting to grab the knife from his hand.

Crying out, she flung up her hands in the air while she begged the intruder not to kill her or her baby.

The lust filled his eyes as he looked over Pepper's body.

Her current frightened state aroused him.

Inching closer, he held the blade up to her face and then flicked the tip of it in the direction of the hallway.

Carefully, he backpedaled into the hallway.

Pepper exited the kitchen and walked into the bedroom while the intruder followed her with the knife aimed directly at her back.

Once she entered the bedroom, she went straight toward the closet.

As she cracked open the closet door, the intruder said from behind, "*Easy*. . . "

Pepper opened the door further and this time more carefully.

Below her was the golden bass statue inside a partially torn cardboard box.

Above her, a small black box, which housed Rook's Glock 21.

The intruder's eyes found the statue in the box below.

As Pepper made an attempt to reach for the other box, the intruder suddenly grabbed her by the arm and pushed her out of the way. The back of her heel snagged on the bottom track of the closet, causing her to trip.

During the fall, the side of Pep's head banged against the corner of the three-drawer dresser, spinning her around until she was facing the floor.

In a dazed state, Pepper landed heavily on her front side, her midsection taking the full brunt of the impact.

The intruder ignored Pepper, who appeared injured—possibly mortally—as she was incredibly slow to move on the floor. He grabbed the statue from the closet and rushed from the house; and then, shortly after, an engine suddenly revved and the throaty muffler of a hatchback screamed into the cold night darkness.

JUAN da Gama was fourteen years old when his father was shot and killed by a stray bullet from one of Señor Blanco's rivals, which infiltrated the heavily guarded compound, leaving Juan with no other option than to flee Nuevo Vera and declare political asylum once he made it across The Border. Juan was bused to a housing center, In-Motion, located within a small town in Washington, where he was enrolled into a one-year educational program. Once Juan graduated from the program, he was adopted by a middle class family, who lived outside Seattle. While he adjusted to his new family, Juan fell in love with music, in particular, grunge music, especially two bands that revitalized the genre, the first being Sponge Cakes and then, the next, Pale and Powdered.

When Juan turned sixteen, one of his guardians passed away from a terminal disease, which left his wife and their son to look after Juan.

When he reached nineteen, he traveled south while on a college-hunt in Colorado where he was approached by a former member of the Chupacabras, who later introduced him to a notorious biker gang, *Los Perros De Fuego*, the gang symbol similar to one of a phoenix, however, the design consisted of a dog with flaming wings. Within a stretch of three years, Juan fell into a life of crime and spent a majority of his formative years breaking the law (shoplifting, breaking and entering, vandalism, *arson*, etc.) until he met a young, blackly dressed woman who, despite her Gothic appearance, was also a great admirer of the grunge band, Sponge Cakes. Her name was María, "*la luz*," Juan's light, and she was the one responsible for pulling Juan from the cavernous depths of hell and showed him that life wasn't always about making enemies or destroying those who tested his masculinity, but rather the opposite.

When Juan was twenty-two, he married María soon after she discovered that she was pregnant with his child; however, before full term, María lost the baby from anencephaly.

Following the miscarriage, María, who, since the age of fourteen, had been working with her mother at a cleaning service, passed away after an off-and-on battle with stomach cancer. Juan strongly believed all of the chemicals María was exposed to at such a young age while cleaning houses had something to do with her cancer.

For the next year, Juan bounced around from one place to another until his older cousin—his "*primo*"—Nicholas López (*hijo de la hermana de su padre*), offered Juan the guest room, which would only be temporary, until he could hold down a stable job and earn a decent income to find a place on his own.

A couple of weeks before the break-in Juan had fallen into similar circumstances, which he escaped when he was fourteen years old, after he reconnected with a couple of his fellow Perros, who reached out to the Chupacabras for work.

With his loses aside, I could only wonder if Juan was aware of what his father had been hiding from him back in Nuevo Vera and whether or not his father's secret played any factor in Juan taking away the one person who brought light into my life.

5

WHEN Rook made the turn from Spring Grove onto his neighborhood street, he was greeted by a roadblock with a police officer redirecting traffic.

With the entire street flickering with flashes of red and blue lights from the tops of cruisers, Rook rolled down the window and more concerned, asked the officer, "What's going on here?"

"You live on this street?" asked the officer.

"I live on 4283," he said, spotting the source of the lights near his house.

"Are you Mr. Carlowe?"

"Yes," Rook said slowly. "Why? What happened?"

The officer stepped aside and let Rook pass.

Rook asked again, this time with more tension in his voice, "What happened, Officer?"

"There was an incident at your house—"

"What kind of incident?"

"Detectives are on the scene—"

"Detectives?"

More patiently, the officer said, "They'll explain everything."

The officer pointed to a vehicle parked in front of Rook's neighbor's house.

"Just pull up behind the black Sea Dan," he said.

Rook nodded and drove to the black car, which was parked behind three police cruisers.

Exiting through the other entrance of the neighborhood was an ambulance. He only caught the tail end of the ambulance driving away, and all he could think about was whether or not Pepper was inside that ambulance. Was she being transported to the hospital or the morgue? If she was alive, did something happen to James? And if so, why didn't she call or text? So many of these questions ran through Rook's mind and left him in a frantic state where his head started to spin with each new question.

Rook pulled himself from his thoughts and rushed toward the house.

As soon as he made his way up the driveway where a group of police officers were combing the front lawn for potential clues, his neighbor, Angela López, who was still dressed in burgundy nurse scrubs, waved him down.

"Mr. Carlowe," she cried out, "you can't go in there!"

"What happened here?" Rook asked Angela, who was clutching a damp tissue in her hand. Her eyes were bloodshot. The mascara was smudged around the corners of her eyelids as if she had been crying and wiping away each tear.

Sniffling, she said, "It's *Pepper.* She was *attacked* just a while ago. She's in bad shape. . . "

At first, Rook didn't understand what his neighbor was telling him. He couldn't make any sense of her words for they sounded foreign to him, as if he was stuck inside a nightmare where he could only make out certain images and the dialogue, turned all the way down, was not entirely on mute, but rather muffled, where words were gibberish, muffled noises jumbled up, as if they were trapped inside a box and an external force was violently shaking that box.

The only words Rook could make out were *Pepper* and *attacked.*

A hot, gnawing rage climbed from the pit of his chest, spreading through his veins, loosening and yet, at the time, tightening everything it touched, as if it was preparing Rook for war.

Through his crackled voice, he uttered, "Where is she?"

"They're taking her to Gabriel," she said, wiping a drop of phlegm from her nose. "Lemme drive you. *Please*, Mr. Carlowe," she begged, "you shouldn't be driving. It's the least I can do—"

Rook's eyes darkened, causing a startled Angela to take a step back.

Closer, he asked, "Who did this to her?"

Angela shook her head.

"I don't know," she said. "When I returned home from my shift, I saw the cops outside your house. Not too long afterwards, an ambulance arrived. Paramedics rushed Pepper into the back of an ambulance—"

"You didn't see what happened?"

Once more, Angela shook her head *no.*

"Then, who did?"

"*Ms. Ingle* called the cops," she said, nodding to the house next door.

Rook turned to his other neighbor's house, as if he knew exactly where to look. Behind the living room window stood a dark figure with a pale face glowing in the red and blue lights. Two opened blinds, slightly cracked upward in a long, upside down V shape, suddenly closed.

As Rook pulled his attention away from the house, he saw a police officer escorting one of the detectives from the house. He motioned toward Rook.

The detective approached Rook.

"Are you the owner of the house, sir?" asked the detective.

"I am," Rook said, trying to control his emotions. "Do you know who did this?"

"As of now, we don't have any suspects," he said, glancing at the notes on a notepad, "however, your next-door neighbor, Julia Ingle, said that she heard a woman screaming moments before a car sped away."

"Did she make out the car?" asked Rook.

"No," he said. "She didn't—"

Rook asked over the detective, "What the hell happened to my girlfriend?"

"It appears as if she might've been struck in the head," the detective said. "When police officers arrived on the scene, they discovered her body lying on the bedroom floor. She was in and out of consciousness—"

Thoughts alone of a woman screaming, his Pepper *screaming*, and then his Pepper *lying* on a bedroom *floor*, rushed into his mind. He fought off the dizzy spell.

"I have to go," Rook said, more directly to the detective.

"Of course," he said and waved down a passing officer. "I'll have Officer. . ." he glanced at the officer's name on the badge, ". . . Jenkins here take you."

"I have a ride—"

"It's no trouble at all," he insisted, flicking his head at the cruiser.

Rook followed the officer to the cruiser, which was parked on the street.

The two entered the cruiser, Rook first mistaking the passenger door for the backseat door. He redirected his hand and opened the passenger door. As soon as Rook closed the door behind him, the officer sped away with the overhead emergency lights flashing. With the rage pumping through his veins, Rook turned his eyes toward his own reflection in the passenger window and for a moment, found himself searching for any lines on the sides of his face, in particular, ones left behind from a headset.

RILEY Boone, the author of the literary classic, *The Undying Hearts of Man*, once wrote: "*Every Man encounters a crossroad, either fabricated through the product of mere spontaneity, discovered*

from a whim coerced by a dash of right timing and good fortune, or forged by the sole actions that led Him to the starting point of a cross-road, which He assembled, both consciously and subconsciously, knowingly and unknowingly crafting a familiar path that He failed to explore in a past unforgotten and He was purely reshaping His own history, a raw and uncompromising tale, in a way He deemed fit. Among these charted paths emerged choices, two paths, two choices, and each choice, he examined, may lead Him to yet another torturous crossroad and then another upon another, like a feedback loop— Is it another wretched one or, on the contrary, does it offer an outcome best suited for Him and His party of One, or, ultimately, will it lead Him to His own fate? But what happens when a path, strange and ethereal, is suddenly conjured? An off-ramp that materializes from unexplainable elements, which promise a more idealistic way out of the madness? Is it Man's transgression to misuse—or reject—the very tools He had been given? If a Man is no longer a Man, then what becomes of Him and His Sanity, which has grown ravenous?" Somewhere, deep beyond a place of Reason, I'd like to think that, all along, I became the very thing that I was supposed to become, not because of fate or, as Boone put it, *"good fortune,"* but because I simply wanted to test my own limits and see, from a vantage point, how far I was willing to venture in order to bring back harmony into my life.

6

AFTER using the siren to speed through red lights and intersections, the police officer arrived as soon as Pepper was being rushed into the emergency room.

Rook thanked the officer for the lift and hurried inside the emergency room. He was asked to wait in the waiting room while nurses and doctors performed a triage on Pepper.

Since Pepper's condition was the most critical due to the severe trauma to her head, she was immediately rushed into surgery to help reduce the brain swelling and stop the bleeding.

While Rook waited for hours in the waiting room as a team of surgeons worked on his girlfriend, two detectives, including the one from earlier, paid him a visit.

The two introduced themselves, the first one, whom Rook had spoken with outside his house, was Detective Soflie, pronounced "So-Flee," but the officers at the station often mispronounced his name as "So-Fly," which was contributed to his slicked back hair and a clean cut appearance, and then, the other one was an older and more seasoned detective, Chuck Giddy.

As the two detectives talked with Rook in the hallway, they asked Rook if he recently had any run-ins with anybody or made any enemies over these past couple of days.

The first two people who came to Rook's mind were his neighbor, Nicholas López, and his cousin. Earlier in the day, Pepper mentioned to him that Nicholas's cousin unexpectedly showed up at the house. The detective followed up by asking him if he had spoken to Nicholas's cousin before, if there was any conflict or altercations between the two, which was a hard "no." Rook mentioned Angela's phone battery being dead and that she needed to use Pep's phone to make a phone call.

When the detectives asked Rook about any potential motives, Rook brought up the statue.

"What statue?" asked Detective Giddy.

"It's a statue of a golden bass," he said. "It belonged to my father, who was big into fishing. It's considered, I guess, a sort of family heirloom—"

"Is this statue worth a lot of money?" asked Detective Soflie.

Rook shrugged.

"I seriously doubt it," he said.

Before parting ways with Rook, Detective Soflie informed Rook that he wouldn't be able to stay at his residence tonight and that he wasn't allowed to return for at least another twenty-fours, which should be enough time for investigators to gather evidence.

He asked Rook if he had anywhere to stay for the night.

Without missing a beat, Rook told the detective that he'd be spending the night at the hospital.

The detectives left Rook and instructed him to try to get some rest.

While surgeons worked around the clock on Pepper, Rook called her younger sister, Auggie, who, despite living an hour and a half away, never visited, except for last Christmas, when Rook and Pepper started to see more of each other, so much that Rook bought a spare toothbrush for Pepper just in case she spent the night at his house. For Rook, it was one of the hardest calls he had to make. He could barely complete his words.

Just before midnight, Rook received word from the head surgeon, who, with a weight over his face and shoulders, informed Rook that his girlfriend, Pepper, was currently in a medically-induced coma to help with the healing process. When Rook asked about the injury, what might have caused it, he explained that Pepper was struck between the upper right temporal bone and the lower part of the parietal bone—which were the most vulnerable areas of the skull—impact of a blunt object, a baseball bat perhaps (as of now, the weapon was pure speculation), caused a hemorrhage, resulting in significant blood loss. The surgeon offered Rook a glimmer of hope, saying that they were able to relieve some of the swelling in her brain; however, that glimmer of hope soon darkened into a cold and pale thought once he said there was nothing that they could do right now and that Pepper's current condition was out of their hands.

Finally, Rook asked him about the baby and whether he was still alive.

The baby, whom Rook and Pepper were going to name James, was, in fact, still alive; however, the chances of the baby surviving were very slim, given Pepper's current state.

After Rook finished speaking with the surgeon, a middle-aged woman who was dressed in a business suit with a green dress shirt and smelled of coconuts paid Rook a visit in the waiting room. She stated that she *worked at the hospital*—Rook thought—but the volume of her voice was turned down, not mute but, as before, distant, incredibly muffled, and he didn't register anything that she said to him, only that she mentioned a *chaplain* and whether or not Rook would like one to visit Pepper.

Once Pepper was settled in a room in ICU, Rook was able to visit her but only briefly.

The right side of her face was swollen and he could hardly recognize her.

He held Pep by the hand and with his head pressed against hers, whispered in her left ear, "I am going to find who did this to you. . . "

All of a sudden, Pepper's eyes bolted open.

"You did this to me," she cried out, her lips shivering. *"You did this to me. . . "*

Rook pulled himself from his thoughts; and as Pepper continued to rest, he kissed her on the forehead.

Pepper's sister, Auggie, and her husband, Alexis, arrived just after four o'clock in the morning, right when Rook dozed off in the waiting room. She tapped Rook on the shoulder, the tap pulling him from his warped fantasy of violence.

Startled, Rook embraced Auggie and Alexis, whom he hadn't seen since last Christmas.

He asked about their three children, who, according to Auggie, were currently staying with a close friend.

Together, the three rode the elevator downstairs to the cafeteria where, over a cup of coffee, Rook tried his best to explain what had happened to Pepper. Investigators didn't have a person or person of interest. He informed them that she was transferred to the ICU, and that he may be able to see her in a couple of hours.

Later that afternoon, after Rook received confirmation from the detectives that he was allowed to return to the house, Auggie suggested that Alexis drive him home to take care of any business that he needed to take care of, such as changing his clothes or taking a shower or picking up his car, since he had left it parked outside his neighbor's house.

Rook refused to leave.

It wasn't until later that evening, after Rook was able to visit with Pepper, that he decided to take advantage of Auggie's offer.

When Rook brought it to Auggie's attention, she reassured him that she'd call him if there were any developments.

While making his way through the main lobby of the hospital, Rook spotted his neighbor, Angela, stepping into the elevator.

Rook stopped for a moment and considered returning to the waiting room.

Alexis asked, "Is there something wrong, Rook?"

"I just saw one of the neighbors," he said.

"Do you wanna talk to her?" asked Alexis.

Rook had a lot of questions to ask Angela, most of them centered around her husband and her husband's cousin. He told himself that the questions could wait until another time.

TWO days before the attack, one of the painters, Marco, who was working alongside me, pulled me aside during the break and showed me a three-minute long video of a woman being carjacked at gunpoint on his phone. The whole incident was filmed and captured by a driver in the car directly behind them. The masked carjacker shattered the driver's side window with the butt of his pistol, struck the woman in the head with his other hand; and then, he eventually forced his way into the backseat of the woman's car. Later that evening, according to the local news report, the woman's abandoned car was discovered on a dirt road along the outskirts of town. Then, after forty-four hours of searching for the abducted woman, the police discovered her body in the desert, six miles from the nearest highway. She had been brutally sodomized with foreign objects and tortured before she was tied to a cactus and burned alive. My initial reaction after hearing the story was disgust: *What kind of person would commit such a heinous crime?*

The disgust soon transformed into a grander feeling—a unified hatred that rippled inside me and channeled through my very bones—strangely, the emotion not directed toward the carjacker or allegedly, the carjacker's pals who took turns torturing the woman, but rather toward the able man who was not only watching the carjacking, but also filming the carjacking with a camera on his phone, only to later post the graphic video on the Internet for the entire world to see, as if he was celebrating the carjacker, giving him a national spotlight, starting a trend and promoting the very act itself. And he wasn't the only one. Several other eyewitnesses also filmed the carjacking. One of the eyewitnesses immediately turned the video over to the police. But did it matter? I asked myself: What would the police do? They'd probably catch the man and then what? Release the carjacker, only to later commit another crime? Who would be his next victim?

Instead of putting down his phone, getting out of the car, sneaking up on the carjacker, and disarming him, even if he was risking his own life to protect another life, he filmed the entire incident as if he was living vicariously through the carjacker; and then, to make matters worse, he unapologetically posted the video, not in a journalistic manner to capture and visually document the crime (Based on his past posts or re-posts, he received gratification in watching other people fail or injure themselves), but rather to gloat about the young attractive woman and her soon-to-be tragic demise.

Then I asked myself: *What kind of a man would stand back, watch a crime unfold before his eyes, and do absolutely nothing, except root for the criminal who, in that moment, overpowered someone who was less powerful?*

Does it make him a coward?

And if so, is it criminal to be a coward?

What disturbed me the most: If I hadn't seen that one particular video of a woman being carjacked, only to later meet her fate, would I have made the same decision?

And if not, what did it make me?

7

FROM the living room window, Rook watched Alexis drive away.

For the next hour or two Rook made a half-ass attempt to tidy up the house, including tossing out the smelly pan of burnt chicken that was left inside the oven, which had been turned off.

While cleaning up the mess inside the living room—again, he asked himself if it was the police who had made the mess or the intruder, who, according to one of the detectives, might have been trying to rob Pepper—his thoughts began to heavily weigh on him, sapping the strength from his body.

As he made his way from the living room, he caught one book in particular protruding from the shelf, the spine of the book jutting outward, as though begging to be pushed back into place. While touching the spine, he looked over the partially visible front cover of the book. Intrigued, he pulled the book, Neil Reddy's *The Dark One At The Landing* (Expanded and Revised 2nd Edition), from the shelf and read an underlined quote from a page, which was dog-eared: *"Tonight, I snipped away a piece of my heart in Loganson, a city which one day I hope to call my own."*

The paperback belonged to Pepper, who preferred to read material that was considered darker by nature. However, the name, *Loganson*, immediately stirred a whirlwind of emotion inside him; and all of a sudden, his mind flooded with violent memories of a life that he buried a long time ago.

Before the stormy violence overwhelmed him, he blocked out the dark memories and decided to wash off the hospital by taking a shower.

Afterwards, he lay in bed with a damp towel still wrapped around his waist and with his head rested against a propped-up pillow, stared directly at the closet before his eyes and tried to imagine what happened to his Pep.

A glimpse of an image rose up inside him: *A dark silhouette standing in the middle of a lit doorway.*

Again, Rook blocked out the image and focused on the recent events.

The questions rose up from the dimly lit bedroom and forced him to confront the demon that was lurking behind the darkness of his thoughts: *What was she doing in the bedroom?*

The closet doors were open, he saw.

Did the investigators open them?

Or, did they leave them exactly how they found them?

They would, he told himself, *if they were good at their job.*

Don't contaminate the crime scene, right?

Leave everything exactly the way it was discovered.

Don't touch anything and if you do, wear a glove.

As questions faded from his thoughts, his mind began to drift. His eyelids became so heavy that he could barely keep his eyes open. Eventually, he dozed off; and when images returned, he was sitting inside his car, parked a few houses down from his. He watched Regina drop off Pep. Once Regina drove away, Rook put on his black ski mask and exited the car.

While Pep was preparing dinner in the kitchen, Rook snuck around the front lawn and entered the house through the guest bathroom window that he unlocked after he excused himself to use the restroom while Angela made a diversion to use Pep's phone.

Carefully, he closed the window behind him and tiptoed into the hallway.

Pep exited the kitchen and walked into the main bathroom attached to the bedroom.

Before Pep exited the bathroom, Rook hid inside the closet and quietly closed the door behind him; and while Pep was changing clothes, he watched her from a crack of the horizontal slat of the louvered door. Both his eyes masked with a horizontal band of hazy light while the rest of his face remained in darkness.

Once Pep was fully undressed, he opened the closet and charged at her while she was opening the top dresser drawer. He drove her body to the floor, pinned down both her shoulders, and began to strangle her. His hands tightened over her throat like an adjustable wrench.

Rook suddenly *heard a car door outside!*

The sound pulled a feverish Rook from the graphic images, causing his eyes to bolt open.

Despite having taken a hot shower, his body was cold and shivering.

After he rolled out of bed, he threw on some clothes and switched off the AC, which had been set to 68°, and then pushed the UP arrow on the thermostat until the temperature read 72°.

Next, he walked into the living room and peeked out the window where he saw Angela pulling grocery bags from the backseat of her van and carrying them to the house. He contemplated whether or not he should talk to her, maybe mention that he spotted her at the hospital. He slipped his feet into a pair of socks and grabbed the tennis shoes from a basket near the front door.

By the time he was fully dressed, he peeked out the living room window once again. The van's side door was shut. Angela was no longer carrying groceries into the house. He told himself that it wasn't the right time and that he'd talk to her later, when he was in a better state of mind. He put down the shoes and finished straightening up the house. Lastly, he rewashed a load of dirty clothes in the washer, which had a rank smell.

While the washer finished its last cycle, Rook walked back into the bedroom and inspected the closet, starting with a broken cardboard box, which once held his father's golden bass statue. As he stood upright, his eyes moved slightly upward, at a box on the top shelf. Inside the box: a Glock. Tucked away behind the Glock was yet another box, this one much smaller, sleeker, and covered in a layer of dust with the white letters, VR-CU, engraved on the side of the box. Next to the version of VR was the name *eLusion*, a questionable company that was basically not existent prior to the highly anticipated release of VR-CU. Not too far away from the small box were safety straps, two of them, one for each wrist, which the makers highly-recommended using while wearing the contents inside that box in order to prevent any serious harm or injury to a user.

Finally, he saw it, the shoebox, as if it had magically appeared on the top shelf. While on his tippy toes, he reached up and pulled the worn shoebox from the back of the closet and opened it, revealing a ski mask lying on top of a stack of old photographs.

As he pulled the ski mask from the shoebox, his phone suddenly rang!

Startled, Rook hurried to the phone, which was resting on the nightstand. He picked up the phone. The screen read "**Unknown**" caller with a 316 area code. He soon realized Auggie had a 316 area code. Usually, he never picked up calls from unknown callers since ninety-nine percent of them were robocallers or scammers or telemarketers trying to sell you satellite radio. He decided to answer the phone.

Sure enough, he heard Auggie's voice on the other end.

As soon as she mentioned Rook's name in an unsteady, defeated tone, his heart began to race. The blood in the veins was cold and drained all of the color from his face. He knew. Once he heard his name being said once again, followed by a sniffle, he knew what had happened.

As Rook sat on the edge of the bed, Auggie explained that Pep died unexpectedly.

The doctors said that they couldn't save the baby.

"James is gone," she said.

She also stated that Pep didn't suffer.

In Auggie's own words, she described it as her sister "slipping away."

Holding back the emotion, Rook told Auggie that he was leaving the house and that he'd see her soon.

After he hung up with Auggie, he immediately burst into tears. He couldn't control himself. All of the emotion that Rook had been holding back for the past twenty-eight hours poured out of him. He tried to stand to his feet, but his knees weakened, both of his legs buckled. He suddenly fell to the floor, his body drooped over the side of the bed. He gripped handfuls of a beige comforter. Soon, the tears felt hot, like boiling water dripping from his eyes, and his grips around the comforter tightened into balls.

As the anger flooded him, he stormed over to the neighbor's house and used the heel of his foot like a battering ram to bust down the front door.

What Rook discovered inside the living room left him in a state of shock, as he stood at the dusty doorway, both of his shoulders, once swollen, deflating like punctured balloons.

Over a dozen of Angela's relatives, from cousins to nephews to siblings to grandparents, all of them were gathered inside the living room. He saw the sleeping bags and pillows on the floor. He saw a small television with poor reception, which was stacked on a cinderblock in the center of the living room. A soccer game was playing on a channel that Rook had never heard of before; and every now and then, the signal would drop, causing the screen to scramble. Two children were fighting over the remote, despite Rook's rude entrance. Except for the two children, who seemed unperturbed by Rook's presence, the remaining people were staring at Rook with wide, almost frightened eyes.

The only words that exploded from Rook's mouth: *"Where is he?"*

Angela rushed from the kitchen and stood at the edge of the living room while Nicholas rose up from the edge of a packed sofa.

"Rook," Angela said, concerned, "what are you doing?"

"Where is he?" Rook asked Angela.

"*¿Qué es esto?*" Nicholas said to Angela.

"Where!" shouted Rook.

Nicholas suddenly hurried in front of Angela and shielded her body. Angela reassured him and told him that there was no *problema*.

As Nicholas became upset, Angela shouldered past him and walked to Rook.

"Where is he?" Rook asked, as he started to shake with rage.

"Where is who, Rook?" asked Angela.

Rook nodded at Nicholas.

"You know exactly who I'm talking about. . . " Rook said, ". . . your cousin. . . where is he?"

Angela said closer to Rook, "Juan is not here."

"You know where I can find him?"

As soon as he heard his cousin's name, Nicholas stormed toward Rook.

Nicholas shouted at Rook, "*¡Sal de aquí!*"

Angela stepped in front of Nicholas and attempted to calm him.

"*¡Ahora!*" Nicholas yelled.

"Please go, Rook," Angela said, waving away Rook.

"*Where* is he? ¡Donde!" Rook shouted at Nicholas.

Frustrated by Rook's persistence, Angela rotated around until she was face-to-face with her husband and in Spanish, told him that she could handle the situation and that he should go back inside "*la casa*" and watch "*el bebé*," which, except for "the house," were the only words Rook managed to recognize in Angela's fiery outburst.

Nicholas eased off while Angela escorted Rook back outside.

"How dare you force your way into our house," Angela seethed. "What gives you the right to kick down our door, like you pay the rent? Where do you get *los cojones?* Huh, Rook? You understand what I'm saying now, huh? Do you see Juan? Do you see Juan's car? ¡No!" Angela answered for Rook. "Juan is not here, Rook—"

More patiently, Rook asked, "Then, where is he?"

"The hell if I know," she said, as she witnessed the pain behind Rook's eyes. Her lips were trembling with a similar

71

anger as Rook. There was a pause between the two, Rook standing in a defeated stance, shoulders slightly slumped, head down. More closely, Angela asked Rook, "What happened, Rook?"

"It's Pep," he said, fighting back the tears.

"Is she better?" asked Angela.

Rook's face slackened into a blank expression as he looked into Angela's eyes.

"What happened?" Angela asked, her voice more tender.

She grabbed Rook by the forearm.

All of a sudden, Rook pulled his arm away from her and backpedaled into the lawn, staring at Angela as if, somehow, she was also responsible for Pep's death. He rushed back to his house and got in his car and drove away.

When Rook arrived at the hospital, he was first greeted by Auggie and Alexis, who were waiting in the hallway outside the ICU. Not too far away was one of the head nurses, who asked Rook if he'd like to see Pepper. She escorted Rook into a curtained-off area in the ICU where he said his good-byes to Pep.

Afterwards, Rook bumped into the detectives, Soflie and Giddy, who were talking to Auggie and Alexis in the hallway. The two first offered their sincere condolences for Rook's loss. Then, they told him about the good news that they recently received during the drive to the hospital.

"We got 'em. . . " Detective Soflie said, referring to Nicholas's cousin, Juan da Gama, who was currently being held at the station. "Police picked him up for a traffic violation. Apparently, he has an arrest warrant out on him—"

"Can I see him?" asked Rook.

The two detectives turned to each another.

Giddy, the older one, nodded.

"We were actually on our way over there right now," he said. "You can follow us, if you'd like."

Rook followed the detectives to the station where Juan da Gama was being held for a failure to show up to court after receiving a citation for speeding. He was given a firsthand look at the interrogation as both the detectives worked the potential suspect while he was seated inside the interrogation room, or what they called, in joking, "the box."

Soflie was a pitbull in the box, whereas Giddy was more conservative, patient and incredibly methodical, as he carefully studied Juan da Gama, his movements, his mannerisms, as well as his words.

Juan pleaded with the two detectives who hovered over him like a dark cloud and stated, on the record, that he was *not* responsible for the death of Autumn Piper. He claimed that he *never* touched her. He did say, however, he was inside the house, but the door was unlocked. He said that he dropped by her house to use her laptop. Juan claimed that he saw it on the counter when Angela used Ms. Piper's phone. Since Juan didn't own a computer, he desperately needed to use one in order to complete a job application. In his own words, when Ms. Piper saw him inside the house, she freaked out and ran to the bedroom. "She tripped," Juan explained, "and hit her head on the side of the dresser." He said that he freaked out as well. He had no other choice than to run.

In his own defense: "Nobody would believe me."

When the detectives were finished with Juan, they walked back into the other room behind the large one-way mirror. For a moment, Juan pulled his head from the table and looked into the mirror. For a moment, Rook saw himself sitting at the table in the interrogation room. His face was milky, as pale and white as a canvas. His eyes carried the look of a guilty man.

Detective Soflie said from behind, *"The guy's clearly lying."*

Rook snapped from his trance and said, "What are you going to do to him?"

The detectives told Rook that they could only hold him for another twenty-four hours and, if they didn't find any evidence, such as a murder weapon, then they had no other choice than to release him—in their own words, "state law."

Rook argued, "But the man confessed that he was inside the house!"

"We don't know that," said Giddy. "We can't charge him with breaking and entering, since there is no sign of breaking and entering. We'll continue to press him until he cracks—"

"Maybe you're not pressing him hard enough, Detective," Rook seethed.

"Easy, Mr. Carlowe," Soflie said and stepped between the two.

He escorted Rook from the station and told him that if they received any relevant information about the case before Juan decided to lawyer-up, then Rook would be the first to know.

Later, Auggie and Alexis spent the night with Rook at his house. Alexis ended up picking up carryout for everybody. Rook didn't eat. Instead, he stayed in bed.

The next morning, after Auggie made breakfast, she brought up funeral arrangements and all of the planning that needed to be done. Rook wasn't in the mood, and the fact that Auggie was bringing up the subject only hours after her sister died left him disgusted. In a polite way, Rook convinced the two that he was fine and that he needed the space. Alexis agreed, Auggie not so much. The two wished him well, said they'd call him later, and then drove back home.

Shortly after, Rook caught Nicholas in the driveway before he left for work.

First, Rook apologized for breaking down his door.

Since his English wasn't good, Angela exited the house and spoke for him.

"Tell your husband I'll repair the door," he said to Angela, who translated for Nicholas.

"We heard about Pepper," Angela said and hugged Rook. "We're so sorry. . . "

Instinctually every inch of him was tempted to pull himself away from Angela as she rubbed his back, but his aching heart welcomed her warm touch. The two embraced one another and not only did Rook welcome her touch, but he also cherished her touch, and if anything, his heart felt lighter and immediately, a deep, humanly connection was forged between the two. As she wrung the tears from Rook, he mustered the strength to look her straight in the eye. Rook never spoke the words for his ironclad pride wouldn't allow him to unburden himself; however, Rook offered a hand to Nicholas, who, after a reassuring look from his wife, shook his hand.

Later that afternoon, Rook stopped by Angela's house while she was working a shift at the hospital. He brought over a brand new door that he bought at the hardware store.

When he entered the house via garage, he spoke with Angela's mother, who couldn't understand a word of English; however, earlier that day, Angela mentioned that *"el vecino"* might stop by the house to repair the front door, which was temporarily secured by a 2 x 4 that Nicholas had in the back of his truck. He nailed the slab of wood into the wall, which prevented the front door from opening.

After Rook repaired the doorway and installed a new door, Angela returned from her shift. She thanked Rook and asked him, if he'd like to join them for supper.

Rook declined at first.

Angela offered again, this time she wasn't taking "no" for an answer.

Eventually, he accepted Angela's offer and told her that he needed to run back to the house and change clothes.

While he was dressing, he received a phone call from Detective Soflie.

He called to inform Rook that he was going to release Juan da Gama.

The reason: He didn't have enough sufficient evidence to hold him.

As far as any punishment, Juan da Gama faced a possibility of jail time for the two offenses, the first offense, which involved not showing up for court on the date provided to him, and then, the other offense, a potential duty to rescue, which fell under civil law, but, more than likely, the overall sentence in both offenses would probably be reduced to a hefty fine.

"As of now," the detective said, "he's a free man."

Enraged by the latest news, the phone slipped from Rook's hand and fell to the floor.

As Rook made his way back into the kitchen, he felt as though he was no longer in control of himself. He first grabbed a hold of both sides of the refrigerator with his hands. He began to shake it, first back and forth and then, once he picked up the momentum, from side to side. The more violent that he rocked the fridge, the more he allowed the anger to enter his body, as if with each shake, each rock, each move in itself, he was pressing his hands harder against his chest and digging his fingernails into his flesh, pulling and stretching open a massive hole, which allowed the anger to pour inside, causing him to rage throughout the kitchen.

The refrigerator doors swung open, the contents, as well as the shelves holding the contents, fell out and scattered over the kitchen floor, making a racket. He continued his campaign of rage and started to yank out drawers and fling silverware across the kitchen. The sound of metal hitting the floor, countertops, or sink was violence—a call to violence—ushering Rook closer to his eternal holy war, which he could no longer win, but rather endure until it pulverized and eventually destroyed whatever bit of soul he had left. He grabbed the candy jar, which was in the shape of a human skull, from the countertop and flung the ceramic novelty against the wall, shattering it to pieces.

The harsh manmade sounds of *clinking* and *clanking*, like two katanas striking one another, rang out through the kitchen.

Next, he turned his rage to the kitchen cabinets.

With the violence strangling his nerves, Rook balled both hands into fists and drove them into the cabinets. He punched holes in the cabinets and then the walls. He opened the cabinets below the drawers and grabbed kitchenware, such as pots and pans, as well as a cast iron skillet, and began tossing each piece across the kitchen.

Rook heard a voice from behind: "¡Ay, Dios mío!"

He ignored the voice for he thought it was only in his head and continued to rage.

From the doorway, Angela suddenly cried out Rook's name.

Rook redirected his attention toward the living room where he saw Angela standing next to the front door, which was opened. The expression on her face was one of great shock and terror.

"What are you doing, Rook?" she asked, as she inched closer to the wrecked kitchen.

With his breath labored, Rook asked Angela if she knew what *they* did to Nicky's cousin.

"They?" said Angela. "You mean, *policía*—"

"You and I both know he was responsible for what happened to Pep. . . "

Angela shrugged, as though both of her shoulders were attached to strings, and above, a puppeteer was pulling on those strings in an exaggerated cartoon-like fashion.

"I don't know what he did. Honestly—"

Rook shouted out, "Don't lie to me!"

"I'm not lying, Rook. *But*. . . " Angela's tone changed, as she lowered her defenses, ". . . I know what he's capable of. He's had a rough life, Rook—" He attempted to interrupt her, but Angela spoke over him, "—and if he had something to do with what happened to Pepper, then he must be held accountable."

A tense, yet, at the same time, tolerable silence built between the two.

Over the rapid pulse beating against his ear, Rook caught a heavy door slamming shut outside the house. He walked over to the kitchen window and first spotted that logo underneath the decal of a swimming pool, "Æ," which stood for the company Aqua Entertainment Creations, on the side of the truck, then Angela's husband, Nicholas, exiting from the truck.

Angela followed Rook's eyes toward the front door where she waited for her husband to appear.

"I must go now," she said more solemnly and made her way toward the front door.

"What do I do?" Rook asked, as Angela walked away.

Angela paused and thought carefully about her response.

With her eyes glossy, she asked, "What would your father do?"

Angela stepped over a pot on the floor.

Before leaving the house, she faced Rook one last time and warned: "He's dangerous."

After Angela left the house, he closed the front door and ambled into the unlit kitchen where he contemplated his first move. Without any plan, he started to clean up the mess in the kitchen but only managed to toss away a few items in the trash: first, a crushed carton of orange juice, as well as an empty—and noted, expired—container of sour cream (he didn't bother moping up the puddle of orange juice on the floor or waste any of his time wiping away sour cream, which had splattered over the cabinet closest to the refrigerator), then, second, a glass bottle of ketchup that he picked up from the floor and placed on the countertop, only to accidentally knock it back to the floor with his elbow, shattering the bottle and causing ketchup to splatter everywhere.

Exhausted from the latest outburst, he sat down on the floor with both of his legs propped up like two acute triangles, his hands draped over his knees, his stiff back pressed against the wall. He ignored any thought of cleaning or repairing—uninspired—and instead, focused on, not only Angela's last words to him, but also the steely look in her eyes when she said those words: *"He's dangerous."*

Rook stood back upright and hurried to the bedroom where he grabbed that smaller box on the top shelf inside the closet, the one with the letters, VR-CU, and brought it back to the kitchen.

For the next thirty minutes, he stared at the two eye contact lenses inside the open box underneath a dim stovetop light and debated whether or not he was going to use them. He specifically remembered the last time he wore them: Four years ago, he recalled, when the entire world was plagued by a pandemic. If he hadn't stop using, then he never would've met Pep. But if he hadn't met Pep, he convinced himself, he would've been spared the pain of losing her.

Tempted to relapse, Rook paced around the kitchen for what felt like another thirty minutes until he heard the *ring* of a doorbell!

More cautiously, he checked the front door but didn't see anyone outside. He flipped on the porch light and stepped outside, only to find a plastic plate wrapped in aluminum foil. He caught only the shadow of a person scurrying away toward the left side of his house. He reached down, picked up the plate, and brought it inside. He carried the plate into the kitchen and placed it on the counter and peeled back the foil. On the warm plate was a helping of carnitas with a side of arroz rojo and frijoles refritos topped with queso fresco and six homemade corn tortillas shells folded inside yet another piece of aluminum foil.

As he pulled his hand away from the plate, he felt a piece of paper taped to the bottom of the plate. He lifted up the plate and peeled away a handwritten note and brought it to the light.

On the note was what appeared to be a home address.

THE triggers were always inside of me, either lying in a dormant state or simply, there.

The certain words or expressions.

Actions and reactions.

Gestures.

Overtime, Pep learned everything single of them, my buttons—the triggers—and used them to provoke me or elicit a reaction from me whenever she gained the upper hand of a conversation (an argument), which often led to a negotiation. In a way, these triggers had become Pep's own little cheat code, her edge over me.

By making myself vulnerable, I had offered her an advantage in a system of checks and balances, which consisted of innumerable checks but not enough balance.

Never underestimate the power of an illusion.

And sometimes, in order to create one, you must mentally perform an autopsy on yourself.

Only then, you can untangle the knots and track down and follow the very roots of your own design.

What rubbed you the wrong way?

What twisted you up inside?

Essentially, what made you tick?

What pissed you off and why did it piss you off?

Then, once you delve deep into that madness, you may ask yourself: How do I defeat it?

By any means necessary, ruthlessly defeat it.

Reach down inside and mentally pull it apart until it no longer serves any value or purpose.

Once you've conquered it, use it to prevent yourself from becoming too powerful.

Convince yourself—*lie to yourself*—that it is the end-all of everything.

Without *it*, this fail-safe, you will erode and ultimately, destroy the very shoulders that were bestowed upon you for the weight of your faculty has become too onerous, imperious and unbalanced, and when you collapse, which, inevitably, you will, maybe not in the beginning, maybe it will take years, decades, to reverse the hardship you have inflicted on those less weighty and fortunate, but once a *chink* in your golden armor has been rightfully exposed by those who yearn to topple you, only then will you crumble and ultimately, wane into nothing more than a two-dollar placeholder who has been shuffled around for centuries by those who provide you with the illusion of faculty along the glass table of time, another top-of-the-hour idiot who jiggles a handful of nickels while speaking half-truths from your rotten stump of None.

It needs you as much as you need it.

Checks and balances, remember?

But don't forget the number one rule: Don't ever mistake *it* for hate.

Because, once you peel back the layers, you'll realize that it's far from hate.

8

AFTER using Pepper's laptop to research the address, which—according to a new version of Gumshoe's ATLAS— was located in an older, rundown neighborhood approximately five miles from Spring Grove, Rook grabbed the Glock, as well as the ski mask from the closet.

With Glock and mask in hand, Rook opened the garage door. He only took two steps toward his car before he spotted the gunmetal gray Caspian parked across the street, as well as the two men sitting inside the car. He immediately recognized the car, the same one that he not only saw parked outside the house after his girlfriend was attacked, but also the same one that he saw parked inside the parking garage at the hospital.

But why were those two dicks staking out the house? Or, he thought, maybe they were staking out the López's?

He made a subtle pivot toward the refrigerator, which held mostly drinks like sodas, as well as Pep's kefir and yogurt. He grabbed himself a grape soda, closed the garage door, and walked back into the house. As a diversion, he flipped on the living room light and hurried into the dark bedroom where he carefully lifted up the blinds and peeked outside. Sure enough, he was right. Sitting behind the steering wheel was Detective Giddy.

Rook took a moment to rethink the next course of action.

As soon as the idea dawned on him, he hurried back into the kitchen and grabbed the spare key to Pep's car and lastly, since the ski mask would draw too much unwanted attention, a black hat to cover up his face. Then, with the Glock tucked behind his waistband and ski mask stuffed into his back pocket, Rook exited via backdoor.

Using the cover of night, he sneaked through the back-yard, climbed over a chain-link fence, and cut through several neighbors' lawns. One incident resulted in Rook running from a beast of a dog and jumping over a shoddy fence, his right ankle coming inches away from the beast's chomping maw. He bruised his side during the landing but managed to exit from the neighborhood in one piece. He then walked along a grassy area on the side of the road until he reached a main highway, and then, from there, he found a sidewalk.

On the way to Under The Hood, Rook walked past a massive movie poster on the side of a movie theater. The movie being promoted was the suspense-thriller, *Final Cut*, and on the poster was a darkly dressed man slashing through a strip of film. Next to grab Rook's attention was a station wagon driving past him; however, it wasn't the vehicle that grabbed his attention. It was the young boy sitting in the backseat of the car. He was pressing a green lizard against the window. Just a couple of days ago, Rook recalled seeing a TV commercial for the popular stuffed animal—"*Lennie*" was the lizard's name. As he turned away from the highway, he was startled by two homeless men dressed in holey, raggedy clothing, both of them sitting against a street post, sucking on vape pens while laughing hysterically. One of the homeless men was laughing so hard that the vape pen slid from his mouth and he started to drool. Rook recalled the vape shop located not too far from his house, and a new sign on the front of the shop advertising a new pen, "Vape+," the plus sign standing for Nicotine plus Nitrous Oxide, or "laughing gas."

Lastly, Rook looked up and couldn't help but draw his attention toward a billboard above the highway. The advertisement was for a new state-of-the-art hard hat, which was specifically engineered to protect one's head from drone strikes. The product was called "*Bully Blocker.*"

Rook forced himself to block out all of the signs and advertisements, which were strangely flooding his senses, and focus on his next plan, which he wouldn't be able to accomplish without a vehicle.

When he arrived at Under The Hood after a roughly twenty minute walk, the shop was already closed. He spotted a surveillance camera on the corner of the garage, which forced him to readjust the hat. He thought about using the ski mask, but he convinced himself that it was dark outside and if he lowered the bill far enough past his brow, it'd conceal his face.

While keeping his head down, he stood on his tippy toes, peeked through the window of the garage door, and noticed several cars inside but none of them were Pep's. He walked around the shop and saw Pep's car parked next to several other cars waiting for pick-up. The cars were parked behind a fence, which was secured with a padlock. He jiggled the padlock, as well as the chain, which was fished through the holes of the gate.

Instead of using the Glock to shoot the padlock, which was his first thought, he decided that it was easier to climb the fence—one, he didn't want to waste any bullets, and two, after his latest escape from the neighborhood, he was used to climbing fences—and use blunt force to bust open the gate.

After climbing the fence, he found Pep's car and as he was about to use the spare to open the car door, he walked past what looked like a contractor's truck with a metal toolbox mounted behind the cab. Out of curiosity, he walked back to the truck and opened the toolbox. Inside was a pair of heavy-duty bolt cutters. He took it as a sign that his actions were justified and used them to cut through the padlock. He pushed open the gate and returned to Pep's car and drove away.

When he approached the address that Angela gave him, "*3668 Pummelo Dr,*" he stopped at a stop sign and saw that the letter "o" in the street name *Pummelo* was scratched off. More than likely, he assumed, probably by bored kids. From what he could tell, the neighborhood wasn't in any decent shape, much worse than his neighborhood. Most of the houses were badly rundown and neglected and from the outside, appeared as if they were abandoned, despite the cars parked in the driveways. The lawns were overgrown and covered in trash. Parked cars lined the streets. Some of them appeared, like the houses, abandoned and ruined. He drove past a car that was plugged with bullet holes. Another one with the windshield shattered by a brick. Small marble-sized pieces of glass scattered all over the pavement below.

As Rook cracked the window, he heard the distant *pop-pop* sound of gunfire.

When he reached the end of the street, he spotted Nicholas's cousin's hatchback, along with six other cars, parked on the street in front of a lit house. He parked in a shaded spot underneath a tree and cut his headlights. For Rook, it was difficult to tell how many people were inside the house and the only way to find out was to sneak around the house for a closer look.

The main problem with exiting the car—and it was considered a problem that he couldn't avoid—Rook had eyes on him and he spotted these eyes from all directions as if the neighborhood itself was a singular entity, and Rook's car didn't belong. He saw eyes behind windows of one house or the many eyes on the dark porch of another or the eyes on the sidewalk approaching from behind.

All of a sudden, he heard a noise coming from the lit house.

There, he saw Nicholas's cousin, Juan, who was casually twirling the set of car keys around his index finger, exit from the front door with another man, who was smoking a blunt.

The two entered the hatchback.

As the hatchback drove away, Rook immediately ducked his head below the dashboard and hid as Juan drove toward him. While he anxiously waited for Juan to pass, he found the rubbery handle of a steering wheel lock protruding from underneath the passenger seat. He grabbed hold of the device and inspected the two-pronged trident-like lock, as Juan noisily drove past by him. The muffler—or lack of muffler—on Juan's hatchback sounded similar to a high-pitch dirt bike.

Once Juan drove away, Rook sat upright and placed the device in the passenger seat and then he switched on the headlights and followed Juan.

While keeping his distance from Juan's hatchback, Rook followed him to the fast-food restaurant, Pollo Fresco, where Rook once more cut his headlights and parked across the street behind a party store and watched Juan stick his head from the open driver's side window and place an order in the drive-thru.

Juan pulled up to the drive-thru window and paid for the food.

From where Rook was parked, he couldn't hear what Juan was talking about with the fast-food worker, but he waved around his arms a lot in a showy, flamboyant manner. Once, he attempted to grab the worker. She retracted her arm in annoyance. Rook could tell that Juan was giving her a hard time, which not only added to Rook's anger, but also made Rook more determined to carry out his plan.

As Juan snatched the bag of food from the worker's hand, he sped away. The tires left behind a trail of smoke. Rook switched on the headlights and pulled out of the parking lot and tried to keep up with Juan. He nearly lost Juan when he took a wrong turn and followed the wrong car. He managed to catch up with Juan once he turned onto the interstate. He followed Juan for another ten minutes until Juan made a hard right on an off ramp and then took a couple more turns before he entered a newer development, which was known to house people who were on fixed income. The houses were mostly one-story and made of stucco, all cookie-cutter.

"What the hell is he doing here?" Rook asked himself.

Finally, he parked the car on a street corner and watched Juan park the hatchback in front of one of those cookie-cutter houses. The two got out of the hatchback and walked up to the house where an elderly woman answered the front door. She hugged the other person with Juan and afterwards, stepped aside and let the two inside the house.

With the steering wheel lock in his hand and the Glock tucked behind his waistband, Rook got of the car.

As doubts pulled him every which way, he immediately returned to the car and pulled out the ski mask from his back pocket.

"Fuck it," he said, removed his hat, and put on the ski mask.

With his face fully concealed, Rook walked around the side of the house and while hiding behind a shrub, peeked through the living room window where he saw both Juan and what looked like his friend sitting on a couch. Juan's friend divvied the food from Pollo Fresco on the coffee table.

As Rook made his way toward another window for a closer look, the motion-sensor floodlight was suddenly tripped, causing the light to shine over him.

Moments later, Rook heard the front door swing open.

He hurried toward the shrubs and took cover behind them.

Through an opening in the shrubs, he caught Juan walking through the front lawn. He was carrying a butterfly knife in his hand.

"Here, *kitty kitty*," he said teasingly, as he waved around the knife as if he was carving number eights in the air. "Where you at, my little *gatito*?"

As soon as Juan walked past the shrubs, Rook stepped onto the lawn and aimed the Glock at the back of Juan's head.

Juan froze in his tracks from a soft rustling directly behind him.

Slowly, he rotated around and found Rook standing only a few feet away, the Glock aimed directly at his face.

"Sup, man," Juan said and raised his hands in the air, "I ain't got no money on me. . . "

Rook yanked the ski mask from his face, his sweaty, messy hair falling into his eyes.

"Hey, man," said Juan, a he recognized Rook's face, "you got it all twisted, man—"

"Shut the fuck up," Rook said.

As he readjusted his grip around the Glock, he felt a piece of debris stuck in the corner of his eye, which caused him to rapidly blink. For a moment, his vision slightly blurred, pulling his surroundings out of focus. For a moment, Rook saw himself standing in Juan's place, both hands raised, knife still in one hand, face sweaty, eyes dilated. He blinked again and finally refocused.

Juan's voice pulled Rook from his thoughts: "*Hey, man, I'm sorry about what happened* to your girl—"

"Drop the knife," said Rook.

Juan dropped the knife on the ground.

"Whatever they say happened, it ain't true—"

"I said, 'Shut the fuck up.'"

Then he heard yet another voice: "*Yo, Don Juan. . .* where you at?"

As Juan's friend made his way through the front yard, Rook closely inspected Juan's attire, in particular, the chocolate brown lightweight jacket and the brand name, "ARLO," written on the breast pocket of the jacket.

Juan suddenly called out, "I'm over here, Dante."

The voice was much closer: "What the fuck is you doing, *cabrón*—"

Rook glanced to his left where Juan's friend, Dante, first acknowledged Rook and the gun in his hand, and then, Juan, who was standing alongside the house. As soon as Dante saw Juan's hands held upward, he darted back into the house.

Despite the action to his left, Rook kept the gun on Juan.

"You're in trouble now, hombre. . . " Juan said with a grin curling along one side of his face. "My boy just got this new piece. It's a real kicker. He's been dying to give it a test ride. Looks like you might be the lucky—"

Rook shouted out, "Shut the fuck up!"

"Is that the only thing you can say to me?" asked Juan, as he took a step closer to Rook. "I didn't kill your girl, man."

Rook heard an elderly woman shouting inside the house.

"Did you hear what I said?" said Juan. "I didn't kill—"

Rook suddenly pulled the trigger.

Nothing.

The gun was jammed.

He made the mistake of pulling the trigger yet again.

In return, the Glock suddenly exploded in his hand, causing a piece of shrapnel to graze the side of his neck.

He dropped the fractured gun to the ground, which prompted Juan to pick up the knife from the ground.

While backpedaling, he caught Dante in the corner of his eye. He only caught a glimpse of the steel in Dante's hand. As soon as Dante lifted up his hand, Rook took off running.

Three booming gunshots *rang* out!

Rook ducked and sprinted toward the hatchback.

Several more shots rang out and each one whizzed over Rook's head. One bullet struck the curb next to the driveway, forcing him to race back to the hatchback and take cover.

With nowhere else to run, Rook searched his surroundings in hopes of creating a distraction, which could possibly give him a chance to make a run toward his car. Rook couldn't find anything at his disposal, except to his immediate left: the access door to the fuel tank.

With a key, he wedged it between the door and pried open the door, twisted the cap until it was removed from the filler, and then yanked the cap from the cord.

Once the cap was removed, Rook peeked through the window and saw Dante approaching. He fired yet again. The bullet penetrated the backseat window, inches away from Rook's head. He backtracked each sound of gunfire and counted at least six to seven rounds, which meant he probably had roughly eight or nine rounds left in the magazine.

As Juan met up with Dante, he cried out, "Shoot that *hijo de puta!*"

Charged by the recoil of the new piece, similar to Rook's Glock, Dante's aim was all over the place as he moved the barrel to each passing shadow below the car. He fired two more shots near the back tire and bumper area, one bullet striking the rear brake lights.

"Watch the whip, *ese!*"

Acknowledging Dante's heightened state, Rook crept toward the rear of the hatchback, the same spot of the two latest shots, and flung the fuel toward the front of the car.

The cap struck the driveway, making a sudden *clacking* sound.

Startled, Dante tracked the noise toward the front of the hatchback and while he popped off four more rounds, Rook made his move.

With the steering wheel lock in his hand, he rushed at Dante, who had the gun pointed in the other direction.

Dante picked up a dark figure in the corner of his eye; and the second that he redirected the gun toward the dark, approaching figure, Rook was already rearing back his arm. He violently swung the steering wheel lock at Dante, who managed to squeeze the trigger and fire off a round while being struck in the head. A bullet grazed Rook's arm but didn't slow him down. Dante, dazed from a partial blow to the head, was struck yet again with a follow-up blow, which caused him to lose his grip on the gun. Dante stumbled backward and dropped the gun to the ground.

Rook eyed the gun on the ground and while anticipating his next move, subtly placed the steering wheel lock in the other hand.

When Dante attempted to regain his footing, he staggered over the flower bedding next to the mailbox and stepped onto a rock, causing his foot to slip. Dante's right ankle suddenly turned, causing him to trip and fall backward and during the landing, the right side of his head struck the top red hat of a garden gnome, who was carrying a satchel of yellow stars.

With the knife in hand, Juan made an attempt at Rook.

As soon as Juan reared back the knife, Rook quickly picked up the gun with his free hand.

Rook counted at least two or three rounds left in the magazine.

Armed, he aimed the gun at Juan and prevented him from taking another step forward.

From behind, Dante asked, "What happened?"

Rook glanced at Dante, who was rather slow to stand. His right eye was bloodshot. While rapidly blinking his eyelid, he struggled to look through the injured eye.

As Dante staggered back and forth, he wandered closer to Rook, who warned Dante to stay away from him.

"Yo, *Juan*," Dante said to Rook, "I don't feel too good, man."

"I'm right here, Dante," Juan, who was standing in the other direction, said.

Dante never turned around toward Juan. Instead, Dante's focus remained on Rook, whom he thought was Juan.

"I told mi abuela about the *cuervos*," Dante said with a slight slur in his voice. "She said she didn't believe in such omens. Believe that?"

All of a sudden, Dante stared directly at Rook with these wide, dilated eyes. Despite Rook telling Dante to back away, Dante took another wobbly step closer to Rook and pulled out a phone from his pocket.

As soon as he brandished the phone, Rook stumbled backward and fired the gun, the bullet hitting Dante in the face, instantly killing him.

Blood splattered over Juan's shocked face.

Rook, who was also in a state of shock, glanced down at the gun and couldn't believe what had just happened.

Juan rushed over to Dante and checked on him, but he was already dead.

While keeping the gun on Juan, Rook backed away and eventually, once he had distanced himself from Juan, ran back toward his car and drove away.

About a mile down the road, Rook had a hard time trying to catch his breath.

As the adrenaline wore off, he pulled the car into the empty parking lot of a Taco Shell fast-food restaurant. First, he checked the two wounds, first the gunshot wound and then, a cut along the side of his neck. Neither the cut nor the gunshot wound appeared life threatening. The bullet grazed his right shoulder and resulted in a laceration about two inches long. The cut bled through the sleeve of his shirt, which was soaked with blood. He told himself that he might need stitches, or if he didn't go to the hospital—which, at this point, was not an option—he could superglue it in order to stop the bleeding. Either way, Rook needed to address the wound. For the time being, he grabbed a handful of spare napkins from the glove compartment and stuffed napkins into the shirt until the sleeve was packed and then rummaged around the car for a string or rope but ended up finding a wire from one of Pep's ear buds and then tightly wrapped it around the upper part of his arm and finally, tied the wire into a knot to keep it from moving.

Lastly, he checked the gun, Dante's gun, one of two murder weapons, the other one being that steering wheel lock, which was partially covered in blood.

He checked the magazine, which had only one round left.

As soon as the idea popped in his head, he immediately shunned it as if it was an awful idea, a leper of a thought, which he would never consider.

Once he gathered himself, his first course of action: Ditch the weapons. Both of them.

As he heard the sounds of police sirens from a distance, he drove to the river and tossed both the steering wheel lock and the gun into the current.

After dumping the gun, he couldn't help but think about the Glock. The gun was destroyed, he told himself, but if the gun was pieced back together, which forensic investigators who specialize in ballistics would after collecting all of the evidence, then, more than likely, the weapon would be traced back to his name. But, again, Rook told himself, maybe even lied to himself, that the gun was completely destroyed and that tracing the gun back to him would be considered a long shot.

The next course of action: Rid any traces of him being at Dante's grandmother's house. He had blood on his shirt, obviously, his blood, but maybe Dante's as well. The fact: He wasn't sure.

The final course of action: Pep's car.

More than likely, he was caught on surveillance camera breaking into the secured fence next to Under The Hood. Although his identity was probably concealed (the hat, as well as the cover of night made it nearly impossible for his face to be recognized), an eyewitness could've seen the car near the vicinity of the crime. Rook assumed that there were eyewitnesses. After all, it was a newer development, which mostly consisted of older residents, who probably didn't sleep much. The first person who came to mind was Pep's mother, a night owl who stayed up to four o' clock in the morning watching true crime shows on TV. Surely, he thought, there was a Mrs. Piper in that neighborhood watching shows like Vadge the Badge when most were watching moving pictures in their heads. Surely, she heard multiple gunshots ring out. Besides, what about Dante's grandmother, who had a front row seat to the whole show?

He decided to drive back to the house.

When he reached the neighborhood, he drove past his street, where, from a distance, he saw the gray Caspian parked across his neighbor's house. He had no other choice than to park the car in a shaded overgrown spot off a secluded dirt road behind his neighborhood until he could figure out what to do with it. He yanked branches from trees and draped them over the car.

Once he concealed a majority of the car, he made his way back to the house, taking the same route as he did when he snuck out of the house. Eventually, he managed to sneak his way through the rear entrance. He checked the front of the house and sure enough, the two detectives were still parked across the street.

Next, he removed the bloody clothes from his body and stuffed them in a garbage bag, which he would discard along with Pep's car as soon as he came up with a plan. He managed to control the bleeding on his arm by wrapping it with fresh gauze.

By the time he managed to change his clothes and slip into more comfortable attire, he was extremely exhausted, and yet, his mind was racing a million miles per hour, trying to backtrack every past movement. He grabbed the VR-CU contact lenses from the kitchen countertop and carefully placed the contact lens onto each one of his eyes and without using any of the required restraints, sat on the couch and rested his eyelids.

A sudden hunger struck him in the middle of the night, leaving Rook restless.

He woke from his half-sleep, reached over the nightstand, and checked the clock.

Blurry red digital numbers gradually appeared in the darkness: 11:11

With his stomach growling up a storm, Rook rolled out of bed and shuffled into the kitchen where he blindly cracked open the fridge. The bluish light temporary hurt Rook's eyes, causing him to squint away the ache. Once his eyes adjusted to the light, he searched through each wired shelf. The inside of the fridge was mostly filled with expired condiments and spoiled leftovers from last week.

Having no luck, he tried the drawer where he found a potential snack: a block of cheddar.

He carefully unwrapped the wrinkled tinfoil from partially exposed cheese, only to reveal a block of moldy, fuzzy green cheddar. He was so hungry that he even contemplated taking a bite of moldy cheese.

Eventually, he closed the fridge and went to bed hungry.

As Rook rested his eyes, he imagined a world without toilets.

ONCE I questioned myself whether life was real or a simulation.

Was my body uniquely made up of a genetic structure, which provided me a road map to the origins of my bloodline, or was I just a series of ones and zeroes inside a boxed void?

Naturally, we are drawn to the Real, the physical and the tangible which cannot be denied by the profiteers who attempt to hijack the brains of those who are the most vulnerable, opposed to the Unreal, the nonexistent. Despite our inherent nature for connection, we continue to oppose what we know as the Real and constantly struggle to remove the ball and chain from corruptive vices, which keep us rooted and imprisoned in a false and idolatrous environment that offers not one single benefit to the progression of Man.

But you tell yourself: They allow us to become the gods of our own creations. And yet, when you question the partiality of their scheme to elevate those who yield to their rules, they attempt to burn you down.

But to whom exactly do they serve, these profiteers?

The operator or the machine?

If they only serve the operator, then how can you continue to rage against the machine when you have become the very lever of the machine?

9

AS Rook leaned up against the kitchen counter, he pulled the VR contact lenses from his eyes.

Disorientated from the recent images in his head, he rotated his shoulder toward the sink and watched the water overflowing from the sink. Stepping over scattered debris of food and kitchen utensils on the floor, he made it to the flooded sink and turned off the running faucet. To the left of the sink was a damp hand towel, which was spotted red with blood—But whose blood?

Images of violence overwhelmed his latest dream (Or was it memory?) of being a seasoned private investigator, whose latest lead led him to a shore where crane operators and divers were pulling a submerged vehicle from the river.

Images of the crime: Rook striking Dante in the head with a steering wheel lock; Dante tripping over a rock and hitting the side of his head on a lawn decoration; Dante slowly standing to his feet, staggering, and pulling out what looked like yet another gun from his pocket, or at least, another type of weapon. Lastly, Rook grabbing a handgun from the edge of the driveway and aiming it at Dante's head.

Rook immediately rejected the thought of a bullet entering through Dante's right cheek as soon as the images entered his head and inspected the ruined kitchen before his eyes.

All of a sudden, Rook heard someone *knocking* on the front door. He rushed to the window where he saw two police officers walking through the lawn.

As panic washed over him, he scrambled into the living room for a better look at the police officers, three of them, he counted, one standing on the front porch, waiting anxiously.

The officer knocked again, all meat, no bone.

As Rook opened the front door, he caught a black bag next to the doorway.

These were the very first images that the officer saw when Rook opened the door: the resident's eyes held downward on the floor, his right foot sliding an object away from the doorway.

Then, when Rook looked up at the officer, he was wearing a look of guilt on his face.

"Can I help you, officer?" Rook asked and cleared his throat.

"Sorry to disturb at this hour of the night. . . " said the officer, as the two others shined flashlights alongside the house, ". . . We just want to check the perimeter and make sure everything is okay."

"Has something happened?" asked Rook.

"There was a shooting," the officer said. "We believe that your neighbor's cousin, Juan da Gama, was involved in the shooting after an eyewitness spotted him fleeing the scene of a crime. Knowing how. . . delicate. . . the situation is between you and mister—"

"Delicate. . . " said Rook, ". . . as in the man murdered my girlfriend?"

The officer held up his hands, as if he didn't want to start trouble.

"If you see anything, please give us a call," the officer said and once he received a clear sign from the other officers, said goodnight.

Before Rook closed the door, he looked for the detectives' car across the street but couldn't find it. He wondered if the detectives were currently at Dante's grandmother's house and if they were, which was likely, Rook told himself that it was only a matter of time before they returned to the house and this time, not to play campers.

As Rook began to straighten up the rest of the house, including stuffing the bloody towel in the black bag of bloody clothes, he heard yet another *knock* on the front door, this time softer.

He figured it was the cops again. Maybe they forgot to ask him a question. Maybe they had some updates about Juan or Juan's whereabouts.

Before answering, he checked the window. The cops had already driven away.

Cautiously, he flipped on the front porch light and answered the door.

Nobody was there.

To his right, he caught a dark and shadowy figure storming away.

Halfway toward his neighbor's house, the one to his right, not Angela but a cranky recluse, Ms. Ingle, the stranger briefly turned around and looked in Rook's direction.

In a glimpse, Rook saw—or at least, thought he saw— Pep's face in a cast of light.

Rook called out, "Autumn?"

He chased after the dark figure; and by the time he reached his neighbor's house, the front door closed behind the dark figure. Rook knocked on the door; and seconds later, his neighbor, Ms. Ingle, answered the door.

"Did you just knock on my door?" Rook asked, motioning toward his house.

"Yes," she stuttered, as she released a tension balled up in her chest with an airy laugh. "That was me. I waited, but you didn't answer. I didn't wake you, did I?"

"No," he said, his voice trailing off. "I was just. . . I spoke with the cops," he said more directly, "but, of course, you already knew that, right?"

"I'm sure you have a lot of questions about what happened," Ms. Ingle said and paused and then, after taking a beat, stepped aside. "Would you like to come inside?"

Rook turned his shoulder and surveyed the dark neighborhood street, which, except for distant traffic noise from the highway, was deathly quiet.

"Sure," he said and entered Ms. Ingle's house.

He was first greeted by a muted gray longhaired Nebelung named "Critter." The cat rubbed against Rook's leg and stared up at him with cloudy lime green eyes with black pupils as sharp as paper cuts.

"He doesn't like strangers, but I can tell. . . " Ms. Ingle said and stopped to acknowledge the cat's interest in Rook, ". . . he likes you."

Rook leaned down and petted the top of Critter's head and paid closer attention to the cat's eyes, in particular, its pupils, which were smaller, not open, as they'd appear in the dimmer light, such as Ms. Ingle's foyer. Rook didn't put much stock into the thought, as he followed Ms. Ingle into a cluttered kitchen where she asked him if he'd like a cup of coffee, since she was about to brew a pot, her reasons being that she was a light sleeper. Plus, she also stated that she needed to get up early in the morning to drive to the studio and didn't want to, in her words, "oversleep."

Based on the many pieces of artwork that he passed in the hallway, Rook guessed, "You're an artist?"

"You hit the nail on the head," she said and grabbed a jar of coffee grounds from the pantry and twisted off the metal lid and grabbed the scooper from inside and scooped out four cups and dumped them into a filter. "I have a studio just off Maple Street."

The name, *Maple*, instantly grabbed Rook's attention. He recalled seeing a street sign for Maple just minutes after he picked up Pep's car from Under The Hood. The images in his head were so heavy and vivid that Rook's eyes began to venture elsewhere.

"You should stop by sometime and check out some of my work. . . "

Rook glanced down at his hands and noticed the dried blood caked around the fingernail of his index finger. He immediately hid his hand from Ms. Ingle.

"Listen, Ms. Ingle—"

"Please. . . " she said and switched on the coffee machine after filling it with a pitcher of water, ". . . Julia. I'm already old enough."

"*Julia*," he said, "about Autumn. . . "

"Before I tell you. . . " Ms. Ingle—"Julia," as she pre-ferred—cleared her throat and walked over to Rook and touched him on the shoulder in an almost motherly way, ". . . I want to offer my sincere condolences, Rook. I had the chance to speak with Jason earlier today when I was picking up the mail. He told me about Autumn. That's one of the main reasons why I came over to see you. I wanted to stop by earlier, but you looked like you were busy. The least I can do is tell you what I saw happened the other night."

"Cops said you called them after you heard screaming," Rook said and studied Julia.

"I'm sure you're already aware that Juan da Gama was involved, right?"

Rook hesitated.

"Cops have him in custody," he lied. His focus narrowed first, then his eyes. "How much did you see?"

"Well, after I heard screaming, I saw him fleeing from your house moments later. Well, let me take a step back. I didn't actually see his face, but I saw his car right before it sped away."

"Was he carrying anything in his arms?" asked Rook.

"As a matter of fact, he was," she said, "but as I told the police, I couldn't make out what he was carrying."

"But he was carrying something, right?"

Julia paused.

"Rook, there's something that I need to tell you," she said, more seriously, "and it's something that I never told the police." She pointed to the living room. "Please. . . "

Julia showed Rook to the living room where the late night talk show, *Late Night With Jack Ballantyne*, was airing live on television. One of the guests on the show was the award-winning actor of his *Tribal* fame, Tom Needles. The musical guest was the pop star, Mayhem.

As Rook did a double take at the well-dressed talk show host on TV, Julia turned down the volume.

The two sat down, Julia in the chair and Rook on the couch. Critter jumped onto the couch and plumped himself next to Rook.

"Shortly after that guy sped away, someone else showed up at your house. . . a woman who was probably in her mid-twenties. Rook," she said sternly, "she went inside your house—"

"Inside?"

Julia nodded.

"Did you ask her what she wanted?" asked Rook.

Julia gave Rook a kind of "Are you serious?" look.

"I honestly didn't know what was going on over there. If I did. . . "

"I didn't mean to. . . " Rook said and immediately retracted any insinuation that she was at fault for not stopping Juan, ". . . It's just frustrating. The not-knowing what happened part. . . "

"She was only there for maybe a minute, not long. She left in a hurry."

"Did you get a good look at her?" asked Rook.

"No," Julia said, thinking. "It was dark, but something told me that she wasn't there to see Autumn."

More intrigued, Rook asked, "Did you see what car she was driving?"

"It looked like one of those crossover vehicles," she said. "There was a crack that stretched across the front windshield—"

"A crack, huh?"

Suddenly, Rook's eyes fell hard into thought.

Only one person came to mind, and it was the same person who had texted him right before he wrapped up work. She texted him as soon as he finished texting Pep about dinner. He specifically remembered that she had something important to tell him.

"You know who it was, don't you?"

"I think so," Rook said pensively. "Why didn't you tell the cops about this?"

"It's none of my business, Rook. . . " she said, ". . . nor is it the public's business what you do in your personal life, *but*, I reckon, the truth always finds a way out. I guess the question that you should be asking yourself: Whom do you want to tell *your* truth? You? Or, someone else?"

"She wouldn't have harmed Autumn," Rook said, looking away.

"Who is she, if you don't mind me asking?"

Rook moved his narrow eyes back to Julia.

"Forget it," she said, waving off the inquiry. She stood up and asked, "Cream and sugar?"

"Black please," he said.

"Black it is."

In the corner of his eye, Rook saw the talk show host, Jack Ballantyne, cue the band to play to a commercial break.

Julia excused herself for a moment and walked back into the kitchen and fixed two cups, one with cream and sugar, the other black, and brought them into the living room where Rook was standing in front of a painting of three dark shapes with glowing white eyes in the center of their foreheads. Julia nodded at the painting on the wall, or what Julia called "*The Three Brothers.*"

"You paint this?" asked Rook.

"I did," she said. "It was inspired by my three brothers."

"You come from a big family?"

"My parents had four children," she said. "I was the youngest."

"Must've been hard growing up with three big brothers."

"No," she said and handed Rook the coffee. "It wasn't actually. I sort of coasted my way through high school. By the time I had reached college, they were already grown up, had families of their own. Throughout my entire childhood, I looked up to my brothers as if they were my protectors. When I was in college. . . " Julia sighed, ". . . they weren't around anymore to protect me, and I guess I had to stick up for myself."

Rook leaned closer and pointed at the glowing white eye.

"Is that supposed to be a third eye or something?" asked Rook.

"Not a third eye," she clarified, "although, it's open for interpretation. For me, it's supposed to be the eye of cyclops, like the ones in Greek mythology." Julia cracked a smile. "It's sort of an 'inside joke,' if you will. My brothers are extremely tall and red-blooded by nature. You can hear them a mile away. Except for my youngest brother, Oliver, who's rather sensitive, I suppose they picked up the traits from my father, who played professional football before I was born. On the other hand, my mother was a sculptor, the polar opposite of my father. . . "

When Rook returned to the couch, he caught the tail end of a TV commercial for the lawyer, Samuel Glasser, who looked incredibly familiar. Even though the volume was lowered, he could read the TV lawyer's lips: *"Been involved in an accident? Call Samuel Glasser today!"*

A "**1-800**" number appeared on the bottom of the screen.

"Is something wrong with the coffee?" asked Julia.

Rook took a sip of coffee, which wasn't as strong or overpowering as he first thought.

"No," he said, savoring the taste. "Thanks."

The two sat back down in their seats.

"So, do you have any children?" asked Rook.

"One," Julia said. "She lives with Spartacus where she and her husband are currently working on their second child—" she stopped midway before finishing her thought, "—I didn't—"

"What's her name, your daughter?" Rook asked, as he shelved the very idea of losing a child.

"Ivey."

"Ivey Ingle," Rook repeated. "Sounds like the name of a superhero."

"Well, not anymore," said Julia. "She hung up her cape for a library card."

"Husband?"

As soon as Rook said the *word*, he immediately acknowledged that he hit a sore spot based on Julia's aloofness.

"Sorry," Rook said and took another sip of coffee.

"Enough with the sorries, Rook," she said, her manner sterner and more rigid as her voice sounded frustrated and frankly, annoyed by her guest's apologies.

Sensing a change in Julia, Rook thought about leaving and mentally asked himself what he was doing here.

At this hour of the night?

With someone whom he looked at as a stranger?

On her couch?

Or, was it considered a sofa, not a couch?

For all he knew, the woman was absolutely nuts.

He looked at the cat to his right, still staring at him.

Those lemon lime eyes penetrating his soul.

He finally mustered the courage to stand up.

"I should be going," he said.

With a deadpan expression, Julia said with a flat, seedy tone, "I killed him, you know?"

"Excuse me," he uttered.

"My husband," Julia said. "It was an accident," she clarified with a strange tenderness in her voice.

After an awkward pause, Rook sat back down on the couch.

More interested, he asked, "What happened?"

"Well. . . " Julia took a deep breath and said more carefully, ". . . it happened three years after I had Ivey. I just found out that I was pregnant *again*. Franklin. . . " she said, as if she hadn't said the name in years and the name shot out like a ball of phlegm lodged in her throat, causing her to take a beat, ". . . Frank and I never planned on having another child. The news was unexpected and. . . " she took in yet another deep breath, ". . . I didn't want to keep it and I know how awful this sounds, but I convinced myself we couldn't afford to have another child. We were already drowning in debt and struggling to stay afloat. When I finally summoned the strength to bring up the subject with Frank, he flipped out. Called me an 'evil bitch' for even suggesting the very idea. I knew, if I went through with it, he'd never forgive me. Originally, we thought bringing a child into the world would help mend our marriage, but honestly, it only deepened our hatred for one another—"

Rook asked, "If you hated him so much, then why'd you stay? Why not just leave before it got messy?"

Julia shrugged, made a noise with her mouth closed.

"I felt trapped, powerless," Julia said in reflection. Then she turned her eyes to Rook: "For some, it's much easier to endure than it is to run. And for some, like me, it was extremely difficult to take that first step, knowing that I was leaving behind a world that I helped create. Sure," she said, "looking back in hindsight, it's easy to ask myself, 'Why didn't you just leave, Stupid? Just take Ivey and get the hell out of here!' I can't tell you how many times I had that conversation with myself." Finally, she arrived at the story: "The night before we got into an argument," she said and placed the warm mug on the coaster. "His pleas turned into threats and at the time, I didn't think anything of them. He said much worse to me before, horrible things, but I wasn't thinking rationally and I was so sick and tired of the verbal abuse. So," Julia said more straightforward, "the next morning, I went behind his back and terminated the pregnancy. As soon as I saw Frank after he returned home from work, he knew what I had done. I don't know how in the world he knew, but he knew. He suddenly cornered me in the kitchen. His eyes went dark, like his soul fled his body. He grabbed a knife from the drawer. I ran upstairs. He chased after me. The next thing I heard, when I made it to the upstairs bathroom, was Frank's voice screaming out below and it wasn't out of rage. It was pain. I inched back to the top of the landing and saw him lying on the bottom of the staircase. The railing along the stairs was bent sideways, barely intact. I remember it being loose and wobbly. Frank was planning to repair it over the weekend. Apparently, as he was rounding the bottom of the staircase, he grabbed hold of the railing with his left hand and swung around it. The railing broke. He slipped and lost his footing, and the right side of his body struck the wall. When his right shoulder struck the wall, the knife in his hand turned around on him and stabbed him in the right pectoral muscle and penetrated one of his major arteries. I rushed downstairs. I freaked out. I pulled the knife out. I've never seen so much blood in my entire life. I called an ambulance," she said, as if she had told the story many times before, especially in front of people whose role specifically entailed the meticulous gathering of details. "Frank died on the way to the hospital. What makes it even worse: Ivey woke up from her sleep and saw the whole thing go down. She watched her father bleed to death. Even till this day, I tell myself, 'He was going to kill me. This wasn't a threat or another one of his scare tactics. *He was*, in fact, *going to kill me.*' I remember, one day when I was dropping Ivey off at my mother's house—this was a few years after Frank's death, and I was done with processing, and I was finally starting to move on with my life—something suddenly came over me when I drove past a playground where there were other kids playing. I felt this emptiness, an incredible numbness, spread over me and cover me like a blanket. I was dead—at least a part of me had died and this. . . *thing*. . . had been hanging over me ever since Franklin's death, and every single time I sensed it—this thing—inching closer, I shunned it away and told myself it wasn't my fault; yet it was everybody else's fault, except mine. '*I was the victim here!*' I know. . . " Julia paused, her voice fragile and shaking, ". . . I was only lying to myself," Julia said to Rook, as tears flowed from her eyes. "I killed a life that was growing inside me. So, what does that make me?"

"A realist," Rook said plainly, thanked Julia for the coffee, walked back to his house, and went straight to bed.

For the next hour or so—Rook lost track of time—he never drifted to sleep. His eyes were closed, both of them, but his mind was wide open, black and gaping as though allowing darkness to enter. He shunned it, the darkness, not only a call to violence, but also an acknowledgement, and rolled out of bed soon after the sheets dampened with sweat.

The coffee, Rook told himself, which he regretted drinking late at the night.

Yet, despite the gnawing frustration of not being able to rest, Rook embraced his alertness; and instead of shunning it, that wide-openness, he took full advantage of it.

Still buzzing from the caffeine, he entered James's bedroom, switched on the light below the ceiling fan, and came across two items, the first item being a painting that he made when he was a child, the other, a plush toy of a yellow star.

Back to the painting: Pep recently had it framed and was planning to mount it on the wall for James. In the painting was a powder blue choo-choo train with wheels that looked like arms riding through a scribbly, hilly green landscape. Directly above the train was an orangish-yellow near-perfectly drawn circle—the sun—with gray clouds parting ways and then standing on top of the hill, a stick figured man waving his six-fingered hand.

The next item was the soft, matted, somewhat greasy plush toy of a smiling star made of cotton, which, when opened along the side, revealed another face, the paler one of a crescent moon, where, at the bottom, a crisscross-like pattern from a sewing job covered what used to be a rip in the material. On the bottom of the moon's face was a frayed white tag with cursive lettering which read the message: "*Only when we let the light in are we able to let the light out.*"

While trying to hold back the tears, Rook thought to himself, *If only it was that simple.*

PRIOR to our conversation on the night of the shooting, I hardly spoke to Julia, whom I knew by the name Ms. Ingle, the "Skittish Lady Who Lived Next Door," "Who, Every Now and Then, I'd Catch Peeking Out The Blinds," "Who Rarely Showed Her Face." Except for the time that she introduced herself the day after I settled into the new house—our conversation lasting as long as it'd take for small talk with a cashier at a grocery store while checking out a half-full basketful of groceries—most of our weekly and at times, monthly interactions consisted of nods of hello or hand waves, me doing all the waving and her taking the gesture as a sign of bad faith. Basically, I knew very little about her, only that she was a widow—her husband's death I'd later learn soon after the shooting—which could've played a factor in the "why" Julia came across as a spiteful, ill-spirited neighbor who had nothing but contempt for those who longed for something as simple and yet, at times, as difficult to reach as contentment.

That night, after Julia spoke about her husband, Franklin, and his tragic death and her choice not to keep the baby, I thought about my relationship with Pep, and how, much similar to Julia, I, too, found myself in a difficult situation, which forced me to ask a question that I had buried underneath a mountainous pile of aged *skins*: Was this really happening to me? Or, did this evasive serpent still have its venomous fangs plunged deep inside me? And if so, would this creature ever release its hold over me?

10

THE next morning, Rook woke to the thought of Juan da Gama still being out there, waiting for him to slip up, which he most definitely would, or drop his guard, again, most definitely inevitable, and whenever Juan found the right opportunity, he'd stick Rook while he was distracted—in a world of constant distractions, it was nearly impossible for Rook to keep his head on a swivel, especially while trudging through a flood of content, whether it be the reps of consumerism flexing a gaudy muscle or playing peek-a-boo from the seam of his back pocket, the eavesdropping lowlife who relentlessly attempts to hijack his every thought by way of algorithmic manipulation.

With not only Julia and her loss weighing heavily on his mind, but also Juan and his mysterious whereabouts, Rook knew that it was only a matter of time before the police started knocking on doors. He reckoned his door would be one of the firsts on the list, which meant he didn't have much time.

Rook rolled out of bed and rushed to the window where he didn't see any cars parked outside. Since it was daylight, he figured that he'd have eyes on him. Aware of the possibilities, he came up with a less-than-ideal plan that, in his own mind, wouldn't draw any unwanted attention toward him. In his next course of action, he threw on a pair of sweatpants and grabbed a pair of running shoes from the living room and then, lastly, found his old mp3 player tucked away in the back of a nightstand drawer. The white wire for the ear buds appeared cannibalized and more than likely didn't work, but, for appearances sake, it didn't matter. At the very last second, he decided to use the wire from Pep's mp3 player but soon realized it was covered in blood. He washed off the blood and replaced the chewed up wire with the other one.

As soon as he headed out for a "morning jog," his phone rang.

Auggie was calling him, and knowing Auggie and how she embodied the common traits of a go-getter—the more time Rook spent around Auggie, the more he began to understand why Pep and her sister's relationship was complicated—she was calling to discuss funeral arrangements.

Rook rejected the call and pocketed the phone.

Before heading out, he grabbed Pep's apartment key from the clay bowel and finally, left the house.

As he first loosened up with a brisk walk, he passed Julia's house.

The garage door was opened, he noticed, which was strange.

When Rook spoke to Julia last night, he recalled her mentioning something about getting up early, for exactly what, he had forgotten. But it had something to do with her art.

Tempted to stop and say hi, Rook decided to continue his jog.

During the jog through the neighborhood, he occasionally looked over his shoulder; and by the time he reached the end of the street, his neck started to ache. He stopped for a moment, took a break—his stomach growled, which was the first time he felt hungry ever since yesterday—and then he returned to his jog.

Eventually, he made it to the dirt road just outside the neighborhood. Once he stepped foot onto the road, he was struck by a momentary nausea. For some reason, he knew that the car was gone; and once he reached the spot where he had concealed Pep's car with tree branches, his suspicions were correct. The car was nowhere to be found. He came across the branches from last night scattered along the ground, as well as the tire tracks, but no car.

Dumbfounded by the car's disappearance, he rushed back to the house, the jog turning into a full-on sprint. He ran past Julia's house and this time the garage door was closed. When Rook finally arrived at his house, he noticed that the front door was wide-open. He grabbed a garden flag of a bumble-bee from the flower bedding and with the metal end of the pole held outward like a weapon, cautiously stepped inside the house. He only took two steps into the house before he heard a toilet flushing in the guest bathroom. Auggie exited the bathroom and gasped from the sight of Rook.

Startled, she grabbed her chest and said with relief, "You scared the shit outta me."

"What are you doing?" asked Rook.

"Alexis dropped me off," she said. "Your door was un-locked."

Rook thought back to when he first left for a jog.

He specifically remembered locking the door, which meant either she was lying or someone broke into the house before she entered.

As Rook closed the door behind him, he saw the black garbage bag on the floor.

He asked Auggie, "Why'd you leave the door open?"

"Oh," she said with a higher pitch, the color in her face slightly paler, as if she was surprised that Rook would ask the question. "Sorry. I was about to pop," she said, motioning toward the bathroom. "I called out for you several times, but you didn't answer. Since your car was here, I figured you went for a walk or—"

"What are you doing here, Auggie?" Rook asked bluntly, his tone more serious.

"You weren't answering your phone, Rook," she said. "Did you not get my texts?"

Rook pulled out his phone and saw several unanswered texts from Auggie, one of the texts mentioning something about "*stopping by, if it's all right with you.*"

He put aside the phone and asked, "Where's Alexis?"

"He went to grab breakfast," she said. "I thought maybe you were hungry—"

"I can't do this now, Auggie," he said, thinking of ways to get rid of Auggie without making it too obvious that he was hiding something from her.

Auggie walked over to Rook and hugged him and told him how sorry she was for him and Autumn and James, then reassured him that he was family and that he shouldn't be alone or shun those who care for him, especially during such a difficult time.

Auggie told him that she and Alexis were here for him.

"Whatever you need. . . " she emphasized, ". . . you don't even have to ask twice."

Rook decided to play along, if it meant getting Auggie out of his hair. He asked her if she could go to his bedroom and grab the phone charger from the dresser.

While only taking three steps toward the bedroom, she stopped, spun around, faced Rook, and then, after a thoughtful pause, brought up her sister's apartment. She told him that she needed to stop by the apartment to collect some of Autumn's thing for the funeral service.

"Most of the stuff is here," Rook said, slightly defensive. "All that's left at the apartment is some of her furniture. Nothing important."

Auggie insisted on going over there; and from the color clouding the sides of her face, Rook saw, he knew that she'd keep pressing him on this particular issue and that his word was meaningless. He could very well tell Auggie that her sister's apartment was empty, and she'd still insist on going over there.

"I tell you what. . . " Rook said, using his words carefully, ". . . I was planning on going over there tomorrow. You're welcome to join me, if you like. . . "

Auggie smiled a closed smile and responded by thanking Rook.

As Auggie fetched the phone charger from the bedroom, Rook grabbed the bag of bloody clothes from the floor and rushed toward the garage.

As soon as Auggie returned with the charger, Rook quickly tossed the clunky bag in his car and walked back into the house where Auggie was standing at the edge of the living room with a phone charger in her hand. As though on cue, he pulled the mp3 player from his pocket and said he left it in the car, which he thought would explain his reasons for scurrying off to the garage. Auggie handed Rook the charger; and even though there was 83% battery left on the phone, he plugged the phone into the charger anyway and thanked Auggie, who addressed the most obvious observation inside the house: the destruction everywhere, mostly inside the kitchen.

As he pulled his eyes away from the outlet, he found the two VR contact lenses lying on the counter. He glanced over at Auggie, who was playing detective next to the destroyed fridge.

Without Auggie looking, he picked up the contact lenses with the tip of his finger and placed them inside the carrying case and pocketed the case.

With a careful survey, Auggie asked, "What in the hell happened here?"

"It was me," he said, again, bluntly. "After I found out the police were going to release that piece of shit, I didn't take the news very well. Obviously—"

"Rook," Auggie said, "you know these things take time. Believe me when I say this: I want to know what happened to Autumn. I'm sure there was a good reason why they released him—"

"The man confessed that he was inside my house," Rook said, raising his voice.

With her jaw tightened, Auggie said more patiently, "Can I at least help you clean up?"

"You know what," Rook said, losing his cool with Auggie. He said again, "I can't do this right now. Stay," he said shortly, as he grabbed his car keys. "Clean. The hell if I care. . . "

"Rook!" Auggie cried out from behind, as Rook stormed away.

After Auggie watched Rook pull his car out of the driveway and speed away, she checked Rook's phone, which he forgot to take with him. The phone was still plugged into the charger, which was resting on the kitchen countertop.

Curious, Auggie tried to use the slider to open Rook's phone but was denied by a four-digit passcode. She didn't even try to enter any passcodes, thought about it, even went so far to press the first digit, the number "8," but ended up placing the phone back in its original place.

What made her start thinking more about Rook and his recent behavior was the percentage of battery, which made Auggie wonder why Rook asked her to grab a phone charger when his phone was nearly charged.

More relieved after leaving the house, Rook mentally ran through a list of places where he could dump the bloody clothes. He ruled out any places nearby the house. He factored in surveillance cameras, including traffic cameras, which could track his car throughout the entire city. The thought of cameras and "tracking" forced him to check his pockets for his phone. He remembered that he left it at the house. Yet, despite a sudden flash of panic, he was in no mood to return to the house while Auggie was playing the irritating role of Nosy, Overprotecting Sister.

Rook's second and most plausible option was burning the clothes. He thought of an abandoned mall along the outskirts of the city—Archway Plaza, or "The Arch," which was what the youth called it. Every now and then, there'd be a group of afternoon skaters using the dilapidated structure as their own personal skating ramp.

Out of curiosity, he drove past Under The Hood; and when he arrived at the shop, it was still closed. The gate, he saw, was wide open but no sign of the owner, which gave him at least an hour or two before the cops showed up.

Three miles down the road Rook arrived at the junky intersection between 7th and Maple, the street name immediately triggering a memory from last night's conversation with his neighbor: Julia mentioned the street while talking about her studio.

He stopped at the intersection and as the light turned from red to green, made a sudden right-hand turn onto Maple Street.

Roughly a mile down the road, he saw what looked like Pep's car parked outside a rundown one-story brick building, which, from the outside, appeared derelict and possibly vacant, like The Arch, as well as countless other rotted, disease-infested eyesores throughout the city, which were not up to code. He made another sudden turn and pulled into the parking lot where he saw none another than Julia's beat-up Surfrider parked alongside the building.

Rook parked a couple of spaces from the Surfrider, which he identified as Julia's car based on many "anti-establishment" bumper stickers covering the back of the Surfrider, one in particular describing her Nebelung as being "*One mean pussy.*"

Next to grab Rook's attention was the driver's side window, which was shattered. At first, he didn't think anything of it. He thought she had rolled down the window to air out the car or whatever. Then, he saw over a dozen pebble-sized pieces of glass settled into the cracks and grooves of the driver's seat.

Feeling sick to his stomach, he slowly made his way toward what he thought was Pep's car and, after a closer inspection, realized it could've been the same car—he was ninety-nine percent sure—after he saw the inch-long ding next to the door handle along the side of the passenger door. Last week, Pep's car picked up the ding from a shopping cart that someone forgot to put away in the corral or lazily and/or inconsiderately left behind in the parking lot, and based on Rook's own personal experiences with shopping carts, he leaned toward the latter. He carefully inspected the dent, which had a red hue to it.

With his temper flaring, the sickness in his gut dissolved and was replaced with a strong desire to inflict punishment on the person or persons who were responsible for attacking the very thing that he held sacred, he stormed into the rundown building and immediately smelled smoke in the air. Thick black smoke poured from the large sliding barn-like door at the end of the hallway. He covered the bottom part of his face with his shirt and rushed through the hallway until he reached the last studio. He heard glass shattering from inside the studio. He leaned closer to the door and called out Julia's name but the only response that he received was the sound of what he believed to be a muffled voice screaming through a gag. He yanked the door opened, only to discover the entire studio engulfed in flames. The fire was recent, Rook could tell, and he saw the black-clad arsonist fleeing through the broken window.

With part of his face still covered, Rook made his way into the studio, dodging several falling canvases, which had been dowsed in various colors of paint before catching fire.

As the flames spread faster due to the many flammable materials inside the studio, including oil-based paints, as well as aerosol spray cans, which, once heated, exploded in the shelves along the wall and sounded like gunfire, Rook dodged the flames until he reached the broken window where he stepped onto an upside down bucket in order to get a better look outside.

There, as Rook managed to barely look through the bottom of the window, he saw the arsonist opening the driver's side door of Pep's car. The arsonist removed the cover from her face, revealing Regina. Both of her gloved hands, Rook saw, were covered with a bright red color, too bright to be blood. After the brief staredown, she got into the car and drove away.

As Rook pulled himself from the window, he heard a rustling sound coming from the middle of the studio. He turned his shoulder, only to find a person, who was bound to an overturned chair, the person's body submerged from head to toe in what looked like blood, while the lower half was partially engulfed in flames.

Rook grabbed a paint-speckled drop cloth, which was untouched by the fire, and smothered the flames on the body.

As Rook peeled away the red-soaked cloth and cleared away some of the blood from the person's face, he realized it wasn't blood, as he first suspected, but rather red paint.

As he pulled his eyes from the cloth, he saw part of Julia's face underneath the paint, which was smeared over her entire face. When she tried to speak, the red paint flowed from her mouth, prompting her to cough and gag and choke. He managed to untie the bounds from her wrists.

With the drop cloth draped around her body, he removed her body from the chair and picked her up with both arms and rushed from the studio. He was sidetracked by a massive painting of a desert, the bottom part set ablaze by yet another ruined canvas that fell in its vicinity. Of all the paintings, it was the only one not defaced by splashes of paint.

Deep, bubbling groans pulled Rook from the rugged mountains of the desert and reinforced the urgency of Julia's current condition.

While carrying Julia's body to safety, Rook hurried from the building; and when he finally made it outside where he could breathe without any obstructions, a crowd gathered in the parking lot.

Among the small crowd, which consisted of at least a dozen people, several of them driving by when they saw the fire from the street, others who lived or worked nearby, three of the spectators were filming Julia as she clung to life.

"What's a matter with you people?" Rook shouted out, as the pedestrians stood like statues and watched and filmed. "Help me, goddamn it!"

One of the pedestrians suddenly rushed to Rook's aide and then another and eventually, the rest of the crowd joined in. One of the pedestrians removed his T-shirt and tried to clear away as much paint as he could from Julia's face.

As Rook stood to his feet and tried to catch his breath, he spotted Pep's car idling on a far corner of the intersection. Suddenly, the car skidded away, the rear tires kicking up a thick cloud of smoke in the air.

Rook left Julia and hurried to his car and chased after Regina, while one of the pedestrians called the police.

As Rook sped through several stoplights, he managed to catch up to Regina, who, after driving erratically, lost control of the vehicle after taking a sharp turn around a curve.

The tires on the left side of the car ran off the side of the asphalt, causing Regina to overcorrect; and by doing so, the car violently jerked from right to left before spinning out of control and crashing into a metal guardrail. From a distance, Rook watched Pep's car flip several times in the air before barreling down a steep embankment, kicking up clouds of dirt and debris.

Rook parked the car on the side of the highway and hurried down the embankment until he reached the woods where Regina crashed the car into several trees. He searched inside Pep's car, which was still intact, but couldn't find anyone inside the vehicle.

With the notion alone of Regina's body being flung from the car, Rook searched the area.

To his surprise, he couldn't find Regina anywhere in sight.

AFTER an extensive search following the violent car wreck, the investigators never discovered Regina Beech's body. The investigators grilled me after I brought up Pep's relation with Regina and told me there wasn't a person named Regina Beech who worked at the credit union. When I asked them to track down Regina's husband, Harold, who was a maintenance worker, the investigators couldn't find him either. Like Regina, not a single record: no driver's license, voter registration, or address. They were ghosts, each and every one of them—at least, before my apprehension following the wild police chase, which ushered me through the scaly doors of the downward spiral express, that was exactly what I told myself because, I knew these people, they once existed in another life, a bold and bizarre one that closely resembled my own.

11

ROOK left the smoky wreckage before the police arrived and drove around the city in hopes of trying to make sense of why Regina would target, of all people, Julia. All of it, Rook told himself, possibly stemmed from what she told him in secret the night before: about Venus, and how she stopped by the house soon after Pepper was attacked.

With Venus on his mind, Rook decided to drive to her apartment.

When Rook arrived at the apartment complex, he saw her car, a crossover with the crack in the windshield, parked in the parking lot and exited the car.

He hesitated, resulting in one foot to hang from the car. He moved his eyes downward at his clothes, as well as the inner part of his arms and hands, not only covered with red paint, but also the charred shavings of Julia's flesh, which had glued onto his skin.

Over the ping-pong of thought, he disregarded his own macabre appearance and entered the apartment complex. He walked up to three flights of stairs; and when he reached the third floor, he felt sick again. Every thought in his head screamed at him to turn around, leave, drive away, don't ever look back—*Go! Get the hell outta here*, he thought.

As he ignored the thoughts by focusing on the upcoming conversation, the first and obvious question being why Venus showed up at his house after Juan attacked Pepper, he made his way to apartment 3E; and as soon as he arrived, he didn't hesitate to knock on the door.

A young woman with tats all over her body, similar age to Venus, answered the door.

Confused, Rook said, "I'm looking for Venus."

"You got the wrong apartment," said the young woman.

"Venus," he repeated. "She lives here—"

"There's no Venus who lives here," she said, saying the name *Venus* with sarcasm.

Before she closed the door, Rook noticed the interior of the apartment behind the woman's shoulder. The inside was completely different: the sofa, the posters, even the color of paint on the walls, as well as the Christmas lights draped under the ceiling.

At the very last second, Rook stuck his foot in the door.

"Please," Rook said, desperate, "there's a woman around your age who lived—" he corrected, "—lives in this apartment. Her name is Venus. Her car is parked outside!"

"I'm not going to tell you again," the young woman said, as she reached her hand behind her back, "either remove your foot from the door or I'm going to call the police."

Eventually, after he acknowledged the seriousness on the young woman's face, he removed his foot, resulting in the door to slam shut followed by the sharp *thud* of a lock sliding across the other side of the door.

Rook inspected the apartment number once more, "3E," and then walked back to his car.

Still determined to speak with Venus—he thought maybe she redecorated her apartment and that maybe she was hiding in another room and that maybe the girl with the skull tat on her neck was one of Venus's girlfriends, who was being over-protective—he decided to park his car in the back of the parking lot and wait for the owner of Venus's crossover to show.

Hours later, while tirelessly sitting inside the car, Rook spotted a person, who was dressed in a dark hoody, entering Venus's crossover. The person was much taller and wider than Venus. At the angle Rook was parked, he couldn't make out the person's face.

He followed the crossover for a couple of miles down the road until it stopped at a gas station where the driver walked into a convenient store to buy a six-pack of soda and a snack.

When the driver returned to Venus's crossover, Rook stepped out from behind a gas pump, startling the bearded, heavyset driver, clearly not Venus.

"Who the fuck are you?" said the driver, as he grabbed the nozzle along the gas pump.

Rook inspected the man's clothes, first the hoody, which was covered in what looked like white dog hairs, as well as orangish crumbs from tortilla chips; and then, lastly, the dark pouches, as heavy as soaked tea bags, underneath his blood-shot eyes.

Then, the man inspected Rook, the blood or paint or both—he couldn't tell which.

With his hands tightly coiled into fists, Rook asked him, "Where is she?"

The man before him shrugged his shoulders and looked at Rook with a furrow shaped like the letter v along his brow.

"Where's who?"

"Venus," Rook said.

The man made a pig-like snort with his mouth, which was supposed to be a laugh.

"Get the fuck outta here," he said and removed the nozzle from the pump.

Rook grabbed the squeegee from the side of the trashcan and held it by his side.

"I'm not going to ask you twice: Where'd you get this car?"

Again, the man appeared baffled by not only the question, but also Rook's presence.

"The car," Rook said to a near shout, "where'd you get it?"

The man hesitated.

"Some dude," he said. "I bought it for hella cheap off Traderz."

"What the fuck is that?" asked Rook.

"It's this online service—you know, Traderz—you never heard of it?"

Rook took a step closer, the dripping wet squeegee still in hand.

"Relax, man." He inserted the nozzle back into the pump and held out his hands. "Why are you so interested in the car? Did it belong to you or something—"

"This dude who sold it to you," said Rook, "who is he?"

"I never got his name," the man said.

"What did he look like?"

The man shrugged.

"I dunno," he said with a stutter. "He had. . . orange hair."

"Orange hair?"

Fiery orange, he elaborated.

"Yeah," he said. "You know, like dyed."

Given the man's current state and how he had absolutely no idea about what was going on—either with the vehicle that he had bought from a popular e-commerce site or the previous owner of the vehicle—he was no use to Rook.

After Rook drove away from the gas station, he only made it just a few miles down the road before he hooked a sudden U-turn in the middle of traffic and headed back into the city where he went straight to Pep's apartment. He couldn't stop thinking about why Venus left the house in a hurry and wondered if Pep and Venus somehow knew each other.

With Auggie on his mind, Rook parked in a shaded spot behind the apartment complex.

When he used Pep's key to enter the apartment, as Rook originally suspected, the interior of the apartment, except for, as he explained to Auggie, several pieces of furniture, the place was nearly empty. He flipped on a standing lamp and snooped around the apartment, first the kitchen where the refrigerator was filled with mostly condiments and an expired bottle of strawberry kefir. Pepper hadn't completely moved out for there were still several items inside the apartment, mostly inside her bedroom, such as a hamper, an air purifier, several palms—which were artificial—and a Himalayan salt lamp perched on top of the desk. He began his search with the desk, first opening the top drawer where he found a stack of copy paper and loose writing utensils. A pen, several of those pump-pencils, an eraser, and a whiteout marker. Lastly, Rook checked the bottom drawer where he discovered a full bottle of Levotrigine. With the glue dried and ineffective, he peeled back the corner of the label, which read "placebos." He twisted open the cap and dumped a pill into his palm and sure enough, it was the same pill that she took on a daily basis.

What Rook found next left him speechless: Pep's face on an identification card. The photo must've been at least ten years old. Instead of her natural salt and pepper, her hair was brunette. The name of the company was called "ONION," the letter O in the word *onion* spiral patterned.

Disturbed by his findings, Rook ended up crashing inside the apartment. Despite sleeping on a stiff futon, he managed to catch at least four hours of sleep.

By the time Rook woke, the inside of the apartment was lit with the pinkish color of dawn. *What was that old saying about a red sky in the morning?*

He rested and thought more about his findings, mainly the ID card.

Minutes after sunrise, he heard two car doors slam shut outside the apartment. He rolled out of the futon and checked the living room window where he saw Auggie and a strange heavyset man—possibly the landlord, based on the massive set of keys in his hand—entering the complex.

Rook rushed to the door and looked out the peephole.

As soon as he saw the two shadows along the hallway—and approaching fast—he darted to the balcony and climbed down three stories, using the two balconies below for footing.

Once Rook made it to the ground without injuring himself, he hurried back to his car and drove away as soon as Auggie and, as he suspected, the landlord entered Pepper's apartment.

With Pep's ID card for the company, Onion, in his possession, he drove to the credit union. He didn't exactly know what he was looking for or what he'd find at the credit union, except for the sign, which he drove past nearly every single day and not once did he ever think twice about the sign or what it read. Outside, in front of the building, was the sign for the credit union, which didn't seem out of the ordinary. Rook closely inspected the bottom of the sign, which, written in small print, read: "*In Association with our Partners at OG.*"

It could've been nothing, he thought. There were lots of words that started with the letter O.

Tempted to enter the credit union, Rook was forced to rethink his next course of action as he spotted the guard standing outside the main entranceway. He was armed, vigilant. Both eyes crossed Rook's path and for a moment, Rook thought he saw the guard do a double take, then, strangely, his lips moving, as if he was talking to someone over a radio.

Rook left in a hurry and made an abrupt turn onto the interstate. He couldn't think straight for he, too, felt equally, if not, more as dumbfounded as that man who was driving Venus's car.

Twenty minutes into the drive he caught the same car in the rear view mirror, the one that he passed at the credit union, and suspected that it was a tail—But who? Again, Rook's mind started to race, fast and spinning, thinking about each person who might've been following him: Venus perhaps or those two detectives or Regina or maybe even that orange haired fellow.

Eventually, after making a hard right onto an off ramp, and then taking several evasive turns below the underpass and charting a path in a staircase-like pattern through an older, rougher, and more dilapidated part of town where traffic was minimal, until winding back onto the same interstate, Rook lost the tail.

After driving three hours, he decided to stop at a motel called Leo's alongside the highway. The area was fairly quiet and secluded and most of the activity came from the nearby Taco Shell, which was attached to a convenient store.

Considering his attire, which looked incredibly suspect, Rook walked across the street and washed up inside a grungy, heavily inked restroom behind the convenient store. He managed to scrub most of the blood from his neck and arms. He removed the shirt, which was covered in red paint and turned the shirt inside out and then made his way back to the lobby of the motel where he bought a room for the night.

The desk clerk, an older gentleman whose hand trembled from a condition while opening the drawer to the cash register, never started small talk with Rook, who struggled to meet his eye. He hardly spoke any words to Rook, didn't know what to say, except tell Rook the cost of the room and lastly, the time of checkout, which was at ten o'clock the next morning.

Once the transaction was made, the desk clerk handed Rook a key to Room #3, which was looped around a key ring alongside a red rubbery fob that read in lower case, "*leo's.*"

Before Rook parted ways, the old clerk tightened a grip around the key, preventing Rook from walking away with it and with a tender voice, said, "Take care of yourself, my friend."

"Sure thing," Rook said, finally making eye contact with the desk clerk, who released his grip from the key.

Rook exited the lobby and walked to his room.

By the time he entered Room #3, which was everything he'd expect from a typical motel room—two king-size beds with floral pattern comforters, which were as slick as plastic, a nightstand with a lamp that separated the two beds, a round poker table with a wobbly leg and a travel brochure of the *Cave State*, a three-drawer dresser made of oak, a hanging mirror, a Luminism-style painting of a red fox wandering through thick woods at the break of dawn, as well as a two-sink vanity with a bar of single serving soap that was almost as thin as a credit card and an airplane-style bottle of shampoo, and a bathroom, which was as small as a closet.

After locking the door behind him and closing the curtains, Rook picked up the brochure, which had a photograph of a limestone cave with pale speleothem appearing like a mouth bearing the massive, knobby fangs of an ancient creature. He sat down on the edge of the bed closest to the bathroom and while listening to distant traffic ambience outside the room, combined with muffled voices talking in a room next door—Rook thought that he heard someone calling out "*Show me!*" over and over followed by the high-pitch laughter of a woman—pulled out the case of VR contact lenses from his pocket and contemplated using them.

With his mind made up, Rook hid the room key inside the drawer of the nightstand where he found a Holy Bible.

He suddenly closed the drawer and sat on the edge of the bed and once more, contemplated whether or not he should plug himself back into the virtual reality game.

Exhausted, he ended up falling asleep; and then moments later, hours later, he heard a *knock* on the door.

Narrow rays of sunlight cut through the cracks in the heavy curtain and ran across the entire room, one of the rays like a glaring katana across Rook's eyes. He woke from both the burst of light, as well as a sound coming from behind the door. He stood fast, resulting in a sudden dizzy spell. He stopped, grabbed a hold of the side of the bed to prevent himself from falling over, and once the spell passed like a creeping sneeze, he walked to the door where, through the peephole, he saw a maid standing outside the room, ready to enter. He checked the time, which read "**10:02**."

AM or PM?

Clearly, he thought, AM, based on the position of the sun. He felt foolish for even questioning the sight of daylight, which rudely awakened him.

Have I been asleep for that long?

Once more, the knock on the door pulled Rook from his mild trance.

"Time for checkout," the maid said and waited patiently for a response.

As soon as she pulled out a set of keys from her pocket, Rook opened the door and told the maid to give him a couple of minutes.

For the time being, the maid moved her cleaning cart to the next room while Rook gathered his things. He only had the one thing, really, the key that he hid in the nightstand.

When he opened the drawer, he couldn't find the key anywhere inside. He decided to check the Bible, which was where he discovered a pistol inside a cutout. He carefully removed the pistol, which fit perfectly, like a glove, inside the gun-shaped cutout. As he inspected the pistol, he soon realized it wasn't any ordinary gun, but it was, in fact, his gun—the Glock—same one that exploded in his hand, pieced back together like a jigsaw puzzle. He immediately checked his pockets. He felt a bump in his right pocket and pulled out the case and more relieved, found the two contact lenses inside the case. He checked his left pocket and found the key from last night.

Before leaving, he looked into the mirror above the vanity and checked for any lines on his face but couldn't find any.

After securing the Glock behind his waistband, he returned the key to the desk clerk and stopped at a continental breakfast and grabbed himself an apple strudel for the road.

During the drive, he only ate a couple of bites from the dried pastry, which tasted like it had been sitting out for hours, and tossed out the rest. He drove westbound for what felt like hours.

Right before he crossed the state line, he noticed a billboard on the side of the interstate; and after a double take, he immediately slowed down and pulled the car in a graveled spot alongside the road. He stepped out of the vehicle and walked up to the billboard, which was an advertisement for the restaurant, Turnstile Grille. The restaurant was known for its "endless buffets," as well as "bottomless plates." Rook wasn't at all interested in a buffet or a bottomless plate—whatever that meant, he thought—but he was more so captivated by the image of the golden statue of a largemouth bass and the so-called *"Great Angler"* challenge. Below the advertisement was a logo of a purple onion, which was cut in half and shaped like a person's head with the organization name, "THE ONION GROUP," below the logo.

Rook said to himself, "The Onion Group?"

The name of the organization immediately sounded familiar; and before Rook could wrap his head around the name, he pulled out that ID card.

Onion?

The Onion Group, he thought, as if repeating the name in his head would help jar any loose memories.

OG?

As Rook made his way back to the car, he suddenly flinched from the sight of the strange reflection in the passenger side window. In that reflection, he saw a glimpse of what looked like Juan da Gama. He even stopped and looked closer into the window, inspecting his face but soon realizing that it was only his mind playing tricks on him.

Since the restaurant was only three miles down the road, Rook decided to check it out.

When he arrived at Turnstile Grille, the place was fairly crowded for lunch. He first saw the sign for the challenge as soon as he walked through the entrance: Any participant who managed to consume a whopping twelve-pound largemouth bass called "Libby" won several prizes, one of them including the golden statue, as well as a special hat that read:

I ATE A 12 LB. BASS.
*WHAT THE F**K HAVE YOU DONE?*

Mounted on a wooden plaque above the hostess was Libby himself: The twelve-pound largemouth bass, which was about the size of a newborn baby.

Perched on a shelf behind a cashier were dozens of those golden statues, each one similar, if not, the same exact one that Rook's father passed down to him.

The hostess asked Rook how many guests were in his party.

"Just one," Rook said, as the hostess grabbed a menu from the post and escorted Rook to a booth in the back of the restaurant.

As Rook skimmed through the menu, a waitress holding a notepad stopped by the table.

The sound of the waitress's upbeat voice as she asked for Rook's "order" rippled throughout his body.

The menu slowly lowered from Rook's face, his eyes finding Venus's. Her face slackened from the sight of Rook sitting before her.

"Venus?" Rook said while trying to collect his thoughts. "Wha. . . what are you doing here?"

"What am I doing here?" asked Venus. "What are *you* doing here?"

"I was just passing through—" he paused and then back-tracked, "—wait a sec. How. . . "

"Rook. . . " she said over Rook and then glanced over her shoulder, ". . . you need to leave. . . now. . . "

A patron walked behind Venus, prompting her to take Rook's order.

She asked, almost mechanically, "Would you like a side of tartar sauce with your flounder?"

"*Venus*," Rook said, sliding closer toward Venus, "what the hell is going on?"

She subtly moved her hand toward the right upper side of her outfit and readjusted the material between the collar and a breast pocket, where the nametag, "*Valerie*," attached to a clothespin, was pinned to her shirt.

While widening her eyes, Venus said to Rook, "Will that complete your order for today?"

Rook was at a loss for words.

Venus wrote down Rook's order and ripped out a sheet of paper from the notepad and then placed it on the table.

"I'll be back with your order, sir," she said and walked away.

Rook picked up the piece of ripped paper with his "order" and read the note: "*They're onto you. Meet me behind the lobster tank after I drop the glass.*"

Moments after he read the note, he heard a high-pitch *crash* of glass shattering in a hallway past the dining room.

Startled from the sound, Rook redirected his attention toward Venus, who was kneeling on the floor and using a damp rag to gather the pieces of broken glass.

Soon after the accident, a janitor brought a broom and a pan and helped clean the mess while Venus walked to the back of the restaurant.

Rook exited the booth and walked over to the lobster tank but didn't see Venus anywhere in sight, only two other wait-resses, one of whom shared a similar profile as Venus.

As he made an attempt to ask one of the waitresses about Valerie's whereabouts, he heard a sharp *psst* behind him. He rotated around, only to find Venus poking her head from the women's restroom.

More urgently, she waved Rook closer.

Rook casually entered the women's restroom.

Venus grabbed him by the collar and yanked him inside and locked the door behind him.

"Please explain to me what's going on," Rook demanded. Then he added: "What's up with the name change?"

"This has nothing to do with me—"

"But it has everything to do with you," Rook said over Venus. "What in the hell were you doing at my house after Pep was attacked?"

"She wasn't attacked, don't you understand?" Venus said, as she began to lose her patience with Rook. "That's what they want you to believe—"

"They?"

Venus paused.

"Onion," she said, her voice trailing off.

He thought about the name on the ID card, as well as the billboard, immediately connecting the two—no—three dots: The poster in Venus's bedroom.

"The Onion Grou—"

Venus suddenly shushed Rook before he could finish the name.

"Yes," she said, more quietly.

"Who are they?" asked Rook. "What does it stand for?"

Venus was confused by the second question.

"How'd you mean?"

"O. . . N. . . I. . . " he began to spell out the name.

"It doesn't stand for anything."

"Who are they?"

"They're a powerful organization that controls everything: They control what you eat, what you see, what you do," she said. "They run everything. . . "

"You mean like a government?"

Venus rolled her eyes.

"You have to think much, much bigger. They run absolutely *everything*. . . " Venus emphasized, ". . . even the government."

"How do you know all of this?" asked Rook.

Venus paused and said even more quietly, not a whisper but close: "Because I once worked for them," she said. "Well," she corrected herself, "technically, I still work for them. I was demoted and placed here in this shithole after I broke protocol and made an attempt to warn you."

"Warn me about what?"

"You're messing with forces that will destroy you," Venus said. "You must turn around and go home."

"Did Pepper work—"

"Your girlfriend," Venus interrupted, "she wasn't who she said she was, Rook. . . "

Depressed, Rook's eyes drifted in thought.

Venus urged yet again: "Rook, go home."

"There's nothing for me back there," said Rook.

"Whatever you do, do not—I repeat—do *not* go west," she said. "*West is death.*"

"Then, where else do I go, Venus? If I go home, I'll be thrown in jail for what I've done."

"*East is peace.* . . But first. . . in order to find that peace, you must confront the demons that you carry inside you. Only then, you will find exactly what you're looking for. . . "

Rook asked, "How do you know what I'm looking for, huh? What do you know about me? Tell me, V—"

"Because you were looking for it with me. . . " she said, as her watery eyes filled with sadness, ". . . and I couldn't give it to you. I couldn't give you love, but I could offer you a way out of the madness, if only for a little while. . . "

"Life isn't supposed to be peaceful," he said, the anger building underneath his words. "It's chaotic. It's violent. Love is death, is it not? A blade and a bandage. To love is to cut yourself, your identity, your being, to surrender your life into the hands of another, ultimately committing yourself to the void. . . "

As the tears flowed from her eyes, Venus said, "I wish that were true. . . "

Rook turned away from Venus and made an attempt toward the door.

Venus suddenly called out from behind: "You're correct, *Juan.* . . about being thrown in jail. But that's not the worst of what's going to happen to you. . . "

Rook paused from the sound of the name, Juan.

Why did she call me Juan?

"You are Juan," Venus said, as if she could read Rook's mind. "You are me. You are everyone—"

He glanced in the mirror above the vanity and caught a glimpse of Juan da Gama standing in his own reflection. He was wearing the same clothes as Rook, same hairstyle, same bags under his eyes, same everything.

Immediately, Rook rejected the guilty stranger peering back at him.

"Stop. . . goddamn it. . . " he said, backpedaling. "Why are you doing this to me. . . "

"I'm not doing anything to you, Rook," Venus said, carrying neither expression nor emotion on her face. "You are only doing it to yourself. . . "

Rook left the women's restroom and made his way toward the exit.

As he walked through the dining room, he suddenly heard a name from his past, the name *Joshua Lamb* being spoken on a news report in the background. He followed the anchor's voice to the television mounted above the waiting area.

The report stated that Mr. Lamb was on the run from the law for the alleged murder of both his girlfriend, Autumn Piper, and their unborn child, and if anyone should come into contact with the suspect, he or she should notify the authorities. The anchor warned viewers not to approach the suspect for he is considered armed and dangerous.

After eyeing the report, several patrons, as well as a cook and a couple of waitresses looked at Rook and froze for a moment, eyes wide and still with dumb expressions on their faces, right before pulling out their phones.

Confused by the report, Rook saw the many eyeballs directed toward his way followed by looks of anger, disgust, and fear.

A patron, who was twice the size of Rook, attempted to subdue, according to the report, the alleged murderer; however, Rook slipped from his grip and ran out of the restaurant and hurried back to his car.

Several people followed Rook outside and from the entranceway, watched him drive away. One of the patrons, not a patron, but rather a gaunt-faced man with dyed orange hair dressed in a plastic-like translucent duster who was wrapped in mystery. As Rook sped through the parking lot, he made eye contact with the stranger's piercing sea green eyes. One side of his face curled with a wicked grin, as if the game had just begun and Rook had scored the first goal.

As Rook drove away from the restaurant and watched the orange-haired man from the rear view mirror, he wondered if it was the same man whom the guy from earlier was talking about, the guy driving Venus's car, and from what Rook gathered, had absolutely no idea what was going on, and if it was the same man—maybe someone who worked for the Onion Group, maybe even a hired gun perhaps, even though he had no evidence to suggest that he was an assassin—Rook wondered how long he had been inside the restaurant, and if he was inside that restaurant, then how come Rook didn't see him sooner (He clearly stood out like a sore thumb with that colorful headful of hair).

After driving for over three hours, Rook eventually ran out of gas, as well as money, and had no other choice than to abandon the car and continue his journey on foot.

Being miles away from the nearest town—the last sign he drove past indicated a town, "Bellamoore," which was thirty miles away—Rook decided to collect everything that he could find inside the car and then he stuffed each item into a plastic grocery bag, including four used water bottles, two of them half-full while the others with only a few sips remaining (the water probably unsafe to drink, he thought, since the bottles had been sitting inside a hot car, but either way Rook figured that he could fill up the bottle whenever he came across any water sources, i.e. rivers or lakes or creeks, which were rather scarce throughout the flat, parched landscape known for its tornados), and then, a Glock, which carried one round in the magazine, as well as loose change, mostly pennies, dimes, and nickels, that, over the years, had fallen underneath the seats, an ice scraper, which could make for a weapon, if he needed it, a lumen meter—Rook didn't see any reason to bring the meter with him during his journey, if anything, it was a re-minder of how he once made a living—then, lastly, the floor

mat along the trunk, which he rolled up like a poster and secured with an old phone adapter cable.

Once he collected everything he needed, he finally trekked
west.

Only a few miles down the road he came across an idled
freight train hauling over thirty cars. From what Rook could
tell, the engineer was inspecting the exterior of the train. He
eyed one of the cars, which door was open, as though inviting
Rook to enter.

As the engineer made his way back to the front of the
train, Rook decided to sneak into the open car near the rear
of the train. Once he climbed inside the car, which, as he first
suspected, was empty, he found a shadowy area in the corner
of the car, unrolled the floor mat, folded it up like a blanket,
sat down, and closed his eyes.

As Rook drifted in and out of sleep, the train made a sudden vibration, forcing him to crack open his burning, itchy
eyes.

The train began to creep forward, unsteadily at first before
picking up speed. The stirring of the train lulled Rook into a
relaxed state.

Darkness descended upon him.

After traveling for miles and miles, the distant horn of the
train suddenly sounded, soon followed by the pulse-like pattern of red blinking lights cutting across tiny, narrow open-
ings of the dusty car, bringing forth the haunting faces of
Joshua's past, as well as his present: Dozens of them, Rook
saw, each one emerging from the shadowy areas at the opposite end of the car.

First to step forward was Juan da Gama, who was staring
at Rook with a blank, almost lifeless expression.

Next to appear was his neighbor, Nicholas, then his wife,
Angela, who was cradling a newborn baby in her arms, as well
as her family members: each one looking at Rook with similar
expressions.

More people emerged from the dusty shadows: his other
neighbor, Jason Mackey, who was mildly shaking his head in
disappointment; and then Venus, who was crying—perhaps
stabbed in the chest by that man with orange hair—her waitress outfit stained with a damp circle of blood; and then Julia,

whose face and neck was badly burned; nonetheless, Julia was very much alive and so, too, were the others who emerged from the darkness.

So many faces, Rook counted, so many stories.

While sitting across from all of these people, Rook neither spoke a word to them nor did he make any attempt to embrace them for he showed no interest in them or where they were headed.

All he knew was that the train would take him to a place where he could finally shed his skin. Based on the direction, he suspected the train was traveling westbound, and what a relief it was to finally rest his blistered feet.

SORRY CENTRAL

As Rook drifted in and out of a warm and restless sleep, his wandering eyes caught a haunting face among the other blotchy faces, which were briefly lit by a right-to-left passing of streetlight outside the moving train.

A sudden bump of the car stirred his flesh, prompting him to fully wake.

The face, Rook recognized, was of Riley Boone.

Despite his greasy, disheveled hair and the dark bags that weighed heavily underneath his tired, bloodshot eyes, Rook was certain it was him, the prolific author, whose words were once hooks which pierced his heart and tightly latched into that wounded muscle until the disturbing age of forced conformity rocked his world.

The hoary author's parched lips parted in a thin, wavering smile.

"Beats flying coach," said Riley, whose voice was much lighter in tone than the gravelly one that Rook heard on audio book.

"You know where they're taking us?" asked Rook.

"Thought you didn't mind?"

"I do," Rook said and glanced around the boxy freight car and pointed out other faces from the dusty darkness, including Ramiel Bouchard—"*Ramie*" for short, whose face Rook confused with the face of a madman with endless appetite for dominance—as well as the scraggly, wiry white-haired member of the ruthless biker gang, White Lightning, sitting against the side of the car.

"But of course you do," Riley said, half-smiling.

Next to grab Rook's attention were the many residents from Autumn Grove, all bundled up in the corner of the car, including Shaquille "BBQ" Godfrey, whose sharp gaze cut through Rook.

Lastly, before Rook shifted his focus back to Riley, he saw the former detective turned private eye, "Backer," who exchanged glances with Rook as if he was mentally sparing with Rook, as if the seasoned investigator was unsure whether or not to trust his Creator, who looked upon his very own extension of Self with both marvel and tepid confidence.

Rook heard panicky whispering to his right, where he saw Angela talking in secret to her husband, Nicholas.

The two immediately stopped whispering as soon as they made eye contact with Rook. Their eyes moved slightly toward their left, where Juan was glaring at Rook, as if he was a word away from avenging his friend, Dante, whose life ended with a gunshot straight to the dome.

Another passing of light flashed over Juan's dimly lit face and suddenly revealed a glimpse of a darker version of Rook: Both of his eyes plagued by shadows, lips nearly nonexistent, his nostrils flared outward like tiny wings.

Another flash of light wiped away Rook's dark face from Juan's like a paint stroke.

"What the fuck you looking at?" said Juan.

Rook said to Juan, "I was just trying to protect myself—"

Juan snapped, "You shot an unarmed man. How does that make you feel?"

"That man was trying to kill me," said Rook.

"Keep telling yourself that, *ese*."

A flash of rage came over Rook.

"If you want an apology. . . " Rook said, more defiantly, ". . . you ain't getting one."

Juan smirked, as if he was hiding an invaluable piece of knowledge, and right when he was about to retort, the train braked and began to slow down.

Red and blue flashes of light gradually filled the inside of the car.

Rook rushed toward the narrow slit in the side of the car and peeked outside the opening.

At the approaching railroad crossing was at least a dozen police cruisers, as well as several black unmarked vehicles, which appeared government owned. He spotted both police officers, as well as darkly dressed agents standing outside the vehicles, guns drawn, ready.

A rush of panic flooded Rook.

From behind, a voice snaked its way into his ears: "*Looks like they found you. . .*"

Rook turned to the voice, Juan's voice, and said to him, "You have to distract them—"

"I ain't doing shit," Juan said, more flippantly.

Another voice chimed in: "*I'll do it,*" said Jack Kenaf.

Rook acknowledged Jack, the drinker who'd melt from the sight of booze, and based on his stern and resilient composure, appeared as if he was a man who had something to prove, not only to himself, but also to his family.

Jack stood up from his seated position and walked over to the door and with Rook's aide, attempted to slide open the door but the door was stuck.

Colt, who worked with Props in film production, found a crowbar in the back of the car and while Jack and several others helped push the door, managed to pry open the stuck door.

"Good luck," Jack said casually to Rook, as he reached out his hand.

Rook shook Jack's hand, *thanked* him, turned his shoulder, and looked back at the others, who, in their own subtle ways, were urging Rook to exit the train.

Without wasting any more time, Rook leaped from the car while the train was still moving. He managed to land on his side along a grassy hill, which helped soften the impact as he rolled down a small embankment next to the railroad tracks. From a distance, Rook watched in horror as the train eventually came to a halt at the crossing where a police cruiser was parked in the middle of the tracks.

Once the train fully stopped, Jack stepped out of the train car and with an object gripped in his hand—more than likely, a crowbar—rushed at the armed police officers, who ordered Jack to drop the weapon and put his hands in the air.

After failing to comply, both officers and agents opened fire on Jack, killing him.

Enraged by Jack's death, Rook had no other choice than to flee. He ran for two miles until he arrived at a small desolate town called Knob.

As soon as he stepped foot onto the Main Street of Knob, Rook was overcome with a sense of déjà vu, as if he had been here but in another capacity.

More alert, Rook wandered through the quiet streets, passing several buildings where he witnessed ghostly faces behind windows. Not one single person could be found, except the ones hiding behind the windows, and even those people remained in a questionable state.

As before with the train, Rook caught a cloud of red and blue lights moving closer towards him.

A colorful, flashing storm.

Everywhere Rook ran, every corner that Rook hid behind, every alleyway that Rook ventured through, every nook that Rook scurried inside, Rook was surrounded by that colorful storm, as if it was drawn to him.

Eventually, after coming across an empty street, Rook was greeted by a booming sound of an intercom shouting at him to "*Freeze!*"

A burst of bright spotlights shone on him, first blinding him.

As Rook's eyes adjusted to the brightness, he saw twice as many police cruisers as before in front of him. Each officer was leaned against a v-shape angle between the door and the windshield of his or her vehicle. Guns were drawn and aimed at Rook, again ready.

"*Hands up,* Lamb!" shouted the police officer.

Rook held up his hands while three officers rushed toward him, threw him to the ground, and handcuffed his wrists behind his back.

Once he was apprehended, two officers carried him toward a cruiser where he was placed inside the back of the car.

He was never read his rights.

Yet, despite the latest events, he felt that, where they were taking him, privileges didn't exist.

"WHAT *was once a heart is now a car battery, plugged into my main arteries, and resting inside a squared cutout in the center of my chest. And that awful smell coming from my mouth isn't a case of bad breath. It's the toxic fumes from a wobbly exhaust pipe,*" Mr. Rebus recites from one of our previous sessions.

"You memorized all of that, huh?"

Mr. Rebus responds with a nod of the head.

"Impressive."

"Well," Mr. Rebus says, "you are aware that all of our sessions are recorded, right?"

"Right. Of course." My voice deflates. "I guess I haven't thought about it in a while."

"That's the whole point, is it not? To be aware without being aware?"

"You've lost me."

"Over time," he says, "we instill deep into the subconscious the very idea of every word you say, every action or choice you make, having consequences based on its severity. Once we feel as though you've reached the end of your Reformity, we then place you in a hostile environment, or what the past reformers refer to as 'the closest thing to the Real World.' From there, it's up to you, Josh, to rely on the very foundation that we've constructed for you."

Mr. Rebus touches my shoulder. His touch only comforts me and makes the hell that awaits me more tolerable.

"With that said, tomorrow is your big day, the final level of your program," says Mr. Rebus. "*The* ever so important *Final Phase.*"

The nerves rattle my insides like a tuning fork.

"Thanks for reminding me. . . again."

"So, do you feel up to the challenge?"

I shrug my shoulders.

"Think so."

My voice is tight, slightly trembling.

"You don't sound too sure of yourself."

"I'm unsure what it'll be like, you know, having to walk around with a chip inside my head. The thought alone scares me to death—"

Mr. Rebus points to the side of his temple.

"Perfectly safe, Josh," he says and then, as we walk past the ice cream parlor, points around Main Street. "Think of Love Town being one giant computer chip." He motions to a vanilla ice cream cone sign on the façade of the entranceway, the material of the cone appearing like a wiry mesh. "*Microphones. . .* " He then motions to a figurine of the brass geese next to a fire hydrant on the sidewalk, the geese's left eye not brass, but rather a tiny black glass ball, ". . . *surveillance cameras.* You, Josh, are aware of these safeguards that we've incorporated into your habitat, but as I've said, over time, once you've become accustomed with living your daily life around these newer. . . elements. . . you'll forget that they're even there." In a more fatherly way, he touches me on the shoulder again, says, this time in a softer tone, "I assure you. In fact, after what some reformers describe as a mild headache, which could last a day or two, like the microphones and whatnot, you won't even know it's there. Trust me. . . it'll be as we discussed. . . Once you leave this town, people will be cruel, callous. . . " Mr. Rebus lists, ". . . vain and most certainly, vindictive, retaliatory, extremely petty, narcissistic, *self*-centered, *self*-absorbed. You'll encounter people who worship the *Self*: you will most definitely run into all of these types along the spectrum of human life but don't you ever forget, Josh, these various types are only a reminder that life is complicated, even for a select few who make life more complicated than it should be and to find yourself perturbed by anyone of these types is a sign that you are, in fact, human. However," he pauses and we both stop walking, "having said that, if you let it consume you—the hate—there'll be nothing left of you but the one thing we cannot remove."

Again, Mr. Rebus points at his ole noggin.

"I see."

Just the thought alone greatly disturbs me.

But again, like Mr. Rebus said, maybe that's the whole point.

Since I have a long day ahead of me, Mr. Rebus suggests that I should rest. We part ways. I spend the rest of a pleasant afternoon walking around Love Town and taking it all in, as if it's the very last time that I'll ever see it.

That night, after I return to my living quarters in the South District, I try to sleep but I can't close my eyes without falling into the haunting memories of a seedy, corrupt world that ushered me straight toward my own reckoning.

I tell myself over and over, "It's not real."

2

INSIDE an empty holding cell, which consisted of four white brick walls and a metal bench that was speckled with stains and splatter and bodily discharge, Rook waited for at least three hours without any food or water until one of the police officers paid him a visit.

The officer informed Rook that he had a visitor.

As soon as Rook laid eyes on the strange man standing by the officer, he immediately recognized him.

Through concentration, he mentally traced the man's face to one in a click-bait news article that he recently read on his phone: A man, middle-aged, was struck by a vehicle while he was playing virtual reality, one of the latest victims of the so-called "ghost walking," which was a relatively new phenomenon spreading across the country, most of the cases happening in more populous cities.

Using a key from a ring carrying dozens of keys, the officer opened the cell and reassured the visitor that he'd be waiting outside the cell while shooting a narrow-eyed glance at the detainee as though he was looking directly into the eyes of the devil himself.

Once the visitor stepped inside the holding cell, he introduced himself to Rook.

The man's identity dawned on Rook as he finished speaking his first name and then his last, "*Huey*," which sprang into Rook's mind before he could finish the first syllable.

"You died," Rook said, stunned.

"I guess you didn't *see* this coming," he said with a grin curling over one side of his face.

"What the hell's going on—"

"I assure you, Mr. Lamb," Walker said to Rook, "I'm very much alive."

More abruptly, Rook said, "I don't go by that name anymore."

"You're still running with that name, Rook Carlowe, huh? Lemme take a guess: Inspired by Riley Boone's Carlow Mote? Quite an interesting character."

Rook didn't respond to the remark, even though Walker was spot on about the name.

"You can't hide anymore," Walker said to Rook. "We all know who you are, *Joshua*."

"How do you know my name?" asked Rook.

Walker said, "You're quite popular around here."

Ignoring the most obvious question, Rook was more intrigued as to how—or why—Walker was still alive.

"There was a story in the news. . . " Rook said, thinking, ". . . it said you were struck by a vehicle—"

"And yet, here I am. . . "

Walker walked over to the bench and motioned toward the seat. Rook scooted to the other end of the bench, making room for Walker to seat.

"I know what you may be thinking right now and the answer is *yes*," Walker said and stared directly into Rook's eyes. "You're still inside *The Hate Train*."

"You're lying," he said, as the heat rose from his skin like a hot flash and dampened each musty area of his body.

"Is it so difficult to confuse the *Real* from the *Unreal*?" Walker moved his eyes down at the bench below him. "Take this bench for example: Does this bench exist? Or, is it virtual? Or, is it merely augmented? And if none of this exist—this holding cell, this police station, this building. . . " he nodded at the cell's door, ". . . those bars which prevent you from escaping—tell me, Mr. Lamb, what's stopping you from unplugging?"

Rook moved his hand up to his face and slightly leaned his head forward and removed the contact lenses from his eyes.

After he rubbed the backside of each one of his achy eyelids, Rook opened his eyes, first his vision blurred. Then, he blinked several times and once again, attempted to clear away any debris, this time from the corner of his eyes. He was still seated inside a holding cell. The strange man, Walker, was no longer sitting next to him.

Repeating the same militant-like movements, the same police officer from before walked up to the holding cell.

"You have a visitor," said the officer.

With a grin attached to his face like a loose sticker, Walker appeared behind the officer.

"You?"

"That's right, Mr. Lamb. . . " he said, the grin sliding from his face, ". . . Me."

Rook glanced down at the contact lens on the tip of his index finger.

The lens melted over his fingertip, causing Rook to rub both his index finger and thumb together.

The officer opened the door for Walker, and Walker entered the cell.

As the officer closed the door behind Walker, Rook stood up from the bench and backpedaled toward the corner of the cell.

"Who are you?" asked Rook.

"I've already told you who I am, Mr. Lamb," said Walker.

"I thought I told you I don't go by that name anymore."

"Cut the bullshit, Josh. Besides, Rook *sounds made up.*"

Rook closed his eyes and when he opened them, he found himself standing inside a subway station.

Before him was a poster of *The Hate Train* on the tile wall. He accessed weapons from the main menu. He immediately scrolled through a variety of weapons before he pulled up one of his favorites, a katana, acquired the weapon; and when he reopened his eyes, he returned to the holding cell.

In his hand was a katana, only different. The weapon appeared faded and translucent, a ghost of a weapon, able to be seen in his hand—in essence, there but *not* there. The blade, as well as the handle, appeared as if it was glass. He ran his hand through the blade, which sent yet another heat wave throughout his body.

"I'm afraid *that* will be useless in here," Walker said, referring to the katana.

Here?

The holding cell, unable to use weapons, the entire vibe, all of it reminded him of one place.

"*The Archives?*"

"Close," Walker said, slightly impressed by Rook's insight. "You're currently inside the beta version of a brand new feature that I like to call—"

Before Walker could finish his sentence, Rook recognized Walker's face, not his entire face, but rather the features on his face, in particular, his eyes, which were the color of the ocean, the same eyes as a man whom he knew as Clark Sax-man, the head of a marketing firm who once offered him a slice of cake. He zeroed in on other features: Walker's thin, pointy nose, which looked identical to Birdie Crimps, owner of a pest control company; Mayor Landon Meyers of New Florida City and his high cheekbones; Colin McGregory and his protrusive brow; and then, lastly, the owner of a software company, Tailorsoft, Ari Phoenix, who, after throwing pallets of cash at McGregory's Farm, renamed the property.

"*Reformity*," Joshua finished while identifying the similar U-shaped receding hairline on the left side of Walker's scalp.

"A reform program, correct," Walker said, impressed. "I must say that you're a quick learner, Josh—do you mind if I call you Josh?"

Rook made a "whatever" half-frown with his face.

"So, we're going to stop using the name Rook, no?"

Again, whatever.

"Maybe you're right," Joshua, not Rook, said. "Maybe it's time to stop hiding."

"No matter how hard you try to get rid of us, we keep returning. Why is that, Josh? Think about it: What do we *all* have in common?"

Immediately, the answer was clear to Joshua.

"We are the antagonists in *your* story, Josh, because that's what *you* designed us to be."

"Designed you how?"

Walker sat down on the bench and waited to speak until Joshua sat down next to him.

"Think of it as a sort of. . . " Walker said, interlacing his fingers, ". . . an expansion package that *we* helped *you* create."

"I didn't create anything," Joshua seethed. "Everything I create, I destroy."

"Whether you like it or not, Josh, you did create some-thing. You created life and what happened to it was not your fault. *But* someone must be held accountable and that certain someone is *you*, Josh. Think about it: Each and every story, each and every character has slowly brought you closer to the truth about what happened on that tragic night, and the act against your fiancée. . . " he emphasized the word *fiancée* as if he was making it clear to Joshua that Pepper wasn't his girlfriend, but rather she was more than a girlfriend, ". . . which forced her to defend herself—"

"Defend herself? It was an accident," Joshua said, pleading. "I didn't kill her."

"Well, it was you who pulled—"

"Stop!"

Walker quieted down and said more carefully, "Whatever the case, it's fair to say you played a key role. And that's why you must be punished—"

"Who are you?" said Joshua. "I mean, *what* are you?"

"I. . ." he said with a deliberate pause, ". . . I work for a company known as Onion—"

Joshua recalled Venus's words, her talking about the company, "*Onion*," inside the restroom of a restaurant. He also recalled those signs, the logo on the bottom of the billboard. Lastly, that sign in front of the credit union.

"Recently, we partnered with the prison systems all across America to develop a new way of rehabilitating those who have committed serious crimes. Like I said, this is a beta version of the program and let's just say we're still working out the kinks, and you, Josh, are one of those noble volunteers who chose to participate in Reformity, which. . ." Walker crossed his index and middle fingers, ". . . if it's a success, will one day abolish *all* prisons—"

"Abolish all prisons," Joshua repeated carelessly. "Right. You still didn't answer my question: *What are you?*"

"On the outside," he said, more seriously, "the real Walker Huey, he was nothing more than a petty thief who was made into an example and served perhaps one of the toughest sentences in one of the most dangerous prisons in the country. After Walker did his time, after Walker barely survived, after Walker experienced the brutal conditions of prison, Walker was determined to fix the prison system. So. . . he made it his mission to reform the way we punish criminals. Using his background in software, he created a new program that would reassess the way we treat those who commit crimes. That program is called Reformity. And you are inside that program as I speak: '*The prison of the mind.*'"

Joshua made an attempt to restate his last question.

"What you are looking at right now. . . " Walker said over Joshua, ". . . is nothing more than a digital version of the real Walker Huey—what you, Josh, used to refer to as an '*avatar.*' I know this may be a lot to take in right now, but it's imperative that you complete the rest of the program—"

Another one of those hot-red waves of panic sent pinpricks underneath Joshua's skin.

With his chest tightening, he said, "So, what you're telling me is that I'm a goddamn guinea pig. Is that it? Huh?"

"*Not* a guinea pig, Josh," said Walker.

Joshua drifted off and heard Walker speaking to him in what felt like another time.

He said the word *trailblazer* and yet, not once did those lips of his move when he spoke such a word.

Trailblazer.

The warmth rushed into Joshua's face, causing him to blurt out.

"Excuse me?"

"A *storyteller.* . . " Walker said clearly, ". . . Using a series of prompts through VR technology, the program is specifically designed so that the offender can create the most lifelike experience which will make the subtle transition back into the Real World feel almost. . . seamless, once he or she has been deemed fit to reenter society. But first, before you begin the final steps into the rehabilitation process, you must be executed—" Walker clarified, "—Your avatar, that is."

"This is some kind of joke, right?"

"No joke."

"I didn't sign up for this," Joshua said, his voice shaking.

"Well, actually, you did agreed, Josh," Walker said, holding back laughter.

As before, while recalling the group, Onion, several images popped in his head, one of them being the first moments soon after he purchased the VR-CU contact lenses: Skimming through all those agreements and then marking a checkmark into a tiny box at the end of all that fine print. He recalled— or thought he recalled—catching those two letters *OG* (ONION GROUP) while endlessly scrolling through that best seller of a user's agreement.

"Don't be upset," Walker said, his voice tender. "You'd be surprised how many people check that box without reading the user's agreement. A hint: It's in the millions—with an m. For decades," he said, "companies have slipped their own little stipulations right underneath people's noses and yet, get this, what's so amusing about it all, those people who know exactly what they're getting into agreed to the terms anyway, which, if you ask me, only points to two reasons: Either the product is so damn enticing that people will sacrifice their own individual freedoms in order to use such a product or people simply don't care. Now, if that's not control, I don't know what is. . . "

"So," Joshua said, thinking, "you. . . " he corrected himself, ". . . *Onion* is controlling all of this?"

"No, Josh," he said. "You are. We only point you in a direction that will have the most impact of your rehabilitation, and it's up to you, Joshua Lamb or Rook Carlowe—or whatever you want to call yourself—to make the decision."

"Free will?"

"Just like free will," said Walker.

"And what if I say no to this execution?"

"We're not executing *you* per se, Josh, only your avatar—your skin—not the user." Walker reiterated, "It'll be like a hard reboot."

"Reboot, huh? So, that's it?"

"That's it," he said. "All you have to do on your part is make a public apology."

"An apology?"

"For the crime you've committed," he said. "So what's it going to be, Josh?"

TODAY is my big day, the beginning of the Final Phase of my sentence.

I wake up as soon as the clock strikes "6:00," and as I roll out of bed, I'm still hungry from the night before.

According to Doctor Parker, except for water, I'm not allowed to eat any foods twelve hours before the surgery.

I arrive at what appears to be an abandoned facility behind the hospital where both Mr. Rebus and Doctor Parker are waiting for me.

As soon as I step through the automatic doors, the two escort me through the main lobby, which, like the exterior of the brick building, appears abandoned.

The receptionist's desk is messy, all kinds of papers and files scattered everywhere. On one of those pieces of paper rests a Styrofoam cup, half full with coffee. Next to the cup are three brown coffee rings strangely aligned in an almost perfect pattern:

"Right this way, Josh," says Mr. Rebus, as he and the doctor escort me to the elevator.

Once those two rickety doors slide open, my chest tightens and both my palms turn sweaty.

Mr. Rebus reassures me yet again that I'm in good hands.

We ride the elevator to the twelfth floor.

Like the main lobby, the floor with a similar hospital-like staleness, appears abandoned, as if both the staff and the patients suddenly vanished into the walls.

"Why is it so quiet? Where is everybody?"

"We're running a skeleton screw today," Doctor Parker, who's not much of a talker, says to me. Despite his reassurance, which comes off as scripted, as if he's taking cues from Mr. Rebus, I still feel more anxious about having a strange object implanted inside my head.

We finally reach a room in front of a nurse's station where I spot the first sign of life. From the lack of expression on her face, the twenty-something nurse appears heavily drugged by sedatives. Her movements are sloth-like. The pupils are larger than normal, making her eyes appear almost black.

Doctor Parker parts ways with us and says that he's going to prepare for surgery.

Mr. Rebus directs me toward a hospital gown on the clothes hanger, which is hooked over the handle of the bathroom door.

The same dead-eyed nurse from before steps inside and hands me an empty bag for my clothes, then leaves the room without saying a single word.

"Who died?"

"You have to excuse the staff," Mr. Rebus says. "They've been burning the midnight oil."

"I can tell."

"I'll step out of the room while you change."

Mr. Rebus steps out of the room for a minute while I slip into the hospital gown, which has a couple of brownish stains just below the collar. More than likely, it's blood. But whose blood? And how many of these surgical implants do they conduct in one day? Mr. Rebus returns shortly after I'm fully covered. I ask him about my clothes and what to do with them. He says to leave them here and that they'll be waiting for me after surgery.

Without answering any of my questions, especially the ones that pertain to the legitimacy of this very practice, Mr. Rebus runs through the details of my Final Phase, which will last exactly ten days. "*Ten days*," he emphasizes. "This is the final stage in the program, making your return to society a swift and easy one. By the end of the stage, the transition from virtual to reality will feel almost seamless."

For others, he further explains, it may last up to twenty days or even longer.

Mr. Rebus says that there was one offender whose Final Phase lasted up to four years.

"Four years, huh?"

"Sounds barbaric, I know."

But for me, I ask, why the number 10?

The number has to mean something, doesn't it?

"Are you *finally* going to tell me why it's ten days?"

"One day for each finger," he says to me. "If you can make it through a day without any thoughts of hatred, which may include but is not subject to *hostility, disgust, scorn, contempt,* or *wishing ill will* on others to name a few—I'll provide you with a list after surgery—then you'll receive a star for the day, which will allow you to keep your finger. . . "

"And if I fail?"

Mr. Rebus holds up a peace sign with his two fingers, tilts his hand to the left like a sideways V, and then closes both his index and middle fingers, which press together and indicate the clos-ing-movement of a pair of scissors.

I look down at my hands, especially my fingers, as if it's the last time I'm going to see them.

"So, why my fingers?"

"The Final Phase matches the offense, and in your case, Josh, your offense is that you use those very *fingers* of yours as lethal weapons against the life of another human being. This is true for all offenders: *Hands*, fingers, legs, feet. . . tongue."

"How does someone commit a crime with their—forget I asked."

"You'd be surprise what a person was capable of doing to another person with the very tools he or she possesses. Believe it or not, Josh, a tongue can be Man's greatest instrument and whether or not Man chooses to use it as a tool or a weapon is up to Man."

"Jeez. You're right about being barbaric."

"Is it barbaric to possess such hateful thoughts? Is it savage to feel such hostility?"

"But they're just thoughts and feelings. That's it."

"And every now and then thoughts and feelings may lead to action. And if that were to ever happen, then it'd be a failure on our part to release a former offender into the Real World with-out being fully reformed. The whole partnership would col-lapse."

"So, what you're saying: 'No bad thoughts or feelings,' right?"

"That's correct."

"Easy enough."

The nurse pushes a wheelchair into the room and wheels me to yet another room where there are three nurses, all of whom carry a similar heaviness in their faces, as if they've been doped up.

Every instinct inside me screams at me to leave.

But I stay.

After surgery, I'm taken to a recovery room where my vision and speech are tested to make sure the chip was successfully implanted into my brain. Then, lastly, I'm shown a series of cards with pictures on them and asked to describe the pictures without speaking. Instead, I'm asked to think of my answers.

When I'm shown a picture of a dog, my mind ventures into a dark territory, which Mr. Rebus warns me to avoid, and all of a sudden, I start mentally breaking down the picture and how it doesn't look anything like a dog, but rather a deer; then, like a flip of a switch, I start to question the person who drew the dog and whether or not this person has even seen a dog before.

Mr. Rebus, who's monitoring the whole evaluation from another room, alerts me that, if my Final Phase had already begun, then I'd have to pay a visit to the Chop Shop.

He reminds me, "No bad thoughts or feelings, remember?"

"Right."

I clear my head and focus on the dog and as soon as I feel that creeping thought of that crap-artist, I immediately reject the thought.

It's a beautiful dog, I tell myself.

3

AFTER leaving the police station, Walker escorted Joshua toward a train, which was idling on a set of train tracks that cut directly through the parking lot.

Baffled from the sight of the train, Joshua glanced over his shoulder at the station, and it was gone, as if it was conjured in his mind. Not there. *Never* there.

As for the train, it was a massive thing, a shiny and silvery beast of a thing with chrome plates over its driving wheels. A soft moonlight reflected over the roof of the train, as though highlighting it in the darkness. From what Joshua could tell, the windows were tinted; and even with a hazy overhead light turned on inside the car, Joshua didn't see any passengers.

The two arrived at a set of steps alongside the train.

Walker stepped aside and said, "After you, Josh."

Joshua hesitantly entered the train and was immediately struck by that brand new sneaker smell, as if the train itself had recently been removed from its package. He marveled at the cushioned seats with cup holders, the interior incredibly spacious with plenty of legroom, as well as air condition. Except for the conductor and several members who worked for Onion, the entire train was empty.

Both Walker and Joshua took the aisle seats and sat next to one another.

Pensively, Walker asked Joshua, "So, why use a different time period?"

Joshua furrowed his brow in confusion.

"What do you mean?"

"You're thirty-eight years old, right? Yet, considering the date, you should be twenty-seven years old. So, having said that, why would you choose to live in a time over ten years ago?"

Joshua shrugged away the question.

He said casually, "You never really know if a year has been good to you until after you've lived that year, and I guess, at that point in my life, I felt like I was finally *hopeful* about the future, especially after having gone through a rough spell four years earlier—"

"You think it had anything to do with your mother having a child when you were twenty?"

"Maybe," Joshua said, "but I'd be lying if I said that I was proud to be Nathaniel's brother."

"Cut the bullshit," said Walker. "If you were so proud to be Nathaniel's brother, then why'd you stop talking to him?"

Again, Joshua's shoulders naturally rose upward for a brief moment and then fell downward shortly after, but this time more heavily.

"Too much going on in my life. I didn't have time to be a brother."

"But you were still hopeful?"

"Yes. . . " he said, ". . . about *my* future, that is until the imminent one ten years later."

"Makes sense with the upcoming nationwide blackouts. I think everyone felt hopeless about the future during that time of. . . " Walker said, searching for the right word to finish his thought, ". . . *uncertainty.*"

"It's fair to say that I wished I was older during that earlier time when I was in my late twenties."

"Then why choose to be thirty-eight?"

Joshua thought about the question for a second, then answered: "I dunno. . . " he said, as he made eye contact with Walker, ". . . I think it's the age when I finally stopped giving a fuck what others thought about me. I was gonna live *my life* on my own terms, without anyone telling me what I could or couldn't do. I wish I had that same mentality ten years ago."

In the subtlest way, the train started to move; and unlike the previous train, the ride was superiorly smooth, which prompted Joshua to gaze out the window where a parched landscape ran like a moving picture before his eyes.

With his eyes still attached to the passing land, Joshua said more thoughtfully, "She's not real, is she?"

Walker said, "You're talking about Pepper?"

He faced Walker and his lack of a response was the response.

"Of course, she is," said Walker.

"But not here, in this fucking virtual hellscape?"

"Unlike psychic constructs that help you navigate through your VR experience, this version of Pepper is nothing more than a performer played by a highly-trained operative of our organization. Even though she is not the real Pepper, she is given the same likeness as the Pepper from your reality; and over time, your mind convinces itself that the Pepper you see in this virtual landscape is the real life version—"

"So, she works for you?" asked Joshua.

"In real life," Walker said, "her name is Claire Cravats."

The name Claire generated an image inside Joshua's mind. He was dressed in a delivery outfit and standing in front of a desk where a familiar receptionist was taking a bite from a blueberry muffin. She dropped several crumbs of the muffin from her lip, causing her to giggle and make a half-ass attempt to catch the sugary droppings. Despite the sweet tooth, she had a peculiar glow about her, a light that drew Joshua close to her. Behind the receptionist was a sign "PRINT USA."

Joshua suddenly snapped from his trance.

"She's one helluva agent," said Walker, "one of our best. Prior to Claire's assignment her likeness was digitally scanned, as was mine, and once we were able to make tweaks to her appearance, we skillfully inserted her into your VR, prompting you to associate any memories of Pep with Pep's replacement—"

"And Regina. . . " he uttered, his voice climbing with rage, ". . . Venus. . . how many more are there?"

"Normally, each user is assigned two agents," said Walker. "A player and a supporter. The supporter's role is there simply to monitor the player and make sure he or she follows the script. There is Claire, the player. Then there was her supporter who was playing the part of your 'fling,' but she was demoted after she broke protocol when she tried to contact you, thus resulting in one of our agents to fill in the role as a supporter. This is a *'reinforcer,'* who remains on standby just in case things get hairy. In other words, the reinforcer, whom you may know as Pepper's coworker, Regina, was activated in order to steer you back onto path—"

Furrowing his brow, Joshua said, "Why go through all of these lengths to help me?"

Walker said, "Like I've said before, Josh, we show you the door. However, it's up to you to walk through it. Free will, remember? But. . . " he said and motioned both hands in a pushing manner, ". . . with slight motivation, whether it be for an example, a billboard sign, or even a particular saying or expression. . . "

The *golden bass*, Joshua remembered.

The *statue*.

That sign on the side of the road.

"Looks like we're here," Walker said, more grimly.

As Joshua pulled himself from his thoughts, he turned his focus toward the window where he saw a gigantic train station past a bend alongside the train tracks.

Protruding from the top of the station was the top of yew tree, which cast shadows over half of the structure.

Left in a state of awe, Joshua asked, "What is this place?"

Walker said charismatically, "Welcome to your last stop, Josh. This is Sorry Central."

DAY One.

I open my eyes exactly at 5:59 and watch the red LED numbers on a digital clock tick to 6:00, marking the beginning of my Final Phase.

I've only slept for an hour or two and knowing Mr. Rebus is tracking my each and every thought has left me in a state of alertness, forcing me to focus on my immediate surroundings: a digital clock with five nature tracks, including the sound of the ocean, a queen-sized bed, a pillow made of a cotton-linen blend, an oak desk, a standard window, a composition book for drawing spirals, which pushes away any unpleasant thoughts and instead, helps me concentrate on my hand, my fingers, those lines—Whatever you do, do _not_ cross the line.

Before the operation, Mr. Rebus specifically stated that my dreams are _not_ included in daily evaluations—he specifically noted the importance of dreams and how dreams are the mind's way of making sense of the chaos that happened earlier in the day and often serve as the body's way of cleansing itself—which determine whether or not I pass or fail; instead, I'm evaluated from six a.m. to my assigned bedtime at ten p.m., which gives Mr. Rebus sixteen hours worth of poking around my so-called "noggin."

Like a switch, it happens, and I'm not even aware until the thoughts slowly make their way to the front of my mind, that idea of intrusiveness and a person having access to my very last private space. I suddenly reject the thoughts before they're recorded and focus on my surroundings.

A digital clock with five nature tracks, including the sound of the ocean.

A queen-sized bed.

A pillow made of a cotton-linen blend.

An oak desk.

A standard window.

A composition book for drawing spirals.

Once the thoughts past, I tell myself that this is going to be much harder than I anticipated.

I'll never make it through one day, let alone, one hour.

IT feels strange being back in Spartacus.

Before I was bussed in last night and escorted to the apartment where I'd be residing for the next ten days, I was given a list of places to carry out my Final Phase. Of all places to choose, I pick the one place where I left so many loose ends.

Mr. Rebus told me that it was a good choice, a noble choice, "_full circle,_" he put it, to conclude your journey in a place that incited such raw emotion.

From what I gathered last night, Spartacus is nothing like the Spartacus that I once knew. It has turned into a major city. Many new jobs were recently brought into the city, including several new film studios, which, after a tax incentive that helped stimulate film production, has been home to tons of movies and television shows, thus branding the city with the nickname "_Hol-_

lywood of the East." These jobs were not included in a list of jobs that I was given, since they were considered "dream jobs," as Mr. Rebus put it while speaking about the movie industry, and as he stated before, anything that dealt with dreams was not included in my final evaluation, which left me with either physical labor or skilled trades, mainly the service industry (There can be a legitimate argument that any job in film production relates to the service industry, being that you are providing a service—perhaps one of the most important services that not only provides a necessary escape from the mundane, but also touches upon each human emotion, and that service is entertainment), but Mr. Rebus is rather strict about following rules.

With little options to pick from, I decide to go with the one trade that requires me to loosen my belt.

For the first half of the morning, after I scarf down breakfast, I shadow the plumber, Lucky, who shows me the ropes. Most of the job consists of house calls: Fixing leaks, tightening pipes, or replacing old parts with new ones.

By early afternoon, I'm still left with a mild but nagging headache from the implant, which Mr. Rebus said would last somewhere between twenty-four and forty-eight hours.

After having shadowed Lucky for most of the morning—a majority of the work can be done with my eyes closed, most of the skills I picked up as a new homeowner—he steps aside and allows me to get my hands dirty.

The last client of the day, a woman named "Betsy Lovitts," begins to get on my nerves. She looms over me while I try to work, her heavy shadow encompassing over me like an eclipse. While struggling to catch her breath, she constantly complains about the water pressure, about the spike in her water bill—which has nothing to do with the service—about the plumber who never fixed the toilet last week, and as she's barking in my ear while I try to fix the toilet, I can feel her spittle hit the side of my face.

As I unclog the toilet with the plunger, the thought rises up inside of me and I can't control myself.

AT 9:00 I hear a *chime* coming from the monitor mounted in the center of the living room wall. I answer the VidChat call. Mr. Rebus's face appears on the monitor. He looks disappointed. He goes through the evaluation; and based on the daily log that

highlights each hateful thought in the color red, I do not receive a pass for the day. He reads one of the thoughts to me: *"Scale back on the blueberry scones, why don't you? She must use a fire hose to wash the dingleberries dangling from her hairy ass. Everyone wants to point their fingers at greenhouse gases as one of the root causes of wide scale pollution, but I'm standing inches away from a literal embodiment of climate change. I hate to be anywhere near this place on Taco Tuesdays. And, what in the hell gives her the right— and authority—to talk down to me after I repair a fucking toilet that has turned into her own personal love seat?"*

Maintaining a professional composure, Mr. Rebus pulls himself from the log and asks me in the most direct way, "Shall I keep going?"

I feel almost sick after Mr. Rebus reads back my thoughts to me.

Was I being cruel? Or, is their honesty in the cruelty?

"But I never said those things to her. Not one word."

Mr. Rebus says, "But you thought about saying them."

Without responding, I listen to Mr. Rebus read another: *"Why don't they build coffee machines the way they used to build them? Built to last. Instead, we have no other choice than to buy these pieces of shit made from cheap material that will probably give us cancer in the future, forcing us to replace them every few years."*

"What? I never thought that."

"You did," he says.

I remember the thoughts scrapping against the side of my skull but never did I actually think them. I practiced meditation techniques that I learned before my arrival at Spartacus, and once I sensed those thoughts manifesting while waiting for the morning brew, I blocked them out.

Mr. Rebus says to me, "The receiver can be rather sensitive at times, so it's best to avoid any confrontation."

Before Mr. Rebus reads another one, which flared inside my thoughts when I was waiting to pick up lunch and in line, I couldn't help but notice in the corner of my eye one particular patron standing next to me texting pictures on the phone, like some kind of modern day caveman, the thought centered around emojis, in particular emoji faces and that yellow-orangish color of an emoji, and wondering if the techs who created these emojis thought humans had cirrhosis of the liver, I hear the *knock* on the door.

Mr. Rebus says, *"Please follow your escort to the Chop Shop."*

"So, this is it? No second chances?"

"I'm afraid not, Josh."

I end the VidChat with Mr. Rebus and answer the door where a physically fit man in a black suit is waiting to escort me to the Chop Shop. I don't put up a fight. I go with him.

4

AFTER Joshua and Walker exited the train, the two entered a massive corridor, which was made of aged brick, the arched entrance shaped like a half-circle.

While crossing the threshold, Walker shared a story about the station and how it had been here for many, many centuries, Joshua's ancestors using the tunnel to seek shelter from Brakemen, who spread disease and death, and once treating the station as a *"safe haven"* from the ruthless high society, the *"gatekeepers,"* whose only expression deemed worthy was their very own, before one day a lone and devious Brakeman infiltrated the Pledgers and swore an allegiance to the known adversary, only to later spread his wicked ways, like *"a venomous serpent slithering underneath people's noses,"* going unnoticed while whispering spells in their ears, the spell taking shape inside a single mind, eventually molding, through trial and error, into a mantra, which, in return, reshaped into an idea that would forever change the very establishment. Decades passed. The wickedness consumed the Pledgers, who converted the train station into what was known as The Gallows, where criminals who engaged in *"corrupt thought"* were hung to death; and over time, the site evolved, from *"death by burning"* to erecting what was known as the *"guillotine,"* all of these executions a form of public display to exercise a collective singularity of The People, who were given power to act as judge, jury, and executioner.

"Fast forward to the present. . . " Walker said to Joshua and escorted him into a pitch black tunnel, which reeked of old metals, ". . . the executions aren't meant to inflict bodily pain on The Physical, but rather The Mental." He touched the side of his temple and asked Joshua, "Isn't that worse than death? Public humiliation. The *assassination* of character. How can one recover from the very image that has been planted inside the mind of The People?"

As he asked Joshua these questions, the side of his face drifted into the darkness.

Joshua followed Walker, who was swallowed whole by the darkness of the corridor, which, within only a few steps of walking blindly over what felt like crushed gravel—Joshua suspected it was crushed bone—led them into what Walker called "Sorry Central."

Joshua was first greeted by a towering broken clock made of solid brass. The time of the clock was stuck on "11:59."

What caught his eye the most was the yew tree, which he saw earlier. The width of the tree covered nearly half of the entire station, its canopy provided shade with lit bulbs hanging from the branches of the tree, creating a more intimate atmosphere for the so-called "public execution."

In a grandiose manner Walker showcased the main lobby, or "gallery," where Joshua's apology would commence on a stage in front of the yew tree.

"In only a matter of hours. . . " said Walker, ". . . this station will be filled with hundreds of thousands of people. All here to see *you*, Joshua."

As Joshua's stomach began to knot, he heard two people laughing from a skybox above the station. Joshua traced the laughing to Regina, who was guiding a group of Onion interns through the skybox. She was dead, he told himself, died in a violent car crash. Yet, she was alive and well.

Moments later, after Joshua was taken to his room backstage, where he was prepped for his apology, Joshua bumped into the agent, Claire Cravats, who was playing the role of his girlfriend, as well as his fiancée. Even though she looked nearly identical to his past significant other, she was not Pep but rather an imitation.

Similar to a movie where an actor plays the part of a real-life person: The actor may look or act similar to the person he or she was portraying. He or she was *not* the real deal, but rather, as Walker put it, a "replacement." Even when Claire pulled Joshua aside for a moment and told him directly that it was nothing personal, "just business," Claire said, and walked away and met up with Regina, who shared a laugh—about what, he didn't exactly know, but he assumed it was about himself—Joshua despised this very person, this imitation, who came off as highly cynical and unprofessional.

He'd even go so far to say that he hated this person, who pretended to be someone whom he once loved.

DAY Two.

I manage to sleep a few hours until the local anesthetic wears off and then I'm rocking and rolling in the sheets, wetting the bed with sweat as I think about the previous night when a garlicky-breathed quack in a white coat who looked like an opera villain severed my left pinkie finger with a Gigli saw. Due to the anesthetic, I didn't feel too much pain—except for an intense amount of pressure—while I was being pruned.

I'm beginning to think the ten-day mind job isn't at all about pain, but rather something else entirely. Nonetheless, I'm required to take a greenish triangular-shaped pill with an imprint code "J-12" the morning after I visit the Chop Shop. Last night, immediately following the cut, one of the nurses placed a wiry mesh-like material over the incision and said it would expedite the healing process. Curious about the condition of my finger, I decide to remove the gauze, which, surprisingly, doesn't show any signs of bleeding or discharge, as well as the special white mesh-like bandage; and strangely, the incision has already healed over and all that remains of the finger is a bare stump. Even the flesh along the incision is as smooth as the tip of a finger.

Since I'm able to continue the job with nine fingers, I part with Lucky, who sends me on my merry way. I'm provided a van, which supplies me with all of the proper equipment for the job.

Within only a few minutes of driving toward the first job, which is located in a middle-class neighborhood, I'm driving the speed limit when all of a sudden a man riding a motorcycle vrooms around me without using a blinker and nearly clips the side of the van before cutting around me, causing me to stop short at the red stoplight, where the biker ends up making a right-hand turn.

I immediately concentrate on the road and try to stay positive and think about the upcoming appointment, which involves a leaky sink. I run through all of the positive aspects of the job: In essence, the service that I provide will be admired, for one, it's a trade that the likes of artificial intelligence is unable to master—at least, not in the next few years, and by then, we'll all be sock puppets for more evolved extraterrestrial species—secondly, its importance in maintaining stability throughout our daily lives, such as washing one's hands with soap and water to kill the gazillion of mega viruses, cleaning a piece of fruit before eating it, or soaking a hand towel in hot water, which might relieve a headache—the thought alone of a hot cloth pressed over the back of my eyelids brings great comfort—a functioning sink offers an abundance of necessities that keep us well and satisfied.

I tell myself over and over that maybe the person whom I provide service doesn't know how to fix a leaky sink or maybe he or she might be too occupied with work to fix the sink and rather seek the services of a professional.

Yes, I tell myself, *I am a professional.*

As I proceed toward the upcoming job without giving the biker any thought, I drive a couple of miles and stop at yet another red light where the same biker is waiting. Standing on a median only a couple of feet away from me to my left is a scraggly-looking panhandler, who's missing a thumb. He's holding up a cardboard sign that reads, *"Fuck you."*

Once the light turns green, the biker speeds off, making several more aggressive maneuvers, one of which causes a driver to move and nearly swerve into oncoming traffic. Despite all of the risky moves, the biker still remains stuck at yet another red light, like the rest of us who drive the speed limit. Wouldn't it be nice to drive without any red lights and cruise through all greens? I fancy the idea of green lights and then, all of a sudden, I feel the engine roar, the ball of my foot presses harder against the pedal, causing the van to accelerate.

As I delve deeper into the thought of a green light, I find myself thinking about trees and all those green leaves on them.

I suddenly snap from my daze, but it's already too late. The grill of the van is bearing down on the motorcycle. The biker glances over his shoulder. Behind a tinted visor, I can see his eyes widen in silly cartoon fashion. All of a sudden, the biker peels away and avoids being struck by the van as it roars behind him.

As I pull my foot from the gas pedal and make an attempt to slam on the brakes, I'm already halfway into the intersection. A car runs through a yellow light and T-bones the side of the van. The sudden jolt causes me to bang the side of my head along on the window. I hear the crack in the glass spreading like a fissure in ice. These are the last images I see before I'm swallowed by the blackness: *Car in the corner of my eye; then, behind the windshield, the face of a driver, pale and slack; then, our two vehicles collide; then bang; then lights out.*

I wake up on the street, only to find two paramedics hovering over my body.

I'm distraught and unaware of my surroundings.

For a second, I try to move but I feel glued to the asphalt. The relief washes over me once I manage to wiggle a finger. These tiny moments bring me comfort and peace as I can feel myself being ushered into another person's arms.

In sudden spells of blackness, the burst of light reminds me that I'm still alive, even though I long for the void. How relieving it feels, the void, and slipping away into it.

Before I realize what's happening, I'm being rushed into a hospital. Yet, despite my entire body throbbing with pain, it feels as if my bed has been replaced by a gurney and I'm still inside my apartment, still sleeping, and as the doctors, the nurses, and paramedics keep telling me that I was in an "automobile accident," I convince myself that it's all a lie, and I'm still inside one helluva dream.

After the drugs wear off, I finally wake up. I'm not lying on my bed. Instead, I'm lying on a hospital bed. My pinkie finger is still missing.

Mr. Rebus is sitting bedside.

He first asks me how I'm doing.

"Shouldn't you already know how I'm doing. . . since you're inside my head?"

"I see your sense of humor is still intact—"

"I don't know what happened. . . One second I was driving. . . I guess I zoned out. . . "

"According to the doctor, the neural implant wasn't damaged. Except for a mild concussion and a bruised rib, no major injuries—"

"What about sleep? I thought you weren't supposed to sleep with a concussion."

"In most cases, sure, you may be right. But you're fine. The doctor wants to keep an eye on you overnight, just as a precaution. Then, you should be free to leave tomorrow morning—"

"What about work?"

"I've already reassigned you to another job."

"What kind of job?"

"I'll save the details for later.   For now. . . " Mr. Rebus's
mood suddenly darkens as he says more directly, ". . . do you
care to explain what you were thinking prior to the accident?
Or, do I need to take a look inside that head of yours?" He pulls
back on his directness and collects himself.   More tenderly, he
says, "It would be so much simpler if you just tell me in person."

"I honestly don't know."

Somehow, I feel as if my answer is not entirely the truth.

"Last chance?"

I shrug.

"I just zoned out.   That's all."

"Can you recall what you were thinking while you 'zoned'
out?"

I remain firm with my answer.

IT'S not until later in the day when I speak with Mr. Rebus, who
gives me a "pass" after he reviews the daily evaluation, that he
informs me about my thoughts during the initial moment of impact. According to Mr. Rebus, I was thinking about trees, the life
cycle of a tree, how it provides plentiful oxygen, such as my
temporary profession as a plumber and how I assist in the unin-
terrupted flow of water, which nourishes life and provides
sustainability.   In a flicker, he explains, the tree was suddenly
struck by a lightning bolt, which caused the tree to split down
the middle and turn black.   Based on his analysis, he doesn't
deem the thought of lightning as a hateful thought.   But he suspects it may be my way of covering up hate and carefully warns
me that attempting to push the hate deep into the subconscious
or—in this instance—mask the hate can often have an opposite
reaction, only exasperating the hatred.   I tell him a story about a
time many years ago when I was a child falling into the deep end
of a swimming pool.   I couldn't swim; and as I descended into the
depths of the heavily chlorinated pool, my lungs began to fill with
water.   I remember a hand grabbing my wrist and then, I felt a
tug on my arm; and as I drifted in and out of consciousness, I
was pulled to the surface, my shoulder slightly dislocated.   Once
water was expelled from my lungs, I found Bill kneeling next to
me.   I'll never forget the day that followed after the near-
drowning experience.   Probably one of the best days of my life
when the colors were brighter and richer than ever before.

Even the air smelled different, sweeter almost, as though each and every breath was a treat.

With Mr. Rebus's warning aside, I don't have to pay a visit to that quack, the Tax Man, after my second day in the Final Phase, which means I get to keep all nine of my fingers.

Small victories, I tell myself.

5

AS the rumble of the audience intensified outside his dressing room, Joshua contemplated breaking the glass and using a shard to cut his throat. If this is all inside my head, he wondered, then I can hit the fucking off-switch and unplug from this horrible nightmare.

The sound of a *knock-knock* on the door pulled Joshua from his morbid thoughts.

Walker poked his head inside and said, "May I come in?"

Joshua faced the mirror and again, fell into deep contemplation.

Walker entered the dressing room, as if he was going to enter despite Joshua's answer.

"I know what you're thinking, Josh," said Walker. "Just a little advice: I wouldn't do *that* if I were you."

Joshua looked at Walker's reflection in the mirror.

"If you die in VR. . . " said Walker, ". . . then you die in real life. . . at least, the part of you that matters the most."

With his face clouding red, Joshua asked, "What does that mean?"

"All emotion," he said, "all reason, all intellect, everything that makes a human. . . *human*, it will be stripped away from you, Josh, and you'll be nothing more than an empty shell of an individual drifting throughout life without purpose or responsibility. You'll be a phantom among the living. Nobody will hear you because nobody will ever listen to you. And your humanity, gone. Any credibility that you once had, dust. Is that what you want, Josh? To be an obstruction? An obstacle? An object? Reduced to a burden?"

"Thought you said this was an execution?"

"It most definitely is, Josh, but *not* of you," he said. "The avatar known as Gaud."

"What do they want from Gaud?" Joshua asked, as the rumbling intensified.

"*They*," Walker clarified, "as in The People?"

Joshua forced himself to nod, his throat too tight to speak.

"They're here for an apology," Walker said and stood next to Joshua, who remained seated in front of the vanity. "And once Gaud has apologized for his crime. . . " his eyes sharpen over Joshua's, ". . . then he will be stoned to death."

The notion alone terrorized Joshua and left his insides in a twisted mess.

It's not real, he told himself over and over.

"But it will *feel* real," Walker said and placed his hand over Joshua's shoulder. "That's the whole point, to make you feel, not only pain, but also humiliation. This is the only way you can be reformed, Josh. Once your avatar is dead, you will finally be liberated from this alter ego that has pulled you down into the depths of despair. You'll finally be able to live a life of substance *and* meaning."

Joshua could feel the vibration of the audience coursing through the dressing room floor, the hums and gibberish chants sending waves of panic throughout his body.

Another *knock* on the door!

Joshua witnessed fire, a beating ball of it, like a glittery floater in the corner of his eye.

The orange-haired man fully entered the room.

He was The Man Who Liked To Play With Fire.

Walker's own right hand.

"It's time," he said, nodding at Walker.

"This here is Aodh," Walker introduced Joshua to a pale-faced man.

While bringing his attention back to the mirror, Joshua caught Aodh's reflection.

Again, the sudden thought rose up inside him. This time, he didn't contemplate using one of the glass shards on himself, not once did such notion of making a quick and abrupt exit from this hell cross his mind. Instead, all of that pent-up rage was redirected toward the fiery-haired man, who had been stalking him.

Walker patted Joshua on the shoulder and said, "Break a leg." While exiting the dressing room, he said to Aodh, "Play nice." He waited for a response from Aodh before leaving the room. All he received from him were the movements of several facial features: A flaring of his nostrils; a thin, closed smile that could pass as a taut leash concealing his barred teeth; and lastly, his eyes, which swelled with a restrained madness.

"Let's go, Don Juan," said Aodh, as he walked outside the dressing room.

After giving himself a mental pep talk in front of the mirror, Joshua stood to his feet and exited the dressing room where Aodh was waiting for him in the dimly lit hallway.

Backstage, the two walked through the hallway, which led them to the main stage.

Along the way, Joshua walked past Regina, who was parting ways with a group of tourists. With Aodh right on his heels, Joshua stopped and asked, "Why'd you kill her?"

Aodh pushed Joshua forward.

Regina, in return, signaled Aodh to cool his temper and made an airy noise with her mouth before responding, "Well, *Gaud*. . . " Regina said with a trace of sarcasm in her voice, ". . . if you hadn't used that magnetic charm of yours on one of our agents, then I wouldn't have killed her."

"She had nothing to with anything of this—"

"Quick being so damn oblivious," Regina snapped. "You and me both know Venus forced my hand after she attempted to contact you." She stopped, turned, and faced Joshua. "She broke protocol. . . " she said, closer, ". . . and someone had to step up and put your ass back on track."

Joshua struggled to register what Regina was telling him.

While reading the confusion on Joshua's face, Regina said more clearly, "You still don't get it, do you? Julia was merely a side of you that strongly desired to move on and accept wrongdoing, which is why we had to *remove* that element of your story, your own little *backdoor*. Pretty clever, I'd say. A spiritual warrior who thinks he's so in tuned with nature and her never-ending song. You still hear her, don't you? Like an echo that only gets louder overtime. According to your contract with Onion, you accepting full responsibility without paying a visit to the ole Chop Shop is an unequivocal no-no. You *can't* move on, Joshua." She gave Joshua a once-over, as if she was sizing him up. "Not yet you can. You see? Getting rid of Julia was an alteration of plan based on the recklessness of a silly, impressionable agent, who broke protocol. Regardless of my spontaneity, that plan—*your* plan—Joshua, it all leads right here. All roads to Sorry Central: the one place where big shots, like you, go to die."

Once again, Aodh pushed him forward, this time harder and causing him to look his balance.

As Joshua and Aodh continued to make their way through the hallway, they soon arrived at a black curtain where only feet away the synchronized stomping and handclapping of the crowd was beating like a furious heart.

Aodh faced Joshua, both his dark eyes penetrating him like a ritualistically-honed blade. He held out his hand, palm side up, showcasing the way for Joshua.

With a stern tone, Aodh said, "If I was you, I'd be honest with them. Otherwise, they'll tear you apart."

Hesitant, Joshua took a step toward the curtains.

Aodh said with a strange awe, "In all my years working for Onion, I've never seen a crowd like this one before." His lips cracked in a wicked grin, which spread across the bottom scarred half of his face. "They're—how do I say—quite an ornery bunch."

He slipped his hand into the slit of the curtain and pulled back, revealing a narrow pathway, which led directly to the stage.

With his chest tightening, Joshua inhaled.

While holding the breath inside his tight chest, which felt as if it was about to collapse from the weight of his heart, Joshua stepped through the black curtains and witnessed the madness that awaited him: Hundreds of thousands of people, as earlier explained, all here for Joshua, each one of their faces filled with contagious rage, easily mistaking humans for rabid animals with their yellowish teeth barred, the corners of their squared mouths covered in foamy discharge, and each expletive or slur that they heaved at him, that rage spittle sprayed from their glossy lips like tiny drops of verbal lubricant that greased the wicked algorithm that drove them.

Hate was all the rage.

And the avatar known as "Gaud" was what they hated.

With Aodh beside him, Joshua was escorted along the opening that snaked its way through the crowd.

So many faces, Joshua saw.

He thought to himself that he didn't know any of these people.

Then, he questioned why they were so angry with him.

What did he directly do to them?

As he peered closer at their faces, he recognized several of the faces.

The first one being his mother, Peggy, who was dressed as if she recently finished playing a game of pickle ball: "*Incompetent wimp!*" Peggy barked. "*Loser! Why don't you get a real job and contribute to society? You waste of flesh! You're dead to me! I wish you were never even born, you fucking disgrace. . .*"

Joshua looked closer at Peggy and realized it wasn't exactly Peggy, but rather a darker imitation of his mother. Her eyes seemed darker as well, sinister, altered. Her voice much raspier, again, altered, as if it wasn't Peggy, per se, shouting these awful words at him—maybe it was a shade of Peggy, a shade that she kept hidden in the darkest corners of her heart—but to Joshua, it felt as if a force had seized control over her entire body, as well as her very mind, like she had been hacked by a techno-pirate and he or she was merely pounding keys on a keyboard.

As Joshua was ushered closer to the stage, he witnessed more faces, some of them being familiar while others foreign, like he had seen them before but in another life perhaps.

Among those faces he saw Natalie's.

She no longer bore any scars on her face and if it wasn't for her eyes, he wouldn't have recognized her. Yet, the peripheries of her eyes, the eyes that once speared his heart, had oxidized, like rust, with a bluish-green color encompassing the love which she once shared.

She never shouted out at Joshua, for the look alone on her face, the disappointment, cut right through him like a thousand knives.

Robert, Brandon, as well as Julia, *not Ingle* but the other one from his past, were also in the crowd and much similar to Natalie, each of them wore looks of disappointment on their faces.

Joshua told himself over and over that these people were not real. They were only extreme exaggerations of the people whom he once knew as friends or family.

Among the swarm of voices, one of them rose up above them, amplified and filtered.

As their voices showered over him, he looked ahead to the main stage where he saw the talk radio host, Buzz Bumble, who was the emcee of the execution.

"Here he is, ladies and germs. . . " Buzz said, waving his arms around in animation, ". . . the man, the myth, the legend. . . Gaud!"

As soon as Joshua heard the name Gaud being spoken, he saw members of the mawb in the crowd: First was Needles, who called Joshua a "backstabber," and then, next, New Jack, who called Joshua a "leech," then Mayhem, who called Joshua a "moron." He saw other members, who all expressed how they felt about him by means of name-calling, as if an insult, like "leech," for instance, was not only an invisible blade that cut the deepest, but also a blunt instrument that crushed the person who was on the receiving end, and the word itself, "*leech*," whose archaic definition once meant "doctor" or "healer," was a weapon used to destroy him.

Again, Joshua reminded himself that all of these people, these faces—imitations—none of them were real. Instead, each one of them were mental projections, or as Walker earlier explained, "psychic constructs," and if, by some organic manifestation, Joshua was playing tricks on his own mind and somehow, these people were a fraction of the truth, then none of the insults carried the least amount of weight or substance for these oral noises shaped by tongues and lips were dumbed-down words expressed by those who didn't possess the mental capacity to deliver anything starkly creative.

Once he walked past the mawb, he saw the faces of his relatives: uncles, grandparents, distant cousins, most, if not, all of them dead, and yet, here they were, alive but not well. Their appearances were ghastly and sickly, almost colorless, their blotchy faces appearing nothing like he remembered from the old photographs.

One of the family members—Joshua couldn't remember which one—spat on him, resulting in the rest of the crowd to follow suit.

By the time Joshua reached the stage, his face, as well as his body was covered in spit, piss, and other bodily discharge.

Buzz, who was dressed in a black and white tuxedo, was first to greet Joshua, who was escorted onto the stage by two muscular bodyguards.

Aodh parted ways with Joshua and then joined the rest of a security detail while Joshua was chained to a wooden post in the center of the stage.

As the bodyguards finished securing the chains around his body, which prevented him from escaping, Joshua gazed up at the godly yew tree running through the middle of the train station and couldn't help but imagine the tree's age, how old it was, hundreds of years old—perhaps even thousands?—the many layers inside, as well as the many stories it carried.

Buzz cried out, "*What a crowd!*" While foolishly wagging his finger, he strutted over to Joshua and said to him, "Man, you are one self-loathing son of a bitch!"

Joshua pulled his eyes away from the tree and in the corner of his eyes, caught Buzz scurrying his way toward him.

With his eyes wide and hella mad, Buzz inched closer to Joshua, covered a bead-like microphone attached to the wire that ran alongside his cheek, and whispered in his ear, "*Don't give them the satisfaction. To ask for forgiveness is to forfeit your dignity. You know I'm right. I'm always right. Once those two words dribble from your lips, Joshy Boy, they will devour you.*" Buzz chomped down, as if he was taking an invisible bite of the air, his top and bottom teeth banging against each other. He removed his cupped hand from the microphone and rubbed the side of his cheek onto the side of Joshua's; and after Buzz pulled his face away, he shouted indirectly at Joshua, "You pitiful creature, you! Filled with so much hate!"

The crowd booed Joshua, screaming all kinds of obscenities at him.

"Lemme ask you fine people that are here today. . . " Buzz said to the crowd, as he stepped toward the edge of the stage, ". . . Should this pitiful creature apologize?"

The crowd erupted in a booming uproar, cheering a resounding "YES!" to Buzz's query.

Buzz faced Joshua, naively shrugged both his shoulders, and said, "You know what that means, Gaud! The crowd has spoken!"

As Joshua mentally rehearsed lines in his head, he pointed out each face in the crowd.

Buzz made it easy for Joshua, as he walked back over to him and leaned closer.

"All you have to do is say those two words," he said and mouthed the words "*I'm sorry*," as if the words themselves caused him great suffering.

Buzz waited for a response.

The beating crowd furiously waited for a response.

"No," Joshua said finally. "I'm not fucking sorry. I won't apologize—"

"But you will," said Buzz. "You must or else. . . "

"Or else what?"

He pointed out one of the faces in the crowd.

A man—Joshua forgot the man's name—but he remembered seeing a story on the news about this very same man being charged with domestic assault after he struck his wife. Yet, here he was in the crowd, demanding an apology as he pointed at Joshua with the same hand that he used to slap his wife across the face, leaving her with a black eye. And from what Joshua gathered, it wasn't just one occurrence. The man struck her multiple times. Used that hand of his like a switch to turn off his wife's mouth. Every now and then, this man treated that hand of his as a close-fisted finger and his wife's mouth was a mute button and he'd repeatedly strike it until it muted.

As Joshua recalled Buzz's words, "*Don't give them the satisfaction*," he began to wonder if the whole event was a test.

"Gaud. . . " Buzz said, his voice more dour, ". . . if you do not apologize for the crime that you've committed, then they will kill you—"

"Isn't that what this is? An execution? Then what are you waiting for? Enough with all of your ridiculous theatrics! Go ahead! Execute me!"

"What part of 'kill you' did you not understand? I hate to be the bearer of bad news, but, if you do not say those two words, you will be dead. *All* of you, including the one and only you. *Here. . .* " he said, more closely and pointed at the jumbotron-like screen above the station, ". . . there. And everywhere. The choice is all yours. . . " Buzz uttered his name, ". . . Joshua."

On the screen: the current "LIVE" video feed of Joshua, medically induced in a trance-like state as he sat on a bench with his wrists handcuffed to a railing alongside a holding cell. Worn on his head a wiry cap, which was responsible for creating such a virtual lifelike experience.

"You're lying," Joshua said and seethed, "I won't apologize!"

"You must!"

Joshua shouted out over Buzz, "I won't!"

Dispirited by Joshua's answer, Buzz lowered his head and said quietly into the microphone, "Very well. You've made your final decision. Now," he said, perking up, "let's move on to the next—"

Before Buzz could finish his sentence, the crowd suddenly erupted in anger.

Buzz attempted to calm the crowd, but he completely lost control over them.

Once the items began to fly from the crowd, Buzz said "*Adios*" to Joshua and while covering his head with his arms, fled from the stage.

The first item to strike Joshua in the head was a ripe avocado, its leathery skin thin and incredibly smooth. The fruit, however, was thrown hard enough that he could feel that very stone inside the avocado as it struck the side of his forehead. Upon impact, part of the skin spilt open, leaving behind a lumpy streak of lime green flesh along Joshua's upper cheek.

More fruit with stones, like avocados, were hurled at center stage, including peaches, mangoes, as well as cherries. Fruit with stones weren't the only items being flung at Joshua. Apples, bananas, oranges were also thrown at Joshua. Next were vegetables, from tomatoes—which was still left to debate whether it was a fruit or a vegetable—to potatoes, which resulted in more significant bodily harm. One member of the crowd ended up throwing an entire head of cauliflower at Joshua, which struck the left side of his chest and temporarily knocked the wind out of him.

The violence raged on, seconds of bloodlust turning into minutes, minutes turning into hours.

One side of Joshua's face was red and badly swollen and so numb that each strike felt like a pinprick against his flesh. One of his eyes was partially swollen shut. The worst of his injuries was a deep laceration on the top of his forehead from where he was struck by a pumpkin the size of a softball, the tip of the coarse and fibrous stem slicing his head, causing the blood to run down his face and nearly blind him.

No matter what was thrown at Joshua and even though there were times that he wanted it all to end, he still did *not* apologize.

Even members of the crowd—The People who carried a sliver of sympathy—begged Joshua to apologize.

Eventually, after the arms of the crowd grew sore and tired, a dazed Joshua was approached by two bodyguards, who removed the heavy chains that were wrapped around his body. Once he was free of the chains, his body fell forward, the bodyguards catching him and carrying him off the stage. They dragged his body backstage. By then, he could barely see inches in front of him, the reddish fog of blood clouding his vision. The bodyguards tossed Joshua's lifeless body back in the dressing room, as if it was no different than the very items used to pelt his flesh. He crashed directly through the carpeted floor and pulled everything attached to the floor with him. Tables, vanities, and chairs: everything that Joshua touched sunk into a deep, dark blackness.

DAY Three.

At 6:01 Mr. Rebus contacts me through VidChat and tells me that I've been relocated to another job.

Even though my pain is rather mild—on a scale from one to ten, ten being the most pain, I'd probably rank it a number three—I take a J-12 pill.

As soon as I arrive on site, which is a depot, I realize that Mr. Rebus either has a sick sense of humor or the ten-day trial is, in fact, all a test.

Despite the recent automobile accident, which I realize could've been much worse, my new job as a bus driver is relatively straightforward and doesn't require me to have all ten fingers in order to successfully drive a bus.

With a new perspective on life after the crash, I make it through the entire day without running into any issues. I'm given a route. I make my stops. I see more of those homeless people during my route. Several of them, I notice, are amputees. One of them is missing an arm and the other, a leg. For I all know, they're Veterans. Maybe they did a tour overseas. Perhaps they lost a limb in battle.

During one of my stops past a desolate intersection along the outskirts of downtown, I catch a glimpse of a child-like figure crawling over the ground inside a grungy alleyway covered in the shadows of a high-rise that blots out the morning sun.

As the two passengers board the bus, I peer closer at the strange person inside the alleyway. Before closing the doors, I see part of the figure; and strangely, the only thing remaining of the man is a part, his entire torso. Both his arms, as well as his legs, are gone, amputated. He uses both his shoulders, as well as his hips, to waddle across the ground. His belly and chest are like the sole of a foot. He uses his chin like an extremity and extends out his mandible to slide closer an empty aluminum can of beans. The sight alone of that limbless man struggling to roll the can on the ground sends chills down my spine.

Tempted to stand up from my seat, a passenger from behind calls out, "*Don't!*"

I look up in the mirror above the driver's seat and find the passenger's eyes in the reflection.

He says to me, "They're beyond helping."

I look closer at the passenger and lose myself in his eyes.

Those eyes.

Mr. Rebus.

Even though the passenger looks nothing like Mr. Rebus, his eyes are the same.

"You're behind schedule, Driver," another passenger says.

I can sense all of their eyes attached to me.

They depend on me.

I ignore the helpless man in the alleyway, close the door, and continue my route.

Surprisingly, while driving this massive machine around Spartacus, I find entertainment in listening in on the passengers and their stories. If anything, their voices pull me from my thoughts.

While driving, I listen to a passenger complain to another passenger about his wife and how she's always getting on his back for not pulling his weight around the house when, on the contrary, he's the one who pays for the house. I overhear three teens gossiping about a latest trend, "Snowcapping." I eavesdrop on an incredibly ill tempered woman, who's recently had a mastectomy, argue over the phone with another woman about a bossy employee at work.

The entire day revolves around driving and listening, as though it's all that is required of the job. I find great pleasure in those two things, which seem so simple.

WHEN I arrive back at my apartment after work, I find myself delving deeper into my thoughts.

It's in those moments of restlessness when I start spiraling.

It all starts with a noise coming from the apartment below me, a thud-like noise similar to a stomp of a foot. I don't think anything of it. I try to ignore it. Then it happens again, pulling me from my thoughts. I find myself anticipating the noise. My nerves begin to tighten. Then I hear it again and again, that *thudding* from, not above, but rather below.

Perhaps a heelwalker who's pacing back and forth on aged hardwood floor like a fiend jonesing for a fix?

Or, an amateur drummer who's practicing how to use the kick drum?

Or, even the headboard of a bed banging against the wall while an impulsive couple revel in each other's flesh?

Whomever—or whatever—it may be that's making the thudding noise below me I make an attempt to drown out the noise by turning on the stereo. The thuds are still there, underneath the music.

After awhile, I completely obsess over that noise below. It's all I think about, the thudding. My mind begins to turn on me and I start to think that maybe these sounds are deliberate, that a member of Onion is living below me, provoking me, trying to get a rise out of me, testing me by making the noises on purpose, as though pushing my buttons, seeing how far he or she can go—what was my limit—before the thoughts warmed like a fever.

Not thinking but, more or less, mentally acting out the crime itself, I lose control.

I ask myself: Why now?

Maybe he or she was out of town when I first moved in.

Maybe I just need to think of something else.

MR. Rebus calls via VidChat at exactly nine o'clock.

Before I answer, I already know that I've failed for the day— the last hour being the worse, with the thuds igniting a series of hateful thoughts.

As predicted, Mr. Rebus informs me that I made it through the entire day without any negative or alarming thoughts. "*However*," he says.

Never have I hated such a word.

However.

Two compatible words.

How and *ever.*

Both joined together in marriage.

I wish for their divorce.

I hope it's a nasty one, which ends in carnage.

Before he can finish his train of thought, I already know his next words, as if I can read his mind.

Sure enough, I'm right.

The noises.

The spiral.

I'll choose my other pinkie finger.

I convince myself that I'll work better with even numbers.

While the Tax Man in the white coat wraps the wire around my pinkie and makes a ring below the knuckle, I drift deeper into my thoughts.

"*According to your contract with Onion, you* (me) *accepting full responsibility without paying a visit to the ole Chop Shop is an unequivocal no-no*," said Regina.

Those past comments alone has me thinking that, no matter what, Mr. Rebus will find anything—even if it's something as mundane as a minor dislike—and if so, then maybe I'm destined to pay a visit the Chop Shop every night, hateful thoughts or not. Maybe the test is not a test, but rather yet another extension of my punishment.

6

JOSHUA felt the blood in his veins throbbing, like vibrations in puddles casting circular ripples.

He powered through the blackness, through that rippling, and cracked open his eyes.

Before his eyes were two muddy boots, black leather, size twelve.

As Joshua regained consciousness, he followed the boots to the wearer, who was the same bodyguard from earlier, one of two who carried him off the stage. He was seated against the well of a tire. He searched for the other one but couldn't find him.

More feeling returned.

The first and most infiltrating one: The side of his face pressed against the metal lining of the truck bed. Each bump and crater in the dirt road caused the side of his cheekbone to bang against the metal lining, sending waves of pain throughout the side of his face.

Despite the most recent discomfort, he felt as if he was finally out.

Even the internal injuries were gone.

Once he regained feeling back in his hand, he touched the side of his face.

The cuts and bruises, once raw and tenderized, were gone, as well as the pungent odor of the fleshy organic products cast onto his body.

Even the pain had vanished, as if he somehow forgot its awful bite and any chance of recalling it was like a softly spoken voice, which echoed through a chatty colony of penguins.

Yet, the weighty humiliation of being stoned to near death still remained, pulling him further into a pit of despair.

As he looked above the bodyguard, he witnessed the tops of the pine trees passing overhead.

He suddenly heard the *squeak* of brakes.

Once the truck stopped, Joshua heard the sound of a door slamming shut followed by repetitive sounds of boots tromping through coarse dirt.

The same bodyguard from before appeared behind the tailgate. He loomed over Joshua. His biceps were about the size of both of Joshua's thighs combined; and similar to the other bodyguard, he wore no expression whatsoever on his blotchy, square-shaped face, which carried as much detail as a smudge of ink.

Together, the two pulled Joshua from the back of the truck and dragged him toward two more figures standing next to a mustard-yellow smart car. Joshua imagined that one of the bodyguards could flick that car over on its side with an index finger as if it was a wind-up toy inside a happy meal.

As the bodyguards propped Joshua's body upright and positioned him in front of two mysterious and darkly shaped figures, one of the bodyguards grabbed Joshua's side as if he was a doll with an elastic neck and redirected it at one figure in particular. The figure, Joshua learned, was none other than Walker, who stepped forward and revealed himself. Behind him was another member of the Onion Group: Aodh, Joshua recognized, who was leaned against that spit of a car, picking at his hangnails and appearing, based on his blatant disinterest, as if he had more important places to be right now.

"I apologize if my men were rough on you," said Walker. "I'm afraid you have forced us to resort to drastic measures."

"Like I care what you do to me," said Joshua. "None of this is real."

With a smirk on his face, Walker stepped forward and kneeled down to Joshua's level.

"I'm going to give you one last attempt to apologize," he said to Joshua. "Think of it as me offering a sort of a lifeline to you, Josh."

"Take your lifeline and shove it up your imaginary ass," seethed Joshua. "You're a fucking figment. A mirage. . . "

Walker reached down and scooped up the sandy dirt and held it in the palm of his hand.

"Hold on your hand," he demanded.

Joshua's hand didn't budge.

One of the bodyguards grabbed hold of Joshua's forearm and brought his hand forward while, at the same time, Joshua resisted. The bodyguard's grip was too overbearing; and after a brief struggle, Joshua had no other choice than to hold out his hand.

With his cupped hand held directly over Joshua's hand, Walker released the palm-full of dirt, which poured over Joshua's hand.

While carefully studying Joshua, Walker asked, "You feel that? Feels different, does it not?"

Oddly enough, Joshua agreed with Walker.

The feeling was eerily familiar, real. Each grain of sand lightly fell over his skin, leaving him in a panic-stricken state.

"Why is that, Mr. Lamb?" Walker asked but answered for Joshua, "Because you're no longer in virtual reality. You see Sorry Central was nothing more than another side-op inside a game you know as. . . *The Hate Train*. . . A kind of simulation meant to elicit an apology for your past crime or shall I say, crimes." He rotated his shoulders in an angle and showcased the dense forest with pine trees that stretched as far as the eye could see. "This here is augmented reality, meaning the forest, even the very dirt in your hand. . . " The comment forced Joshua to glance down at the traces of dirt on top of his hand, ". . . this whole environment around you is *all* real, Josh. As far as the augmented part. . . " All of a sudden, he thought he saw a person behind Walker, ". . . I'm sure you're questioning yourself right now as I speak: What is actually real?" Walker followed Joshua's eyes drifting over his shoulder. "One thing is for certain: This. . . " he said and grabbed yet another handful of dirt from the ground, ". . . this is real." He stood to his feet and pointed at the rectangular-shaped hole in the earth, deep enough to fit a body, or in Joshua's case, Joshua's body. He pointed at Joshua's soon-to-be grave and said more casually, "*That* is real."

More alert, Joshua asked, "What do you plan on doing with me?"

"The question is 'What are *you*, Joshua Lamb, going to do with yourself?' *Lifeline*," Walker reminded Joshua. "I'm only going to offer it once. And if you choose to disobey me, well then. . . " he looked up at the cloudy sky, ". . . even that God of yours won't be able to save you."

Walker flicked his head in a nod, motioning to the bodyguards to stand Joshua to his feet.

As Joshua was propped upright, the bodyguards walked Joshua to the hole in the ground.

Along the way, Joshua's foot stepped on a weed.

Walker stopped suddenly and turned his shoulder, causing Joshua to stop as well.

"If I were you, I'd watch where I step," he said coyly.

Despite Walker saying that he was back in reality, or better yet, a "semi-reality," Joshua was forced to pause and take a closer look at his surroundings.

"What is this place?" asked Joshua.

"This is *The Forest of The Damned*," Walker said and faced Joshua. "The resting place for your God's banished children, those who were unable to move forward and accept wrong-doing. These poor souls will spend decades, centuries. . . " he kneeled back down, touched one of the weeds growing from the earth, then dramatically held up his hand toward the hazy sun, which was blotted out by the thin newspaper gray clouds, ". . . crookedly reaching up to their Maker, hoping He will save them from this hell where they languish. They're given four years. . . " said Walker, standing upright, ". . . four years of darkness, four years of desperately longing to touch a tiny glimpse of light at the end of their dark tunnels. If they fail to atone for their wrongdoings, then I'm afraid nothing can save them from the fire—"

With his voice trembling, Joshua said, "Fire? What fire?"

"Every four years, Ferrymen administered what is known as controlled burns—"

"Controlled burns?" Joshua uttered.

"Correct," Walker said. "Cleansed by fire."

With slight hesitation, Joshua confirmed: "By Ferrymen?"

Nodding, Walker said to Joshua, "They mostly consist of ex-members of an elite squad you may know as Reapers. A rather interesting bunch, they are."

Walker proceeded toward the hole.

When they arrived at Joshua's hole, the bodyguards released their grips from around Joshua who leaned forward over the hole and peered into it.

Once more, a wave of panic overwhelmed Joshua.

"What the fuck is this? Some kind of joke? Stop playing around. If you're here to scare the shit out of me or teach me a lesson, then you've succeeded. Now, bring me back to reality—"

"Did you not hear a single word that I said to you, Josh?" Walker said, as he began to lose patience with Joshua. "This is reality. *Your* reality."

Joshua closed his eyes and repeated over and over to himself: "This *isn't* real, you fuck. I'm in a holding cell, get it? I can wake up at any point. . . "

Walker said more amusedly, "Then why don't you? While you're at it, why don't you click your heels three times and *whoosh* yourself back to reality?" Walker's narrow eyes darkened like storm clouds stirring the heavens. He said closely, "Whether you like it or not, Josh, this is your reality right now and either you ask for forgiveness or. . . " Those gloomy eyes fell below, ". . . down in the hole you go."

"Fine," Joshua said shortly. "I'm sorry—"

"Not good enough," Walker said and nodded at the bodyguards, who forced Joshua into the hole.

After the initial impact, Joshua immediately attempted to climb out of the hole, which was roughly eight feet deep. His attempts were blocked by the boots of the bodyguards, who prevented Joshua from escaping.

"Apologize, Josh. . . " Walker said, as he towered over the hole, ". . . and all of this will be over."

"I said I'm sorry—"

"Mean it, Josh."

"I'm sorry goddamn it," he cried out.

"Not good enough," Walker said and stepped away.

"Where are you going?" asked Joshua. "Huh?"

Once Walker and the bodyguards were no longer in view, another person who was carrying a shovel stepped forward.

"Nate?"

Joshua's younger half-brother, Nathaniel, drove the sharp end of the shovel in the mound of dirt next to the hole and pulled out a shovelful of dirt, which was filled with all types of insects, but mainly worms.

"You're *not* real," said Joshua.

"Just what I expected," Nate said with a scowl. "I've *never* been real to you."

Before Joshua could respond, Nate threw the shovelful of dirt onto Joshua's head.

In a last-ditch effort, he attempted to cover his face from the dirt, which showered over him.

"Nate. . . " he shouted out, ". . . you know I didn't mean that! You are real, but not in here, in this fucking hellscape! Don't take it so personal!"

"You're pathetic," Nate said with rancor and walked away.

As Joshua cleared away the dirt from his face, he looked up and towering above him was his cousin, Gabe.

"Sup, J," Gabe said, his voice gentle and caring.

"What are you doing here, Gabe?" asked Joshua.

"Make it easy on yourself, will you—"

All of a sudden, Gabe's spiteful mother, Marlene, who was a manipulating bitch, snatched a shovel from her son's hand.

"The hell if I'm going to let this lowlife piece of shit drag you down with him," she said bitterly and scooped a shovelful of dirt and tossed it on Joshua.

Joshua's aunt stormed away, calling for Gabe.

"Just apologize, 'k," Gabe said while Marlene was ordering her son to leave.

Eventually, Gabe walked away in a similar fashion as Nate.

Next to step forward was Robert, or "Old Jack," whom Joshua recently saw in attendance at Sorry Central.

Old Jack didn't say a word to Joshua. Instead, he tossed a shovelful of dirt at Joshua's feet.

After Old Jack was Joshua's brother, Christian, who said to Joshua, "I told you so—"

"Oh yeah," Joshua said, the anger clouding over his red face. "What did you tell me, Christian?"

"Didn't I tell you that you'd wind up in a hole sooner than me?"

"Because you think you're better than me, huh?"

"No," Christian said to Joshua, as he stood atop a mountainous bluff on the side of the hole. "I'm not better. Believe it or not, but I wish I was more like you. I wish I took more risk. I wish I spoke my mind. Instead, I chose to live a safe life and keep my head down and my mouth shut, unlike you, who never held back, especially after you traveled overseas and found your way back home and it was like you conquered the world. I couldn't have done any of those things you've done, Josh. But. . . what bothers me the most: You actually attempted to live a normal life." Christian readjusted his grip around the handle of the shovel. "But I don't blame you one bit. Nah. I pity you—"

"Fuck your pity," Joshua seethed.

"You know. . . there's nothing more boring than living a life padded with bubblewrap where every step you take is like walking through a minefield. I mean, you could've achieved great things, but instead, you chose to be *normal*." He shook his head in disappointment. "What a shame."

More people from his past showed up, sharing their own two cents' worth about Joshua and all of his shortcomings.

Each one of them tossed a shovelful of dirt on Joshua as soon as they reduced him to insults and whatnot.

Dirt continued to fill up the hole, each wounded remark resulting in yet another fling of dirt.

By the time he was waist-deep in dirt, he could only move the upper half of his body, whereas the bottom half remained still, cemented into the cold, relentless earth, and any attempt that he made to escape was fruitless.

Once Peggy, still dressed as if she recently finished a game of pickle ball, loomed above like a dark silhouette, Joshua was already neck-deep in dirt. Any iota of forgiveness left inside of him had dissipated, leaving him with only rage, so raw and infinite that it stretched throughout centuries. She should've been dressed for my funeral, he thought, instead of that stupid costume. He told himself—convinced himself—that his mother wasn't real and that her presence was merely a cruel fabrication, which had been augmented into his surrounding environment.

With a stern composure, Peggy shared a story to Joshua about a time when she was younger and how she had an abortion after she had unprotected sex with a stranger whom she was using to retaliate against a neglectful boyfriend and the whole time while she told the personal story to Joshua he suddenly realized that he was about to die. He floated outside his own body and witnessed himself being pulled out of VR after he blacked out in the holding cell; then, after he regained consciousness, his body was loaded into the back of a truck.

"I'm sorry. . . " he interrupted Peggy before she finished telling the rest of her story, ". . . for everything. I was selfish. I let my own personal issues get between us—"

"It's too late, Joshua," she said, unflinching. "You're already dead. You died before you entered my world."

The very last words that Peggy spoke to Joshua sounded incredibly odd and were delivered in a deeper and much sinister tone, not her tone, not even close to her natural tone, but rather the tone of a darker entity with a force as contagious as The Plague, as if it had used words as sharply-honed projectiles and when they left her mouth, these airy, invisible things, they struck their target with godly precision.

As soon as Peggy fulfilled her obligations, which forced Joshua to hold up his chin, as if he was doing pull-ups with his head, Bill, who was dressed in a spotty-pale blue hospital gown that appeared like an oversized dress over his frail body, shuffled closer with a gingerly pace until he arrived at the only part left exposed on Joshua's body, which was his head. Bill appeared exactly how Joshua last remembered him: His face, pale and ghostly; his cheeks, as well as his eye sockets sunken inward; his eyes as murky as stagnant floodwater; body riddled with a disease that was crawling through his insides and consuming all of his internal organs like a gluttonous spider.

The only words that Bill said to Joshua: *"I'm sorry, son. . . "*

Tears ran from his flooded eyes, as Joshua struggled to keep his head above the ground.

After a painful pause, Bill finished, "I'm sorry that I introduced you to Hate. I thought that, if you knew Hate and you learned what drove Hate, maybe you could do something that I never accomplished: Defeat Hate. I was wrong, Josh. Hate is a cancer," Bill said, as the tears left behind glossy snail trails along his cold flesh. "For some, it's also a friend. And sometimes. . . the two can be mistaken as the same." The words dripped from his quivering chapped, crusty lips: "Josh, I *never* wanted you to carry Hate inside your heart. But it doesn't matter what I want. It's what *you* want."

Bill suddenly drove the sharp end of the shovel into the small mound of dirt like a spear next to Joshua's head and decided to abandon the shovel without fulfilling his obligation.

As Bill shuffled away, Pep was the last one to visit Joshua.

Not once did she ever speak a word to Joshua.

Instead, she pulled the shovel from the earth, scooped up the last remaining dirt, and threw it on Joshua's face, nearly blinding him.

Finally, after all of the people from Joshua's past left The Forest, Walker appeared, marveling at Joshua as he choked and gagged and spat dirt from his mouth.

Once he was able to violently shake the dirt from his eyes, he first eyed Walker looming above him and then inches away from his face, an ant, which appeared much larger than any average ant. To Joshua, the ant appeared as large as a rat scuffling around him and every now and then, taking a nibble from his flesh as though sampling Joshua.

"Please. . . " Joshua begged Walker while spitting mouthfuls of dirt, ". . . make it stop already. You win goddamn it!"

Walker kneeled back down to Joshua's level, this time ground level, and admired the curious ant. Where there was one, there was another and another. Then another.

More ants.

Dozens of them.

Multiplied into hundreds.

All making their way to the parts of Joshua's exposed face.

"Remarkable creatures, aren't they?" Walker said to Joshua while carefully examining the ants falling in lines, like soldiers. "Humans are no different than ants, are we not? I'd even go so far to say that humans are ants, but on a much larger scale. Or, even bees, for that matter. How are these creatures able to exist? Protect the hive. Protect the colony. But most importantly, protect the queen. The *mother* of your child," he said, as he stared Joshua directly in the eyes.

Once more, Joshua saw—at least, thought he saw—Pep standing behind Walker and carrying a dead fetus in her arms.

Joshua focused on Walker, his words.

"You failed to protect Mother," Walker said.

"It was an accident," Joshua cried.

"Yes," Walker said over Joshua and dismissed his apology. "You've said that over and over before, but I'm not sure you actually mean it."

"I do mean it!"

Walker stood up and grabbed the handle of the shovel.

"I don't believe you," Walker said to Joshua and scooped the remainder of dirt from the mound and then tossed dirt onto Joshua until his face was completely covered in dirt.

DAY Four.

After speaking with The Board, Mr. Rebus contacts me via VidChat.

Based on recent events, The Board concludes that my temporary employment as a bus driver makes me a liability. Their reasons are centered on the fact that I have eight fingers, and the majority of this so-called "Board" unanimously agrees that, in order for me to safely transport passengers, I should have at least nine fingers. Where they came up with that number is beyond me. I'm beginning to see a pattern emerging with the "10-Day" trial, exercise, or whatever, a primary focus being on the importance of fighting temptation to hate in order to salvage my fingers.

Mr. Rebus never says it, but I think he's trying to teach me a lesson that it's better to use the very digits that I was provided at birth than it is to carry any hateful thoughts.

By early morning, Mr. Rebus has already set me up with a job as a custodian at a local museum, which doesn't require all of my fingers. Most of the work consists of sweeping, mopping the floors, cleaning the bathrooms, and removing streaks and fingerprints from windows, which I can manage with eight fingers. As with the bus driver job, I find the work as a custodian rather relaxing, despite its degrading and often negative connotation of cleaning up the filth that people leave behind. What brings me the most comfort is the quiet environment of the museum and being around so many great works of art, paintings and sculptures.

During late afternoon, I take a half-lunch in the courtyard outside where I'm surrounded by sculptures that could pass as aliens.

Only an hour after I return to work, I hear a loud commotion coming from the Renaissance section.

As I make my way to the action, the noise becomes clear: A baby is wailing throughout the museum, causing museumgoers to scramble toward the exits. Those fleeing from the harsh sound of a baby's cries bottleneck at one particular exit, which result in several injuries. A couple of fights break out between museum-goers. One person falls to the floor while trying to flee, and then moments later, a stampede of people trample the person on the floor.

As much as a crying baby annoys me, I never—not once—become upset at the baby. Instead, it's the people—most of whom are adults—who irritate me the most and their reaction to a natural sound, such as a baby crying, and how these people handle the situation, which could've easily been resolved by doing the complete opposite. Instead, they yell at the baby and curse its very cries, as if they've forgotten what it was like to be a baby—which makes sense because I myself don't remember what it was like to be a baby, for all I have are hazy images and foreign smells, and I'm sure that I'm not the only one who can't recall on the fly what it was like to be a baby, considering our brains are still developing and absorbing and trying to make sense of this strange fucked-up world that we've entered.

As more museumgoers pile up in front of the exits while the mother pulls the baby from the carriage and tries to calm the baby by rocking and gently shushing it, the thoughts flare up inside my mind, and all of that hot rage is directed at the traffic jam by the auditorium.

Later that day, I pay a visit to the Chop Shop.

DAY Five.

Three fingers down, six to go.

I'm back at the museum, only this time under the title of "SE-CURITY GUARD."

My only suspicion as to why Mr. Rebus sends me back to the museum even though I'm reassigned to another job: Perhaps he expects—or at least, anticipates—there to be another incident like the one yesterday, which will require me to get a more up close and personal look at the very people whom I scorned; and instead of me watching from the sidelines, Mr. Rebus wants me right there at the center of the action, face-to-face, breath-to-breath with those who drove me to a series of internal outbursts while I angry-mopped a floor that I had already mopped earlier that day, most of my thoughts revolving around brutal, bloody imagery of what I fancied on doing to those people. Such ugly thoughts, they were. The ugliest. No man should ever experience these ugly thoughts.

With my left hand looking like one of those grabber-claws inside a plush toy machine after I have my ring finger lopped off, I make my rounds around the museum.

Halfway through the day, I realize how much I'd rather be a custodian. It gets pretty boring, either sitting around or making rounds through the museum, looking for trouble, but really, it's a waiting game. You're waiting for trouble to take place and when it doesn't, it can cause an idle mind to wander.

Around mid-afternoon, before the crowds start to pick up, I'm called to the main entranceway to help escort a homeless man from the premises.

As with the ones from earlier, he, too, is also missing a valuable piece of his body.

In his case, a nose.

The sight of those two open holes in the center of his face makes me question whether or not a majority of the homeless population in Spartacus consists of past offenders, not Veterans.

Turns out, I learn from another guard after I spot a slight discrepancy in Leonardo da Vinci's *Mona Lisa*, all of the artwork inside the museum are replicas and the original works are kept in a secured bunker deep in the earth. The transition, according to the guard, Ralph, took place over the course of several months without the public's knowledge, all carried out in the middle of the night, all hush-hush.

Ralph's comments linger over me throughout most of the afternoon, and it's not until I walk past one of the museumgoers sitting in a slouched position on a bench in front of Edvard Munch's The *Scream* that I suspect the reasons as to why the museums resorted to such drastic measures.

With his beady eyes glazed over and lost in the screen of a phone, the museumgoer watches a commentary video on the Internet, which, based on my first impression, sounds like a warped confession that reveals a more troubling condition.

The so-called "content creator" makes a living off bashing other people's work; and yet, despite his title, he doesn't possess a single creative bone in his body.

Everything is about destruction, either destroy or be destroyed.

Hypercritics scrape the surface level of a piece of work—in the case of one of these creators, "*T-bagger,*" teabag being a euphemism for scrotum—a movie.

As I eavesdrop over the audio from the video, it's clear to me that T-bagger's envy is set on full-blast. Never does he delve deep into the movie, like a surgeon with a scalpel, and make any attempt to dissect the work. Instead, he comes off more as a street sweeper, uses a lot of sound bites and labels the videos with certain "headlines" to trick algorithms into generating more traffic. He possesses a parasitic-like nature, attaching himself to the host (The Artist) while attempting to monetize from the blood that has been spilled by The Artist.

Of all people, why does society choose to elevate those who'd rather destroy than create?

T-bagger is nothing more than a blunt instrument played by those who contribute to the end of Art and the devout creation of Art.

As I spiral into my own world of hatred, I begin to pick apart T-bagger's words, as if he's an Artist, and I can't help but draw parallels to extremists who deface a monument or ruin a painting or crush a totem which one held as sacred. By all means, those, like T-bagger, who struggle to grow up and live a meaningful life, must destroy because somewhere deep inside they want to obliterate the nostalgia that has metastasized like a cancer inside their bodies.

For the first time ever since I started the Final Phase, or "The Lop," which it should've been called, I'm glad to pay a visit to the Chop Shop at the end of the day. Never have I been so content with having one of my digits lopped off.

I won't miss it.

Maybe I'll stick it in a jar.

Or, maybe I'll even make a sculpture out of it.

7

"HELL-LOW?"

Joshua remained in a trance.

"Sir?"

The young lady's voice rushed past Joshua like wind.

Finally, Joshua pulled his attention toward the wide-eyed server before him.

In the server's hand was a greasy white bag of two orders of chicken souvlaki, one over rice and another with French fries.

"Your order," she said, her voice curvy like a question mark.

Joshua grabbed the bag from her hand and said, "Thank you."

As he exited the popular restaurant, Gorgon's Café, which was run by three ambitious sisters, he shouldered his way past the pickup line that stretched through the front of the restaurant and spilled out onto the sidewalk alongside the building. He carried the bag of food to his car, which was parked at the far end of the parking lot. Upon arrival, he reached down to open the driver's side door and while doing so, noticed a dark stain a couple of inches above the left breast pocket of his brown scrubs. He couldn't remember where he picked up the stain, if it was from a drink or beverage (coffee or soda being his best bet), perhaps blood, or even vomit. He carefully pinched the material along his chest, pulled it outward, like a small teepee, held it close to his nose, and then gave it a cautious whiff but still couldn't identify the stain.

Pushing aside his suspicions about the stain, he placed the carryout food securely on the passenger seat and drove three miles to his first floor apartment where he ran into his neighbor, Mr. Backer, from apartment 101, who was sniffing out a new lead into a curious case: "Who's been clogging the trash chute?" So far, Mr. Roberts, from 112, had narrowed it down to three potential suspects, one of them being Joshua's neighbor, Orlando, who recently moved from New York City.

Exhausted from work, Joshua skipped the small talk with Mr. Backer and wished him well in his search and entered his apartment where his fiancée was lying in bed and from her slothful state, appeared as if she hadn't left the bedroom all day.

Once when he placed the carryout food on the kitchen table and called out to Pep, she didn't budge an inch.

"What took you so long?" Pep asked from the bed, as Joshua divvied out the food.

"Hello to you," said Joshua, as he placed the rest of the pocket change from the recent purchase of Mediterranean food inside the glass pumpkin cookie jar on top of the refrigerator. He was using the jar as his own personal piggy bank, most of the money inside the jar he was saving for a vacation with Pep, possibly Florida.

Pep made a comment under her breath and continued to watch TV.

"Well," he said, acting as if he didn't hear the comment, "it took me forever to place the order. You should've seen the line when I got there. It was wrapped around the building."

Again, no direct response from Pep.

Frustrated, Joshua left the kitchen and leaned into the bedroom and asked, "Are you going to eat or not? Food's getting cold. . . "

As Pep rolled out of bed, Joshua excused himself while Pep made herself a plate and began to eat without him.

Trying not to make any sounds, Joshua closed the bathroom door behind him. While using the sink, he splashed his face with cold water. The feel alone temporarily relieved the pressure, which wrenched behind his cheeks. He downed a blue pain pill with a sip of water from the faucet.

During mid-swallow, Pep called out his name.

"Just a sec," Joshua said back.

He flushed the toilet and exited the bathroom, only to find an expressionless Pep standing in front of the doorway. Her eyes cut right through him like those of an ill child.

Startled, Joshua grabbed his chest.

"Why so jumpy?" asked Pep.

"You trying to give me a heart attack?" Joshua asked over Pep, who, in return, furrowed her brow.

"What? No," she said and motioned toward the phone on the vanity. "I need to check my emails real quick. I'm expecting a message from Tom."

"Don't you think it's too soon to return to work?"

"Beats lying around here all day—"

"But Pep, you think you're ready?"

She gave Joshua a look: Her head angled downward with her eyes up and penetrating, as if she was staring directly through her eyebrows, again, child-like.

Joshua stepped out of the way, allowing Pep to pass.

Before sitting down at the kitchen table to eat dinner, Joshua stopped at the bedroom window and caught a wren and a robin having what appeared to be a territorial dispute. For the past couple of days, Joshua witnessed the two birds fight with one another, surprisingly, not a mockingbird, but rather the wren being incredibly aggressive and territorial, especially toward the robins.

In the background, he heard the name *"Backer"* coming from a movie on the TV.

Not Mr. Backer from apartment 101, but the other one.

The scene involved a district attorney and the captain of police walking through the hallway of a courthouse, the DA bringing up one of the captain's unconventional detectives—Backer—who was making *"quite a reputation for himself."*

The sound of a toilet flushing pulled Joshua from the thriller; and before Pep exited the bathroom, he made his way into the kitchen where he couldn't help but wonder if Pep really needed to use her phone or if she used it as an excuse to watch over Joshua, as she had been doing lately. Everything he did, either a chore around the apartment or scrolling through a news article, he felt as though he had eyeballs on him—*her* eyeballs—always watching and analyzing him, her presence lingering over his shoulder like a bad angel.

Pep joined him at the kitchen table where she didn't waste any time digging into the chicken souvlaki.

"Yum," she said and chewed through one side of her mouth, as if she hadn't eaten in weeks, which, on the contrary, made him wonder what else she was doing in the bathroom, and taking one of her "antacid pills" was merely yet another excuse to conceal the truth. "See why they were so crowded. Best Greek food in the city—"

"Mediterranean," he corrected.

Pep stopped eating and gave Joshua yet another penetrating look, this one carried out with a tilt of her head.

"Same thing," she said and continued to eat.

"So. . . " Joshua said and cut through the tension with a sigh, ". . . the wren out back is at it again. Yesterday, the little dude was chasing away mockingbirds. Now, he's fighting off robins. If they don't chill out, I might need to play a mediator."

"So this is what you do now when you're bored? Speak to birds?" said Pep. "You can't interfere with nature, Joshua—

you know what. . . " Pep said in a sardonic tone, ". . . maybe you should return to that fantasy world of yours. I heard on TV there's another version. It's like they keep updating that shit every year."

"I'd rather speak to birds," Joshua said expressionlessly.

"Well, next time you speak to your friend. . . " she said, taking a bite from the skewer of chicken, ". . . make sure to tell him that his cousin tastes delicious."

With his mouth closed, Joshua smiled away his anger and the comment that he was tempting to say.

After chewing the rest of her food, Pep said while sensing the defeat in Joshua's eyes, "I was thinking: Why don't you open up your own *bird shop*? You know," she said with her beady eyes aimed at Joshua's fallen eyes, "since you love 'em so damn much—"

"Enough already, Pepper," said Joshua. "It's been a long day, okay?"

"Oh-kay," she drawled with exaggeration. "Okay what?" She stopped pecking at the half-eaten skewer. With her elbows fixed on the table, she leaned forward with both of her shoulders open in an offensive position. She snapped, "Like you're the only one who's had a *long* day!"

"You know what I mean, Pepper," Joshua said, restraining his anger. "I'm not trying to pick a fight with you—"

All of a sudden, he was interrupted by thunderous sounds of godly footsteps pounding the ceiling.

"This fucking guy," Joshua said, more frustrated.

The guy, whom Joshua mentioned, Mr. Heelwalker, as he was known as, who never left his apartment, who, at times, sounded as if he was literally trying to bring down the ceiling. Neither Joshua nor Pep was aware of what he was doing up there all day and night, if he worked from home. As far as they knew, he was the only person living above them. Yet, at times, based on that thundering coming from above, it felt as if there were many more.

With the soon-to-be argument put on a temporary hold, Pep said with similar frustration, "I feel like sometimes he's doing it deliberately."

"Maybe he doesn't know—"

"What? Doesn't know that there are people living below him?"

"I'll talk to him—"

"Should've heard him earlier this afternoon," said Pep, her voice more piercing. "He was so loud I had to put on headphones to drown his ass out."

"That bad, huh?"

Leaning back in her chair, Pep said, "I don't know how much longer I can live like this. This is no place to raise a child." As though catching the words from leaving her lips, she suddenly paused, the word *child* spoken shortly, the letter "d" dropped from the pronunciation, bludgeoned by the deep regret of stoking such pain. More hesitantly, Pep said, "That is, if you want to try again. . . ."

"Why would you bring that up?" he said more defensively. "With everything going on right now? What was this whole thing about you returning to work?"

"But I don't have to work," she said and leaned closer to Joshua, this time with her guard down. "We can start looking again. What about this weekend? I just say we get the hell outta here—"

"There are three houses that I've been keeping an eye on," he said, unsure, as if he was reciting a past line that no longer carried any truth. In a subtle way, he cleared his throat, said, "All in a good location."

"What's gotten into you, Josh?" Pep asked, as if she could spot the lie, not in his voice, but in his gestures, the way he struggled to meet her eye or the slight tremble in his bottom lip.

He faced Pep and said in return, "What do you mean?"

"*What you mean?*" Pep said mockingly, as if she was doing her best "Poor Little Ole Joshua Lamb" impression. "Be a man!" she said, her voice attempting to drown out the thundering upstairs. "Go up there and wring that asshole's neck!"

"And go to jail?" said Joshua. "Yeah," he said, losing his temper. "Very cool, Pep."

"Yeah," she said back. "It is cool." Her chest started to pound faster and each throb of her heart rattled each and every word that projected from her mouth. "I'd rather be with a man who shows bravado, opposed to some boy," she seethed, referring to Joshua as a boy, "who shrivels into a frightened, passive mouse every time there's a conflict."

"A mouse, huh?" Joshua said, his voice throbbing as well. "So, you want me to go up there, beat my chest, and make a bunch of loud voices, like some kind of animal?"

Pep snapped, "You can at least talk to that little shithead! Is that so much to ask?"

Joshua suddenly pounded his fist against the table, causing the glasses and plates to rattle.

In a fit of rage, he stood up from the table, kicking the chair from below him with the heel of his foot. He stormed away, grabbed his car keys from the kitchen counter, and then slammed the door on the way out of the apartment.

After driving around the city for thirty minutes or so, he decided to blow off steam by seeing a movie.

When he arrived at the box office in front of the theatre, he picked up the first movie with the closest showing. Of all the movies, he chose to purchase a ticket for *Firebug*, a thriller about a former cop, Fickle, who was left with no other choice than to take the law into his own hands after his partner was murdered by a notorious serial arsonist named "Firebug."

Halfway through watching the movie, the anger melted from Joshua and left him in a more forgiving state, ready to apologize to Pep for storming out of the apartment.

Everything was going well for him until one of the movie-goers decided to pull out his glowy toy of a smartphone. The bright glow of the phone pulled Joshua's attention away from the movie. The texting carried on for about ten minutes or so, as if he was writing his next great American novel. Joshua attempted to ignore the glowing light in the corner of his eye by angling his body away from the texter and using his hand as a headrest, hoping it'd block that distracting, intrusive light. His attempts were unsuccessful.

By the time Joshua played a back-and-forth eye job with the texter, he completely lost interest in the movie and was unable to piece together the many twists and turns in the plot, one being that Firebug had gathered a devout cult following and most of the fires were *not* started by Firebug himself, but rather some of his loyal copycats. By then, Joshua was ready to walk out of the theatre. He contemplated confronting the texter. He even ran through a couple of lines in his head and each one was, more than likely, destined to receive an unpleasant reaction from the texter. He decided to leave.

With the anger still lingering inside him like an unwanted guest, he drove back to his apartment.

By the time he arrived, it was a quarter past nine and all of the lights were turned off, which Joshua thought was unusual since Pep was a night owl, who'd stay up to midnight watching late-night shows. He flipped on the kitchen light and saw the mess everywhere, leftover food thrown on the countertop, contents from the fridge scattered on the tile floors. He found an empty bottle of Chardonnay in the trashcan, as well as a broken wine glass in the sink.

When he crept into the unlit bedroom, he saw Pep's silhouette sitting in a chair in the corner of the room. In a jittery-like state, she was rocking back and forth in the chair.

The sight of her silhouette triggered an image inside his mind: A dark figure standing in the lit doorway of a dark bedroom, a gun in hand. Joshua lying in bed. *Eyes flick open.*

Joshua shook away the image.

Concerned for his fiancée, he switched on the light, only to find Pep still awake. Both of her eyes wide open as if she had invisible staples attached to the edges of her eyelids and not once, when the light switched on, did she ever turn those wide eyes toward Joshua. Instead, they were aimed directly at the floor, as if she was somehow trapped in a thought so raw and violent that it left her feverishly frozen in a restless yet robotic state, as if the thoughts were screwed in tightly by vise grips, which prevented any mobility.

"Pep," Joshua said carefully, "baby, what are you doing?"

Pep's eyes shot upward, stabbing Joshua.

In a deeper and unsteady tone, Pep asked, "Where've you been?"

"I just needed to get some fresh air," he said, more concerned. "Listen, Pep, I'm sorry—"

She suddenly blurted out, "Sorry!" She made a noise with her mouth. "You're pathetic."

"Pep. . . " Joshua said, holding out his hands, palms open, ". . . let's just call it a night and go to bed. We'll talk in the morning, okay?"

Pep made yet another noise with her mouth, then mumbled a series of insults underneath her breath.

"How much did you drink?" he asked, as Pep unveiled a half-full bottle of wine that she was holding beside the chair.

In a defiant manner, she took a swig of wine.

"Don't you tell me what I can put inside *my* body—"

"Pep," he said, stepping closer, "you need to sleep it off, okay?"

"Stop saying that fucking word!" Pep shouted out. "Okay! Do I look oh-kay to you?"

"You need to calm down."

"Need," she said, more hysterically. "You have no idea what I need!"

When Pep spoke the word *need*, the bands along her neck flexed like muscles.

"You need rest," he said.

Pep cried out, "Fuck you!"

Shocked by Pep's hostility, Joshua couldn't help but look over his fiancée, her current state, and how she was shaking with rage—Where the rage had come from, he didn't know, but whatever it was, either rage or worse, hatred, its hold over Pep had been tightening to the point where it was cutting off, not only the blood supply, but also the signals inside her brain that controlled memory, creating a faulty imitation of a person who neither looked nor acted like the Pep he once knew, but rather a stranger, an outsider who was considered a threat to his own safety.

"What's a matter with you?" Joshua asked, his voice more sympathetic towards Pep's plight.

Pep screamed, "What's a matter with me? What the fuck is a matter with you!"

He tried to console Pep, but his touch alone on her body was like the slick scales of a serpent rubbing against her skin.

She cried out, "Get off me!"

Again, Joshua tried to get a better handle over Pep.

"Pep," he said over her screams, "you're not yourself!"

She pushed, shoved, punched, and kicked.

Joshua eventually backed away.

Triggered by outburst, Joshua punched a hole in the drywall. The pain along his knuckles, if anything, heightened the rage, as if the pain itself was a quick hit of a potent drug and he desperately wanted more of it, handfuls of it, stacks of it, pallets of it, all of it consumed.

Enraged, he started to throw things around the apartment, first a vase, which shattered feet away from the chair that Pep was sitting in, the pieces nearly hitting Pep, as she ducked for cover, and then, a flat-screen TV, which Joshua grabbed with both hands like a wrestler, raised it above him, and suplexed it onto the floor, causing Pep to scream out in horror.

He charged at Pep, as she cursed him. Both of his hands, palm-side held out, arched slightly downward as though each was positioned to push Pep.

At the last second, Joshua's hands flexed outward, all ten of his fingers spread as far as it could stretch them.

Joshua snatched Pep by the throat and slammed her to the floor where he straddled her. She swung at Joshua, who, in return, blocked and redirected each blow with his left hand while his right hand remained over her throat, squeezing. Both thumbs, index and middle fingers, tightened over Pep's esophagus, thus obstructing any air that reached her lungs. A lack of oxygen slowly dwindled her energy. Each punch and slap gradually weakened and appeared as if she was raking the eyes of an invisible monster. Veins swelled alongside Pep's forehead. Her eyes were bloodshot, still as wide as ever.

As her face changed from red to blue, Joshua released his grip from her neck. The guilt immediately left him in an awful, shrunken state—*What have I done?*

Pep coughed and rolled over on her side, trying to get more air into her lungs.

Joshua pleaded with her and couldn't apologize enough.

"I don't know what came over me, Pep," Joshua cried, the guilt overwhelming him.

Once Pep was able to breathe freely, she stood to her feet and pushed Joshua away.

While he sauntered into the kitchen, his head low, both of his shoulders deflated as if he recently committed the crime of the century, the crime of laying his hands on the mother of his late-child, Pep hurried to the closet, grabbed Joshua's gun from the lockbox, and returned to the kitchen where Joshua was attempting to cool off by sticking his head inside the refrigerator. He heard a sudden *clink* from where Pep stepped on a piece of broken glass.

Joshua rotated around, only to find Pep standing inches away from him, the barrel of the gun pointed at his chest.

"I'm tired of all your games, Joshua," Pep said manically. "It's time to end this once and for all. You got that?"

"Pep," Joshua said and raised his hands in surrender, "put down the gun."

"No," Pep said, determined to shoot him where he stood. "You don't get to tell me what to do—Not now, not ever!"

"Pep. . . please. . . " Joshua said, his voice soft and tender, ". . . I am now begging you to put down the gun. . . What do you want me to do? Please Pep. . . whatever issues you're going through, we'll go through together and we'll work them out, like we always do."

The tears ran down the sides of Pep's face.

She cried, "You know what I want, huh?"

"Anything," said Joshua.

Pep clenched her jaw together.

"I want you to die," she said through her barred teeth.

"You don't mean that—"

Pep suddenly pulled the trigger.

Nothing.

No gunshot.

No sound.

She gasped.

Joshua gasped.

The round in the chamber jammed.

Relieved, yet at the same time aware of the danger that his fiancée posed, not only to himself, but also her, Joshua said to her, "Whatever you do, do *not* pull that trigger again. Trust me. . . "

While crying, Pep muttered through her wavy lips, "Fuck you. . . "

Joshua attempted to reach for the gun.

Pep retracted the gun and once more, pulled the trigger.

Joshua shouted out, "No! Wait!"

The gun suddenly backfired, causing the barrel to explode in Pep's hand.

A piece of shrapnel struck Pep in the neck, striking one of her main arteries.

Joshua flinched and once he realized he hadn't been hit, rushed over to Pep, who was clutching her neck. He applied pressure to the wound, but blood kept pouring out through tiny narrow spaces between his fingers and knuckles. More frantic, he grabbed a hand towel from the sink and pressed it against the neck wound.

Pep, who was left in a state of shock, tried to speak but he told her not to worry, that he was going to call for help, that she'd be okay when, in fact, he knew she wasn't going to be okay.

As he tried to stand, Pep grabbed him by the forearm. In an unspoken way, her eyes were telling him to let her go. She was tired, her eyes told him. She wanted to rest, they said.

With his brow furrowed, Joshua said, "No. . . "

He stood up, fetched his phone from the bedroom, and called the police.

When the dispatcher asked about the injury, Joshua said, "Gunshot wound."

Considering the nature of the injury, the police were the first to arrive at the scene.

By the time the two officers entered the apartment Pep had already lost consciousness.

Her pulse was incredibly faint.

Despite Joshua applying pressure to the wound, she was bleeding out.

The paramedics arrived shortly after the police.

Once the two paramedics loaded Pep onto the gurney and wheeled her to the ambulance, one of the paramedics lost a pulse as the other one pumped oxygen into her nose and mouth.

Joshua followed alongside the paramedics, urging Pep to hold on. Even though the police had many questions about what happened, the paramedics allowed Joshua to ride with them in the back of the ambulance. During the drive to the hospital, the paramedics aggressively worked on Pep and tried to revive her.

When they finally arrived at the hospital, Pep was declared DOA (dead on arrival).

As the paramedics transported Pep to the morgue, the police pulled Joshua aside in the ER.

Shortly after Joshua gave his statement to the police officers, two detectives—Joshua was so distraught that when the detectives introduced themselves, their names went straight through one of his ears and then out the other—as well as a couple of forensic investigators talked to him in the hallway. One of the detectives, Detective So and So, asked Joshua to ride with them back to the police station.

Joshua gave the detectives a confused expression.

"Am I being arrested?" he asked.

Detective What's-His-Name said to him, "We wanna talk about what happened tonight."

Joshua paused.

Then asked the scarred-face detective: "Do I need a lawyer?"

"Not at all, Mr. Lamb," the other one said. "We just wanna talk. That's it."

"Isn't that what we're doing now. . . *talking*?"

"You have to look at what just happened from our perspective, Mr. Lamb," Detective Flattop said, pocketing his eTablet. "A woman—your fiancée—fired a weapon, which backfired and ended up killing her. And all we want to know: Why did she pull the trigger? Was, as you said, she the aggressor who was trying to kill you? Or, was she trying to defend herself from you?"

Another investigator brought up Joshua's clothes and the blood splatter all over them, as well as both his hands, his fingernails, which were also covered in his fiancée's blood. His entire body was a walking, talking piece of evidence.

"Also, if you don't mind, your clothes, Mr. Lamb. . . " Detective Bat Ears said, pointing at Joshua's shirt in particular, ". . . we need to collect them. We can either do it here or down at the station. I'd recommend the station."

Joshua was left with no other choice than to ride with the two detectives back to the station where forensics collected evidence, as well as his DNA.

When the detectives began to take a familiar route, Joshua began to question where they were taking him. Surprisingly, they ended up driving back to Joshua's apartment, which left him in a more confused state.

"Thought we were going to a police station?" said Joshua, as the detective parked outside the apartment complex.

"Not yet," said Detective Steely Eyes. "Why don't you grab an extra pair of clothes? After all, we're going to have to collect everything that you're wearing. . . "

"But won't I be. . . "

Joshua was tempted to finish, "disrupting a crime scene," but he thought to himself that the comment might make him look guilty.

"Be what, Mr. Lamb?"

Joshua didn't answer.

"Go on," the other one said to Joshua. "We're not going anywhere."

More flabbergasted, Joshua stepped out of the vehicle and closed the door behind him.

He only made it a couple of steps away from the detective's car before his friend, who worked with him at the nursing home, said from behind, "*See you bright and early tomorrow.*"

Frank?

A thorny sensation suddenly ran though his body.

Frank's voice was like pinpricks against his skin.

Cautiously, Joshua rotated around, only to find his friend and coworker, Frank Lazar, also an orderly like Joshua, sitting in his parked station wagon, the upper left side of his body leaning from the window.

The two detectives were nowhere in sight.

"You good, man?" asked Frank.

Joshua drawled, "Yeah. . . "

"Fuckin' lightweight," he teased, referring to the two beers that they drank at a neighborhood bar after work. "Have a good night."

"Yeah. . . " Joshua said again, ". . . You too."

As he walked back to his apartment, Frank drove away.

Curious, he glanced over his shoulder and searched for the detectives but they were gone.

Joshua fished out his keys and entered the apartment. As soon as he closed the door behind, any thought about the two detectives was gone as well, as if they had been deleted from existence.

As the hallway light poured into the dark bedroom, Joshua found Pep laying in bed, awake, her back turned to Joshua, pillow tucked between both of her thighs.

"How was your day?" asked Pep, who didn't turn to acknowledge Joshua.

"Good," Joshua said strangely and exited the bedroom.

As he was searching through the pantry for a bite to eat, he received a text from Mime, who, in the text, wrote: "I want to see you."

Joshua secretly texted back: "You have any food at your place?"

Mime texted: "I have enough to feed an army."

With Pep still in bed, Joshua contemplated his next moves for a minute before replying: "Be there in 10."

He skimmed through the pantry, as well as the fridge and grabbed any food that was near, or past, the expiration date and tossed them in the trash. He walked back to the bedroom and stuck his head inside and said to Pep, "I'm going on a food run. Need anything?"

Pep didn't answer.

"Pepper?"

"No," she said shortly. She said before Joshua left, "Eggs. We need eggs."

"Already on my list," he said. "Anything else?"

"No," she said. "That's it."

On the way to Mime's house, Joshua stopped at a gas station and put several dollars worth of gasoline in his car. He stopped by a convenient store to pay for the gasoline, as well as pick up several groceries, which could act as filler since he didn't plan on actually driving to a grocery store. While waiting to purchase the groceries, mostly snacks and junk food, a strange man with tattoos entered the convenient store. Of all the tattoos on his body, Joshua noticed the tattoo of a fiery *phoenix* behind his right ear, not emoji-small, but large enough to make out from where he stood.

Immediately, Joshua's internal radar alerted him of a potential—and more than likely, imminent—threat in the vicinity. Plus, a distinct limp in the stranger's walk caused Joshua to freak out. His thoughts spiraled out of control, the theme of his thoughts being that "They had found me," *They*, as in *The Ghosts of His Violent Past.*

Without attracting any attention, Joshua followed him in a warped reflection of an overhead mirror.

Based on the way the strange man walked—not including the limp—as well as the stiff, rigid posture, Joshua suspected that he was ex-military.

Once Joshua spotted a gun holster protruding from underneath his armpit, he knew that the strange man was either ready to take him out, an eye-for-an-eye type of deal, or simply keeping tabs on him—But for how long, he didn't know for he had been distracted, not only with work, but also Pep and all of her baggage. He was ninety-nine percent sure that the stranger worked for Orwell. But, if he was correct, how in the hell did they find him? Joshua covered his tracks. He did exactly everything that he was supposed to do; yet, Joshua thought, *these fuckers were still hunting me down* like a rabid dog.

Joshua managed to pay for the gasoline, as well as the groceries without any trouble.

Before leaving the store, Joshua grabbed a couple of extra bags. Even if he was completely wrong about the stranger, he thought to himself that he still needed an excuse to leave the house and returning back home with a couple of bags of potato chips and cookies was not going to cut it, and if anything, it would only draw more suspicion.

As Joshua returned to the car, the strange man exited the store. He drove away and obsessively checked the rear view mirror to make sure that he wasn't being followed. Roughly three miles down the road, Joshua didn't see anyone following him, which made him breathe a little easier.

When Joshua arrived at Mime's ranch-style home, she answered the front door wearing only a pink bathrobe.

With slight paranoia, he scanned the neighborhood street, which prompted Mime to speak out about her lover's erratic behavior. "Don't worry about her," she said, touching Joshua on the wrist.

Once she grabbed Joshua's attention, she grabbed him by the collar, pulled him into the house, and closed the door behind her without locking it.

Before they had unadulterated sex, Joshua first stopped by Mime's refrigerator and opened the carton of eggs. He found three eggs missing.

"You mind?" Joshua said, showing Mime the carton.

"But won't she know? There's three missing—"

"I'll just say that they were broken," Joshua said, grinning. "Clerk gave me a discount. Women like discounts."

Mime grinned back.

"We sure do," she said, flicking her pencil-thin brows at Joshua. "Very clever, I must say."

A tense, hot silence grew between the two as they stared in each other's eyes.

Mime asked, "How much time do you have?"

"About an hour."

"Then, we don't have a lot of time to waste—"

The two embraced one another, Joshua taking the lead by first kissing her on the lips while rubbing and squeezing her breast.

Eventually, as the two locked lips, they moved their way to Mime's bedroom in the back of the house. Each one of them couldn't remove their clothes soon enough.

By the time the two reached the bedroom, they were undressed, except for Joshua's socks, which he left on. While passing the threshold of the bedroom, he attempted to turn on the light switch.

"Don't," said Mime, as she flipped off the light switch. "You know I don't like it when we do *it* with the light on—"

"Why not?" Joshua asked, kissing Mime's neck.

"I just said so," said Mime.

"Whatever," he said, carrying Mime to the bed. "You're the boss."

After the two had sex from various angles and positions in bed, they rested in the dark with their bodies entangled. The hazy light from a lamp in the living room cut through the doorway. The sword of light cut across the bed, highlighting their naked bodies.

All of a sudden, while Joshua rested his body, he heard a noise coming from the kitchen.

"You hear that?" he said and arched his head upward with both ears open like a cat.

"Hear what?" Mime mumbled.

Joshua heard yet another sound, a *creaking* sound.

He whispered in Mime's ear, "I think someone's inside the house. . ."

"Grab the gun from the nightstand," she said abruptly and grabbed hold of Joshua's side as if she was ready to use it as a shield.

He rummaged through the drawer on the nightstand until he pulled out semi-automatic pocket pistol, which was already loaded. He flipped "off" the safety and once more, heard a sound coming from just outside the bedroom.

With his shoulders squared, Joshua rolled over on his right side and aimed the pocket pistol at the lit doorway.

All of a sudden, he saw a lanky shadow over the carpeted floor.

Mime ducked behind Joshua, the top of her head poking over his left shoulder. His aim was steady, surgical almost.

As Joshua's heart pounded against his chest, he witnessed a dark manly figure—possibly the same strange man from the convenient store—step into the doorway.

Mime's fingernails dug into his back, as if she was bracing herself.

In the hand of the silhouette was a gun, much larger than the one in Joshua's hand—at least, Joshua was certain that he spotted a gun.

As the intruder lifted the potential gun, Joshua aimed upward and then pulled the trigger.

One gunshot.

The intruder grabbed its neck and stumbled backward.

With the intruder on its heels, Joshua carefully rolled out of bed.

Mime trailed off, "Josh, *I don't think*. . . "

He checked on the intruder, who fell to the floor.

Once Joshua stepped from the bedroom, he first found a phone lying on the floor.

Immediately, Joshua recognized a turquoise casing of the phone. Next he found Pep lying on her back.

As the pistol slipped from Joshua's hand, he rushed over to check on Pep, who was bleeding from a gunshot wound in her neck.

By the time Joshua rushed into the kitchen to grab a hand towel, Pep was already bleeding out.

Mime, who was still frightened, exited from the bedroom and as soon as she saw her lover's fiancée on her living room floor, screamed out in a bone-chilling horror.

"What the fuck did you do, Josh?" she cried.

"I thought she. . . "

"Thought she was what?"

"But she had a gun."

"It's a goddamn phone, Josh!"

As Joshua tried to stop the bleeding, Mime fired off dozens of questions at him, the most important one being: "*What the fuck is she doing here, Josh?*"

"She must've followed me from the apartment," he said, his breath labored.

Mime called the police while Joshua tried to save his fiancée.

By the time the police arrived, she was already dead.

Two detectives were next to show up.

They had lots of questions for, not only Joshua, but also the woman whom he was having an affair with behind his fiancée's back.

For hours into the night, Joshua sat in a cramped interrogation room, retelling his story over and over to the detectives.

Apparently, the night before, both Joshua and his fiancée had gotten into a heated argument. Pep specifically told one of her friends that she feared for her safety and that, the detective made sure to quote, "*he might kill me.*"

It wasn't until earlier that next morning, when Joshua was still left in the interrogation room, when a detective entered the room with a pair of handcuffs.

"What the hell is going on?" asked Joshua.

He suddenly retreated inward, as if the world itself began to cave in. Even the detective's face began to change as well. Like his facial features were slightly rearranged.

"*You're being arrested* for the death of Autumn Culpepper," Detective Baggy Eyes said, pulling Joshua from his trance.

"It was an accident. . . " Joshua said, the color leaving his face. "I thought she had a gun."

The other detective explained while his partner secured a pair of handcuffs over Joshua's wrists: "That's not what your fuck buddy told us. She said that she saw a phone in her fiancée's hand. Said she saw it as clear as day—"

"That's bullshit," Joshua seethed.

"As for the marks on Autumn's neck—"

"Marks? What marks?"

"Strangle marks," said the detective.

"I swear I didn't touch her," Joshua argued. "She did that to herself—"

"Save it, will you?"

Before Joshua could resist, the Detective Man looped and tightened the final handcuff over his wrist and escorted him to his holding cell.

After spending nearly an entire day inside a cell, which was about half the size of his bedroom, Joshua's case was reviewed by the prosecutor, District Attorney Cece Gama, who brought the case to Judge Rimy Bateaux. Once acknowledging the seriousness of the crime, the judge set the bail at two hundred fifty thousand dollars. A bail bondsman issued a bond; and since Joshua didn't have enough money to pay for the premium of that bond, which was posted at twenty-five thousand dollars (10% of 250,000), Joshua's so-called "knight in shining armor" ended up bailing him out after word traveled about his arrest. The knight was none other than Peggy's husband, Ralph, a Pharm Bro, who carried around 25k as if it was pocket change. If it weren't for Peggy's demands, Ralph never would've showed up. Even during the drive back to his apartment, which had already been processed by the forensics unit, Ralph shared his animosity toward Joshua made it clear to him that his latest actions would be the death of Peggy.

According to a near-flawless track record, Gama was quite an excellent prosecutor, who never overcharged; and based on all of the evidence, it seemed likely that Joshua would be charged with manslaughter. However, a driving factor for the 2nd degree murder charge were the marks on Ms. Culpepper's neck, thus suggesting she was acting out of self-defense. As far as Joshua's fiancée showing up at Mime's house, the front door was unlocked and there were "no signs" of breaking and entering.

Shortly after Ralph dropped Joshua off at his apartment, he discovered a sign for a "NOTICE" on the front door, the landlord giving Joshua ten days to vacate the building.

During those ten days, Joshua found another, more affordable apartment on the other side of town in an older, established section, which had declined over the years, and met with a defense attorney. Surprisingly, Joshua couldn't believe how many defense attorneys were calling him on the phone after his release, as if his name was broadcast to every single lawyer across the country. Despite the many options, Joshua wasn't picky. He decided to go with the lawyer, Jack Fisk, a local who, after hearing Joshua's story, was convinced that he could reduce and potentially drop the charges and convince a jury that his fiancée was the aggressor based on a mountain of evidence that Joshua had collected over the past few months (texts, emails, eyewitnesses, Pep's blood work, which showed antidepressants in her system, etc.), all indicating an abusive relationship, which could potentially lean in his favor, Joshua being the victim and the shooting being nothing more than an accident.

Regardless of his circumstances, he felt that it was best to try to get things back to normal even though nothing would ever be normal again. Joshua's reputation, image, face, name, all of it would be attached to one of the most violent acts that a human being could commit.

At night, when the grocery store was the least crowded, Joshua picked up groceries an hour before the store closed. He wore a black hat and while picking up basic items (bread, milk, eggs, etc.), made sure to keep the bill of the hat low and nearly covered his eyes. He never received any strange looks from any customers or the cashier, who gave Joshua a closed smile when she read the total of his purchases. Many times, he thought about using a drive-thru option, which the grocery store offered, or one of the many food delivery services, but he feared that the driver may recognize him and contaminate the food (i.e. spit, boogers, loogies, bodily fluids).

As he left the store without any trouble from any shoppers or employees, Joshua felt relieved about re-entering society, despite the serious charges against him, until a lanky man who was dressed in a suit made of corduroy approached him from behind. Joshua stopped loading the rest of the groceries into the back of his car and caught the sound of rubbery soles scraping along the gritty pavement. Joshua turned his shoulder and through the dim, randomly flickering floodlight, spotted the suited man who called himself, "Walker Huey."

The stranger reassured Joshua, "I'm not here to judge you, Josh—"

"How do you know my name?" asked Joshua.

"By now, if you're not living under a rock, I think the entire country knows your name," he said, referring to the "entire country" as some sort of singular entity, which spoke directly about itself with unanimity.

Joshua looked him over, a quick skim from head to toe.

He told himself that he didn't look like your average day citizen.

The obvious giveaway: The suit.

Nobody wore them anymore, he thought to himself, even the ones who spoke from The City of Dreams or—depending on your current allegiance—The City of Nightmares.

Walker pointed at the remaining grocery bags, one of the bags filled with a frosty tub of chocolate ice cream, inside the shopping cart and said to Joshua, "Let me give you a hand."

Joshua stepped forward and pulled the bags from Walker's hands, causing the banana from a cluster to slip from the bag.

"I can manage," he said, loading the rest of the bags into the car.

He shut the backdoor and walked around to the front of the car.

"I can have the charges dropped, Josh," Walker said from behind.

"Right. . . " he said with his back to Walker, ". . . a lawyer. Just as I suspected. Have a good night, Lawyer."

"Not a lawyer, Josh," Walker said, as Joshua reached for a door handle. "Think of me as a problem solver. I can assure you that you won't even step foot inside a courtroom."

Joshua paused midway while opening the driver's side door.

"If you're not a lawyer," he said, facing Walker, "then who are you?"

Walker said, "How about a drink?"

Joshua once more looked over Walker, this time more skeptically.

"Just one drink," Walker said. "By the time I finish telling you my proposal, you'll be back home before your ice cream melts. There's a bar next door," he said, motioning to a small dive at the end of the strip mall. "What do you say?"

Joshua glanced at the bar on the far end of the strip mall. The sign "BAR" lit up on the front of the window. A fairly low-key place and dimly lit. Only several cars parked in the parking lot. To the left of the bar was a closet design business called Closest Thing.

"One drink," Joshua said and followed Walker to the bar.

When the two arrived at a spot called The Crescent with a symbol on the façade appearing like a glowing smile, they sat at the bar where three long-faced bar flies with upside down crescents on their faces were slumped over their drinks. Each one was either watching a ball game on TV or staring into the deep, dark abyss; nonetheless, neither Joshua nor Walker's presence distracted them from the dullish escape before their tired eyes.

Once Joshua and Walker ordered a beer from a bartender, who spoke in nods, Walker cut straight to the chase and said, "I started a company, which has developed a partnership with the prison system, in order to provide a brand new approach in treating those who have committed crimes. Our goal is to one day abolish *all* prisons from around the country. What I'm about to offer you, Josh, is a chance of a lifetime," he said and sipped from the foamy beer. "Along with a selected few who have already chosen to volunteer, you will be at the forefront of the next phase of rehabilitation and reintegration. You'll be part of history and set a precedent for the future—"

"Enough with the bumper sticker lines," Joshua, who hadn't touched his beer, said with mild frustration. He asked, "What's the offer?"

With his chin raised high and his throat doing a pull-up, Walker took a gulp of his beer.

After swallowing the beer, he looked Joshua directly in the eyes and asked, "Have you ever heard of a neural implant?"

"Yeah," he said strangely. "I've heard about it. It's mostly for quadriplegics or those suffering from mental disorders—"

"Not anymore," Walker said and pulled out a VR-CU contact lens from his pocket. "Using the very same VR technology, we have managed to take one of these. . . " he said, as he held a contact lens on the top of his fingertip the same way a waiter or waitress would hold a tray full of food over his or her palm, ". . . and converted it into an implant no larger than a grain of rice that has been thoroughly tested. It's completely safe. To put it in the simplest terms: The implant is a switch inside your brain, and if the switch is open, then it allows you to experience virtual reality the way it was intended, without any external devices, such as contact lenses or those clunky, god-awful headsets—"

"So, you want me to be one of your guinea pigs?"

"*Not a guinea pig,*" said Walker. "*A trailblazer.*"

For a moment, Joshua lost himself in Walker's beady eyes. His eyes didn't lie, Joshua thought.

After digesting the remark, he asked Walker, "*What if* this switch is closed?"

"If so, then it'd be no different than you sitting right here, drinking a beer. The images before you are real, not virtual." He pointed at Joshua's beer, which, except for Joshua's hand cooling over the glass, was untouched. "That glass in your hand is exactly that, a glass. And inside that glass is an ice-cold draft beer. Now, if the switch is, say, opened, instead of drinking a beer, you may want to drink water. All you have to do is think it, Josh, and it will appear. Whatever the case. . . " he emphasized, ". . . your mind will convince you that the beer is not beer but water. As far as your virtual reality experience, we collect and piece together stories, which we believe will reform you."

"Reform me?" said Joshua. "What in the hell makes you think I need reforming?"

"Well, you are soon going to trial for the murder of your fiancée, are you not?"

The sound alone of Walker's words, especially those two words *murder* and *fiancée*, caused Joshua to tighten his jaw.

"Think about it, Josh," Walker said, as if he was trying to make his case, "How many people enter prisons, criminal or not, and come out worse than when they entered? You're forced to revert to your most basic, *most* primitive self in order to survive in a prison. Believe me: Prisons don't have to be hard. But the environment—that cage—it only forces you to become something *less* evolved, *less* human. It forces you to become an animal, Josh. Prisons are archaic. . . and I guarantee you, once our neural implant catches on and becomes the new standard, prisons, as we know them, will be on the brink of extinction. Let's face it: America's prison system is broken, and something radical needs to happen in order to change the way we treat those who have committed crimes." Walker pointed his finger to his head. "This here is the glue that'll restore order to the chaos that our system has deliberately created. . . " He then reached his hand over the bar and grabbed a loose, wrinkled dollar bill that was sitting next to a wash station and showed it to Joshua before the bartender could fetch his tip, ". . . all for this." Money. Walker handed the bill to the bartender, who gave Walker a sleepy-eyed glare. "And before you ask. . . " he said, as though reading Joshua's mind, ". . . No. We don't receive a penny from donors and outsiders, who want to use our technology for their own personal gains. The money is clean. . . sort of speak. . . "

Walker's slight hesitancy in where he was receiving money to fund his program didn't bother Joshua. For all he knew, Walker was born into money. Perhaps a wealthy father who struck oil. He could care less how much money was in this guy's wallet, which was probably made from a preserved hide of a human.

"So," Joshua uttered, as he tried to unpack and jerry-rig Walker's offer, "who controls the virtual reality. . . What I mean to say. . . How do you know when to turn this so-called switch off?"

Walker said, "We provide you with the blueprint and it's up to you to create a story that will help you become a better, more contributable member of society. Then, once we feel as if you've reformed, the program will be complete."

"And where does this so-called *experience* take place?" he asked with growing suspicion that Walker's whole pitch was a pipedream, a glorified scam, some hack idea from an idealist who was cut and molded from the virtual fabric of a nonexistent reality. "You and I both know that mixing virtual with reality isn't exactly safe in reality? There must be safeguards in place, right?"

"Glad you asked, Josh," he said and sipped from his beer. "The program is conducted at a state-of-the-art facility where each volunteer will be monitored around the clock—"

"So, you're replacing prisons with another prison?"

He pushed aside his beer and squared himself to Joshua.

Serious, he said, "More than likely, if you're convicted by a jury of peers, you're facing up to twenty-five years to life in prison. This new program—if successful—won't even take twenty-five days."

"*If successful?*" Joshua repeated, as he began to pull his ear away from Walker. "*What if* it's not?"

"Based on the early trials, one of which included Ramiel Bouchard—"

The name immediately grabbed Joshua's ear.

"*The* Ramiel Bouchard?"

"The one and only Cordon Bleu."

"That monster belongs in a tombstone, not a prison."

"The program is designed to work best with most offenders—"

"Most, huh?"

"Each subject varying from three weeks to three months," Walker finished without addressing Joshua's concern. "However, we decided to try the neural implant on serial killers, the latest being Ramiel Bouchard, and turns out Bouchard didn't exactly fall into the pattern of a serial killer, who are known to have a lack of function in their prefrontal cortex, that important part of the brain that regulates the one important feature that separates human from animals: *empathy*. Of course, the prefrontal cortex is also responsible for a wide-range of functions, including decision-making, as well as impulse control. By the second week of the program, he was transformed into an invaluable member of his community."

Joshua uttered, "Ramiel Bouchard?"

"Correct," Walker said, unflinching.

"If I do commit to your program, how long will it take?" asked Joshua.

"As I've said earlier," Walker said carefully, "for some it takes around a few months or so—"

Skeptical, Joshua interrupted, "Or a few decades?"

"Think about it," Walker said, more patiently. "Naturally, sleep—from what we have learned—is the brain's best way to rewire itself. So, while in the program, it'll feel like a dream—at least in the beginning. Over time it'll begin to feel real, as real as me sitting right here in front of you. The question is 'When does the dream turn into a nightmare?' And, essentially, how do we pull ourselves from that nightmare? That's what the program offers you, Josh. A way out of *your* nightmare. But it's up to you, Josh. . . " he said, touching Joshua's arm with the tip of his finger, ". . . whether or not you want to wake up."

Thinking, Joshua asked, "And *what if* I don't wanna wake up?"

"Then, it's simple. You'll stay in the program until you're ready." He paused and asked, his voice softer, "If you don't mind, Josh, can I ask why your fiancée was scared of you?"

Once more, Joshua gave Walker a once-over.

He threw a five-dollar bill on the bar and said to Walker, "Thanks for the offer. But I'm sick and tired of solving my problems through fantasies. I'd rather deal with them in the real world."

As Joshua stood up from the bar stool, Walker pulled out a beige-colored business card from his breast pocket and slid it along the greasy bar.

On the card was a tiny graphic of a red onion, split in half, revealing the many layers inside.

Intrigued by the minimalist-looking card, Joshua grabbed the card from the bar and flipped over the card and found a telephone number on the back.

No name or company, just a bunch of numbers.

"Sleep on it, Josh," Walker said. "Just think about all of those people who are rotting away in a jail cell. People, like you, who desperately long for a second chance."

He looked over the card and slid it back to Walker.

"That's where you're wrong," Joshua said. "I don't want a second chance."

After Joshua said his goodbyes, he left the bar and drove back home where he unpacked the groceries.

By the time he pulled the damp, squishy tube of ice cream from one of the bags, the chocolate ice cream was melted and dripping along the sides like brown ooze. The ice cream was so runny that it could pass as chocolate milk. With his hands and fingers covered in sticky ice cream, Joshua tossed the tub in the trash and finished unloading the rest of the groceries.

That night, while tossing and turning in his messy bed, he couldn't stop thinking about the strange encounter moments after he left the grocery store. Those words, Walker's words, occupied Joshua's head, twisting each and every thought and aiming each one back at him. He'd be lying if he said the offer wasn't tempting. Mostly, he couldn't stop thinking about the jury, if he were to go to trial, which, more than likely, was the next course of action in the drawn-out process of the law, and whether or not the jury had the stomach to send a man to prison without living every second in his shoes, understanding what life was like for someone who was constantly treated like a doormat. He recapped the past few months of living in the same apartment as Pep and all of those nights when she'd talk down to him as if, in a matter of months, she had transformed from his fiancée to a smothering, ill-tempered, resentful, and incredibly possessive mother with all of her strategic manipulation, her trying to burrow underneath Joshua's skin through certain under-the-breath comments or random insults, her aggressively carry out chores or deliberately making noises around the apartment like some bratty child, if Joshua didn't pay her enough attention, the door being one of Pep's most common avenues, shutting it loud enough to wake him whenever he was trying to rest from a stressful day of work. The truth was that Joshua no longer found Pep attractive; and each and every day of dealing with her insecurities, complexities, and rigorously combating Pep's crafty vindictiveness, he started to pick out each of her flaws, either physically or mentally shining a flashlight on them until he found them repulsive. Each day that they lived together she became bossier and more critical of his every word, as well as his behavior, analyzing his every single move as if she cast a spotlight on him twenty-four hours a day. Naturally, Joshua began to resent Pep, with all of her nagging and constant badgering. At times, when he looked at Pep, he felt as if he was looking directly at Peggy; and the notion only made his insides cringe.

As Joshua thrashed around his damp bed sheets from late in the night to early next morning, his thoughts turned against him, and he began to think that maybe something was, in fact, wrong with him. Not Autumn.

Why the fuck did you stay, Joshua screamed at himself, knowing it *wasn't going to end well* between the both of us?

You, coward, you should've left!

Yet, despite her death, he still talked about Pep as if she was still alive, her presence like a ghostly shadow shapeshifting around his thoughts.

Joshua pulled himself upright from bed, face and body all sweaty.

As he sat along the edge of the bed and both of his warm feet touched carpet while the upper half of his body propped upright with both straightened arms, which acted like anchors along the damp mattress, he imagined himself inside a prison and not just any prison but a maximum-security one where, in order to survive, he'd have to become a monster. All of those so-called "impulses," as Walker described to him while referring to the brains of serial killers, would be front and center.

In order to survive, Joshua thought, he figured he'd have to destroy that part of his brain and possibly beat the front of his head against a wall, crush and crumble his prefrontal cortex as if it was a delicate wad of paper and with enough blunt force, as well as pressure, he'd significantly reduce the size of that special area of the brain that regulated his very impulses to destroy a once beautiful, thriving world, which was becoming cruel and more unjust.

His worst fear: What if *that* particular *area* of his brain had *already* been *compromised?*

He eyed the car keys in the bowl on the nightstand and more thoughts crept inside his head.

Thoughts of *driving away* ran through his mind, thoughts of fleeing to perhaps another country where he'd be reduced to an outsider, a man without a country, thoughts of *looking over his shoulder* chased after him.

With his chest tightening, he pulled himself from his running thoughts and walked into the kitchen where he poured himself a glass of water from the faucet.

As he stared at a glass of murky water, he suddenly questioned the purity of the water and thought about its cleanliness, if there were any added chemicals or contaminates in it that would harm his body.

He could only imagine what water would be like in prison.

As he dumped out the water into the sink, his eyes crossed a cluster of bananas perched in a basket on the kitchen countertop. The corner of a business card was protruding from a narrow crack between the two bananas.

Carefully, he pulled the card from the cluster; and as he anticipated, it was the same card that he earlier refused at the bar. He recalled handing the business card back to Walker.

Joshua retraced his steps, pressed rewind on his thoughts, and wondered when—or even how—Walker slipped the card between the bananas. He wondered if it fell out of a sleeve and dropped into the bananas when Walker attempted to help him unload the groceries from the shopping cart.

Or, what left Joshua even more dumbfounded, *what if* he deliberately slipped it between the bananas? Like a magician?

After spending a majority of the morning wide-awake in bed, Joshua finally decided to call the number on the back of the card.

Walker picked up after the second ring.

"Mr. Lamb," he said, not surprised by the call, "I see you found my business card."

"It would appear so," said Joshua. "Cute trick."

"I figured an offer such as the one I proposed to you last night would scare you away. But, no doubt, it's a kind of offer that's no different than marinating a piece of meat. The longer you marinate it, the tastier it'll get. So, I assume you thought it over. Didn't get much sleep, did you now?"

"I have your word that I'll serve absolutely no jail time?" asked Joshua.

"I assure you that you won't spend a second in a jail cell," he said, confident about his promise. "You have my word."

"So, this program, it's legit? I mean. . . " Joshua stuttered, ". . . You said I'll be volunteering."

"If you're asking whether or not it's been tested on humans, like you, then the answer is yes. The implant has been approved by FDA. It's basically a medical device, meant to serve only one purpose: *You*, Josh. It serves you, your needs."

Joshua asked, "So, it's safe? I'm not gonna turn into some vegetable, am I?"

"Do you want to turn into a vegetable?"

Joshua paused and said, "I just want my life back."

"I understand," Walker said and used his next words more carefully. "Before we begin with the next stage, I need to ask you one thing and it may seem out of the blue. But I assure you it'll help with the healing process. . . " Walker paused yet again, ". . . Did you love her, your fiancée?"

Joshua would've had a different response for Walker if he asked that very same question last night.

After spending an entire night dissecting their relationship, especially the last few months together, Joshua welcomed the question.

"I did. . . " he said more clearly, ". . . at least, in the beginning I did. One might say I loved her too much, obsessively even. . . so much that I found myself turning into someone I wasn't. Everything I did, either for her or our baby, I tried to do so with perfection, but over time, I learned that was my problem: Not realizing that people aren't perfect. They're *far* from perfect. They're fucking messy."

He pulled himself from the phone and thought about the time after he learned he was going to be a father, then weeks afterwards a distance wedged between the two of them, like an invisible wall separating two egos, resulting in less talking, less seeing one another, Joshua working overtime to support a life which was growing inside Pep, not being there around the clock for his fiancée, searching and finding a much easier and quicker fix to tame a wicked plight behind her back, then, afterwards, when Pep had a miscarriage, Pep pushing Joshua, mentally driving him through that wall, blaming him and his cursed blood for *"her"* baby not properly developing inside her womb.

Feeling the sting of love in his gut, Joshua swallowed the ache and climbed his way from his painful thoughts and said to Walker, "My relationship with Pep was moving way too fast; and I guess, in the end, when I failed to witness that love turn into hatred, I desperately wanted to rewind it all, slow things back down, just like the time when I first laid eyes on her, when everything moved in slow motion."

Once Joshua ended the call with Walker, the next few days moved lightning fast, and Joshua had a hard time processing it all.

After meeting with the district attorney, Gama, Judge Bateaux, and Walker Huey, owner of the Onion Group, Joshua, while accompanied by his lawyer, Jack, cut a deal, which gave Walker and his company custody over Joshua. While staring at the contract before him on the table, mainly the two words, which were highlighted in bold print, the first word, "**neural**," and the second, "**implant**," Joshua inked his signature on the dotted line at the very bottom of the paper.

Holding out his hand, Walker reminded him, "Trailblazer, remember?"

As a photographer captured the historical moment, Joshua unsteadily shook Walker's hand, as if it was all a front.

Shortly after leaving the courthouse, Joshua parted ways with Jack and rode in a heavily secured truck with Walker to the airport hanger where they boarded a private jet and flew directly to a landing strip outside LAX; then, from there, the two rode in a helicopter, which flew them to a helipad on top of a skyscraper in the heart of Hephaestus City, which was formerly known as San Francisco, a Mecca for the tech industry.

Once Joshua arrived at Onion Group's headquarters, he was escorted to a private wing, which housed the other volunteers, who had their own private living spaces, which could pass as bachelor pads, and then taken to what Walker called "The Green Room," green being a color which helped relax the mind, where he was prepped for surgery.

Before Joshua could process the last twenty-four hours, he found himself lying on an operational table with three doctors wearing surgical masks looming over him.

Next to the doctors was a tray with all sorts of metallic instruments on it, one of them being a circular bone saw.

With his gloved hand, the head doctor showed Joshua the near-microscopic implant that was going to be inserted into his brain.

All of a sudden, the room turned smaller.

Joshua struggled to catch his breath.

Everything suddenly sunk in: The past twenty-four hours reduced to one moment.

Endless possibilities ran through his mind, none of them good or promising.

What the hell have I gotten myself into, he thought as the room started to shrink and spin.

"Relax, Joshua," said the doctor.

The tips of Joshua's fingers started to tingle.

His entire body tingled.

All five of his senses were amplified.

He wanted it gone, all of it: Doctors, as well as the strange figures standing around him, that hospital-like smell, the metallic taste in the back of his mouth, the prickly touch of cold steel on his back, the hum of a beastly machine running in the next room.

As the nurses try to calm Joshua, he pulled out one of the greatest magic tricks that Man had ever invented: He switched everything to black.

"HELLO, Josh."

All of a sudden, Joshua gasped for air.

Images of being covered in dirt pummeled his mind.

He could feel his chest caving in from the weight of earth bearing down on him. The smothering. Not be able to reach down for a single breath. Head noise amplified to a point of clipping each thought. That harsh distortion like a famished blade churning inside his mind.

While catching his breath, Joshua cracked open both eyelids and followed the voice to a blurry face.

The very last memory flooded his mind: A feeling of being buried alive.

"Rise and shine," the voice said.

The grayish blur cleared from his eyes, revealing Walker's face before him.

Startled, he scanned his environment but all he discovered was a dimly dark grayness surrounding him, or as Walker informed him, "The Recovery Room."

"Or," he said, glancing around, "The Gray Room, as I like to call it. Research has shown the color grey has been proven to comfort the mind."

Blue Room.

Green Room.

Now Gray Room?

As Joshua sat upright in bed, he asked, "Am I dead?"

"No, Josh," Walker said, "you're not dead. Instead, think in terms of 'phases.' Right now, you're in a type of limbo-like phase, ready to move on to your next phase. The fellas like to call it the 'Sweat Shop.' Don't ask me how they came up with the name. Maybe it has something to do with being on a hot seat—"

Joshua said over Walker, "You wanna a confession from me? Well, you're not getting one—"

"I never asked for one," said Walker. "I assure you we're done with the theatrics. The next phase is sort of a nuts and bolts approach before you reach your Final Phase. You'll be assigned to one of our finest caseworkers who'll be in charge of conducting the sessions. The whole point of the sessions is for you, Josh, to share your feelings. A mental exercise to purge the hatred inside you." He tilted his head in thought. "Maybe that's why they call it the Sweat Shop. '*Sweat out the hate*,'" he said charismatically, "I like the sound of that."

"When is all of this gonna end?" asked Joshua.

"It ends when you want it to end, Josh," said Walker.

"Then, I want it to end right now," he said.

"You don't mean that. . . "

A flash of animosity suddenly rose up inside Joshua, a hatred for Walker and his games.

"See. . . " Walker said. "It's still there," he said and leaned closely as if he was provoking Joshua, ". . . can't you feel it? Crawling through your head like a spider. You want it out of you—"

"You don't know what I want."

"You want what every man wants. . . " Walker said coolly, ". . . respect, peace, *love*. You wanted all of these things. Yet, you continued to surround yourself with people who didn't offer you any of these feelings. In your eye, all they did was fuel the hatred inside you. And all we want is to know why. Knowing that these people were toxic to you, Josh, why did you keep them a part of your life? And, if somehow you felt as if you had an obligation toward these certain people, then why Joshua Lamb, why couldn't you push past your resentments, *your hatred*, and learn how to love them. Best way a man can receive love is, first, he must love himself, and value his worthiness. So, tell me, Josh: What do you truly value?"

DAY Six can't arrive any sooner.

The rays from that ball of fire in the sky are like hot tines raking across my eyes.

I awake to the bright light, which leaves me in a rather foul mood.

I should be welcoming the light, but the sight of it urges me to venture back into my dreams, where I feel more at peace.

Four fingers down, five days left.

Both of my ring fingers have turned into ghosts.

Altogether, I'm left with six digits, three on each hand.

Again, I like even numbers.

I work better with even numbers.

Of all the jobs that Mr. Rebus assigns to me, I must say it seems the most fitting—being that my hands look like three-prong cultivators.

He says that I can use the fresh air, especially after my string of petty grievances. Maybe I am grasping at straws. Maybe I'm just trying to grasp at something real, which is extremely difficult to accomplish while being surrounded by so much superficiality.

Since the three other landscapers don't have any proper garden gloves to fit my alien hands, I'm left with the standard five-fingered gloves, the pinkie and ring fingers empty and lightweight and flop around like useless things and at times, get in the way while I pull weeds from flower beds.

Of all the jobs that I have worked, landscaping, perhaps, seems like the most peaceful one. I thought that I wouldn't enjoy the job when Mr. Rebus first brought it to my attention. I must say that it's starting to grow on me. Being around so much plant life and clean oxygen. Getting both of my hands dirty. It's like a tiny yet massive world right underneath my nose. Forget about the lawn equipment and all of those fumy machines, which make it more *convenient* to finish the job. I find more comfort when my hands dig and sculpt and manicure and nurse the very life, which supports our existence.

It's not until lunchtime that one of the landscapers pulls out a strange device from his pocket and places it against his mouth like an inhaler and starts sucking away on it similar to a pacifier and then, afterwards, blows out a strange yellowish cloud. It doesn't have that tobacco cigarette smell, which gives you cancer—not the smell but the inhalation of secondhand smoke—or a synthetic fruity gagging odor from vape pens, which also gives you cancer, but rather a sharp vinegary stench that penetrates the nostrils like acid. The closest I can identify the stench is the smell of dried, caked over sweat. Whatever these fumes are—I never ask for each hit he takes rattles the locked cages that contain my ugly thoughts—it makes the air harder to breath; and I find myself moving away from him in order to catch my breath.

All I can think about while I watch the other landscapers breathe in that strange substance in the air, is the infamous "Gasp Movement," which took place many years ago when millions of protestors filled the streets in nationwide protests against air pollution.

What will result in breathing in this foreign substance? Will it affect my body? Weeks from now or will I feel the effects when I'm older, when my immune system is compromised?

A northern breeze suddenly blows the stench toward me.

As the hatred fills my lungs, the thoughts turn black.

The doors to those cages spring open.

I find myself imagining what I'd like to do to him: First, I picture duct-tapping his mouth to the exhaust pipe of a heavy-duty truck, a real gas guzzler of an automobile, and as he's blowing cold steel, switching on the ignition and revving the engine while the truck is in park.

Thumb, I tell myself.

I'll let them take my thumb.

I stare at the roses, which pop with color and vividness.

The sun above provides the flowers with vitality.

Yet, at the same time, too much exposure to the sun can be deadly, maybe not in a day, but in the long term.

WHEN Day Seven creeps up like a bad habit, I start to feel as if, no matter what the results in the evaluations, I'll always visit the Chop Shop at the end of the day, hateful thoughts or not. As far as the one finger that I manage to keep on Day Two—or was it Day Three? (I've lost track)—I think maybe it was Mr. Rebus's way of offering me a sense of hope when, in fact, hope only exists in alternate realities and multiverses.

Making coffee has become a challenge, but I mange to brew a pot without showing any frustration.

After Day Six, I'm left with only five fingers.

Two on my left hand, my index and middle finger.

Three on my right, same as the day before.

After losing my thumb, I realize it may be one of the most important fingers on the hand. It is the backbone of the hand, the stabilizer, and without it—let alone those other two at the end of the line—it's much harder to grip things. There's only so much one can do with two fingers, except for maybe picking your nose or scratching your ear or pushing buttons.

With my limited range and capability, Mr. Rebus sets me up with a caregiver position at an Assisted Living Community called Lakeview. He says I don't need many fingers to carry out the job. All is required of the job: An ear for listening, preferably two of them, which works in my favor. I've always been a good listener, perhaps it's one of my strong suits; however, it does have its downsides, *always* listening, *always* hearing other people's problems and complaints. When you listen too much, you have a tendency to fill your head with all kinds of voices and some can be as bitter and vile as the venom of a cobra, which can be difficult to filter out.

When I pull up in the parking lot, a tree removal service is working next to the facility where a maple tree was fractured down the middle, possibly from wind or maybe even lightning, half of the tree lying on the ground while the other half still remains upright. Workers are sawing off the limbs of the tree and tossing them into the back of a wood chipper.

Upon my arrival, the head of the staff, Carol Wheedle, shows me around the place. She first introduces me to one of the residents, eighty-three year old Jonah O'Brien, "Jo," as he prefers— and before I have a chance to introduce myself, he makes sure to emphasize the correct spelling of Jo. *"Like a cup of joe,"* he says, straight-faced, *"only spelled without the letter e."* Despite his preferred name, the sour man insists on me—the "spoiled brat"— calling him by his last.

I reach out my hand to shake O'Brien's hand. His eyes flick downward at my three-fingered hand and pretends as if my hand doesn't exist. The rejection neither upsets me nor does it cause me to take offense; however, I find it rather strange for a man who moves his arms so slow and mechanical to refuse my hand, as if, in an unspoken way, he doesn't want me to touch his hand.

According to O'Brien, who doesn't mention a word about my hand, I haven't earned the respect to call him by his first name.

Carol, who's been working at Lakeview for eleven-going-on-twelve years, four of those years caring for Jonah O'Brien, still calls him *"Mr.* O'Brien" while emphasizing the title of Mister.

After being in O'Brien's presence for no more than four minutes, I make the conclusion that O'Brien is more like a bucket of joe opposed to a cup. Clearly running on overtime, he is nothing like one would expect from a man his age. For some, when being close to the end, it's fair to say that they can be reflective about life, appreciative for every remaining breath, waiting for that final chapter, especially for those who believe in an afterlife. Not O'Brien. He's full of piss and vinegar, his words burn long and slow like a bed of hot coals, his face like a raisin with each line and wrinkle surrounding his eyes a story where by the third act he turned into a punching bag for those whom he made part of his life.

A staffer relieves Carol after she's called to address a pressing matter in another wing of the facility and shows me around Lakeview. During our walk, she informs me that I'll be shadowing O'Brien for the remainder of the day.

"The job asked of you," the staffer says, "will consist of assisting O'Brien with whatever he needs. Mostly," she says closer, "you will be an ear."

Before parting ways, she advises me not to engage.

Her words fade into the background, as I come across a framed black and white photograph on the wall. In the photograph is the destroyed interior of what I soon conclude is the very same hallway before me. Ruined debris scattered every-where. The waterline ran up to four feet along the drywall.

"A flood," says the staffer, as she stands next to me and looks at the same photograph on the wall. "Many years ago this entire building was flooded. What you're looking at is the aftermath of the flood. This entire wing, from what I was told," she says, marveling at the hallway before her, "was completely renovated."

I take note of the photograph and follow the staffer to the recreational room where the man of the hour is waiting on my ear.

Back to O'Brien, she whispers into my ear, "Just nod your head and agree with whatever he says."

She says the words as if she knows from personal experience.

First off, when O'Brien and I are alone in the recreational room, he finally makes a remark about my hands, which doesn't surprise me.

As with the recent rejection, I don't take offense from O'Brien's remark considering most of the losses are my own doing, especially Day Six, when I welcomed such thoughts of violence.

Only a few minutes into our conversation, it doesn't take me long to figure out that O'Brien is a man of hate. Again, I can't help but think about Mr. Rebus and if setting me up with Jonah O'Brien was deliberate, a test. He hates everything: The world, as well as the people occupying it, especially those younger than him, those whom he believes are going to drive the country into the dirt. O'Brien only sees corruption and moral decay in the world.

As he lists all the things he hates, I begin to feel lighter, as if a weight has lifted from me.

Everything he hates in the world, from the taste of toothpaste to one of the orderlies and how he smells as if he hadn't taken a shower since the last election, "Greasy ball of snot," he calls the orderly, seems so petty and vain.

After playing a board game in the recreational room, I walk O'Brien back to his room where two people are arguing in the hallway. One is an orderly, not Stinky, but a heavyset woman with a bob cut whom I walked past on the way to the recreational room—the glare on her face is clear indication that my presence isn't welcomed. The other is a resident, an elderly man who goes by the name Charley, a rather sweet and effeminate man. She grabs him by the arm and points at an orange-colored spill of liquid on the tile floor, as though tempted to rub his nose in it, as she talks down to him in the same fashion an abusive parent would talk to a child or worse, a pet.

As soon as O'Brien rants about society without any filter whatsoever—the one that he observes from the safety of his recliner in front of a television—the thoughts suddenly flare up like a toothache.

Despite the two of us not seeing eye-to-eye on anything, I agree with every word that drips from his thin, shriveled lips, as well as his hatred for the orderly and those who belong in a zoo, not a place caring for the vulnerable or the compromised.

As O'Brien shoots off at the mouth, I dissect the way people treat one another in society.

The way we talk to one another.

All of the certain expressions we use, the bumper sticker-like "Phrase of the Week," repeating the same thing over and over again and again, constantly evolving and devolving.

What does it say about a species that routinely mimics itself?

A society filled with posers and copycats?

"I'd like to stick those keys where the sun don't shine," says O'Brien, as he refers to the set of keys on the necklace wrapped around the orderly's neck.

I start to wonder about the staffer and what she said to me earlier.

For the rest of the day, I spend most of the time contemplating which finger I should choose: Either the index or thumb.

I list through all of the pros and cons for each finger.

So far, it's probably one of the most difficult decisions I've had to make in a long time.

DAY Eight is staring me directly in the face.

Rebus stills keeps me on as a caregiver.

Four fingers left.

Two on each hand.

My odds aren't looking good.

Even though my left hand has been spared, it pains me to lose another finger.

Knowing the importance of the thumb, I'm left with no other choice than to have my index finger removed, my trigger finger.

I tell myself that, when the whole Final Phase is over, maybe they'll grow back, like a lizard that regenerates its tail.

Rebus is convinced that the best way for me to learn how to rid the hatred is by being around those who are equally, if not, more hateful, like, for example, he mentions, O'Brien, an individual who is just brimming to his eyeballs with hatred.

When I arrive at Lakeview, one of the staffers escorts me to O'Brien's room where the door is cracked open. I follow the staffer inside the room and before I can only make it two steps inside, she suddenly pauses, "whoops," does a swift one-eighty, and then redirects me from the room.

As I remain still and observant, I catch a glimpse of an orderly, who is standing over a wobbly O'Brien at the foot-end of his bed. With both of his arms held outward as though bracing for a hug, the orderly makes an upward motion and appears to be guiding O'Brien's legs into a pair of pants. I spot flesh, pillowy soft and doughy, folds of flesh bunching into layers, as the orderly maneuvers the waistband past O'Brien's upper thighs.

As the staffer closes the door, the orderly shifts his weight and partially exposes O'Brien's butt cheeks, like two saggy pouches of water inside thin, wrinkled bags.

The staffer holds her arm behind me like a backwards letter C while she guides me from the doorway and walks me back into the hallway where we wait for the orderly to finish doing whatever he's doing.

Moments later, the orderly and a nurse exit with colorful yet tightly pressed smiles on both of their faces.

"He's all yours," says the orderly.

The staffer guides me into the room where O'Brien is sitting in his recliner.

The first words to slip from his mouth: *"You again, huh?"*

"You can't get rid of me that easily."

With his arm stiff and rigid, he points to the top of the dresser.

"Gimme that pair of socks, will you?" asks O'Brien.

The staffer chimes in and says that she'll leave the two of us alone.

As I ask about O'Brien's plans for the day, I catch yet another glimpse of flesh.

His toes.

Except for the big one, he doesn't have any.

As O'Brien grabs the socks from my hand, he follows my eyes downward.

"Work related," he says.

I ask O'Brien where he worked.

He says that he's worked hundreds of jobs, one in particular left him with four missing toes.

"Lumberjack?"

Surprised by my response, O'Brien asks, "How'd you guess?"

"My grandfather accidentally chopped off four of his toes while he was cutting firewood in the backyard. . . at least, this is what my father once told me."

"That's the thing about an axe. . . " O'Brien says while stiffly sliding his foot into the sock. ". . . It doesn't have eyes."

Once he's fully dressed, slippers and all, we make our way into the recreational room where O'Brien suggests that we grab a game from the locker and play it outside in the courtyard. I first ask him what game he'd like to play and without missing a beat, he suggests *Snake Eyes*, which is similar to the classic strategy game, *Connect Four*, only instead of using a grid of six rows and seven columns, the game uses *ten* rows and *eleven* columns. Also, instead of connecting the four matching colored tokens in a single row, a player must match the two identical snake eyes. Each player is given a nest carrying fifty-five grassy green tokens, which, after about a minute into the game, can easily get confused with an opposing player's tokens, if you don't keep track of where you placed a token. The catch: Players are only given *two* tokens with snake eyes, which can be found on the backside of the tokens. The other catch: A player cannot see an opposing player's snake eyes since one side of the tokens have snake eyes, meaning players must use each of their tokens wisely. Last but not least, the player who matches their snake eyes first wins.

Halfway through the second game, the grid, which is made up of plastic, suddenly breaks in half, causing all of the tokens to scatter over the picnic table.

At first, O'Brien blames the pills that he's taking and how they have affected the mobility in his fingers, making them, at times, stiff and hard to move.

He shifts the blame toward the game itself, the makers of the game Snake Eyes, the material used to manufacture the product.

"Plastic," O'Brien emphasizes, "cheap fucking plastic!"

After he rants about plastic, he veers, almost fluently, into a common complaint among older people: Why aren't things built the way they used to be built? In O'Brien's eye: "Built to last."

These days, everything is replaceable.

Which makes me wonder if O'Brien's parents or grandparents said the same thing when he was younger?

He talks about corporate greed, cutting corners, taking shortcuts or worse, taking advantage of people.

He hates corporations, hates everything about them.

Most importantly, he hates the idea of being replaced.

For a man who has worked many jobs throughout his lifetime, I'm sure he knows a thing or two about being expendable.

O'Brien grabs a token, tosses it back on the table, and says to me, "Everyone is replaceable, like these very board games."

I'd be lying if I said I didn't agree.

When we return from the courtyard, I walk past a staff member who's carrying a small cup of meds to one of the residents. I can't read the imprint code on the pill for it's too small and I'm too far away. The color is what catches my eyes. The pill is the same exact color as the one I've been taking ever since Day Two. I part ways with O'Brien and piddle around the building and wait until the employee leaves the closet-like room where all of the medicines are stored. While searching through the shelves of meds, I locate a bottle of placebos with the imprint code "J-12" on them. After inspecting the small green pill, I place it back in the bottle.

DAY Nine.

So long, Thumb.

Nice knowing you.

With two days left until my Final Phase is complete, I can say, regardless of how things pan out, that I'll be glad when these last two fingers are gone, leaving me with only one finger.

Before the day starts, I decide not to take the pill, since it's practically useless.

I never brought up the subject with Rebus during the Vid-Chat call last night and I don't plan on bringing it up either.

As for experiencing any pain, my thumb feels no different than that feeling you get after you stub a toe against a hard object, only much more subdued, as a tamer radiating sensation that can easily be ignored if I focus my mind elsewhere.

For a majority of the morning, O'Brien remains relatively quiet and mostly keeps to himself. It's not until after lunch that he finally opens up while we take a late afternoon stroll around a serene Lake Holden. His eyes are darker and telling, brow stiff and rigid, thoughts as heavy as the earth.

"Out with it already."

"Please excuse my reservedness today, Joshua," he says, his voice as taut as roots twisting in dirt. "Today is the anniversary of my wife's death."

"You never told me you were married."

"You never asked."

I clear my throat and feel somewhat ashamed for not even asking him—Or did I?

"When did she die?"

"Forty-five years ago," he says. "Seems like the older you get the faster time gets. I reckon, when you're so close to the end, you spend so much time waiting to die that you forget about living."

O'Brien walks through a clearing along the trail, which opens up and reveals Lake Holden. He stands along a parched knob of land along the edge of the shore. His eyes lost in the still water.

"What was your wife's name?"

"Maggie," he says. "Her name was Maggie. When I was around your age, I did something unspeakable toward her. I don't know how it exactly happened," he says in deep reflection. "It just happened. At the time, I was working as a bartender—"

"Lumberjack, deliveryman, bartender: Where haven't you worked?"

O'Brien thinks for a moment as if he's combing for a joke inside that gray matter of his but ends up offering me a thin-lip smile instead.

"When Maggie and I moved further into the city," he says, "it was easier to find a job than it was to lose a job. And if for some reason you did lose a job, it was mostly your own doing. For me, I was only a bartender for two years."

"Why's that?"

"Way too much temptation."

"So, I get it now. You were a ladies man, huh?"

The charm doesn't work on O'Brien.

His eyes remain dark and fixed on water.

"Maybe once, but when I met Maggie, I never looked at a woman the same way ever again. . .until I met Sheila. She was a clerk who worked at a nearby police station. Spent her work-days around cops who wore their badge as if it was an excuse to be an asshole. She'd stop by where I worked after her shift. She drank. She talked. I listened. After weeks of Sheila having my ear, the guard that I put over my eyes was lifted. All of a sudden, our eyes connected. It was like the Fourth of July."

"Did you love her?"

"No," O'Brien says. "But I was attracted to her. Unlike Maggie, she was. . . " the words catch in his throat, ". . . how do I say?"

"Wild?"

More relieved, he says, "Extremely."

"Maybe it had something to do with being around cops all day."

"You mean like swimming in all that testosterone?"

"They have women cops."

"Sure," he says. "But not as many back then."

"Must've been pretty wild. Not having a counterpart to keep you in check."

"You can say that," he says in agreement. "Her father was also a cop. He was abusive. She carried that resentment around with her. It wasn't until things got rougher and more. . . physical between us that I knew someone was going to get hurt. Two days after I broke it off with Sheila, Maggie found out where I was going after work. She followed the laundry trail—"

"Laundry trail?"

"Let's just say Sheila tore through my clothes like a tigress. A real man-eater, she was. After a while, I started to run out of excuses as to why my clothes had rips in them."

"She must've been something."

"She was," he says, head down. "But she had her issues. We all do. Maggie never forgave me, and she hung my mistake over me, used it against me to gain leverage over me. I wanted to leave Maggie, but I didn't want to be the guy who left a woman like her."

Like her?

"What do you mean?"

"I questioned myself at times why I even married Maggie: 'Was there something more sinister at play?' 'Was I punishing myself for leaving Jamie, my high school sweetheart?' Maggie had this condition, Liebenberg syndrome, an autosomal genetic disease that affects the limbs. In the beginning, when I first met Maggie, I wasn't aware of her condition but it was obvious to me that she had a condition. Her hands," he says, holding out both his liver-spotted hands, "weren't shaped anything like mine. But after awhile, after spending more time with her, I never saw her abnormalities as a weakness. I saw them as a strength, advantages that she could use in her favor, even though many others looked at her much differently. Knowing that, I was always on the defense, vigilant about what others said about her, even the way they stared at her. I was ready to fight for her. . . "

As O'Brien talks about Maggie, I drift inward and think about Natalie, and I can't help but notice the stark similarities in our relationships.

O'Brien steps away from the lake and continues down another trail, a more narrow one, as if he doesn't want the water to hear what he's about to tell me next. I follow him through the woods until we reach yet another clearing away from the lake. He walks up a step embankment where we reach a set of train tracks. O'Brien tells me that he needs to rest.

As he sits down on the tracks, he uses his right arm to ease his lower body onto the tracks. I help lower him down. He tells me that he can manage. I pull my hand away and as he sits down on the tracks, I notice his elbow pop slightly out of joint. Yet, O'Brien doesn't make any sign or sound indicating that he's in distress.

"Don't worry," he reassures me, "there hasn't been a train on these tracks since I've been at Lakeview."

"Something happened between you and Maggie, didn't it?"

"One night," he says and catches his breath, "we were spending a night on the town to celebrate our wedding anniversary. We had a couple of drinks. I admit that I had one too many. A man made an unpleasant remark about Maggie's hands when we were leaving the bar. Something came over me. I snapped," he says and snaps his middle finger and thumb together, which makes an unnatural sound. "I would've killed him if Maggie hadn't intervened. When she tried to pull me off of him, I accidentally pushed her away. She tripped and hit the side of her head on the curb. During my drunken rage, I heard the man's friend telling me what I had just done to my wife. I stopped punching the man and then, when I turned around, I saw Maggie on the ground and all of that red puddling around her head."

A sudden image of Pep lying facedown on the kitchen floor flashes through my mind, forcing me to return to O'Brien's words.

I block out the violent image and train myself to focus on his words.

They're just thoughts, I tell myself.

It never happened.

"I killed her," O'Brien says. "Me—"

"But you didn't know it was her, right? It was an accident?"

"No," he says and then corrects, "I didn't know it was her who tried to pull me off cuz I was too focused on trying to kill this man. But. . . " he pauses, ". . . there's still this part of me that questions whether or not I was looking for this one particular man who would finally say the wrong thing at the right time. Like I was waiting for this man to say something about Maggie." He looks up at the cloudy sky above. The tears fall from the corner of his bloodshot eyes and run down the side of his face. He says, "Maybe that man who I was beating was myself."

O'Brien leans forward and runs his papery hands over his forehead. While doing so, part of his unbuttoned collar peels open, revealing, first, a gold necklace around his neck, and then, second, a similar scar, shaped like a starfish, on the lower part of his chest. The scar is not only in the same spot, but also the appearance of it is nearly identical to mine. I motion toward the gold chain and ask him about the necklace. He pulls it from the opening of his collar and shows me a golden pendant of a wing. He tells me that a close friend of his had given it to him many years ago and he just started to wear it again over these past couple of years and when I ask him why, he says that, in the past, it had brought him "good fortune."

By the time he finishes telling me about the necklace, I decide not to ask him about the scar.

Instead, I sit down next to O'Brien on the tracks.

The words spill from my mouth.

"*I hate Rebus.*"

"You hate Rebus, huh?"

"I guess you can call him this parole officer-type counselor who's been helping me navigate through the program—"

"I know who he is."

"You do?"

"Everybody at Lakeview knows who he is—" he corrects himself, "—well, most of them."

"Can you tell—"

"That pirate who they sent over here before you told us all about him. If I were you, Joshua, I wouldn't trust him. Not a single word that comes out of his mouth. Whatever he says to you, more than likely it's bullshit. So," he says with an unusual sarcasm, "how's the program treating you thus far?"

"I hate it"

"Is that so? You don't like my company?"

I hesitate to answer.

"Don't worry," he says. "I wouldn't like my company either."

"I especially hate Rebus for putting me in a position where I must confront my demons. For awhile, I was fine with leaving them alone, the demons, like spiders in their own web, not bothering anyone, every now and then they'll descend from those webs above, give those around me a brief scare, and then, they'll return to their webs, not bothering anyone unless provoked, merely languishing in their own unique design and looking down at the living."

"All demons come from somewhere," says O'Brien. "Where do yours come from?"

"A dark place."

O'Brien attempts to sit upright but struggles.

I stand to my feet, as O'Brien holds up his hand as though asking for me to grab it.

"Would you?"

I grab O'Brien's hand and immediately notice the strangeness of his rubbery hand.

With a slight tug upward, I help O'Brien to his feet. His arm suddenly slides farther out and before the prosthetic falls from his shoulder, he grabs hold of the arm with his other hand.

More frightened by the sight of the arm, I take a couple of steps away from O'Brien.

"Who the hell are you?"

O'Brien says, "Just a tired, broken down old man who, once, was just like you, Joshua. But even worse. If you thought my heart is filled with hatred now, then you should've seen it when I was your age, after Maggie's death. The hate completely consumed me—"

"Who are you, really?"

"Jonah O'Brien," he says.

"But your arm—"

"Arms," he corrects and removes the first prosthetic. Highly detailed and realistic. Even the liver spots have been painted on with an airbrush.

He nods at the other arm, motioning for me to remove it from his shoulder.

Once I remove the other arm, he says to me, "Not shocking enough?"

"You were in the program as well, weren't you?"

"You know you're right about Mr. Rebus," O'Brien says. "You should hate him, Joshua."

"You know that he's listening to this very conversation, right? Every single thought inside my head is being recorded right now."

O'Brien says nonchalantly, "Yes. A parasite that has latched itself onto you." He squares himself to me, looks me straight in the eyes, and says more seriously, "He will eat you alive until there's nothing left of you."

Signaling to O'Brien, I move my last index finger toward my mouth and warn him to be more careful about what he says, since I'm basically a walking tape recorder.

"I'm eighty-three years old, Joshua," he says. "Does it look like I care?"

I look over the prosthetic that I hold against my body, my armpit surprisingly being a temporary replacement to hold items. I still can't get over the arm and how the arm itself looks identical to a human arm, only it feels much different on the skin of my palm.

I hold my eyes on the prosthetic.

"What is it?" asks O'Brien.

"Why do I feel like agreeing to join the program was me signing my own death warrant?"

"Because," O'Brien says seriously, "for some, it is."

"What happens after the Final Phase?"

"Who knows, Joshua? What you need to be asking yourself: Do I want to wind up looking like this? Because, if you continue down this path you're on, then you will, and you'll look back at this moment with a regret so deep and infectious that it'll rot away your very core. I sensed it the first time we met. You know the feeling, don't you? That feeling of regret. . . "

"When I was much younger, I did something I regret even till this day, and for the next ten years or so, I was forced to live life on the run, always looking over my shoulder, always on my toes, always on the defensive. I felt as if I had to prove, not only to myself, but also to others that I was capable of surviving on my own. After this. . . party of interest stopped pursuing me, that sharpness disappeared, that hunger gone. Was it for the better or the worse? I dunno."

"Trust me," O'Brien says. "Whatever you were running from, it sounds like you've already faced it and now, it's time for you to move on with your life. And that is why you don't want to repeat the same mistakes over again, right?"

"Curious. . . what did you do after you were released?"

"I lived a quiet life," O'Brien says.

"A quiet life, huh?"

He says, "It's not that hard. Maybe you should try it."

Easy for you to say.

⊗

DAY Ten, the final day of my Final Phase, and I'm left with only two fingers.

What's more appropriate than to wind up with both of my middle fingers?

I can't help but find a devilish amusement from the sight of my hands.

I'm sure the sight of my hands will cause a rise from onlookers.

Either way, the final day of my Final Phase can't arrive soon enough.

When I arrive at Lakeview, I meet up with O'Brien and within only a few minutes of talking to him, he's already neck deep in his hatred and all of it is directed toward a staff member, who made a cheap crack at O'Brien's body odor behind his back, and the sound of his voice and how he speaks about the staff member makes me sick to my stomach.

As I attempt to block out O'Brien by focusing on pleasant thoughts—after all, this is my last day and I'm still hoping to salvage these last two birds—an orderly, who looks incredibly familiar, pokes his head inside the room after knocking twice on the door.

"You got a visitor," says the orderly.

At first, I assume he's referring to O'Brien.

He shakes his head and points directly at me.

"No," he says. "*You*."

"Me?"

"He's waiting for you in the main lobby."

"Off you go," O'Brien says suspiciously. "Not like I'm going anywhere anytime soon. Well, I take that back. . . "

Before O'Brien can rant about where he's going—a part of me already knows what he's going to say—I leave the room and follow the orderly to the main lobby area.

From the end of the hallway, he points toward the main lobby and says, "Right this way."

I catch up to the orderly, who ends up falling behind. I stop and turn my shoulder. The orderly is nowhere in sight. I search through the hallway but can't find the orderly. I check several closed doors nearby, but still, he's gone, like a phantom.

An eerie feeling comes over me and I hurry back to O'Brien's room.

He's gone as well.

I check other rooms and can't locate a single resident inside the building. The same goes for any staff members: They're gone as well.

I decide to make my way toward the main lobby where I suspect to find people; and when I arrive, the lobby is empty as well, except for a mysterious man standing by the fireplace with his back turned to me. The beating glow of fire flashes over one side of his face and I soon realize it's Rebus.

I inch my way through the lobby.

"What's this all about?"

With his back still facing me, Rebus says, "*You*, of course. This has always been about you, Josh."

I glance around the lobby; and strangely, it appears different from the lobby in Lakeview.

I've been here before.

"Yes," Rebus says, as though he's reading my mind, "as a matter of fact, you have been here before."

"Why are you doing this?"

"I'm not doing anything, Josh," he says and finally, faces me. "This is all *your* doing."

"I don't believe you."

"Believe whatever you want, but you created all of this: *A man is nothing without worth* and you, Josh, believe a man's hands are his *only* worth. Hands meant for creation, not violence."

"I never said that—"

"But you thought it," he says and steps closer. "Am I right?"

Once more, my eyes veer slightly toward a reception desk, which also looks familiar.

"We're currently at Mother's Grace," Rebus says, "the place where you worked before. . . " he trails off, ". . . you know, the incident. Or. . . " he says teasingly, ". . . as you constantly refer to it as *the accident*. Pretty noble of you I must say, Josh, for helping out those who are in need. While combing around your thoughts, I noticed that arts and crafts were an activity that you enjoyed the most with patients. I take it time you spent with Natalie rubbed off on you—"

"Don't mention her name."

A flash of anger jolts me, and I'm urged to rip out of his tongue for speaking her name.

Rebus holds up his hands in surrender.

"You're the boss," he says and waves me into another room.

"What do you want?"

Rebus stops and waits for me to follow and when I don't, he walks back toward me.

He says back to me, "What do you want, Josh?"

The answer can't be clear enough.

"*Closure.*"

"I'm afraid the program doesn't work that way," he says more directly. "The program—the one you're currently in—is specifically designed to take a user's worst fears and turn those fears against the user by way of deception and manipulation."

An image creeps into my mind, slowly and steadily, like a drop of black ink spreading over delicate fabric, splitting and fracturing across each fine thread: *A homeless man in a dark alleyway crawling along his belly's-side, no arms or legs.*

Rebus holds up both hands, flashes them at me as if he's taunting me, and says, "You, Josh, think Man is no Man, but rather a useless Man if he's unable to use these. . . what Man is able to do—or not do—you think *these*. . . " he flashes his hands once more, as if they're merely things in his way, ". . . are what measure the weight of His functionality. . . " He points at his head, and in that glimpse, I see the other four fingers on my right hand, each one of them translucent like a jellyfish, ". . . Did you ever stop to think, Josh: *What if* the era of Man is over, finished?"

"I'm not finished. . . Not yet."

"*Now that I do believe,*" he says amusedly, voice loud and booming. "And why do I believe that, huh? I'll tell you why. Because when I peek inside you my friend all I see is darkness. But there is light at the end of the tunnel, *your* tunnel. You just don't see it. . . Not yet. But I believe you will. Do you know why? Because, once, in another life, you were a decent man, Josh, who cared for others. . . "

Again, he waves me into another room.

I follow him into the room.

He switches on the light, revealing my apartment.

He walks me into the apartment where he shows me the kitchen.

I stop at the doorway.

As Rebus stands next to the kitchen counter, I feel paralyzed.

He asks me, "Is there a problem, Josh?"

"I know what you're doing, and I'm not going along with your plan."

"And what exactly am I doing, Josh?"

I hold out my hands, my two middle fingers.

"Look at what you've reduced me to. . . "

"I didn't do anything to you, Josh. Like I've said, you did this to yourself. Now, it is time for you to stop running from your own self. Now, it's time for you to accept the truth."

The name suddenly dawns on me.

I remember seeing a similar name in one of my father's manuscripts.

Right before my eyes, a title in courier font appears on the first page of a bound manuscript:

```
        The Crippler
            by
        Bill Lamb
```

While digging through his old stories, I remember this particular one, *The Crippler*, and the script's condition, which, from the wear and tear, appeared as if it had been read many times and many hands had touched it. Maybe my father had shopped it around the market or showed it off to fellow writer friends or editors or agents. Or, maybe my father's hands were the only hands to touch the script. The paper was off-white; the corners of the manuscript were curled inward like the tips of dead pedals. But why this one particular script?

The Crippler.

The main character of the story, I recall, was named "Rebus."

I remember.

Rebus.

I vaguely remember the story. Spotty details emerge from my hazy thoughts. The story was centered around a hacker who crippled a small town's power grid for one week. Eventually, the hacker, I recall, "The Crippler" was his name, was caught by authorities. The hacker was only a fraction of the story. Most of the story was focused on the townspeople and the effects of losing electricity, especially for those who relied on electricity to survive.

According to *The Crippler*, his motives were what you'd call "grandiose." By switching off the power, he hoped to cleanse the world of the hatred that social media companies were spreading throughout the town. The hacker's plan helped one particular person, who was addicted to a particular unchecked algorithm, which was governed by hate. By the end of the story, when power returned, all of the townspeople were back to their same ole ways, except for one person, who was forever changed and *less* hateful.

"*You. . .* you're not even real, are you? Your name isn't even Rebus, is it?"

"I am exactly what you've made me to be, Josh," Rebus says to me. "A *medium* standing in between fact and fiction, *the truth* and the lies. The choice is now yours. I can either guide you to freedom or I can step in your way and prevent you from ever leaving this place—"

"What place?"

He doesn't answer, not at first.

The silence strangles me.

Tightens.

"Your head," he says finally.

I step forward into the kitchen.

The space behind Rebus opens up, revealing a dark sound-stage. The entire kitchen is split in half. One side of the wall is missing. Somewhere, I can imagine a director or producer sitting in one of those chairs in the darkness of the studio, watching with great intensity, nitpicking at each movement, each gesture, like a digger mining for gold. Each detail of the kitchen is precise and exactly the same as the apartment that Pep and I once shared. Everything on the set, like the kitchen cabinets, isn't real but rather a prop. Even the apples resting in a metal basket on the countertop aren't really apples but rather fake plastic apples.

Using the palm of my hand, I cup one of the plastic apples and show it to Rebus.

"The truth, huh?"

I fling the apple into the darkness behind Rebus.

"Please, Josh. . ."

Rebus holds out his hand, as though he's ready to show me the truth. He steps aside and in a glimpse, I catch the soles of shoes behind the corner of the counter. I follow Rebus's hand toward the two legs of a woman lying facedown on the kitchen floor.

Before I step closer toward the countertop, I immediately move my eyes away.

"You must accept the truth, Josh," says Rebus.

"The truth. . ."

I flip Rebus the bird.

Without thinking, I suddenly turn on a garbage disposal and stick my middle finger into the drain.

I'll give you truth.

The feel the blades spin round and round, chewing through flesh and bone.

Surprisingly, the cut is clean.

When I pull my hand from the garbage disposal, the air punches the open wound. The pain suddenly hits me, and it feels so intoxicating. The pain. I cling to it, like a drug.

As I stick my other hand into the garbage disposal, Rebus attempts to stop me.

I push him away with my elbow and jam my hand into the garbage disposal.

Drunk with pain, I stumble away from the sink and glance down at my blood-soaked hands.

Feeling lightheaded, I stagger and fall to the floor using the backside of the cabinets to cushion the landing.

"No more piggies."

In the corner of my eye, I notice a motionless Rebus is lying facedown on the floor.

Finally, I manage to stand to my feet and walk over to Rebus.

Using my hands and forearms like shovels, I turn Rebus over on his back.

He's not Rebus.

"Pepper. . . "

The side of her forehead has a massive gash.

The last images that fill my head: *While I stand next to an open fridge Pep argues with me, her shouts cut through me like a razor. I suddenly black out. I can feel myself leaving my own body and watching from the outside. This person, this dark stranger, who is now occupying my body, pushes Pep. She trips, her heel slips. She falls backward; and during the fall, she strikes the side of her head on the corner of the countertop.*

I return to my body.

"Stop lying to yourself, Josh," says Rebus, as he returns to the floor. "Accept the truth. . . "

More images, raw and undeniable, frontal: *I'm lying in Mime's bed, a pocket pistol aimed at a dark figure approaching the bedroom. The shadow of the figure's upper body crosses a column of light along the carpeted floor. Mime ducks for cover behind me, her left hand claws into my ribcage. The silhouette appears at the doorway. Her silhouette. I pull back on that sweaty trigger. A bullet strikes her in the neck. She falls backward. She bleeds out.*

"But it wasn't her—"

More images: *The phoenix-tattooed man from the convenient store appears at the doorway, his gun is drawn. His silhouette appears behind the doorway.*

He works for Orwell.

He's sent to rebalance the scales.

Make sure that I never speak a word about them.

Or, the job they asked me to carry out.

An eraser.

A delete-pusher.

Ready to wipe me from existence.

It was him.

A hired gun.

But how did *they* find me?

"*Not him,*" says Rebus. "Remember the truth. . . "

"It was him."

The Assassin Man.

"But it wasn't."

"Was too."

"Joshua," Pep says plainly. "*Shut the fuck up already* and look at what you did. . . "

I stop talking, stop thinking, and hold my dead fiancée in my arms.

I finally feel the weight of my own actions.

A deep and violent fissure courses its way through my entire body.

I can't control the tears as they pour from my burning eyes.

"You don't know what it's like, Pep, to wake up everyday, wondering how the fuck I ended up like this, in this situation where I dragged an innocent woman into my messy life. I'm sorry, Pep. I'm so sorry I got involved with you. I should've ended it sooner. I should've. . . "

The words, as heavy as weights, jam in the back of my throat.

Even trying to speak the words feels like one of the heaviest reps.

"You made me feel trapped. You pushed my back against the wall—"

Suddenly, Pep's dead eyes open.

She's staring directly at me.

"I never pushed you against the wall, Josh," she says.

"You did. You cornered me. . . "

"You shut off, Josh," she says over my cries. "You built a wall around yourself because you were scared to raise a child—"

"Shut up!"

My ghost fingers attempt to squeeze her matted hair.

"You are scared to face yourself, Josh."

Her words run through me, like water.

A squirt of blood jets from the bullet hole in her neck.

The truth streams from the wound, the truth snaking its way over my hands and arms.

"Maybe one day," she says and places her hand over my left cheek, "when you learn to love yourself, like you did with Natalie," her lips part with a smile, "like you did with me—at least, in the beginning—you'll open yourself to the world again and love will find its way back into your heart. That's the beauty of love, Josh. It has a strange way of filtering out the hate. But it won't happen over night. It'll be gradual, Josh. One day, maybe years from now, you'll find yourself in a state of reflection, wondering what happened to that man I used to be. Did he leave for good? You'll never know, Josh, because who you become is who you've *always* wanted to be."

Pep's glossy eyes suddenly still and glaze over, as she closes both of her eyelids.

I pull her lifeless body to mine and hold her closely.

Somewhere, in the back of my mind, I'm waiting for a director to shout out the word "*Cut!*" behind me.

I never hear such a word.

Instead, I imagine myself being lifted onto a crane, which pulls me away from the scene that I've been avoiding ever since I killed the one person who forced me to become a man.

8

FOR the remainder of the day, that one question still rattled through Joshua's head.

What do I value?

The question rolled over into the next day, which marked the first day of Joshua's sessions.

The Sweat Shop.

Joshua followed The Curator's instructions via a VidChat call and walked about half a mile through the main housing facility until he reached a room where his sessions would be conducted.

When he knocked on the door, he was greeted by a man who called himself, "Mr. Rebus."

Joshua entered the white interrogation-like room.

The White Room?

In the center of the room were twelve black chairs positioned in a perfect circle. Ten people, or what Mr. Rebus called "NPCs," were seated in the chairs. Mr. Rebus took a seat in the second to last chair. Joshua followed suit and sat down in the last remaining chair.

"Not the kind of Sweat Shop you were expecting, is it?"

Joshua shook his head no.

"This is where we sweat out the disease, Josh—May I call you Josh?"

Joshua shrugged as if he didn't care what he called him.

"Disease?"

"Hate," Mr. Rebus said clearly and placed a clipboard on his lap. "A highly contagious disease that can affect us all, even those who are the strongest of character. After we have purged the hatred inside you, Josh, you must complete the Final Phase of the Reform Program. For you, based on the crime, it'll consist of a ten-day trial. And if you pass the final evaluation, you will be able to reenter society."

Joshua asked, "And if I don't pass?"

Mr. Rebus said, "Then, the Final Phase will run as long as it has to—"

"What is that supposed to mean?"

Mr. Rebus cracked a smile as crooked as a seesaw.

"It means: Just follow the rules and everything will go according to plan," he said.

"So," Joshua said, thinking, "why ten days? Why not a week?"

"Ten days," he emphasized, his voice resonant. "Compared to most of the offenders, I'd say that you have it rather easy. I've seen an offender reduced to a single eyelash on the tip of your finger. A single blow of your breath could send him away, whooshing through an eternity. So. . . " he let out a sigh, ". . . before we get ahead of ourselves, let's focus on The Now. As Walker explained earlier, it will be up to you, Josh, whether or not you are willing to rid the hatred that drives you. If not, then I'm afraid you'll suffer from the consequences. With that being said, tell me, Josh, when you think about the word *hate*, what's the very first thing that comes to mind?"

The first images to enter Joshua's head: *Pushing his fiancée*, who tripped and struck the side of her head against the countertop, thus killing her.

Mr. Rebus said while Joshua drifted further into thought: "Try to go deeper," he clarified for Joshua. "Don't focus on the images. Focus on the word itself."

Mentally, Joshua witnessed that word in all caps pushing closer.

Next to appear was a man's face.

Orwell.

His name was Orwell.

First name, Maron.

While sitting next to him inside an airport, Maron Orwell offered Joshua a job in Loganson, West Virginia.

Joshua accepted.

"Deeper, Josh," said Mr. Rebus.

Joshua returned to the word *hate*.

He replaced the first letter of the word with the first letter that came to mind.

If only I stayed with Natalie, then I never would've returned to Spartacus.

Which means I never would've wound up doing that one job, which nearly killed me.

What if *I was supposed to be in Tokyo?*

He replaced other letters with the word: *Late, Mate, Rate.*

Each word carried meaning and each word held significance in Joshua's life and each word was almost always attached to the word "*If.*"

If I wasn't late *with dinner*, would she have freaked out?

If I didn't mate *with Pepper. . .*

If I didn't constantly rate *my relationship with her, trying to compare it to everyone else. . .*

These were only words, Joshua thought to himself.

Words are a form of expression.

They are the glue to a functioning society.

But they were just words, he told himself, and actions often speak louder than words.

Did these words represent how he truly felt?

To hate is to possess a strong dislike.

But where and when did a like turn into a dislike?

Joshua then arrived at a like, which soon evolved into a passion.

Where there was passion, there was love.

Joshua did love Pepper.

But when did his love for her begin to corrode?

"*Myself,*" said Joshua.

Mr. Rebus chimed in, "You hate yourself?"

"No," he clarified. "I don't hate myself, but I hate the man I became when I was with her."

"Your fiancée, Pepper?"

"Yes."

"Did you love her?" asked Mr. Rebus.

"In the beginning," Joshua said thoughtfully. "*Yes.* I did. When I returned home after being away for what felt like years, I guess it's fair to say that I came back kind of like an old soul. Being inside so many different people—"

"Inside?"

"*Their thoughts,*" Joshua corrected himself. "Being able to easily read their thoughts and experience their experiences firsthand aged me, not physically but mentally. Years passed. I jumped around from job to job. And yet, everyday was the same." He shrugged both his shoulders. "Just me trying to get by with what little I had. But I never complained about what I had or did not have. It was just enough for me, except for one thing—"

"A partner?"

"Yes," said Joshua. "Eventually, I found a decent job as an orderly at a nursing home where I assisted mostly seniors. It was rewarding, in a way, helping people, especially those in need of help. Most of them didn't have much. Their families rarely visited them. Some felt abandoned, betrayed, ashamed for winding up in a home. At times, it was like a dog pound for the elderly—strays wrangled up by people who pretended that they loved their mother or father or brother or sister, that they were doing it for their own good. No person—I mean, not a single one—should ever feel like a burden on another person, especially a family member. The job, of course, came with its highs and lows. Then, one day, she walked through the main lobby. I was immediately attracted to Autumn, even though she was much older than me. Right off the bat, I could tell that she had already been through the rodeo, which was marriage. She already rode the bull, and that bull was one helluva kicker. He had done much damage to her but never broke her per se. Instead, it was that damage which made her more attractive. She had a sense of humor and while spending time with her, I felt, dare I say, young again, lighter, like a weight had been lifted from my shoulders. When I asked her what she was doing here, she told me that she was visiting her father, who was on the floor above where I was stationed. I've heard from other staff members about Mr. Piper and how he had a tendency to sneak out of his bedroom in the middle of the night and wander through the hallways. She said that she and her mother could no longer care for him and that he needed to be watched around the clock, twenty-four hours a day. Even as she told me these things, I thought to myself how much I didn't care about her father—"

Mr. Rebus asked, "Why not, Josh? He was the father of your soon-to-be fiancée. . . "

Joshua shrugged.

"I just wanted to get to know her and her alone," said Joshua.

"That's not how it works, Josh," Mr. Rebus said. "To love someone—unconditionally—you must, at the very least, respect the people in their lives."

Joshua laughed.

"Respect?" Joshua repeated, still astonished by the comment. "So, you're telling me I'm supposed to respect a man who constantly abused his wife? Treated her like she was less than zero? Is that what you're saying?"

Mr. Rebus narrowed his eyes.

"*There it is,*" he said. "Why does Autumn's father upset you?"

"He doesn't upset me—"

"But, clearly, he does."

"I know what you're doing to me right now," Joshua said, more directly at Mr. Rebus.

"What am I doing, Josh?"

"You're trying to get me to admit that I'm no different than Mr. Piper—"

"Are you?"

"Of course, I'm not like Mr. Piper," Joshua said, his voice climbing to a near shout. "I lost my temper one time! One fucking time—"

"Which indirectly resulted in the death of your fiancée."

More hysterically, Joshua cried out, "It's not like I woke up one day and said to myself, '*Hey, I'm going to kill my fiancée today.*' It was an accident, plain and simple."

"According to a key witness, it was *not* an accident, Josh," said Mr. Rebus, who, on the contrary, remained cool, calm, and collected. "Moments before, you threatened her because you felt as if you no longer had control—in essence, you felt powerless—and the only way for you to retain power over her was to reacquire it by any means necessary, mentally or physically. You're right about your fiancée, Josh. She was broken when you first met her. So, what does that say about you, Josh? Are you broken as well? Or, are you a man who likes to repair broken things?"

SURROUNDED by woods, I'm standing in a gravel parking lot in front of a historical blue two-story hotel in the middle of nowhere. The building is aged, rundown. In the shadowy corners of the ceiling above the first floor are spider webs, thick, white, and gnarly, as if they have an established date, which isn't too far off from the grand opening of the hotel. The paint is cracked and starting to peel and chip, especially in those areas around the hotel room doorways. The mosquitoes dance haphazardly over a puddle of stagnant water from a moldy ceiling leak, which appears as if it's been there since the last election, along a sidewalk underneath a walkway above the first floor.

As I point out the detail of the hotel, including a mildew-like odor that feels as if it's sticking to my skin, I suddenly spot a dark, wavy object soaring above me.

I move my eyes upward and slightly squint from the sunrays cutting through the heavy overcast sky and during my narrowed glance, witness a pale blue onesie descending from the opening of the second-story window of the hotel.

Once my eyes adjust to the warm brilliant light I first notice two feet, each one fitted with a white sock. Next, I see two hands and those fingers, which appear like tiny pink capsules. Then, lastly, I see his round face screeching past me like a motion blur, each facial feature exaggerated and distorted.

As my heart drops from my chest and sinks into my stomach, I attempt to catch the baby.

Everything happens so fast.

Yet, everything moves so slowly.

The baby's legs slip right past my fingertips, as I reach out to catch him.

I hear the sudden *thud* first and then feel the crack, as a fissure crookedly streaks through my entire body like a bolt of lightning.

The side of the baby's head strikes the side of a parked van and instantly kills him.

Everything inside me, all feeling, all thought, all sense, is wrung like a damp towel.

As the lifeless baby lays in the parking lot, I read the name "*Doug*" written in cursive above the breast pocket of the onesie.

The name is short for Douglas.

His middle name "Woodruff."

The sight of the name further stretches the fissure inside me, as though I'm being split right down the middle. Each and every muscle in my entire body twists and knots with a kind of rage that I have never encountered.

A primitive kind of rage.

Seek and destroy.

As the rage overwhelms me, my hands tighten and curl and ball up into hammers.

All of the triggers that make me upset, all of the hate that I feel clawing its way through my skull, all of it is suddenly amplified.

A short and obscure man with obscure features deliberately blows a cloud of strange smoke directly in my face. I feel incredibly sick from absorbing the smoke, which fills both my nostrils and slithers its way like a serpent into my lungs, traveling through each cavity. The smoke destroys each vital cell inside my body. Eventually, after days, weeks, months, and years of allowing the obscure man to blow smoke in my face, I'm diagnosed with cancer. Terminal. The actions of the obscure man result in a grim timeline for me. I'm placed on a conveyor belt, which will guide me to my inevitable doom. I'm dying, not fast but slowly, and yet, I stand on the belt, riding through the clouds of smoke while allowing vessels of obscurity to violate me and my vital organs, the obscure man with his smoke violating my lungs or an obscure woman who shoves handful of food down my throat, violating my stomach, or the obscure pistons on each machine in the factory, which pound relentlessly, violating my ears. The hate boils-hot inside me when I think about the very inception of their plights, each one passed down from one generation to another, their blood tainted by the greed of a corporate entity, which has cast a corruptive spell on the weak, the vulnerable, and the undetermined.

Driven by raw anger, I sprint toward the door which leads to the staircase.

I swing open the door, nearly breaking off one of the hinges.

In the darkness a strange face emerges before my eyes.

Then, among that darkness, a toothy smile bends into the shape of the letter U.

The gravelly blast of a shotgun grates through the darkness.

Hot pellets flash from a barrel below that wicked smile.

I'm hit directly in the chest. The forceful blast lifts me off my feet and sends me backward into the parking lot.

The punch of buckshot straight to the chest knocks the air from the lungs.

As I try to catch my breath, my vision blurs and I drift in and out of consciousness.

The deafening screams of a familiar woman nearby force my eyes back open.

I hone in on the woman's face.

She's a friend of Natalie's.

A model friend.

One of Natalie's mentors.

Sasha is her name.

The head of a pit bull emerges from the darkness of the open doorway.

The dog's teeth are barred with strings of drool hanging from the corners of its mouth. Both of its eyes are big and black, as if the pupils themselves have their own tiny gaping mouths.

A hand grips the backside of the dog's red collar, as if it's holding onto a live weapon, ready to explode. The face, as well as the body of the owner concealed by shadows.

All of a sudden, the mysterious owner releases a taut grip from the collar, freeing the bloodthirsty pit bull.

The pit bull immediately charges at Sasha and leaps at her throat.

Sasha falls backward from the weight of the muscular dog, allowing the beast to bite her in the neck.

While Sasha thrashes around with her screams reduced to gargles of frothy blood pooling in her throat, the pit bull begins to chew at her face, tearing off mouthfuls of flesh.

In the opposite direction, I notice, as I pull my chin upward and dig it into my chest and look past my two feet, two men are standing next to the van. One of the men is helping the other one suit up with protective gear, mostly around the vulnerable areas of his body—neck, groin, thighs, armpits.

I focus on the man's face and recognize him as well.

Philippe, I think.

Or, Mateo?

I forget his name, but I have met him once before in another life.

As soon as the gear is secured onto his body, he attempts to lure the pit bull away from Sasha, whose body remains motionless on the ground. The pit bull charges at him, first leaping up at his chest. He uses his arm as a shield. The pit bull's bites his forearm and latches onto it with its sawtoothed mouth, which is locked in a death grip. The pit bull violently shakes his arm back and forth as if the man's arm is one of those rope toys. The gear on his body makes his movements slower. His arm slackens, wiggling back and forth like a wet noodle. The pit bull clamps down harder, his canines piercing the suit and then digging into his flesh. The pit bull releases its death grip and backs away.

Before he can return to a defensive position, the pit bull attacks him yet again, but this time it charges straight toward his groin.

The pit bull chomps down, its canines chewing through the material of the gear. The pit bull yanks its head backwards and suddenly rips off the man's genitals as if it's ripping off a chunk of hard and fibrous gristle from a tough piece of meat. The pit bull eats them whole. The blood is everywhere, all over the dog's mandible and face, as well as streaming from the man's groin region.

My vision starts to blur again; and before I can cling onto the images before me, I black out.

I hear a voice to my left: "*You awake, Buddy?*"

I crack open my eyes and find myself back at the beginning. Back in Loganson.

Back in a memory—or a dream?

My chest is wrapped with bandage. The gauze covering the gunshot wound is spotted with a damp circle of fresh blood.

"I need to change those bandages soon," says the voice.

I follow the voice to Levi's face.

"Easy there, cowboy," he says, as I attempt to sit upright.

The pain, as heavy as a twenty-pound dumbbell, shoots through my chest and races throughout my entire body.

"You need to rest," Levi says and touches me on the shoulder.

I move my eyes to his hand and never move them until Levi eventually releases his hand.

"Still defensive," he says. "I don't blame you. I would, all things considered. . . "

"Where's the other guy?"

Levi pauses and forces a thin smile on his face, as if he's holding back words.

"You must mean André?"

"Yeah. Him."

"He'd hate me for using that name."

"Interesting fellow."

"*He's*—how'd you say—complicated," says Levi.

"I see. So, are you two. . . "

"Ancient history," Levi says.

"*What's your story?*"

With his mouth closed, he makes an attempt at a laugh.

"I mean, like, what do you do?"

"Well, I do a lot of things."

"Job?"

Levi smiles.

"Veterinarian's assistant."

"I assume this is all new to you."

"What? Treating humans?"

"Yeah."

"At one point in my life, I wanted to be a nurse."

"Why didn't you?"

"Humans tend to bite."

"Opposed to animals?"

"They can bite, but not nearly as much as humans."

Once more, I attempt to sit upright. I push through the pain and finally managed to sit up on the bed. I rest my back against the headboard and peek outside the crack of the window.

"Storm finally passed," says Levi, as he helps open the blinds for me after I attempt to reach for the hanging tassel. "Fortunately, we dodged one heck of a bullet. . . " He acknowledges my injuries, ". . . Sorry. You know what I mean. Anyway, we were spared from most of the flooding. Can't say the same about most of the surrounding area outside Loganson—"

"How long have I been out?"

"*Three days*," he says, the words sounding as if they belong somewhere else. Or, *was it three hours?* "River receded yesterday. So. . . " Levi says, as he crosses both arms over his chest, ". . . while we're on the subjects of bullets, you gonna tell me how you wound up with one in your chest? And do I need to be scared?"

"Why would you be scared?"

"I dunno," he says. "You tell me—"

"You're safe."

I manage to shift my body to the edge of the bed.

"Mind giving me a hand?"

I hold out my hand.

"I don't think that's a good idea. There's a possibility that you might reopen the wound."

I don't move my hand an inch.

"Fine," he says, annoyed. "Don't say I didn't warn you."

Together, we walk outside the ranch-style house.

Debris from the recent storm is still scattered along the street, as well as the other lawns.

"What a mess."

"Well, like I said, we got it good compared to others."

"Hate to see bad."

Farther down the street several uprooted trees are lying across the street, preventing any cars from passing.

Levi walks me to the river, which is not even a quarter of a mile from the house.

When we arrive at a bridge above the river, Levi asks again, "So you gonna tell me who shot you?"

"Doesn't matter."

"Never heard a peep on the news about the shooting. Weird, huh?"

"I assume you didn't hear anything because they didn't want you to hear anything."

"What exactly do you do for a living, Mr. Lamb?"

"Drop the mister crap. . . it's Josh. . . "

I take a moment to soak in the scenery, the raging river below, and the glassy blue skies.

"I sell shoes, at least I did in another life."

"You're a shoe salesman?"

"You look surprised."

"Is that like a cover or something—"

"It's only part time."

"Any plans besides working as a shoe salesman?"

"I was saving up money to buy a new car, but. . . "

"Yeah?"

"But things sort of changed."

"Changed how?"

"Does the name Maron Orwell mean anything to you?"

"Orwell?" Levi says with his face slack. He reiterates, "*The* Maron Orwell, the son of Baron Orwell?"

I nod my head.

Levi asks me, "How'n the hell you'd get involved with one of the most powerful men on the planet?"

"Let's just say: *Unusual* circumstances which led me to here."

"And what's here? Of all places, Loganson?"

"Maron wanted me to do a job for him."

"What kind of job?"

I make eye contact with Levi.

More than likely, the next words out of my mouth will put Levi's life in jeopardy.

No loose ends, I tell myself.

"He wanted me to kill a man named Harvey Crum—"

"Why does that name ring a bell?"

"Crum's company AëR was interfering with Maron's work— surveillance—mostly drones and whatnot. Ring a bell?"

"The name sounds familiar," Levi says with drifting, thinking eyes.

"I suppose Maron figured that Crum, who used to be close to Maron's father, Baron, knew that he was going to be a problem. So Maron sent the one person who Crum would least expect: *Me*."

Levi's face turns ghostly pale.

His eyes tell me that he should stop asking questions.

Curiosity is one seductive bitch.

"Why you?"

"The Orwells were working on a secret project: an end-all cure to finally beat cancer or any disease for that matter. It was going to be the next breakthrough in evolution. While researchers were developing this so-called 'all-in-one cure,' their plan backfired. Somehow, I was caught in their biological crossfire and infected by the entity, which they were experimenting on—"

"Entity?"

"*Frankie. Her name is Frankie.*"

"Her?" The confusion spreads through his face like creased paper. "A person?"

"Collateral damage created by Man's own arrogant attempt to dominant others by flexing its military might."

"What is that supposed to mean?" asks Levi.

"She is the end. . . and the beginning. . . "

"The beginning of what exactly?"

I walk away from the bridge, as though I'm leaving the past memory—or dream—and traveling into part of another one, an altered one where the present has fully caught up with me.

Levi follows me down an embankment. I stop at the edge of the river and stare down at my wavy reflection in the water.

"For the longest time, I've been running away from a monster. Now, it's time for me to face it."

"We all have monsters," Levi says. "Some of us call 'em demons or skeletons—"

"I'm afraid this isn't that kind of monster. This is a kind of monster that seeps its way into your soul and corrodes everything it touches. Overtime, I allowed this monster to wear me down until there was hardly anything left to salvage. I let this monster use its scare tactics on me. And for a while, they worked."

More concerned, Levi asks, "What are you talking about, Josh?"

"*The greatest trick a Doomsayer could ever pull was to convince the public that the world was going to end* and that his so-called 'act' wasn't a grift, but rather a *prophetical message from a higher power who had blessed him with an individualistic knowledge that couldn't be obtained by others, only himself.* Now, imagine millions of these Doomsayers, each one trying to one-up one another in order to trick the algorithm that he or she was someone of influence. Now, that'd be the ultimate crime, wouldn't it? Taking a person's *hope* for a brighter tomorrow and tossing it into a fucking blender."

All of a sudden, I sense its presence closing in on me.

I can hear their brakes *squeaking*.

They step out of their vehicles and close their doors behind them.

Not Orwell's men.

Millions of them, *copycats*, all rolled up into one collective being, approach me, ready to use certain words or expressions to infiltrate my mind and send me down a pathway of despair.

Over my shoulder, I witness a bulky, multi-armed creature in the reflection of the water.

The shadowy figure storms over me.

I suddenly wake and pull myself from the images, not memories but something close to a memory.

One side of my face is lying against gravel, which presses against my cheekbones.

I'm back at the hotel.

The beast looms over me, its bloody, drooling mouth inches away from my face.

At any moment, it can peel away my skin no different than skin on a baked chicken breast.

As I brace for its deathly bite, the beast makes a moaning sound and leans closer to me.

All of a sudden, I feel its warm tongue lick the side of his face.

The beast licks my chin and cheek area and leaves behind streaks of blood and drool before it darts away.

As the beast vanishes into the woods, I manage to sit upright. I shake off the creeping dizzy spell by concentrating on one particular object: The tiny bead from the buckshot in the center of my palm. My chest is riddled with more of these beads and even the slightest movement causes the beads to dig further into the flesh and tissue, like tiny blades stabbing me.

Once I stand to my feet, the sight of that dead baby lying on the ground reignites that anger inside me, like hot coals burning underneath my skin. First, a sharp flicker and then a heat wave of anger push past the pain, making it feel irrelevant, yesterday's news. I don't want to look at it, can't look at it, but it reminds me of the innocence, which was brutally ripped from me. Once I've acquired that horrific image, I use it to push me forward.

I make it to the doorway; and before entering, I tell myself that, if this is my final level, then there must be a Final Boss.

With the showdown looming, I step past the doorway and brave the darkness.

As my eyes adjust to the dim lighting, I come across a staircase leading up to a second floor. I walk up the staircase and make it to the first hotel room on the right.

The door is open.

I step inside, as though I'm being lured into a trap.

First, I hear a person *sniffling* from somewhere inside a living room, but I can't see a damn thing for it's too dark to make sense of my surroundings.

I follow the noise to the corner of the room where a trembling Natalie is sitting in a fetal-like position against the wall.

I'm reliving the scene over again in my mind.

Just minutes ago, I argued with Natalie.

The argument was about me and my lack of desire to be with her.

She wanted to break up with me. She does break up with me.

She said that I've been distant lately, that I've lost interest in her.

And it's true.

She's right about everything.

I did lose interest in her.

I stormed out of the hotel and left and I never turned back.

It's not until I hear a racket coming from the bedroom that I realize that we're not alone.

Natalie isn't frightened of me, but rather the presence in the other room.

I stop in the kitchen and grab a butcher's knife from the holder.

As I make my way toward the bedroom, I witness only part of the dark figure pacing around a window, which is opened.

That horrific image returns from the sight of the open window.

The anger is like gasoline coursing through my veins.

I reach the bedroom doorway where I find what appears to be a shapeshifting creature standing behind the bed. In the darkness, its shadowy face constantly transforms and contorts, changing shape and size, only to reform. The face shifts from man to woman, almost seamlessly, as if its skin is made of a thick liquid, which stirs from one gender to another, then hardens like mold, then melts again, only to harden yet again into a darker or lighter tone.

"You. . . *you* took everything from me. . . "

The shapeshifter smirks a thousand smirks before it turns its back on me.

The rush of anger flows through my body.

"Don't turn your back on me!"

Despite the weapon in my hand, I'll never be able to defeat the shapeshifter for its too strong and powerful in numbers.

I brave the shapeshifter once more and shout out at it.

Finally, as though impressed by my tenacity, as well as my willingness to face it, the shapeshifter rotates back around and squares itself to me.

I look the shapeshifter directly in the eyes and not once do I blink or bat an eyelash.

For fifteen seconds, I stare down the massive shapeshifting creature.

In my mind, I count each second.

And each one lasts for what feels like an eternity.

BOTH my hands are curled into fists.

I'm ready to fight.

When I crack open my eyes and shake off what feels like a nightmare, my grip loosens and my fingers finally uncurl.

The side of my face is pressed against soft, damp weeds.

I pull my face from the ground and find myself in a ditch alongside a desolate road next to a gutted, abandoned industrial park. All that's left of the historical park are its chipped and perforated bones, which have become a gaudy canvas for the artistic youth to express themselves.

I stand to my feet and once more, look down at my hands and all ten of my fingers, each and every one still intact. I turn my eyes toward the road rash along the underside of my forearms.

As I survey my surroundings, I come across fresh tire tracks where a vehicle skidded away.

Is it finally over?

Or, is this something else?

And if it is something else, why does it feel so strange, like a hangover without the sickness?

Next, I check my body for any injuries. Except for scrapes along my arms, I only find one: My head. I carefully run my hand over the side of my head where I'm missing a section of hair, which has been shaved. More carefully, I touch the serpentine-like incision along the bare spot. I map out each detail of the stitch job.

The panic slides over me like a melting ice cube. I come across a broken piece of glass from a side view mirror on an abandoned car and inspect the side of my head where the neural implant was inserted into my brain. The stitches appear recent, perhaps days old.

Was the implant removed?

Or, is it still there, like a *splinter* inside my brain?

The only way to find out is to remove the stitches.

Based on the stagnant surroundings, as well as my current condition, this isn't the right place or the right time to conduct a half-ass surgery.

While tracking the sun, I hear those words, "*West is Death*," inside my head.

Based on the position of the sun—if I had to guess, it was probably around eight o'clock in the morning, give or take—I decide to walk toward the direction of the sun.

During my travels alongside the road, I attempt to piece together the last images in my head before I woke: I can't remember much about the dream—or was it still part of Day 10, the last day of my Final Phase, I'm not sure—but I do remember the graphic images before they vanished into the fog of my thoughts. I recognize the familiar man whose manhood was devoured by that beast. His name was Philippe. How can I forget his name? Natalie and I met him during our travels in Rome. He was nice to Natalie—perhaps too nice—which was why I felt so jealous. I remember we had a heated argument later that night, all of it spawned by my jealousy toward Philippe. I should've confronted Philippe but didn't want to make a scene in front of Natalie. Not too long after we both returned home, I ended my relationship with Natalie. Unlike what the images in my head suggested, I was the one who broke it off with Natalie, *not* her, but she'd argued that the feeling was mutual.

After walking for a couple of miles, I return to Hephaestus City, which is left in utter ruins, except for the massive skyscrapers that tower over the filth.

Along the upper façade of one particular skyscraper is a familiar name:

ORWELL

The helicopter ride, I recall.

Then the building, previously the headquarters for a company known as the Onion Group, I remember, was the same building that I entered after I signed my name on the dotted line of my contract. *"My own death warrant."*

But *what if* I wasn't duped by that snake oil salesman and my case went to trial?

I ward off the notion of jail and stare at the name high above. *"Orwell."*

Maron Orwell.

A man who knows a thing or two about upgrades.

I can't help but wonder if he upgraded his own ambitions.

Or, in this case, downgraded.

If my suspicions are true about Orwell and how he used his drone surveillance and applied it to Huey's VR technology, then I suppose there are many others like me.

Either imprisoned or liberated.

Walking around with stitch jobs on their heads.

In the span of an hour, I witness several shootouts among the residents who appear enhanced by augmentation. One person is shot only feet away from me. I watch him take his final breaths before he succumbs to his injuries. Other crimes include hack jobs, violent assaults with the kind of hardware that I've never seen or heard of before, carjackings via phones, a flash mob, robbers using deep fake technology like modern day surgical masks to disguise their identities, and many other crimes that force me to seek cover.

One detail catches my eye while a young man is performing an impromptu surgery in an alleyway behind a looted convenient store. As he extracts a newly printed kidney from the back of a rival, I look closer at the *blueberry* decal on the back right shoulder of his leather jacket. All of a sudden, I'm struck with a sinking feeling. A punch in the gut. I need to get the hell outta here, I tell myself. Immediately.

Somehow, I locate a train station along the outskirts of the city, which, surprisingly, is still operable, despite the violence that recently regurgitated me like a bone.

With no money to purchase a train ticket, I end up turning back around and once more, braving Hephaestus where I come across an open cash register inside a convenient store that was recently looted. I yank out the empty drawer. My hands, especially my fingers, fumble around the drawer, as though I haven't used them in decades and now, I'm relearning how to use them once more. Everybody knows they keep the big bills underneath the tray. Yet, when I *finally* pull off the tray, jackpot.

Amateurs, I tell myself.

I walk back to the train station and use the money to clumsily buy a ticket, as well as a black hat with the logo "*MW*" from the gift shop.

With the stitches covered up, I board the train.

My next stop: "Spartacus."

After riding the train across the country, I'm finally back in Spartacus.

On a whim, I check out the apartment where I was staying while inside the Program. I can't remember much about the Program, only the rough location of the apartment complex.

When I arrive at what I think is the location, the details return but only in waves. I did stay here, in this precise location, if only for a while. For *ten days*, I remember.

The only catch: There is no apartment complex, only a section of barren land and a sign that reads, "NO TRESPASSING."

Was it torn down?

Bits and pieces of memory are still there, randomly flaring up.

At times, distant and fragmented while other times, incredibly detailed and vivid but only in a glimpse: There was a *man*. I remember *his face. His name was Rebus*.

I focus more on that name, *Rebus*, and continue to make my way through Spartacus.

The signs are everywhere I turn, all kinds of signs, like the day I broke up with Natalie, like the day my father died. Was I looking for these particular signs to help make sense of a difficult time in my life? Or, was there a higher power casting out these signs, as if it was making an attempt to warn me of the hardships that awaited me? With Natalie, all of the signs were focused on the "breakup," each and every sign connected, both literally, as well as symbolically, and involved things breaking. The most obvious one: A waitress dropping a glass inside a café while I stepped away for a moment to grab a cup of coffee before I met with Natalie. Was it a sign? Or, was it merely a coincidence? Or, was I simply looking everywhere for signs? And what did a glass have to do with our breakup? Maybe nothing. But maybe everything. At times, whenever I was about to experience a tragic event in my life, it felt as if my mind was an open doorway. The door was gone, hinges removed, and all that remained was a doorframe, which allowed the universe to course through me.

The first sign that I come across is exactly that, a sign in the shape of a massive billboard on the side of the highway with the words "2 *Days Left* Until The Grand Opening!" The sign is for a new entertainment center, of all things, an escape room. Below the sign along the bottom left-hand corner is a code: "**XP-4143**."

The next sign outside a bookstore: A promo for Rickie Trace's new techno-thriller *Second to Last.*

I walk past a restaurant called "*Trolley's.*"

The logo on the façade is a picture of two brothers, The Trolley's, pushing a handcar made of a submarine sandwich on wheels.

Then, the next is a poster for the new Gladiators playoff game: The final battle to the end in the "*Final Finals!*" Two of the star players, first one wearing jersey number "15" and the other "1," are standing side-by-side, thunder spike in hand.

Another sign: "*One more to go!*"

One more what?

One more day?

One more hour?

One more minute?

One more second?

The signs are posted all around me, as though toying with me.

Another one grabs my eye: A movie poster for Dalivia Plaut's serial killer horror flick, *Serpiente.* On the poster is a humanoid train, fleshy and dark, traveling through a dark hellscape.

Finally, as the memory slowly starts to return, I decide to stop by Lakeview. The building appears similar; however, the sign no longer reads Lakeview, but rather The Golden Swans. When I make it to the front entranceway, there is plywood covering the windows and main entrance. The sign reads, "Closed."

A local on a bicycle pulls up behind me.

I turn and face him.

"What the hell happened here?"

With a cynical tone, the local says, "What always happens when you neglect the very thing you create."

The expression on my face alone warrants a further response.

"Flood," he says and trails off, "from what I heard. Broken water main, something like that. I heard there was so much water that it was pouring out from the doorways and windows. . . " he points at the parking lot, ". . . and onto the street."

"No shit."

"I shit you not."

As he squares his body toward me, I notice a tattoo on both of his wrists. Each one is a tattoo of a dotted line wrapping his wrists with a scissor icon along several dots.

The sight of the tattoos immediately reminds me of a staffer, who worked as a nurse at Lakeview. He was much older, but he had a similar—if not—the same tattoo as the young man before me.

He says, "Pretty wild, huh?"

"Yeah. Wild."

The young man rides away on his bike.

I find an opening in the corner of the loose plywood, peel it back, and barely sneak into the abandoned facility without cutting myself on the serrated metal frame. Immediately, a musty odor hits me in the face. The entire floor is destroyed, swelled, buckled, and chewed up. I notice the debris everywhere, all ruined and wrinkled from being waterlogged.

As I make my way through the lobby, I spot a glimmering light among debris on the floor of a narrow hallway.

I walk past an insect-infested coffee station behind a reception desk where one corner of the granite countertop has been chipped off.

An image of violence flickers through my mind.

I'm lying in Mime's bed, a pocket pistol aimed at the dark figure approaching the bedroom. Mime ducks for cover behind me, her left hand claws into my ribcage. The silhouette appears at the doorway. Her silhouette. I pull back on that sweaty trigger.

I focus my attention on the glittery object.

The sunlight pours through the gaping hole in the ceiling and hits an object on the floor, randomly casting bursts of light.

Mindful of each step I take over the ruined debris, I arrive at the shiny object, which is surrounded by broken pieces of drywall.

With the air escaping my lungs, I touch my chest but find no scar.

As soon as I reach down to pick it up, I hear a noise behind me.

At the end of another hallway to my right, the exit door suddenly opens.

I witness a strange person scurry from the doorway.

"Pep?"

I rush back outside and chase after the trespasser.

The door swings close behind me.

I attempt to catch the door before it closes but nearly jam my fingers.

The door is locked.

When I turn back around, I can't find the trespasser anywhere in sight.

More focused on tracking down the person, I decide to leave the facility and make my way back to the main road where I walk past yet another sign next to a tree, which has been split down the middle after being struck by lightning. Parts of the trunk have exploded. One half of the trunk is black and charred.

Next to the partly overturned tree the sign reads, "*O'Brien's Auto Repair.*"

That name, O'Brien, immediately jars loose a memory.

"*Now, it's time for you to move on with your life.*"

Suddenly, I move my eyes to my chest and once more, pull the collar of my shirt downward and search for the scar from a gunshot wound but can't find one.

For the remainder of the day, I explore the rest of Spartacus, which, except for several newer developments, hasn't changed much since the last time I was here. Along my travels, I'm drawn to more of those signs, from advertisements, which share a common theme of counting down to a big event, to strange encounters with locals, who look eerily familiar, as if I've seen them before in another life. I have to remind myself that it's just my mind playing tricks on me.

5. THE OCTOPUS

"THE FUGGY FOUR," AS LONDON VERBALLY BRANDED HER NEW PROVI-
sional B-List group of awesome besties before throwing back
yet another round of gagging Hämmerhead shots at the neon-
soaked, psychedelic-themed, Nineties-esque Bubble where a
compilation of Sponge Cakes albums, including their very
first demo when they were called Josey "Rockberry" Rose &
The Talisman of The Purple Urinals, was constantly played
on repeat throughout the damp night.

The Four left the Bubble bar and stumbled their way to a
hipster-like "from-farm-to-street" taco stand, Shock Taco.

Journey, the devoted assistant for the spiky-haired auteur
Boris Mour, who was used to waiting in long lines whenever
she was "on the clock," displayed her annoyance with a faint
rolling of her eyes accompanied by a *whooping* police siren of a
sigh. Although London and Gee-Gee couldn't make out a
single word from her protest, Caitlin, the youngest member of
Fuggy Four, detected a general complaint about the current
state of service, as well as employment, and somewhere
within those watered-down grumbles about the stay-at-home
"*influencer*"-types, who were capitalizing on one helluva wicked
algorithm that would pull down all of humanity into the
depths of despair and in return, funded by hack social media
companies and their sponsors whose only glory came in the
impulsive shape of a carved-out hole in a dank bathroom
stall, influencing "*a society to return to self-sufficient hunter-gatherer-
like days*" where, soon, "we'd have to kill, pluck, and cook our

own chickens or you might *look at it from a more strategic and sinister plan conjured by elites*—elites spelled in lower case even though these gluttonous shape-shifting assmouths act as if they're deserving of upper case when, in Malldough's Theory, they're undeserving of such case and positioned on the same level as the malicious platforms that they artificially support—*to make everybody dependent on a centralized governmental entity which provides goods and services.*"

"Whoa!" said London and emphasized the *n-e-y* in "Easy, Never-Bend-The-Knee Journey."

Despite slow service, the line was moving or at least, appeared to be moving at a penguin-shuffling pace.

"Thee Fugally Four shall *not* wait in thee lines," Caitlin Acker animatedly blurted out, as if she was reciting lines from Shakespeare for everybody in a hundred yard radius to hear.

The other three, including a rambling Journey, as well as London, who worked in hair and makeup, and then Gee-Gee, wardrobe, all laughed at Caitlin's drunken antics.

"*Fugally?*" said Gee-Gee. "It's Fuggy. Get it right, PA—"

"Hey," London said in Caitlin's defense. "Watch it, G. She has a name."

"I'm just teasing, gurl."

Caitlin, who had grown accustomed to the title while on set of the latest production for the film *Crosscut*—working title—which recently wrapped three hours ago after a month and a half of shooting on both location, as well as several sound stages, including a water tank at Gold Reel Studios, never let the bitch-in-wardrobe's sarcasm dampen her spirits. Instead, while running off the fuel of liquid courage, she focused a comeback on Gee-Gee's nightly attire: "Says ole Blackbeard who works in war-*de*-robe," Caitlin said from one side of her mouth in her worst squinty-eyed pirate impersonation. "*E'rrr* you going to play a game of *black* jack at thee ole tavern after you eat your meat wraps? Cuz if you *e'rrr* I'd like to show you a trick I can do with me peg leg! *E'rrr. . .* "

More laughter erupted from the three, including Gee-Gee, wide-eyed and impressed, as she stared at Caitlin, whose comment about the puffy pirate shirt landed like an uppercut.

"Ouch," Gee-Gee said superficially. "That stung."

"Wait to you feel me peg leg," said Caitlin, still using the throaty pirate voice.

The joke didn't nearly pack a punch.

Still tipsy from Hämmerhead, London was the only one of the Fuggy Four who found Caitlin's impersonation amusing.

With a flat tone, Journey uttered under her breath, "You two should get a room."

Gee-Gee leaned over toward Caitlin and bumped shoulders with her.

"Sorry, friendo," she said, stressing the "dough" in *friendo*. "Not available."

"That's too bad," Caitlin said with a lustful gaze. "Guess I'll have to settle for carnitas."

Stunned by Caitlin's drunken humor, Gee-Gee said more carefully, "I'm gonna have to keep an eye on you."

After the teasing, Caitlin made an attempt to skip the line but was immediately met by a vocal majority. Caitlin brushed off the attempt as a mere *"Gotcha!"* moment, which didn't sit quite well with the rest of The Fuggy Four, who were waiting in the back of the line.

Eventually, they placed their orders and found an open picnic table where they waited until their "group" was called. London suggested that, after the tacos, they should hit up the trendy bar Hops & Scotch, most commonly known by deodorant-free locals as "Hopscotch," for more drinks.

Journey and Gee-Gee were definitely "down to clown" and also, enthusiastic about capping off the festive night at a place where they could work off the many carbs that they were about to ingest. Caitlin, on the contrary, wasn't at all thrilled about London's suggestion and her lack of enthusiasm was written all over her deadpan expression, which prompted Gee-Gee to chime in on Caitlin's demeanor.

With a smirk melting from her face, she asked, "What's wrong, PA?"

London chirped, "Gee-Gee!"

"*Caitlin*," Gee-Gee reiterated, "was it something I said?"

"No," Caitlin said with deflation. "I think I might call it a night after we eat—"

"What?" said London. "Why? We're having so much fun. . . *e'rrrn't* we?"

Her pirate impersonation sounded like a gremlin and put to rest any other attempts at recapturing the pirate flare.

"Yeah, it's just. . . " Caitlin said, as she searched for an excuse to end the night much earlier than expected but came up empty, ". . . I don't care much for Hopscotch."

"Really? I thought that was your go-to spot? I mean. . . " Journey buzzed from across the table, ". . . you talkz aboutz it allz the timez. Why the one-eighty, Lady?"

"You're trying to dodge a stalker, aren't you?"

"No," Caitlin said abruptly, "well, I mean—"

"She is," shouted Gee-Gee, who turned her aim at Caitlin. "You skank!"

Defeated, Caitlin lowered her head in a quiet, shrinking manner as if the air in her lungs was sucked out, her spirits squeezed and deflated, which caused the three Fuggies to pay closer attention. Methodically, based on the sweet chin music that Caitlin, the night's "wild card," had been playing ever since the group stormed their rowdy-ass way from London's apartment, which was located within walking distance of the art district and the most ideal spot to pre-game, she'd have an unfiltered crack, a hashtag-worthy clap-back for Gee-Gee.

Concerned, London leaned closer to Caitlin and asked, "What's wrong, Cat?"

"It's weird. . . " she said, struggling to lift her head, ". . . I. . . ya'll probably think I'm crazy for mentioning it."

"Out with it already!"

"Remember the weekend when ya'll went to Lake Holden during—what was it? The first or second week of shooting?"

"Second week," Gee-Gee said confidently. "Too bad you didn't tag along. You missed out on all the fun. London found a rat snake in her sleeping bag—"

"Can you let her finish please?"

Gee-Gee eased back, listened.

"Well," Caitlin said, "forget about it. . . " she waved off the story, ". . . it's nothing."

"No, Caitlin," London said sincerely. "Tell us. We promise we won't tell anyone."

She nodded at the other three, especially Gee-Gee.

"Not a peep," Gee-Gee said, as she twisted the invisible key next to her lips and with her hands, motioned chucking the key across the parking lot, that ghost of key bouncing and skipping into a sewer drain, into shitty water, swirling round and round into a lost realm until landing in a great Nothing where keys had clipped wings.

Relieved and more confident, Caitlin said, "That weekend, a friend of mine whom I went to college with—Jessie was her name—she was in town and she asked me if I'd like to meet up for a drink." She shrugged her shoulders, no big deal. "So I decided to met her at Hopscotch. Also, it was the night after we filmed that *spicy* scene earlier that same day."

"Spicy is one way of putting it," Gee-Gee said from the corner of her mouth.

"Anyway," Caitlin said and made a soft jab at Gee-Gee, "it was fair to say I was feeling a bit *skanky*."

"Skanky, huh? Not slutty?"

"Nope," Caitlin said shortly, her letter p pronounced like a spit of air. "One-hundred percent unadulterated skanky. So. . . " she sighed, causing Wardrobe to back off and allow her to finish her train of thought, ". . . Jessie and I were at Hopscotch when, after my second WIPA, I saw this guy from across the bar, standing alone, deeply disturbed but way confident. We made eye contact several times." Caitlin fell into a momentary trance, as she tried to recall his features. While drifting deeper into thought, Caitlin saw herself mindlessly scrolling through a news article on her phone. For the life of her, she couldn't remember the article, what it was about, who was in it, but she saw a distorted face in the article, recognizable yet unrecognizable. "He's tall," she said vaguely, as she scraped and clawed through gummy thoughts, "maybe just shy over six feet. He's gotta long face, high cheeks. . . " she listed, as if she was compiling a whole bunch of faces and assembling them all together, like a glittery collage posted on the bedroom wall of a sappy, starry-eyed twit of a tween, ". . . but handsome in a strange European kind of way, like a reincarnation of Dean Geraldo—"

"Who's Dean Gerald?" asked Gee-Gee.

"Geraldo."

"The actor from *No Leaf Left To Turn*."

"Never heard of it."

"Serious? It won like an Oscar for Best Picture back in the Seventies."

London said shortly, "Tory Cline absolutely killed in it."

Caitlin shot a bloodshot-eyed glare at London, who, in return, held up her hands, allowing Caitlin to finish her story.

"So," said Caitlin, "we were definitely connecting with one another, and he's got these blue eyes, like Geraldo, that seem like they're glowing. I was hesitant about talking to him."

London asked, "Why?"

"He looked weird."

"Thought you said he was handsome?"

"He was. . . but he. . . there was something strange about him. . . like he was super nervous, like he was about to jump out of his skin."

"But confident?"

"Yes—I mean—I dunno."

"Could've been bloomin'?"

"Blooming?"

"You know, dandruff diving? Sweetening the snout?"

"He wasn't a junkie."

"So, what'd you do?"

"So," Caitlin repeated, sighed, "I cast my lure—"

"*Order for The. . . Fuggy Four!*" a man on an intercom says in the background.

"That's us," said London.

Journey interrupted, "I'll get it."

"You sure?"

"Yeah," she said casually. "Just fill me in with the details later."

She stood up and sashayed to the pick-up window.

"Should I wait for her to return?" asked Caitlin.

"No," London said and waved her hand. "Finish."

"Where was I?"

"You and Jessie at Hopscotch. Second drink in. You eye-fuckin' a hornball Dean Geraldo look-alike from across the bar."

"Things got crazy-weird after that," Caitlin said unsteadily. "He walked over and talked to us. His name was Oswald, I think, no, Osprey. . . Wait. . . Oswald. . . "

"You don't know even his name?"

"Hold up a sec," Gee-Gee interrupted. "You're not talking about Osprey-*Osprey*? Not really a name you hear a lot—"

"No," Caitlin said, as an image of a warped face flashed in her mind. His face, she thought, but *not* his face. She cleared her throat and said, "Not the same one, of course."

London nudged Gee-Gee on the arm, allowing a blushing Caitlin to finish.

"He buys us a drink and after we finish our drink, Jessie calls it a night. I don't remember a thing after Jessie leaves. Only fragments."

"Shit, Cat, you got roofie'd—"

"No," Caitlin said suddenly. "I mean, we only had one more drink and I paid for mine."

"How about when he bought you a drink?" asked Gee-Gee.

"I specifically watched the bartender make it and afterwards, he handed it directly to me."

"Did you ever leave him alone with your drink?"

Caitlin rolled her eyes at London.

"Come on," she said. "You think I'm that dumb?"

"No," said London. "It's just—"

"How much did you drink?"

Caitlin shrugged.

"My limit, I guess," she said. "I wasn't shitfaced, if that's what you're asking me?"

"So, what did you—"

"Sorry it took so long," Journey said, as she returned with a tray of five yellow baskets, four with an order of tacos and one with a stack of nachos, which was piled high and dripping with a volcano of melted cheese. "That dude behind us accidentally took our order. How do you mistake Fuggy Four with, of all names, *Bryan*?" she said the name "Bryan" sarcastically, as if it was an archaic thing, dare she'd say, foreign.

Neither London nor Gee-Gee caught a word that Journey said.

Again, Gee-Gee asked Caitlin, "Did you hook up with him or not?"

"I dunno," Caitlin said, ignoring the basket of tacos. "It felt like a strange dream that's hard to explain. I ended up going back to his place. I don't remember many details about his house. I remember it was really clean, like brand new, like a house used as a model home. Like spotless. Like you could eat off the floor, if you wanted to. There weren't any picture frames hanging on the walls. Not one photograph throughout the entire house. I didn't think anything of it, at least not at first, I didn't. I remember we had sex in the dark, sloppy sex, like he was playing *Headbanger's Baller's*, no rhythm whatsoever, a full-on sprint toward the finishing line—"

"Thought you said you didn't have sex."

"We did, but we didn't. I mean, he didn't even finish—"

"I hate to admit it to you, PA, but once his cock touches your vadge, that's sex."

Caitlin said over Gee-Gee, "I do remember, very specifically, a light from the hallway shining into the bedroom, and I could still see his face and those sweaty blue eyes. He was on top. But then, all of a sudden. . . " Caitlin said slow and carefully, as she tried to recapture the moment while she was deep in a reflection, ". . . he *wasn't*." She turned to the other and said in side note, "If that makes any sense. I mean. . . what I'm trying to say: He was not the same person anymore. His face was different. I freaked out. His face started changing."

"What do you mean *changing*?" asked London.

"Like he was wearing different faces, like a mask or something."

"What'd I miss?" asked Journey.

The question went unanswered for both London and Gee-Gee were left utterly speechless by what they could only describe as Caitlin experiencing a hallucination.

"We stopped having sex," said Caitlin. "Like I said, he never, you know, finished. I turned on the lamp next to the bed. He rolled out of bed. He was talking about these '*voices*,' and how '*they would not shut up*.'"

"Please tell me you got your ass outta there," Gee-Gee said, aghast.

"I wanted to, but I felt bad in a way—bad for him. I could tell he was in excruciating pain. Next, I remember I started yelling at him. I dunno why. It's just something came over me and I got angry with him. Then I *think* he started to pound his head against the wall. So hard that he left behind dents. His forehead was, like, bleeding."

"You think?" said London.

Caitlin said, upset, "It felt like a dream. Then he grabbed a knife. No!" she corrected. "An envelope opener from the nightstand and then he started to stab himself in the ears."

"What?" Journey cried out. "That most definitely sounds like you were dreaming, Cat."

"Please tell me that this was the part where you Roadrunner your *bee*-hind outta there."

"I checked on him to make sure that he was okay, but he didn't want my help. So, then, I left. I think he might've had a mental breakdown maybe—"

"That's one way of putting it," said Gee-Gee, as she delved into her pollo tacos, which were getting cold.

"Yeah, but Caitlin, for real," London said seriously, "what proof do you that have you went home with this guy?"

Caitlin paused, her drunken eyes flooding with tears.

"I dunno," she said, teary-eyed.

London wrapped her arm around Caitlin's shoulder and consoled her and afterwards, slid the basket of carnitas closer to her.

"Here," she said motherly. "Eat. You'll feel better after you get some food in you."

Caitlin ate soggy tacos and strangely, started to feel much better.

3-2-24:

The first week of the shoot was a shitshow plagued by one fuck-up after another. After yesterday's mess while shooting one of the most vital scenes in the film, my confidence level has fallen six-feet-under, and I fear that nothing can save me now from an inevitable weekend of rewrites, which, by Monday morning, will be food for trashcans. Working alongside Boris has turned out to be more challenging than I originally predicted. The man is a complete sociopath with skin as thin as rice paper and his inability to handle any constructive criticism that I offer him has been put on full display after a week of hell. He runs a tight ship, too tight, if you ask me. Despite any animosity I feel toward Boris, I'll give him credit where it is due: His "NO PHONES ON SET" policy is a good model that, fingers-crossed, I hope future productions adopt...that is, if we still have jobs after enduring yet another spoiled-rotten generation who are making their A-plus effort to squeeze the money from the pockets of those who are trying to keep this once magical industry alive. It has become evident that Boris would die before revealing a single detail of the film before its release, and I can only imagine what heinous acts he'd commit if any actor or crewmember were to leak any footage from set. I reckon Boris has his own personal "Company Men" on speed dial.

While I'm on the subject, the scenes with The Company Men is the foundation, in essence, the glue that binds the entire story together and without them, the story has no footing whatsoever (Our next scenes with The Company Men aren't till the 6th and 7th week of the shoot and based on what we've already shot, those scenes don't look promising and knowing Boris, he might end up cutting out the scenes, as well as the scenes with the detectives trying to track down the mysterious killer of each host). No matter how much I stress the importance of The Company Men, Boris has very little interest in developing these two vital antagonists who are responsible for shaping the character arch of our protagonist. Instead, he'd rather portray them as these nameless, faceless "things" that take orders from a man of many resources who takes the form of a shadowy figure in a smoky room (For Boris, highlighting such a clichéd character, like Mr. Smoky, is his own poke at the cliché). He even scrapped the name "Braces," which, in my opinion, made for a very compelling name for a villain. He didn't like the second option either: "Stilts." A type of protagonist who had a higher vantage point over others. The type who saw everything from every angle. Not too close to the action but not too far away. The Sole Survivor who made damn sure that his shoelaces were always knotted and tied tight. Most importantly, he saw the big picture and in that picture was the enigmatic viral-being known as "The Entity."

As a screenwriter, I must swallow that awful pill of passing off what I created to someone who shares a completely different vision and force myself to realize that this is not my story. Not any-

more. Now, it's Boris Mour's story. And I'm a mere observer watching my own words being twisted into something that I can no longer call my own.

2

WHILE everyone on set, including the dozens of fully-nude background actors, waited anxiously for the *"Rolling"* cue, the second assistant cameraman held the film slate in front of Camera A.

The film slate read:

"CROSSCUT"
Roll **A018, B012, C009** Scene **32A** Take **15**
Director **Boris Mour**
Camera **Lionel Gauche**
Date **3/8/24** NIGHT **INT. MAT STR**

The players involved in the scene: A-list actress from the psychological thriller *The Manipulator*, Libby Foxe, who's playing the role for The Entity's fourth and most controversial victim, or as described in the script, *"Host #4,"* Everleigh Mince, who transmits the mysterious virus to a recently-separated home inspector, Osprey Gortana, played by the seasoned actor Kenneth "Net" LaMaine.

"Scene thirty-two," the second assistant cameraman articulated clearly for everyone to hear and opened the film slate to a sixty-degree angle. He said, "Take fifteen."

London made her last-second adjustments to Osprey by using a squirt bottle to spray a mist of water on his shoulders, as well as his lumbar and glutes, to demonstrate a man who was sweating bullets. Once she achieved the amount of moisture on his body, she hurried out of the scene.

As soon as the slate was closed, which made a reverberating *clapping* sound, the second assistant cameraman stepped out of the way.

The jittery assistant director, who was dressed as if he recently rolled out of bed, his hair as messy as a Yorkie, shouted out from behind the monitors, *"Roll cameras!"*

Finally, Director Boris Mour, who was seated in a director's chair next to the AD: "Action!"

Surrounded by fifty-seven background actors—all naked—Libby and Kenneth resumed their missionary position on a bare mattress, which was lit up by an overhead spotlight, whereas the surrounding areas outside the spotlight were dark and the dedicated fifty-seven extras, who were standing motionlessly around the mattress in a ritualistic-like circle, appeared like ghostly manikins in a dim, flickering candlelight.

Moments later after the assistant director's cue, Libby returned to her malevolent character, Everleigh, the flirty masseuse who was hiding a secret that would forever alter the life of the gullible sack of bones whom she picked up at a seedy dive bar, while Kenneth, who was wearing a sock over his dick, returned to his character, Osprey, the intoxicated home inspector.

The two began to have simulated sexual intercourse, a perspired Osprey on top of Everleigh, riding her, and then once Boris shouted out the cue, "*Now, The Entity transfers from Everleigh to Osprey!*" Everleigh suddenly rolled over on top of Osprey and switched positions.

Boris made sure to emphasize for the character, Everleigh: "*The pain of recently losing your friend is overwhelming! All the frustration, the rage, the hate, it all surfaces! The sex is the only thing to rid it away! He's deep inside you, driving out the hate! Your skin is now on fire. . .*"

Three different camera angles picked up the raw emotion pouring from Everleigh. Her neck muscles flexed tight like cords. Tears ran down the sides of her cheeks, as she angrily thrust her hips over Osprey. Her moans grew raspy and harsh, cries of both pain and pleasure.

All of a sudden, moments before the spectacle of her hateful climax, the overhead spotlight flickered and then exploded into a thousand pieces. Sparks flew everywhere! Tiny pieces of glass rained down on both of the actors' naked bodies.

Boris yelled out from behind the monitors, "*Cut!* What the fuck, you fucking fucks!"

The cameras stopped rolling.

The lightning department was equally as flustered as Boris, scrambling around the set, first making sure the actors were not injured (they weren't), and then trying to fix the electricity malfunction, double-checking, triple-checking cables.

Tension swelled over the set, as Boris removed his headphones and slammed them onto the floor.

As Boris and the lighting guy, Dwight, argued about the lighting, the assistant director corralled the covered extras and told them to "break for lunch" while the crew sorted out a lighting issue. Gee-Gee handed Libby and Kenneth a black robe to cover their bodies while their assistants ushered the actors back to their separate trailers. The assistant director, who was still scatterbrained by the recent scene, passed the covered extras to Caitlin, who wrangled several strays who wandered into restricted areas, and then escorted them to a cramped room away from Stage 3.

While the weary extras waited on the rest of the film crew, who received first dibs on lunch, which was catered by a highly-rated local food truck, Caitlin decided to hand off the reins to another PA and grab herself a hot chicken skewer, as well as a lamb's lettuce salad with mozzarella cheese, tomatoes, and black olives topped with a lemon vinaigrette from the buffet.

When it was their turn to be called, the extras were left with limited options at a crafty stand, which was supplied with snacks, including crackers and artificially flavored fruit bars, as well as beverages. The clear pecking order on full display, as a novice extra pointed out, the extras being pushed to the bottom rung; however, for many extras who enjoyed being on set, so much so to adjust their full-time schedules around a shoot, they didn't mind being treated as if they were second-class citizens.

During lunch, Caitlin, who was still feeling aroused by the latest scene despite it being simulated, read from a news article about the "real-life" Osprey Gortana on her phone. The article mentioned Mince's unusual death and how Gortana discovered her body in bed the morning after the two engaged in a one-night stand. Coroners were dumbfounded and had no explanation as to how Mince died. According to Gortana, before he fell asleep, she was, in his own words, "Fine," and didn't see anything out of the ordinary. The next morning, when he discovered Mince, she was dead, clearly, somehow her internal organs melted—"*liquefied*," was a term used by coroners—and were oozing from both eyes, nose, mouth, as well as ears, all of that gooey organ sludge pooling over the white bed sheets. Even till this day, Gortana maintained his innocence. Authorities never charged him with any crime. The bizarre event—or considering the trail of bodies which were connected to Mince's death, *events*—caught the cryptic eye of a filmmaker who delved into the realm of the phantasmagorical, an auteur who, before he could utter the word "*action*," was handed a script that he could not turn down.

Based on the timeline of recent events, Caitlin could only ask herself: "Too soon?"

Or, one could argue in fast-paced age of trying to stay relevant: Was soon not soon enough?

⬢

3-10-24:

One of the grips pulled me aside and referred to the scene as "The Fuck of the Century."

From the amounts of takes Boris shot before he was satisfied, the entire day sure as hell felt as if it lasted a century. The script supervisor, Marci, said it was around sixty-eight takes. Let's round it up and say seventy. I think by the thirty-something take everybody stopped counting. Boris may even hold some kind of Guinness Record for longest takes while shooting a film. Most directors, on average, use around seven to ten takes. Not Boris. He'd make a perfectionist look like a lazy hack.

During the eleventh hour before the start of production, Boris, being the kind of filmmaker who, not only liked giving shout outs in his films, but also taking a production-ready script and cutting out key scenes, or what he called, "the fat," changed the name of the restaurant from The Drunken Clam to The Fox Hole soon after Libby was brought on at the last minute following the abrupt departure of Pat Melonie, who dropped out of the role due to a scheduling conflict. Despite Boris's antics, again, I must give credit where it is due.

After Libby joined the cast, Boris deliberately hid Libby from her co-star Kenneth and during Scene 31B (INT. ~~THE DRUNKEN CLAM~~ THE FOX HOLE), moments after Libby (Eve) arranged a get-together with Kenneth (Oz) whom she met on a dating app, the two saw each other for the first time. This was part of the genius in Boris, wanting to capture, on camera, an authentic moment between two people who have never met in person. In the industry, they call it "capturing lightning in a bottle." At times, Boris, regardless of how many actors complain about his style, acts as if he comes from a different era of filmmaking where Greek Gods and Goddesses once ruled the world. To sum the scene up as best I could: Instant chemistry. Which brings me to the next two following scenes, the Mattress Store Scene and Everleigh's "Death" Scene, where significant changes were made. Boris and I couldn't be farther apart when it came to the flesh trade in movies. For me, personally, I'm not at all interested in writing about sex in a scene. If anything, it brings down a story and distracts from other areas of the script that may need further development. I was more focused on the events that transpired after Everleigh and Kenneth hooked up. Boris was the complete opposite. He wanted to highlight the Mattress Store Scene and focus more on the metaphorical side of it, with these Strangers "watching," as if it was his jab on modern day society, where people (or Strangers) are more interested in watching other people screw than actually screwing themselves, sort of like people living vicariously through other people, not only a jab at the porn industry, but also social media as well, with people "following" other people and being so invested in other people's lives except their very own. Below is an example of the script "BEFORE" Boris used his pen like a katana to edit out what I had already written and then "AFTER" he bled that script red with ink. The differences couldn't be more evident.

In the first script, the story is focused on The Entity and what physical effects it has on Everleigh's body. The Sex Scene is short, a brief moment to convey to the audience that the two are being intimate without, no pun intended, shoving it down your throat.

In the second "edited" script, it's the complete opposite and most of the story is focused around Everleigh and Osprey having sex.

FULL STOP

INT. EVERLEIGH'S BEDROOM - NIGHT

We see QUICK SHOTS of Everleigh and Osprey having sex
on a messy bed, clothes strewed about the room, as well
as the furniture. While embracing Osprey in her arms,
Everleigh's head jolts backward, her wide eyes rolling
over white. The lamp on the nightstand flickers, as
Everleigh opens her mouth in a gaping yawn.

We CUT to moments after sex, with Everleigh and Osprey
resting in bed, a wash of pale moonlight soaking over
their bodies. Everleigh rises from the pillow, moaning
in severe pain. Osprey violently wakes from a deep
sleep and checks on Everleigh.

                    OSPREY
              What's a matter?

                    EVERLEIGH
              Pain...

Osprey gently touches Everleigh on the shoulder, his
touch alone feels like a knife pressing into her skin.

                    OSPREY
              Where?

Everleigh pushes Osprey away and grabs her head, her
eyes squinting.

                    EVERLEIGH
              (grimacing)
              Everywhere.

Osprey rushes to the bathroom and fills a glass with
faucet water. He brings the glass of water to Everleigh, who backslaps the glass from his hand, causing
the glass to shatter against the wall. Everleigh convulses, her internal organs began to melt. Osprey attempts to console Everleigh, but her body is piping hot
to the touch.

Screaming in horror, Everleigh's eyes burst and ooze
from the sockets of her skull. Brain matter turns to
mush, dripping from her nostrils.

Osprey rolls off the bed and stands back and watches
Everleigh's insides turn inside out.

AFTER:

INT. ~~EVERLEIGH'S BEDROOM - NIGHT~~ *MATTRESS STORE - NIGHT*

~~We see QUICK SHOTS of Everleigh and Osprey having sex on a messy bed, clothes strewed about the room, as well as the furniture. While embracing Osprey in her arms, Everleigh's head jolts backward, her wide eyes rolling over white. The lamp on the nightstand flickers, as Everleigh opens her mouth in a gaping yawn.~~ *Camera A - Start w/ OVERHEAD SHOT of Eve and OG on mat., we slowly pull down on the tw.*

~~We CUT to moments after sex with Everleigh and Osprey resting in bed a wash of pale moonlight soaking over their bodies. Everleigh rises from the pillow, moaning in severe pain. Osprey violently wakes from a deep sleep and checks on Everleigh.~~ *Camera B - Cut to 'BOTs' standing in dark, watching EVE, OG, eyes candlelit - CUT to CA→*

A SERIES OF SHOTS : Doggystyle, 69,

Camera C - CLOSE UP of 'BOT' touching itself

          OSPREY
    What's a matter?

missionary, reverse cowgirl, The Lotus, Oral, *Upstanding Citizen, Ends w/ (Missionary!)

          EVERLEIGH
    ~~Pain...~~

~~Osprey gently touches Everleigh on the shoulder, his touch alone feels like a knife pressing into her skin.~~

          OSPREY
    ~~Where?~~ *B During climax the light flickers. The Entity transfers into OG*

~~Everleigh pushes Osprey away and grabs her head, her eyes squinting.~~

INT. EVE'S BEDROOM - DAY

          EVERLEIGH
      (grimacing)
    Everywhere. *QUICK SHOT of Eve, lying facedown in bed, dead, crying bloody RED tears.*

~~Osprey rushes to the bathroom and fills a glass with faucet water. He brings the glass of water to Everleigh, who backslaps the glass from his hand, causing the glass to shatter against the wall. Everleigh convulses, her internal organs began to melt. Osprey attempts to console Everleigh, but her body is piping hot to the touch.~~

~~Screaming in horror, Everleigh's eyes burst and ooze from the sockets of her skull. Brain matter turns to mush dripping from her nostrils.~~

Osprey rolls off the bed and stands back and watches Everleigh's insides turn inside out.

These changes, both subtle and greatly significant (Scene 33, which was originally three pages long before the rewrite, reduced to a quick shot that may or may not even make the final cut), can either make or break a script. What it really boils down to is how much we show on film. Is it too graphic? And if so, will it lose our audience? Does it contribute to the story?

The most important question we should be asking ourselves: Is sex and violence any different from one another?

On that note, I suppose Boris and I aren't so different after all.

3

FOLLOWING yesterday's production of the Lake Holden Scene, which took three days to shoot in a 187,000-gallon massive water tank inside Stage 8 at Gold Reel Studios, allowing filmmakers to use a controlled-environment to capture a dramatic scene involving the suicidal Osprey Gortana and his final demise, the exhausted crew endured yet another grueling day while filming the beginning part of the scene on location, which involved Kenneth's stuntman driving the car off the bridge and into Lake Holden. The scene that followed, which was filmed inside Stage 8, showed the moment of impact: an interior shot of the car hitting the water, Osprey, in return, striking his head against the steering wheel, requiring the special effects team to use at least a pint's worth of movie-magic blood for the head wound, which rendered Osprey unconscious, thus contributing to his ultimate demise.

After an intense amount of safety precautions were addressed and given a green-light—each rig triple-checked (*After all,* the AD emphasized to the crew, *it's just a fucking movie and it's not worth dying over!*)—the dangerous stunt went exactly by the numbers and according to plan. No injuries.

The rest of the afternoon was less stressful and most of the filming was conducted by the second unit: Exterior B-roll shots, as well as shooting the crucial final two scenes of the film, the first being a shot of a postcard-like sunset over the foggy Lake Holden as the heavy-duty wrecker lifted Osprey's waterlogged car from water while the two nameless detectives talked to Osprey's elderly aunt, who was played by legendary actress Silvia Bleu, who was known for her iconic role as "Lola" in the cult psychological horror flick, *Day of the Cackle*, and the second being the sprawling crane shot, which started out with a stoic police lieutenant—again, nameless—giving a sure update to the pool of news reporters from various networks and then gradually—and gracefully—pulled away, high above, revealing the active scene with police and divers and rescue crew scuttling around the scene like beetles while curious onlookers waited behind caution tape.

Moments after the lake scene wrapped, Caitlin, who was tasked to babysit a handful of extras, including police officers, detectives, divers, as well as members of the news media, received a text from her friend, Jessie.

With her phone switched to silent, Caitlin instructed the extras to hang back inside a white tent, which was specifically erected for extras in order to keep them away from the set until their roles were called, and wait for Props to collect any remaining accessories (i.e. belts, guns, holsters, badges, cameras, microphones). She stepped aside for a minute and surveyed the area to make sure nobody was around before unlocking her phone.

She read the text from Jessie: "Is this the guy you were talking to at the bar news.one8.art/4332."

Once more, she checked her surroundings as though Boris the Bully was somewhere hiding in the bushes, waiting for her to use her phone. She clicked on the link, which redirected her to a news article about a *"Missing Person."* The name of the individual missing was, to her surprise, *"Osprey Gortana."* She scrolled through the article before reaching the photo of Osprey, who was not the same person from last Saturday night—or so she first thought—this so-called "Oswald" fellow, who remained nothing more than a vague blur to her.

When Caitlin tried to mentally picture what he looked like and combed through the murkiness, she only picked up bits and pieces, only partial features. Yet, none of those features looked remotely similar to the photo in the article. What haunted Caitlin was one suspicion: *What if* his name was Osprey? And if so, *what if* he was the same Osprey?

Brushing away the thought, Caitlin texted back: "Different guy"

Then, she continued to shoot a series of texts at Jessie before she could respond: "But this is so weird"; "The missing guy is based on the same character from *my* movie"; "Unless there are two Osprey Gortanas???"; "But that couldn't be true cuz, from what I read, this Gortana also has connections with Everleigh Mince! WTF"

As Caitlin was about to send more texts, she spotted Gee-Gee walking toward the tent, ready to check the wardrobes. Caitlin, who didn't trust Gee-Gee or anyone on set, including that Prop Guy, considering the "back-stabbing" nature of the industry, put away the phone before Gee-Gee caught Caitlin in her field of vision and made sure the extras were behaving.

⬢

3-22-24:

The Film Gods shall giveth and thou taketh away.

After a productive week of shooting the Lake Scene (there was still much debate on whether or not we wanted to film the final scene on the third week since Boris was notorious for filming in chronological order, but scheduling conflicts made it nearly impossible for us to wait till the final days of production to film the Lake Scene), the fourth week is plagued with one hurdle after another, from one of the lighting guys slipping on a puddle of blood and hitting the side of his head while filming Brooklyn Hart's Death Scene to the special effects team not getting Brooklyn's prosthetics to work properly. Despite the disastrous week of shooting, I saw a glimpse of the footage from Brooklyn's Death Scene and it's, by far, some of the most graphic material that I've ever seen on film. The scene involves lots of prosthetics and practical effects, which are meant to convey the look of Brooklyn's skin boiling after being infected by The Entity. Lots of blisters exploding. Blood-pus splatter. Skin melting. Not in an over-the-top schlock-y B-rated way, but grounded and incredibly realistic. We're talking Chernobyl-esque.

Since Libby's character, Everleigh, visits her former college roommate and bestie, Brooklyn, over the weekend before Brooklyn turns into human pepperoni pizza, she makes a brief appearance in the Hospital Scene.

Originally, the scene was written without Everleigh; however, opposed to incorporating a scene with The Detectives inside Brooklyn's apartment and a QUICK SHOT of a framed photograph of Brooklyn and Everleigh on a bookshelf, Boris felt it was necessary to ditch the scene and instead, add Everleigh to the Hospital Scene in order to hone in on the idea that each and every character acts as a breadcrumb, each character "connected," with The Entity using these characters as a way of playing "Tag! You're it!" This is yet another difference between us. Boris often treats the audience as if they're complete idiots while spoon-feeding them scenes, which could be addressed in a glimpse of an image, like the photograph in Brooklyn's apartment. I'd rather let the audience figure out the connection between each of the characters. But these days, Boris would argue, it's too esoteric. This is coming from a man who's obsessed with using imagery as symbolism.

The largest hurdle, however, are the events surrounding Osprey Gortana...that is, the real life Oz. Every now and then, Reality has a way of rearing its butt-ugly head and sinking its jagged teeth into you and pulling you back down into the muck.

I have a golden rule when writing: "Never let OUTSIDE FORCES interfere with a project."

I'm afraid the situation with Oz cannot be ignored. When I found out about Gortana's disappearance last week on a lazy Saturday morning following a drunken night out with the crew, who, to be fair, deserved a drink or two or three or four, especially after filming the taxing Lake Scene, I immediately contacted Boris about our next course of action. When Boris picked up the phone, he was already aware of the news. He had no plans of "re-shooting" the Lake Scene, despite the recent news about Gortana. His simple fix: Scrap the names, replace them with other names. As far as the names used for the remainder of the shoot, he came up with a plan to "limit" the amount of names used in dialogue. Instead, he relied on fixing the issue in Post and using voice-overs to change the names that were already captured on set (*My buddy Sam is a Wizard when it comes to everything audio - the guy's ears are so sensitive he can hear a gnat's fart). You'd think the recent news would slow down production and force it back to the drawing board. On the contrary, it ramped up the production. Boris told me, "Gotta strike while the iron is hot, right?" Did I say the man is hardheaded?

I suppose Boris is right to some degree. Since the film is loosely "inspired by true events" (I use the word loosely with caution), I don't see any point in twiddling our thumbs, waiting to find out how the whole "Oz Situation" pans out. Since it's been over a week after news broke about his disappearance, more than likely Osprey Gortana is dead. And if I'm right (please tell me that I'm wrong and Gortana is on an exotic beach, flipping the bird to a society which once labeled him as a "Murderer"), I can't help but ask myself: Is it disrespectful to continue on with the production? A part of me says, "Yes." But another part of me says, as though I'm reminding myself: Clearly, it's a fictional story inspired by real-life events. I make sure to stress the word fictional.

In the original script, the final scene ended with Oz, still alive, still grieving after the gruesome death of Everleigh, whom he watched die horrifically after a one-night stand, still traumatized by the whole freakish incident, driving to the cemetery where his mother was buried. Gortana, who apparently had a complicated relationship with his mother, had said in an interview after his name was cleared of any wrongdoing that his mother used to abuse him with a scolding hot iron when he was a child. By the age of eleven, his mother left him, leaving him with no other choice than to stay with his aunt. Even as a grown man, he was still left with "abandonment issues." So, after reading about Gortana's story, I felt as if it only made sense to write a scene with Oz looking back in reflection, especially after having experienced such a traumatic event. Of course, the scene never made it to the final "Boris-approved" script. Boris thought it was better that Oz died at the end. If you look back at Boris's catalog, most, if not all of his films end with a death, either the main character dies or someone close to the main character, which makes sense, considering Boris's tragic background: When he was sixteen years old, he watched one of his older brothers die in a car accident (Boris was seated in the back-

seat of the car, the front of the vehicle received most of the major damage, Boris made it out alive with only a scratch); he watched his elder brother die from a heart attack after he returned home from Los Angeles; he held his mother in his arms as she passed from lung cancer; he held his father's hand as he died after a freak lawn-mower accident; he describes in great detail about losing his best friend, whom he watched fall into a vicious cycle of heroin addiction, which ultimately killed him.

4

"QUIET on set!"

The second assistant cameraman held a film slate in front of Camera A. On the slate, the scene was described as "INT. HOSPITAL - DAY" and then the date, "Date **3/26/24**."

The cancer-ridden nurse, Sandra Brown, played by thirty-year-old actress Brit Millie, who, based on her last three blockbusters, was no stranger to wearing prosthetics. The last movie that she starred in she played an angelic river nymph, Ravine, who slowly and painfully mutated into a ghastly sub-terranean-like creature that terrorized a small town along the polluted river after being infected by manmade chemicals in the dark fantasy horror, *Look At What You Did!*

As the assistant director shouted out an order to roll cameras, Brit fell back into her character, Sandra. Her breath became extremely labored, chest inflating and deflating. Despite the exaggeration of her breathing, Brit had help portraying a sick woman who was being eaten alive by infectious tumors spreading throughout her entire body. While cramped inside a CT scanner that had a massive fracture running alongside the machine, Brit wore at least a hundred extra pounds of prosthetics and makeup, which made it difficult to move; and at times, it felt as though she was being smothered. Flashes of panic overwhelmed her. A constant flight or fight. Each and every time she was struck by that feeling, she chose the latter. Each and every time, she fought through the immediate urge to yank off all of that shit covering her body. She fought through the urges, focused on her lines, and stayed in character.

From behind the monitors, Boris cried out, "Action!"

As soon as Boris said the word, Sandra groaned in great agony.

One of the members of the special effects team, Antonio, was operating a hydraulic system, which was attached to the crafted CT scanner, and working a remote control to pull it apart as the character, Sandra, ripped through the machine with her massive arm, which was the size of a tree trunk.

Another member of the SFX, Dillon "Dill Pickle," used another remote to inflate the tumors along Sandra's skin. Each tumor was fed through tiny tubes, which were concealed by makeup, and those tubes ran into an air pump positioned below Sandra.

More special effects deliberately took place throughout the entire shot: Sparks flying from the cables attached to the CT scanner; the release of smoke from a smoke machine; the flickering of overhead lights; several of those balloon-like tumors exploding with blood and skin fragments.

Sandra's groans turned to painful screams of bloody horror as the radiation emitted from the CT scanner caused the massive tumors to swell over her entire body, crushing off her air supply.

All of a sudden, the sparks created a fire and as the flames began to spread throughout the X-ray room, Boris yelled out the word, "*Cut!*"

The firefighters, who were waiting on standby, rushed to put out the flames with fire extinguishers.

Boris removed the headphones from around his head and rushed over to Britt to congratulate her on her performance.

With their director being more than satisfied with the shot, members of crew erupted in cheers and applause.

Caitlin made a strange face and could no longer hide her disgust after witnessing all of that blood and gore. She hurried from Stage 5 for a breath of fresh air.

With her skin feeling as though it was crawling with thousands of spiders, she stood behind the food truck, which was parked next to a holding area in the lot, and waited until nobody was around before taking a couple of drags from a vape pen, which contained a dab of marijuana concentrate.

As she made her way back to the stage, she bumped into London, who was escorting the actress, Lassie Durden, to Stage 5 for her scene with Brit Millie. Lassie was playing the character, Brooklyn Hart, the radiologist and next host for the so-called "Entity."

London's eyes fell upon the vape pen in Caitlin's hand.

"Misbehaving, are we?"

While tucking the vape pen behind her back, Caitlin said suspiciously as the weed-high crept in, "What are you talking about?"

"Please," said London, who picked up the change in Caitlin's eyes, which were more bloodshot and shrunken, both of her eyes and eyelids like two raisins. "You can't fool me. . . "

Caitlin begged, "Please don't tell anyone."

London furrowed her brows in disappointment.

She felt old, not like an older sister, but old, like a mother.

"You kidding?" said London. "Who do you think I am?"

"Wanna hit?" asked Caitlin.

London's eyes lit up.

"Hell'z yeah," she said and took a drag from Caitlin's vape pen.

Caitlin offered the vape pen to Lassie, who was already prepped for the scene.

"No thanks," she said. "That stuff makes me paranoid."

Caitlin said, "Could work for your character?"

"The last thing Brooklyn needs to be is paranoid," said Lassie.

London handed the vape pen back to Caitlin and said, "Our little secret."

Caitlin commented on "Brooklyn's" bracelet.

"You like that?" London said and showcased the friendship bracelet worn around Lassie's wrist. "Kurt the Prop Guy pulled it from *Fyrbawler*. Same one that Mayhem wore."

"No shit."

"I shit you not," London said. During a brief pause in the conversation, she cut through the silence with a question: "So you still following the whole Gortana story?"

"Obsessively," Caitlin said and pulled out her phone to check on the latest updates. "Rumor has it that, after the film was green lit, he was so distraught that he thought about filing a lawsuit against Gold Reel."

"Good luck with that," said Lassie. Then, added: "On what grounds?"

"I know, right," London said over Lassie. "It's *fic*-tional." She checked her watch. "Listen, um—"

"Caitlin," she filled in. "Cat for short."

"Apologies," London said, pinching her face. "I'm not good with names. We must get going. You know how The Bully is when we're running behind schedule."

"I know, right?"

"Thanks for the puff," London said and winked at Caitlin, "you magical dragon."

"No prob," Caitlin said, wearing a grin over one side of her face.

London and Lassie left and shortly after, Caitlin followed suit.

Distracted by her phone, she accidentally bumped into one of the writers, which resulted in him dropping a journal to the ground.

"So sorry," said Caitlin, as she attempted to fetch the journal.

When she kneeled down, she witnessed a dark and disturbing sketch inside the centerfold of the journal.

She peered closer at the highly-detailed sketch of a muscular man who was in great agony, his roars speeding across the centerfold like a freight train ready to run off the paper as he ripped off his *skin* in similar Clark Kent-fashion, only instead of a suit and tie it was flesh, which the tormented man pulled and stretched away like bubblegum from his body, revealing his ribcage, as well as his skull underneath.

Over his left shoulder: Another disturbing sketch, this one depicting what appeared to be another man with the tentacles of a strange creature bursting from his body.

To his right: The silhouette of a young man with a handgun, stalking through a desolate parking lot during an apocalypse, another strange creature, possibly the one chewing its way from the another man, hovering over a wrecked car in a cross-like pose. Narration and dialogue boxes suggested that it was some kind of sketch for a graphic novel. She only caught the first line from the narration: "*I hate remakes. . .*"

Carefully, she picked up the journal, grazing arms with the quiet writer, who had spent most, if not, all of the production seated by Boris's side.

She handed the journal to the writer, who closed the journal and with a straight face, said while nodding at the phone in Caitlin's hand, "Do you control *it* or does *it* control you?"

"I dunno," Caitlin mumbled and excused herself.

"Be careful," the black-clad, slick-back haired writer said and walked back to the Stage 5.

5

THE assistant director, Hogan, shouted out after convening with Boris, as well as a couple of producers behind the monitors, "That's a wrap on *Crosscut* everybody!"

Great relief and exhilaration washed over the crew, including the two actresses, Brit Millie, who was playing the role of Sandra Brown, *pre*-transformation, as well as the seasoned day player, Isabella LaBrusca, who was playing the role of the dying Ruth Angelo, the first host to transmit The Entity to Sandra Brown.

Despite being the final scene to be filmed before the production finished, the scene was one of the opening scenes of the film, mostly due to scheduling conflicts, Isabella, being a regular on the popular TV show *Playing Rico*, wasn't available until much later in the shoot.

Considering the scene took place during a thunderstorm at "Mother's Grace," which was filmed at an abandoned hospital before set design converted the old and rundown and allegedly "haunted" building into a nursing home, the lighting team played a crucial part in the scene.

Boris left his chair and walked over to Isabella, embraced her. As she sat upright in Ruth's deathbed, Boris raised her arm in the air as if she was a boxer who recently defeated her greatest opponent, the opponent being the scene, which, as expected, she killed: One of the reasons why Boris was so determined to have Isabella played the part of Ruth.

After the celebration, London, who was responsible for giving "Ruth" that pale, deathly look by heavily applying a white foundation to her wrinkly face and then adding darker tones underneath her eyes, and then, Gee-Gee, who fitted Ruth into a white bathrobe made of modal fabric, pulled Caitlin aside and asked her if she'd like to go for a drink to celebrate the end of the shoot.

Later that same night, after Caitlin and her new friends London, Gee-Gee, and Boris Mour's assistant, Journey, went out for drinks and capped off the night with tacos at Shock Taco, Caitlin, who was feeling sick to her stomach, decided to call it a night.

During the rideshare home, Caitlin played detective and backtracked the origins of her illness, starting with the moment when she had her first drink at London's apartment: A sangria-type of drink known as "Crimson King," not exactly a beer, didn't fall into the rules of the ole saying, *"Beer before liquor, never sicker,"* whereas the other saying, *"Liquor before beer, you're in the clear,"* was more like a national motto for partygoers; however, from the standpoint of a heavy drinker, the ole sayings didn't mean diddly-squat to Caitlin.

After a Crimson King, she mentally pushed the hazy timeline forward. Her second drink: a Rum and Coke at the dive bar downtown called The Gallows. Then, her third, fourth, fifth, sixth, and seventh (?) drink: Shots of Hämmerhead at Bubble Bar. Caitlin didn't recall running into any issues while ordering the drinks. She watched the bartender pour each shot from a bottle that he grabbed from the top shelf. She thought back to the careless, chatty bartender at The Gallows and she wondered about the cleanliness of the establishment after finding a greasy smudge on the glass.

Finally after drinks at Bubble: tacos at Shock Taco. Of all the places that she visited throughout the night, Shock Taco was the only place where Caitlin could've picked up on something, maybe food poisoning or something else that threw her stomach out of whack. If it was food poisoning, she knew it wouldn't have hit her so quickly. She backtracked once more, recalling several key moments throughout the night, the first one taking place right after they left Bubble, walking past a tank of octopuses inside the trendy Korean restaurant with a lively bar, and then after they left Shock Taco, walking past the same exact Korean restaurant, less crowded than earlier. She protested London's wishes of stopping by Hopscotch for a nightcap and snuck into the Korean joint and grabbed one of those octopuses from the tank and attempted to put it in her purse as though she was trying to liberate it from its inevitable demise. The owner of the restaurant was furious and threatened to call the police. Gee-Gee came to Caitlin's defense and apologized for her actions and somehow, talked the owner out of calling the local authorities.

With her head spinning, Caitlin focused on the moments of grabbing hold of that slippery, sticky, slimy octopus, its rubbery tentacles coiling around her fingers, as well as her wrists as if, in Caitlin's mind, it was begging her to save it—she couldn't quite tell its sex, whether the octopus was male, female, or whatever and in that spontaneous (or deliberate) moment, she could care less about whatever pronoun it preferred. She saw life in desperate need of rescue.

The owner of the restaurant, "YEONG," as the name read on the tag above the breast pocket, attempted to pull the octopus from Caitlin's arms; and in that moment, right before Yeong yanked the clingy octopus from Caitlin's forearm, the two, both Caitlin and strangely, the octopus, shared eye contact as if time stood still and together, the two of them connected like magnets, *not* physically but rather metaphysically, or dare she'd say, spiritually, as if the world around them vanished, the people, Caitlin's so-called "new friends," the owner Yeong, the furniture, the restaurant, the cooks, the chef, sous-chef, sushi-chef, the waiters and waitresses, even Korean music playing in the background turned all the way down, and in that black abyss only they remained—two energies, two life forces, two spirits.

Recapturing the feeling of the octopus and its tentacles moving over her flesh made her sick to her stomach.

By the time she made it back to her parent's house, which was located in the suburbs, a fifteen-minute ride from downtown, she could no longer hold it in. She stumbled to a holly alongside the front porch and blew chunks behind the shrub. She resorted to sticking her finger down her throat in a desperate attempt to expel every drop of wickedness inside her body.

During Caitlin's violent purge her mind started to race, her thoughts spiraling out of control: *a swarm of glow sticks running past her vision like coked-out fireflies,* she visualized, then *bubbles, that octopus, beads of sweat zigzagging down the side of London's neck, shots of Hämmerhead, the tentacles of the octopus like suction cups over her cold, clammy flesh, more shots of Hämmerhead, Journey mentioning some "dude named Bryan who accidentally" took their order by mistake, another shot of Hämmerhead,* Stop! Her mind returned to a dude named "Bryan," that mysterious person who was waiting behind them in the line outside Shock Taco. She couldn't rid the images from her mind and the uncertainty only filled in those gaps in the timeline with her own conclusion: A guy slipped something into their food—or better yet, *her* food. None of the others felt ill before she parted ways with them. London, Gee-Gee, Journey, they all drank the same drinks as her, mixed drink for mixed drink, shot for shot. The only difference, Caitlin concluded as she began to dry-heave, was the tacos. Gee-Gee ordered chicken, London veggie, Journey carne asada.

As Caitlin pulled herself from the holly, she saw the yellow package of rat poison right there at the front of her mind, as if it were suspended in the air, so close that she could touch it.

All of a sudden, she started to experience a severe pain in her stomach, worse than a cramp, a knife twisting and digging into her gut. She stumbled through the pitch-black house and trudged upstairs and when she finally made it to her bed, the entire room began to spin. Her breathing was shallow and each inhale she took felt constricted, like she had a weight pressed against her chest.

Staggering around the moonlit bedroom while removing articles of clothing, she convinced herself that what she was experiencing wasn't from the alcohol. She was a drinker, the "weekend warrior," who often spent nights, especially during liquor-fueled weekends, delving into blackness, as if she was a time traveler, a walker of various realms, and that blackness, her old friend, was a tiny black box, which could be anything, a closet where she could place her daily troubles on clothing hangers or a filing cabinet where she could store the pain that she felt each and every day for living a life as a ghost, invisible and unseen by those whom she wretchedly longed to *see* her and touch her in a world that felt so binary, regardless of smugly claiming that it was anything but binary. She told herself that the difference was in the food, those tacos. The action was intentional. Someone *was following her.* Someone *who had her number.* Someone *had committed a terrible act.*

Feeling extremely dizzy, she fell to the side of the bed and collapsed to the carpeted floor.

Behind her, she heard the bedroom door *squeak* open.

A young man in his late twenties, dark gelled hair, dark eyes, darker clothes, stepped out of the shadows in the hallway and entered the bedroom. He tiptoed toward Caitlin and stood over her, as her eyes began to swim around her head. Each and every breath shallower.

The darkly dressed man with the tattoo of a phoenix engulfed in flames on his neck glanced at Caitlin's hand, as well as her fingers, which were covered in traces of black ink from an octopus, and kneeled down onto the floor and with a thick bluish gray glove made of the same material as a lead apron worn on his hand, pressed his hand against Caitlin's nose and mouth, restricting all oxygen from entering her body.

Since Caitlin was barely clinging onto consciousness, she didn't put up much of a fight. Her body jarred slightly, like a violent spasm, and she made an attempt to grab the intruder's arm, but the weight of his body was too overwhelming.

Eventually, she succumbed to the pressure of his body, smothering her, killing her. The cold hand of Death washed over her like a tide scrambling over the shore; and once He retreated back into the darkness, both of her eyes stilled, her breath stilled, everything about her stilled.

The tattooed intruder pulled out a phone from his jacket's pocket. He accessed an app that detected heat signatures of what was written in the script as "The Entity." He found no traces of the unique presence inside her. The signal was gone. After leaving the house without waking Caitlin's parents, the intruder made a phone call to his boss, Maron Orwell.

Orwell answered, *"What's the word?"*

The intruder said with confidence, "It's done. Her days of jumping are finished. So, what's next?"

Orwell said, *"Tie up* all *loose ends."*

The intruder said, "Yes, sir."

He ended the call and once he reached his car and entered, he pulled out Caitlin's phone and checked her latest messages. He scrolled through her contacts. He found a recent message from a person named, "Jessie."

He read a text from Jessie, which, in it, contained a link to a news article about a man named Osprey Gortana and his recent disappearance. He searched for one of Caitlin's contacts, this so-called "Jessie" character, and within only a few minutes of scouring through the Internet, found the address of where she lived.

The week after CAST wrapped a kayaker found Osprey Gortana's vehicle (the real life Gortana) at the bottom of Lake Holden, just three miles away on the other side of the lake where we filmed the final scene of CAST, previously titled, Crosscut, which, according to Boris, was, to my surprise, inspired by a Bible passage, John 8:7. In a statement, the kayaker said that if it wasn't sunny that day then he probably never would've seen the glare from the vehicle below the water's surface. The investigators called in Gortana's next of kin to identify the body, and turns out the body that the divers pulled from the vehicle belonged to Osprey Gortana. The whole thing is bizarre to say the least. It's like the old saying: Often times, "Life replicates art." And other times, "Art has a strange way of replicating life." I keep coming back to what happened only hours after the production ended, with one of the production assistants, Caitlin Acker was her name, being found dead in her bedroom the very next morning after her and several other crewmembers went out to celebrate the end of the recent shoot, and how, during an investigation, coroners found deadly amounts of arsenic in her system, which were ruled the cause of death: Was it an accident? Was Caitlin to blame or was someone else involved? And if it was intentional, then who would want Caitlin dead? And why? These are the many questions that have been asked but have not yet received any answers from the police or any of the investigators responsible for handling Caitlin's case. Time and time again, I have to remind myself that I'm an observer who's made the choice to sit back on the sidelines and watch from a clearer vantage point while the players continue to sacrifice, not only their bodies, but also their credibility for a game that demands blood in order to appease an audience who has fallen victim to one of the greatest tricks of all time.

- Z